THE
MAGNIFICENT
RUINS

THE MAGNIFICENT RUINS

a novel by

NAYANTARA ROY

ALGONQUIN BOOKS
OF CHAPEL HILL
2024

Published by
ALGONQUIN BOOKS OF CHAPEL HILL

an imprint of Workman Publishing
a division of Hachette Book Group, Inc.
1290 Avenue of the Americas,
New York, NY 10104

The Algonquin Books of Chapel Hill name and logo are registered trademarks of
Hachette Book Group, Inc.

Printed in the United States of America.

Design by Steve Godwin.

This is a work of fiction. While, as in all fiction, the literary perceptions and insights
are based on experience, all names, characters, places, and incidents either are products
of the author's imagination or are used fictitiously.

The publisher is not responsible for websites (or their content)
that are not owned by the publisher.

Library of Congress Cataloging-in-Publication Data
Names: Roy, Nayantara, [date]—author.
Title: The magnificent ruins / a novel by Nayantara Roy.
Description: First edition. | Chapel Hill, North Carolina :
Algonquin Books of Chapel Hill, 2024. |
Identifiers: LCCN 2024030027 (print) | LCCN 2024030028 (ebook) |
ISBN 9781643755847 (hardcover) | ISBN 9781643755878 (ebook)
Subjects: LCGFT: Domestic fiction. | Novels.
Classification: LCC PS3618.O892653 M34 2024 (print) |
LCC PS3618.O892653 (ebook) | DDC 813/.6—dc23/eng/20240812
LC record available at https://lccn.loc.gov/2024030027
LC ebook record available at https://lccn.loc.gov/2024030028

10 9 8 7 6 5 4 3 2 1

First Edition

I love her, and that's the beginning and end of everything.

—F. SCOTT FITZGERALD

LAHIRI FAMILY TREE

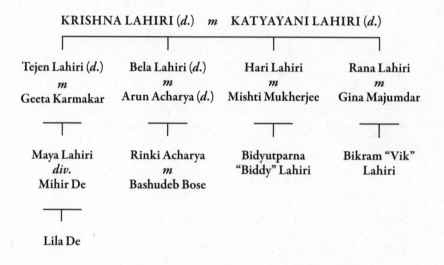

KRISHNA LAHIRI (*d.*)   *m*   KATYAYANI LAHIRI (*d.*)

Tejen Lahiri (*d.*)
m
Geeta Karmakar

Bela Lahiri (*d.*)
m
Arun Acharya (*d.*)

Hari Lahiri
m
Mishti Mukherjee

Rana Lahiri
m
Gina Majumdar

Maya Lahiri
div.
Mihir De

Rinki Acharya
m
Bashudeb Bose

Bidyutparna
"Biddy" Lahiri

Bikram "Vik"
Lahiri

Lila De

d. deceased   *m* married   *div.* divorced

THE
MAGNIFICENT
RUINS

A secret is a terrible thing. It starts as a single inhalation, a fragment of bacteria that enters your bloodstream, multiplying immediately or over centuries, a thousand neural networks of secrets emerging from the first. As a family, we were long practiced in the art of secrets, trading one deception for the other through generations, weaving an intricate silk screen that prevented the outside world from knowing who we might turn into. But that night on the terrace, confronted by the body that we had taken life from, I wondered if there would be no hiding this time.

A secret is a terrible thing. Unless there was honor in keeping it.

BROOKLYN, 2015

1

IN THE MIDDLE of that summer, I inherited my grandfather's house in India. There were five sprawling floors of it, home to my mother, my grandmother, and their extended family, eight thousand miles away from my apartment in Brooklyn. The first time that my mother called that day was at 7:15 a.m. I let the phone ring through, because we had not spoken in fourteen months, and I was steaming my skirt, and I did not know yet that my grandfather was dead. It was my birthday, and I assumed that despite the countless others she had missed, this year she had decided that she would like to talk to me. It would not occur to her that I might be late for work if I stopped to take a call from a mother who had remained silent for fourteen months.

It was my mother's way to remain silent. We might have argued about a minor difference (I did not like stew, thereby her stew) or a crevasse of a grievance (at sixteen, I had allowed my stepmother to formally adopt me, to be able to live with my father and her in Connecticut. Indian law did not allow a man to take his child out of the country unless he had a wife, i.e., a caregiver, nurture considered the prime function of femininity). After that, my mother had said, "My doors are closed to you forever" (a favorite phrase, which had meant six and a half weeks at the time).

The pattern, like the infinite loops of a familiar blanket, was always the same: no words exchanged until she had forgotten her wound. This worked, in part: The long spells of quiet (whether weeks or months or, once, almost two years) served to charge the relationship, as a drained iPhone might gather battery from a socket. And then the phone would ring again. With the familiarity of old scars, we would slip back into Saturday evenings when my phone would light up, euphoric and neon: *Hi???!!*

The first conversation would be stilted on my end, exuberant on hers. I would revel in a universe where my mother wanted me. Over time, she would begin calling regularly again. Those weeks would inevitably lull me, slightly tipsy from the largesse of her motherhood, into a maternal buzz. And then I would say something that would hurt her feelings, which always meant the punishment of disappearance.

In this manner, we had passed almost three decades. My mother was not an old lady. She was beautiful and fragile and cruel in the way children can be, and she frightened me.

THAT AUGUST WAS the hottest that Brooklyn could be, sudden warm showers permeating the mugginess. There was more steam than air in the subway, bodies stacked alongside, the whole thing reeking of damp rage and hot dogs. I was the first stop on the L train after spending an hour on the 1, inching back from Manhattan. Williamsburg was filled with photogenic parents with bamboo strollers everywhere. I was finally earning enough to occupy their neighborhood, an aberration in a railroad apartment, the kind with a unifying corridor trailing from kitchen to bedroom to living room; you had to walk through every room to get to my couch and TV—the first-class compartment, I liked to say. It was around the corner from Williamsburg Cinemas, and I had made it look like a real place—with rugs and books and plants. I was twenty-nine, and there had been enough cities and apartments—I knew how to make a cup of instant home.

A few blocks from the water, there was an Indo-Chinese restaurant serving hot green chili sauce mixed up with glistening soy Hakka noodles, vinegary chicken on top, exactly the kind I had grown up eating. The owners were descendants of Chinese migrants in India—Hakkas—who had settled in Kolkata over a century ago, adopting the goddess Kali as their own, intermingling woks and scallions with Indian spices and heat, creating the Gobi-Manchurian marriage of my dreams. I had not lived in Kolkata since I was sixteen, and having the restaurant nearby was a whiff of jumbled, salty memory that I would breathe in as I passed by.

Every morning, I left the house at eight fifteen, to get to work before Gil did. Gilead Edelman had hired me not long after I'd graduated from Columbia, where he had adjunct-taught undergraduates for two years before leaving for a publishing job, and where I had spent four years planning the novels I was going to write after a bachelor's degree. Instead, I found myself reading the manuscripts that my classmates wrote, making notes on their revisions.

Columbia had been filled with ideals and libraries and anger, and we were all trying to have some sex. In the stacks of Butler Library, I felt at home. Toward the end of senior year, I found myself a boyfriend from the graduate physics department and a job as a waitress at the café below his building. That first year after I graduated, I tried to write after my shifts—a few sentences here, a page there, of what I assumed my first novel would be. It was a lot of trying to guess at what first novels might be.

When Gil was promoted to editorial director at Wyndham, he asked if I wanted to be his editorial assistant. I gratefully shut down my many trails of Word documents and accepted the job. Seven years later, I was a fiction editor with an instinct for other people's work. My own stories were abandoned ghost ships. But when I read a sentence, I could see past its bad-shit swag, into its spine. It felt like luck that I had found a career that included me in the world of writers yet gave me my own place, my little throne on the margins of their manuscripts. The writers, unlike my mother, kept in touch. Constantly.

MY MOTHER CALLED again in the early afternoon. Lunch had blitzed past after a series of meetings, and the phone glowered again, with the word *Ma* vibrating up at me as I bent over the manuscripts on my desk. There were so many sentences to read to uncover one that might offer up the promise of plot, one that might deliver a few crumbs of riches. Since Wyndham had been acquired by the e-commerce company Phenom a year ago, the authors I had to placate had multiplied, alongside the number of meetings. Still, I loved the job and sought validation constantly, because the publishing world doled it out so teasingly; despite prestige, my salary had struggled for years to meet expenses. But it was hard to complain aloud about income when the plethora of barely paid interns only increased every year, each the cream of their Ivy League crop.

To my father and stepmother in Connecticut, rarefied literary circles meant as little as the long sentences we put in our books. They were attorneys, with a shared love for paperbacks. In the evenings, they drank rum or whiskey, ate kebabs or a casserole, and put their feet up in front of *Criminal Minds*. Still, they extended many a loan and shoulder, turning up for book launches, drinking wine in corners, bewildered and loving.

WHEN MY MOTHER called the third time, it was the middle of the night in India. It felt unbelievable that the idea of my birth, of my body aging until it began to resemble hers, was the reason she was impatient to reach me, but if it was, I was in no hurry to let her in. It was her way, after all. Just as my mother pursued her silences, she was relentless in her need. A thought might take form, and in seconds she would be possessed by it, caught within the wheel of her imagination, spinning in unending narratives. Everything was enlarged in these moments.

The phone lit up again. I answered. "Hi, Seth."

I had met Seth three years ago, on a dating app. With the same impromptu vision with which she transformed Wyndham's children's literature from preachy to astonishing, my friend and colleague Molly had signed me up for the app. I was single at twenty-six after a long relationship, and I had taken like a fish to the waters of solitude, but Molly insisted that I had gone long enough without any action. It wasn't healthy, she said, as if prescribing me an omega-rich diet of salmon and men. Besides, what if I forgot what sex felt like? And so Seth was the second man from the app whom I had gone out with. We had had dinner at a bar in Brooklyn, followed by good sex—which I had not forgotten how to have. I was confused by how handsome he was and by his interest in me. Seth was charming, if in a constant state of despair. In the weeks and months that followed, we continued to spend time together that held no promises. The closest we came to sweetness came months later, deciding that we would have unprotected sex only with each other. This was practical, and Seth looked relieved when I suggested it, since it provided our relationship with a clear outline.

One night, after dinner, I settled into his bed as he was brushing his teeth, and looked at his bookshelf, a precarious, teetering stack, perched on a single slab of wood in the wall, which threatened to bury us as we slept. I reached toward the Mavis Gallant, to the white stack below it, which I knew was his new manuscript. Seth, I knew, was embarrassed to solicit me for both sex and a sale, and so had never asked his agent to send it to me. This suited me, but when I looked at the manuscript's first few pages that night, I was unable to stop reading, long after an apprehensive Seth had fallen asleep next to me. The next day, sleepless, I went into the office very early and had an awkward conversation with Gil, outlining the "circumstances." Gil had read half his manuscript by that afternoon, and that was how I became Seth Schwartz's editor.

Now, Seth was one of our banner writers, nearly done with his second book—a luminous rumination on a futuristic, sinking Venice struggling under a dystopian government.

He was rarely joyful on the phone, but tonight was an exception.

"I've been thinking about Amy," he said. "When she realizes the prime minister's program she's been peddling doesn't allow single mothers like herself to fall in love, her image of herself as a good person cracks. By the time she meets Marcus, she uses that rule as a guardrail against him—but really, she's just self-sabotaging."

It was a good idea. Seth had been writing a character that could not have fallen as headlong in love as he had written her.

"That's great," I said. "Think of her as suffocating every feeling that comes up, in that paragraph where she realizes that she wants him to make her breakfast."

"I've also been thinking that act two should be in Amy's voice," said Seth. "If we just switch that section entirely to her POV, we'll see Marcus through her lens as he rises to mayor and marries his first wife."

This was not a good idea. At least he had had one of each.

It was his fourth attempt this month to douse a raging writer's block. Seth was in his early thirties and had written a first novel titled *Reminders*, which was, as every editor had told his agent, too close to the plot of a popular thriller. The slew of rejections had sliced him open. *Sinking* was his second novel, told through the eyes of a young Italian boy, the son of a villainous prime minister. In the book, after watching a friend drown while ice-skating, the boy becomes obsessed with the idea of sinking objects. In adulthood, he goes on to become the mayor of Venice, on a crusade to save his city from climate change and corruption, only to morph into his father and the bureaucracy he had spent his life fighting.

Seth was Jewish, from the Upper West Side, and spoke only broken Italian, but the manuscript saw through his issues with his own father, and so he wrote with fluency. So much so that Gil and I had asked if we might take a look at *Reminders*. And then Wyndham had published *Reminders*, after all, and Seth Schwartz was called a writer now, and it had brought the color back into his cheeks.

IN MY OPINION, Seth took too many pills. In my Indian family, pills had been considered a last resort, when the human body and mind had failed. We did not approve of much failure, so we did not invest in much medication. Seth's bottles of Ritalin and Lexapro made me nervous. But through Seth, I had learned that, like a migraine or a cold, when depression descends, you treat it as any recurring condition, with prescription and baths and compassion. It was the opposite of all that my own kin believed in.

When I was nineteen, my father and I had taken a trip back to India, the last of two visits I had made since becoming "an American," as my mother liked to put it. Lying next to my mother's mother, Geeta, on her four-poster bed, the fan overhead a steady hum, I had asked if she had ever considered taking my mother to a therapist. My grandmother had blinked for a moment, a flicker of doubt passing through, and then rebounded, on the offense. "So everyone in America runs to a therapist for every little thing?" she had whispered in Bengali, frowning even as she looked away. We both knew that my mother's problems were no little thing, but it was only years later, faced with the open, shame-free medicine cabinets of my friends at Columbia, faced with Seth's Monday-to-Sunday pillbox, that I relaxed righteous judgment toward prescribed pain relief. Years later, I understood that my mother had remained undiagnosed her entire life, untreated and alone, swinging between extremes.

"MARCUS IS YOUR guy. *Sinking* is his story. If the middle section doesn't get into his head, is it still his story?" I asked Seth as my assistant poked her head into my office, signaling that I had another call. I wondered if it could be my mother, but I had never given her my work number. I signaled to Harriet to take a message.

Seth did not answer. I could hear the hum of a jazz playlist, soft chatter, a barista calling out a name, from the abyss inside the phone. Small things could spiral Seth into a bleak vacuum, from which he would then struggle to swim out of and stay afloat. What I had not learned about him as his sporadic lover, I knew intimately as his editor. In our professional relationship, his writerly anxieties meandered easily to the surface, past his sheen. He had been born into wealth and bred in Manhattan; at his book launch, his friends were familiar faces—occupants of the middle ranks of the *Times*, the *New Yorker*, the *Paris Review*, and my bookshelf. It was territory I knew how to navigate, and I prided myself on having reached the same literary circles without pedigree or trust fund or whiteness.

"Maybe I can just stay with him for now and see where it goes," said Seth, a grudge in his voice.

It was a version of "Pussy Cat Dues," from *Mingus Ah Um*, that was playing in the café he was at, I realized.

"God, Lila, I hate this chapter. This book, this guy. I have no idea what's true about him. Remind me again when you go on your big vacation?"

A little wave of pleasure coursed through me at the mild panic in Seth's voice.

"Next week," I said. "I'll be back in two weeks."

"You're deserting me. In my hour of need."

I laughed. "I haven't had a holiday in three years. You'd think it would be my hour of need. Besides, I've paid for it already, so there's no going back." I closed my eyes in pleasure at the thought. It had taken me almost a year's savings to be able to afford a week at a cliffside retreat in Maine. I envisioned myself walking along the ocean, my laptop floating away from me, tossed to the waves.

"Maine, right? Do you want company? My dad's cottage is probably not too far from wherever you'll be doing yoga under the stars." I heard a glint in Seth's voice, the unmistakable note of a suggestion. His easy switch back and forth between our identities as professionals and lovers flustered me.

"Don't you have a book to write?"

"Yes, well, that's all going to the dogs."

I laughed again. "Not if I have anything to say about it."

"See you tonight?" he asked.

"Tonight?"

"Yeah. You busy?" There was a faint note of concern in his voice.

"For . . . work?"

"No," he laughed. "Not for work."

"Oh. Yeah. Okay. Tonight is cool."

Seth must have heard the heat in my cheeks, because he laughed again.

"Cool," he said gently as he disappeared into the ether.

It was all cool. I was as cool as ice, still figuring out the ways of Brooklyn. I pressed line two and immediately panicked that it might be my mother. There was no one on the other end.

HARRIET WAS EATING pistachios at her desk, bright as I approached.

"Hiya, Lila."

I frowned at her. "What was so important?"

There was a 1960s romance novel flipped over, steamy cover side up, on her desk. Harriet's gaze slid to it at the same time mine did.

"Oh. Molly was looking for you," she said.

"Harriet, Seth's got a couple of months left until the deadline. There's a small chance it makes Wyndham as much money as *Reminders* did. Which would make Gil very happy. Which may even get you a raise. So, please, allow me to make that happen."

Harriet looked chastened.

"Time for coffee," I sighed.

"I'll get it," said Harriet, standing up so fast that her chair spun back.

I raised my eyebrows. Harriet Chen was not known to volunteer for non-literary tasks.

"Just, y'know, to make up for the Seth Schwartz call. Sorry 'bout that." She grinned at me. "And because you look so tired."

"Why, thank you."

A murmur of anxiety whispered through my veins. It was almost sunset, and the Brooklyn skyline was bathed in pink and orange, a zigzag of Midtown towers spread out in the distance across the water, my precarious reflection a blur of shadows in their center.

Suddenly, Molly's arms folded around me, squeezing the breath out of me. Others sang "Happy Birthday" around her. Harriet, all-knowing, carried in a cake. I blew out the candles, and Harriet set to slicing wedges onto too-thin paper plates. The cake was a mixture of whimsy and richness, bits of grapefruit punctuating sharp cream cheese, a two-tiered monster, sweet and bitter, typical Molly. I could see some people recoil from its extremes as they ate, but I adored it, and her.

Eleven years ago, Molly and I had shared a dorm room at Columbia, teenagers jostling past harried New Yorkers to get to the green campus, a respite from the city. With her family in Queens and mine in Connecticut, we had alternated our combined laundry between either home on long weekends. In those days, we had had no need for separation, and when the opportunity to work for the same publishing house had presented itself, it had felt only natural. In the absence of any real sense of belonging, it felt like Molly was family I had found.

Now, as the office party wound down, she insisted we go downstairs to the bar, school night be damned. I was agreeable because it meant that I could not be expected to answer a phone at my own birthday celebration.

I LOOKED AROUND the corners of the crowded bar. Molly had invited all of our friends, our colleagues at Wyndham, and anyone else she thought would wish me well on my birthday. Seth was chatting with Penelope, the new wellness editor who sparkled as she placed a hand on his shoulder.

Molly's arms encircled my shoulders. "Are you having fun?"

I nodded, happy.

We squeezed onto barstools as Chris, the bartender, brought us a martini and a spritz.

"There's a line of people who want to buy you drinks," he said. "This one's on Gil."

Molly looked radiant. Bringing a community together, watching them create new threads and channels, was her superpower. I looked around the room and felt a warm buzz.

"Thanks, love," I said to Molly.

She looked pleased, lifting her glass. "To Lila, the best editor and friend," she said.

Gil and Seth planted kisses on my cheeks and made toasts, raising their glasses. "To Lila." *Clink.* It felt like a trickle of sunlight that could suffuse your body on a winter's day, enough to brave the rest of the season.

Gil looked like he had had a long day. Going from editorial director at Wyndham to being owned by Phenom was like managing a bodega one day and Whole Foods the next. Everything was amplified—resources and problems—and a team that wanted our books on every shelf in America was asking him too many questions. Gil knew exactly how to run our office when it had twenty-five people in it. He knew how to curate literature, patterns forming a quilt, arriving at a rarefied "Wyndham sensibility" over the years. But now we had entered the lion's arena, needing beach reads and social presence around magnum opuses. In 1976, Edgar Morgenthau and Kathleen Walker had started publishing poetry chapbooks with three-hundred-copy print runs, and Wyndham had been born in their garage. Kathleen had died three years ago, and Edgar had moved back to their family home in Vermont. He had taken the check from Phenom and gone, leaving Gil stranded in board meetings all day, navigating moguls and marketing people and excessive print runs for books that inevitably became warehouse stacks and held the promise of near death to literary careers, and so we were now the most frightened that we had ever been.

"Gil," urged Molly. "Tell us what Aetos is like."

Gil, conspiratorial, leaned forward. "I think he's made of silicon."

We roared, firmly on Gil's side.

Molly interrogated Gil. "Does he talk about family? What does he order at lunch? Does he want an office in the building?"

Molly wanted to understand Malcolm Aetos, the billionaire businessman who had founded Phenom, so that when the time came, she would be able to connect with him in a specific way that only Molly knew to establish. Gil sighed. Chris, the bartender, put a Smiths record on for us.

"The man doesn't sleep," said Gil. "He drinks only green juice and gin, eats almond butter by the spoonful, and does seven things at the same time. He's making a decision, texting with a CEO somewhere, dictating a memo, and coming up with an idea, all in ten minutes. And they're all good ideas," said Gil, forlorn, running his hand through thinning hair.

"I can barely come up with the one idea I'm supposed to have," said Seth, melancholy.

Gil and Seth admired moguls instinctively—a taste for soldiers and superheroes.

Gil had been a ladies' man through the 1990s and early 2000s, to the point where his former employers had gently tapped him on the wrist for dating several of their female authors. But he cut a dazzling New York social figure, throwing Wyndham parties that were legendary for their debauchery as much as for literary glamour.

I loved Gil. He had brought me into his world, and he had turned around a small press enough to self-sustain it and attract the eye of Aetos. Learning from Gil his consumption and understanding of the world and, thereby, fiction, had made me a better editor and a freer person.

"Let's dance," said Seth, scooping me by the waist.

"Girlfriend in a coma, I know. I know, it's serious," sang Seth, along with Morrissey, into my ear. He was fluid with his body when dancing, completely unlike his usual, anxious self. The heat enveloped us, coming in through the open windows, but we didn't care anymore.

Molly put on Tito Puente, her Afro a perfect halo around her face, her nipples jutting through her thin vest, effortless in the center of the room.

My hair formed sweaty clumps of tendrils around my temples as Seth and I twirled around, knocking into Ingrid from nonfiction and Gil as they cha-cha-ed their way around the tables.

At two in the morning, I pulled out my phone to look at the time. My mother had called three more times. I stood on the sidewalk a few minutes later, waiting for an Uber. Seth appeared, grabbing my hand, just as the car rolled up.

"Going home already?" he asked, wistful, his dark hair fanning over his sweaty forehead as I opened the car door.

"I'm tired. No good for anything else."

I let my fingers link through his. The minute we were out of the bar, out of work, out of sight, we took on the shape of lovers.

"Okay, okay. Did you have a good surprise? I helped, you know."

"I know."

"Lila *Day*?" asked the driver.

"Absolutely not," said Seth to the man.

"That's me," I said to the driver, smiling at Seth as something electric and familiar passed between us.

I wondered if it wasn't too late to take him home, after all.

Penelope appeared at the entrance of the bar and lit a cigarette. Spotting Seth, she lifted her hand in a half wave to us. I unlinked our secret fingers gently.

"I think Penny's looking for you," I said.

He turned around.

"Oh," he said. "Yeah, we were just . . . y'know. We might hang out later, yeah." He grinned at me, his hand sweeping his hair away from his face. "That is, unless you've changed your mind?"

I liked looking at Seth Schwartz—he was like a painting in a museum that had no place in my apartment.

"Good night, Seth." I smiled up at him.

He kissed my cheek, shutting the car door behind me. "Happy birthday, Li."

Penelope waved at me, and I waved back. The car sped through the empty streets, past a few bars with dim lights still on, the last revelers emerging into the night. I rolled down the window, drying my sweaty hair, grateful for the brief gust of coolness from the August breeze.

WHEN THE UBER stopped in front of my apartment building, three men were stretched out, sleeping, on the street, each perpendicular to the other, arms splayed against the heat. As I got out of the car, I realized one of them was a woman, her dark hair fanned out, a book spread open on her chest as if she had fallen asleep, reading, as I did so often. Williamsburg by night was at its most truthful, revealing the spaces that people occupied in sleep—insiders versus outsiders.

As I made my way up the stairs, I could hear what sounded like an action movie, coming from my Pakistani landlady Saba's apartment on the ground floor—muffled gunshots and sirens. Locking the door of my apartment behind me, I slipped out of my blouse and skirt, eager to hide in the safety of my bed, eager to leave birthdays and my mother behind.

In the bathroom, sitting on the toilet, looking at my phone, I saw that a distant cousin in Singapore had posted a photo of my maternal grandfather. He was laughing that deep belly laugh of his, and even before I finished reading the caption, I knew that he was dead. The post was long, and I had to click on it to be able to read the whole thing. In it, my cousin grieved the loss of a good man. My grandfather had been in bed, chained by his kidneys failing him, for over two years. All I remembered was the bear of a man whom I had had secrets with. A man with a giant stomach that vibrated with laughter like a shaking hill when I had climbed it as a child. I felt a seizure of grief, winded by its intensity, as I stared at the phone in my hand.

My grandfather's death was all over Instagram and Facebook and Twitter in the matter of an hour. I looked at pictures of him, the man who had made my childhood better. I tried to imagine the world without him but found it impossible, even though I had not seen him in person in ten years. I willed myself to cry and release the thudding in my chest, the despair that choked my throat.

My phone buzzed again and again, the metal slippery with sweat, as if screaming at me from between my clutching fingers, but since I did not want to hear it from her, I did not answer my mother's call.

It felt like my grandfather's death might melt me down, throw me back into the waters that threatened to dissolve the life I had built in New York. We would share a date now, he and I—my birthday, the day he had died. It felt like another of our secrets, like the hard-boiled sweets I would sneak into his big, dry palm when my grandmother would leave the room. Pythagoras, the Ionian Greek philosopher, had believed that when a human died, the soul would leave its body and search for a new home. Pythagoras had said that home could be the first plant or animal or living creature that the soul took a fancy to. But what if home was Williamsburg, Brooklyn, across an ocean? My brain was warm with gin from the party, and standing in my bedroom, I imagined my grandfather's soul possessing me, his laugh radiating through my own body.

Something in me wanted to pretend to my mother that I did not know that he was dead. What would make her comfort me? Or me her? Fourteen months ago, I had broken an elbow, a week before we last spoke. I wondered if she would ask me about it if I were to call. We were perennially at the precipice of holding each other to bitter trial.

I picked up the phone and held it against my ear. It was cold, and then quickly, hot, the metal warming like fire as it began to ring. There were things my mother had done to earn my rage—for instance, to throw away flowers sent to my grandmother or let them die unseen. Forgotten to invite me to a family wedding. Stopped speaking to me for imagined slights. I had never understood, but I was ready for battle, scimitar raised. She picked up on the third ring.

"Hello."

"Hi, Ma."

"Lila. How are you?" She was polite, even concerned.

"I'm okay, Ma. How are you?"

"I'm okay," she said. "I have to be okay, for the kids."

My mother was a professor. The kids she referred to were her students. Not the daughter she was speaking to.

"Dadu died last night, Lila," she said. Her voice had turned gentle, a rarity, and my eyes burned for the first time as I imagined my grandfather, never again in a room with me, never again delighted to see me.

"He died in his sleep," my mother said. "It wasn't too bad."

She said this as an act of kindness, I would learn later.

"When is the funeral? I want to be there for the kaj," I found myself saying.

There was a silence. Polite again, she said, "The cremation is tomorrow. I called you. Many times."

"Yes, I'm sorry. I wasn't near my phone," I lied.

In her silence, I felt caught, as I always had with her, trapped under the microscope of the person who knew when I was lying.

"You have work," she said. "And your life. It's so far—there's no need for you to come."

A rage began at the bottom of my shoulder blades, spreading quickly, meeting the prickling at the base of my skull.

"Of course I'm coming," I said. "He would have wanted me to come."

"He left you the house," she said.

There was a pause. My mother had always loved a scoop, so there was a certain excitement in her voice, for she was finally certain of giving me news that I could not have known.

I said nothing, and so she began to explain, hot and impatient, as if I did not know which house she referred to.

"Our house," she said. "305/B. It's all a big mess. There's no explanation for it. He must have just gone senile. How can a sensible man leave a house to a child, just like that? The lawyer will sort it out," she continued, a torrent now. "The lawyer will sort it out," she said again.

I heard her breathe, heavy. *I'm not a child, Ma,* I thought.

"Lila," she said softly, in the distance. "Lila," she said again, this time with less confidence. "Are you still there?"

I heard a muffled sound behind her and recognized it to be my grandmother's polite cough. I realized that a panel of my relatives were waiting to hear what I might do. What the new owner of their home would do.

In 1987 in Kolkata, my mother and father had divorced in the eye of a storm when I was eight months old. She had been twenty, my father twenty-two, her first lover, a good reason to run away from an Indian home where her young uncles were adored, primarily for being male. At seventeen, when she met my father, she had taken matters into her own hands. Three years later, they were the only two people in Ballygunge who were divorced. It was the most privileged neighborhood in Kolkata at the time and entirely primed for a scandal. It struck me that my mother was the only one in her family with real experience of how the gossip mills of Ballygunge might speculate and dissect the fact that a far-flung foreigner had inherited her beloved family house

"I told you, Ma, I'm going to come to the funeral. Ask them to wait to do it until Monday."

2

I SPENT THE next few hours in a panicked examination of my bank account, trying to estimate what last-minute flight tickets across the world might cost. A one-way trip to India, as it turned out, was triple the partial refund that one got after canceling a wellness retreat in Maine. I tried not to think about money or my emptied savings as I finally drifted to sleep. *I had planned to be in Maine for two weeks,* I thought in a haze. *Surely, Gil would not care that it was India that I would be going to instead, that it might be a little more time than I had planned on?*

In my dreams, all I saw was my grandfather's face, the sorrow in his eyes.

DESPITE THE NIGHT, I felt extraordinarily awake in the morning, as I stood in line at the Starbucks on Twenty-Third and Park, below Dr. Laramie's office. I trusted Dr. Laramie, once every two weeks, with things that nobody else knew about me. Therapy felt like a shape-shifting myth across cultures. So acceptable in the Brooklyns and Manhattans of the world that it would be an aberration to not to have a therapist, to not have problems. Everyone in New York was ravaged by their love affairs and debt and childhoods, by race and geography and loneliness. In Kolkata, people had fewer problems, because one did not talk about them.

I stared at a patch of the Hudson River in the distance, out the window of Dr. Laramie's office, while he watched me.

"How many people live in this . . . joint family?"

"My grandfather had three siblings: two much-younger twin brothers,

Hari and Rana, and a sister, Bela, who died a few years ago. The brothers are in the house with their families. They're more like uncles to me, closer in age to my mother, only eight years older than her. She was raised like a sibling of theirs. Hari and Rana have wives and children, plus my mother and grand-mother are there." I counted on my fingers. "Eight total, plus the maid."

"Everyone has their own . . . room in the house?"

"More like everyone has their own floor in the building, but with a free-wheeling, zero-privacy policy—everyone up in everyone else's business all the time. Nobody ever shuts or locks a door."

"How many floors?" He seemed riveted by the idea.

"Five. My grandfather's name was Tejen. If I ever have a son, I'd like to call him Tejen."

"You've never talked about having children before," said Dr. Laramie, his pencil swooping into his notebook, making small curls, as if drawing.

"It was just a thought," I said.

Dr. Laramie looked up, his pencil relaxing against the spine of the book.

"I'm just not used to the idea that he's—my grandfather—is gone."

"It's only natural," he said, gentle. "Was your grandfather close to his siblings?"

"He was more of a father figure to them, I think. All the Lahiri siblings were afraid of their actual father, my great-grandfather Krishna Lahiri," I said, feeling tiredness settle into my bones. "Everyone was, even the beggars of the neighborhood. He was ninety-four years old when he died of a heart attack, midway through a rewatch of *Gladiator*, his favorite film."

"Were you afraid of him?"

"No," I said. I squinted at the piers. "I was only five when he died, but he liked me. When someone's nice to you, it's hard to remember their bad side."

"We do forget," said Dr. Laramie.

A silence hung over us, filling the room. I looked at the clock. Ten more minutes.

"It wasn't just me he liked," I said, hearing the defense in my own voice. "Krishna loved his wife, my great-grandmother Katyayani, too. She was a musician. Hari and Rana both inherited it from her. She would host harmonium and ghazal concerts in the courtyard, although she never sang or played herself, because performing in public was considered slutty behavior for women of her social class. She was a hoot, though, loud and funny and rebellious. Didn't care that the ladies of old Brahmin families were expected to be well-read, have sons, and live lives of quiet elegance. She didn't really have a maternal side. She turned over the care of her younger kids to her oldest son, my grandfather."

The words tumbled out of me, a manic chattering to my own ears. Dr. Laramie wrote in his notebook again.

"There's water on the table next to you," said Dr. Laramie.

I poured the water, slices of cucumber floating in the pitcher like at the spa that my stepmother, Iva, liked in Hartford. The cold of the liquid spread through my chest, the taste of the cucumber metallic and pronounced.

"It sounds like your grandfather was his father's favorite son," said Dr. Laramie. "Since he got the house?"

I nodded. "The oldest and the most responsible of the brothers. Rana and Hari just live off their inheritances, always between businesses that they start and fail at."

"You sound fond of them," said Dr. Laramie.

"Do I?" There was a spiral of a painting behind his head, red, white, and black, like the poster for *Vertigo*. "I was the kid whose parents were divorced." I shrugged. "People were nice to me."

"How long did you live in Kolkata?"

"I left at sixteen," I said.

The room felt humid, my underarms prickling with sweat. Dr. Laramie watched as I shifted. He was never in a hurry to extract me from these moments.

"How far is your mother's house—the house you inherited—from your father's house?"

"The house I inherited was my grandfather's house, not my mother's. My dad has an apartment down the street, about half a mile from it."

Dr. Laramie paused. "Is there a reason your mother didn't inherit the house? And you did?"

I looked away. "I don't know." I shook my head. "My mother isn't exactly the kind of person who would put family before, say, her career or something."

"And you would. You are."

Panic rose in me anew at the thought of Gil and Aetos. I took another sip of water.

"You must have been close with your grandfather," murmured Dr. Laramie, as if solving an equation.

An image of my grandfather telling me a secret joke, his big nostrils flaring, his baritone laugh at the ready. It dawned on me that I would have to prepare a hot defense of this unearned inheritance for the world, starting with a therapist who in three years of knowing me had never heard me mention my grandfather.

"I'm going to miss our next session," I said instead. "I'm going to India for eight weeks. The office can't do much about it since it's a personal . . . loss, and I have accumulated PTO. Gil is always telling me to take a vacation anyway."

"How does the prospect of taking so much time off make you feel?" asked Dr. Laramie, uncrossing and crossing his legs, elegant, as if at a dinner party.

"I haven't been back in years," I said, too bright, the fear of risking my career cramping its way into my stomach. "It'll be a break from work."

"And how is work?"

"Good," I said. I finished the water. "A lot of meetings all the time since the takeover." I paused to focus on the spiral behind his head, which, absurd before, felt like I might be circling within it. "Kolkata will be a good break. And I'll sort out this house thing. I mean, my grandfather must have had a good reason for leaving me an old building filled with his weird family," I said with a laugh.

Dr. Laramie regarded me from his armchair. "Your mother will be there."

He said the words gently, as if mixing egg yolk into flour with his thin fingers, careful not to overmix, careful to keep light and air in, careful not to allow it to clump and harden. He closed his notebook. I looked over my shoulder; it was 9:53.

"There are things we have been practicing in this work," he said, the tips of his fingers touching in a triangle, like a namaste. "Maybe you could put them to use, when you need it."

Yes, certainly, I will reframe my thoughts and meditate in Kolkata. I did not say it aloud, but I felt myself smirk.

"A prescription might work too," I said as I reached for my purse.

"What if she didn't exist?" he asked.

"Who?"

"Your mother," he said. "You've barely mentioned her."

"What about her?"

"What if we . . . you and I"—he gestured to me and then himself, as if this were the part that needed explanation—"were to pretend that your mother was gone? Disappeared. Dead." He offered up the word like a small gift. "Would you be unhappy? Would you still be angry with her?"

"She would have existed once," I said.

"Would you still feel as though she were responsible for all of your grievances in this life?"

"I don't know," I said. "You're asking if I would forgive her for my childhood, in the event she disappeared or died?" Something was piercing upward through me.

"Lila, what if we took the hatstand away. Where would we hang your hat?"

God in heaven, please let him write a book, so I can shred his aphorisms to pieces with a pencil.

He looked at the clock. It was 9:54. "Good luck with the house," he said.

"Thanks." I rose, like sourdough he had baked.

"What will you do with it?"

"With what?"

"The house. It's yours now? Will you sell it?" Dr. Larami looked genuinely curious.

"Blow it up, raze it to the ground?"

He laughed, since we were off the clock. "See you when you get back, Lila."

3

WHEN I ARRIVED at work, Harriet informed me that Malcolm Aetos had asked to see me at one. Gil and Aetos had met with Molly that morning and had promoted her to head of the Kids and Young Adult Division, and Ingrid in nonfiction had been let go. Molly had texted me all of this information with equal amounts of joy and despair. When a big company takes over a smaller one, it is often with the intention of absorption and not assimilation. Aetos had bought us because he wanted to own our voice, amplify it, and integrate it into Phenom. That his people would be replacing us with their own hires was a foregone conclusion that I had forgotten. I was already the senior-most person in my division, excepting Gil, which meant that in an up-or-out environment, I was most likely out. Molly brought lunch into my office in an attempt to distract me.

"I mean, it's your house now. You *could* sell it." Molly said excitedly. "You could finally pay off your student loan, mine too, buy an apartment, maybe buy me one. I mean, can you imagine?" She ate lentil soup out of a sturdy paper cup, savoring the spoon. "Mm, a summer home."

"I'm inheriting a house, not a country," I said. "Plus it's a hundred degrees in Kolkata in June—you'd have to leave your bikini behind—and with my ulcer, I'll be sick within the first three days."

Molly's eyes widened. "Really?"

My shoulders deflated. "No. Yes, it's hot. Well, yes to all of that, but it's also . . ." I shook my head, unable to summon up the words, the smell, the exhilaration of Kolkata. I sighed. "It's incredible food, and everyone will want to hug you and talk to you and feed you. It's a lot of beautiful fabric and old furniture, and the friends I had as a kid."

"Dreamy," said Molly. "If you sold the place, could you keep all the money, or would you have to split it with everyone who lives in it?"

"I . . . Of course I would take care of them."

"How long have they lived in the house?"

"All of their lives. It's been in the family since the 1800s."

"Jesus."

"Mol, don't ask me these things," I said, irritable. "I don't have a fucking clue. I thought you were trying to get me to relax."

"That's what the soup was for," said Molly, remorseful. She let out a sharp exhale. "I wish we could just go back to the way things were, y'know? When it was just Gil and us and our people."

"Yeah," I said. "I think about that. But you're doing great . . ." My voice trailed off, and because there was nothing more to do but wait, we focused on the soup, which had an oddly comforting effect.

Harriet opened the glass door of my office a sliver. "Malcolm's ready," she said.

Molly straightened as a gob of lentil soup dropped to the carpet. Harriet looked at the stain, horrified.

"It's going to be fine, Li," said Molly.

My shoulders knotted together. I shrugged.

"We'll see," I said. "Harriet, would you book my four p.m. with Raven Hubbard in the conference room? Unless she likes stepping in lentil soup, in which case we can do it here."

Harriet allowed a smile. She was ambitious, and her job depended on mine. Molly looked upset.

"If they fire me, I could really use the break," I said, smiling at her. "But they shouldn't. I'm overworked and underpaid—a real deal."

My sciatic flared like an insect standing on its hind legs. I kissed the top of Molly's Afro, coconut and lavender wafting up at me. I was happy for my brilliant friend. If I was asked to leave, I knew she would call every publisher in town to get me hired.

"Well, at least you own a big house worth millions," said Molly.

On my way out, I winked at Harriet. "Even if I get fired, they are going to hang on to you for dear life. Only you know where all the bodies are buried."

She smiled at me, sympathetic, because she knew it was true.

MALCOLM AETOS'S OFFICE was an exercise in minimalism—a large, empty suite with Aetos swiveling behind the expanse of a glass-topped desk. A lone, muscular bust of a rearing horse stood on the windowsill behind him, as if in preparation for war. There were no papers on his desk, only a glass paperweight that reminded me of a snow globe, and a cell phone that blinked unceasingly, like a hazard signal. I thought of my own messy desk and felt like a guilty teenager. Aetos rose, stretching a palm in my direction.

"Lila, I'm pleased to meet you in person. It's taken us too long."

When a powerful person is in a room, even if you have no idea who the person is, you sit up a little, because the person exudes something: I had read that somewhere about movie stars and the personas they carried with them like handbags. When Aetos stood, he radiated something, like the muscle-men buying protein milk at my bodega. What must it be like, to think of oneself as truly great.

There were no chairs across from Aetos's desk, so I stood in front of him, trying to match his smile. Aetos turned his neck and palm to his right, and gestured toward a large armchair I had not noticed at first, its fabric so white that it blended effortlessly with the walls. I sat down in it and was immediately enveloped, my knees and legs too high, the effect that of being a child again.

"We met at the party you hosted for us after the sale," I said.

His skin was as clear as a child's, as if untouched by the time that ravaged ordinary humans.

"Yes, of course," he said, gracious, though we both knew there had been no need to correct him.

Aetos sat back down and relaxed into his springy, leather chair. At five foot five, he was shorter than I was, but that was not how it felt. I realized

I was drumming my fingers, silent and frenetic, on the arm of my chair and stopped.

"Is Gil joining us?" I asked, looking at the glass door to Aetos's office, which had shut behind me.

"Not today," said Aetos with a buoyancy. "But he was running the fiction numbers by me earlier. I hear that we are up one point eight percent in the first quarter. And it's mostly due to strong performances from editors like you."

I smiled at him again, grateful.

"Our literary fiction has been selling not just nationally but globally," continued Aetos. "Plus e-book sales have been climbing steadily." Watching me, he picked up the paperweight and turned it around in his palms.

It was an hourglass, I realized, and not a snow globe. I wondered where Gil was and if he knew that his boss had summoned me to either fire or laud me.

"Are you feeling good about the books for the coming year, Lila?" asked Aetos

"I feel pretty certain that the Jenna Beam and Miriam Thambi could be big," I said from a place far-off from my own ears. "As Gil has probably told you, the Thambi is being considered for a national book club, and we should know soon. The Beam novel has a powerful voice, and the book is set in Utah, where she was born—a queer examination of the interiors of Mormon life. They're both solid debuts. Plus, Raven Hubbard is finishing her sequel."

I reached for the bottle of water in front of me, twisting its cap off. "My only concern is that we aren't really reaching our audiences anymore."

Aetos swiveled his body in my direction. I shrank back, apologetic.

"Are you suggesting we're not doing enough?" he asked. "I've put in a significant investment in advertising this quarter."

"Yes," I said, hearing my voice floating at a distance. "But we are setting ourselves up for failure if we limit ourselves to the same outreach and ads we always have. Print media ads are tougher to get in front of readers than ever before. No matter how good the books are, we have to find new ways to get them to people."

"What do you suggest?" asked Aetos from his distant satellite.

I have thought about this so many times, but, Gil, you would have dismissed the idea, so I will tell this smooth-skinned man.

"We should appeal directly to readers. Let's find them in their email inboxes and their Facebook and Twitter accounts, and make sure they know the best thing about each book and why they have to preorder it. It's not expensive—we would just need to create our own accounts and a fan base, like musicians, who would spread the word and create buzz. Authors could engage directly with their readers too."

Aetos frowned. "That's impossible. Are you saying we should try to reach consumers individually?"

"Think about the way Facebook created communities. What if we took advantage of groups like that, across all of the new platforms, and gave ourselves a solid online presence. Readers would have a place to hear about books and talk about them together. All we would have to do is create posts. These days Facebook even allows you to make little videos."

"A paid video advertisement?" murmured Aetos, reflective.

"Maybe, but even readers could talk about our books and post their opinions online, and we could share them," I said. "We could take advantage of the biggest audience in the world—the internet. Isn't that the point of having Phenom's resources?"

The left edge of Aetos's lips curled in a half smile. "Feels naive. People could hate a book and be vicious about it. Could sink sales ten times more than a bad review. But I'll get Jonathan's team to build a model. I know how to listen to ideas. Gil wasn't wrong about you."

I felt a warming guilt at articulating ideas that I knew Gil thought of as silly, that Anna from Wyndham's marketing team had looked confused by, but there was something in Aetos's face that gave me permission to continue. I owned a house now, and somehow it had relieved me of my sanity.

"The thing is, Wyndham was doing fine. But if Phenom wants us to sell books in the same volume as their other products, we need new hires on the marketing team, who understand social media and love books," I said. "Who will think through crucial marketing strategies. Books aren't like your other products. Our campaigns are creative, and they change for every book and writer. We've got to play into individual strengths—race, culture, new styles. Marketing can't be doing it from a template, like it's the launch of the latest headphones."

"I wasn't aware that we were confusing books for headphones," said Aetos, his face a flat, smooth canvas.

"I didn't mean—"

Aetos waved my sentence away. "We, Gil and I, have been talking about your future here at Wyndham . . . at Phenom. I want to promote you."

I felt a sweeping rush of relief.

"To co–editorial director," said Aetos.

I wondered if I had heard him correctly.

"But Gil is editorial director," I said.

"Yes, that's correct," said Aetos, affectionate, cheerful, as if faced with his own, slow child. "But we need a young, diverse voice as much as the older, experienced one. You will both run the show, side by side. You've been here nearly the same number of years, and it'll be great—the yin to each other's yang. You'll balance and thrive." He held up his palms to illustrate scales, his right hand sinking as his left hand raised, then his left hand sinking as his right hand raised.

"But I'm not even an executive editor. I'm a senior editor now."

Aetos set down the hourglass on the desk. Fine sand began to trickle through an invisible funnel within the glass.

"You do want this, Lila, yes?"

Something in his face sent a chill through me.

"Of course, yes," I said. "I just, Gil—"

"Excellent. That's what matters. Titles are about earning them. That's all you need to focus on." Aetos laughed suddenly, a higher sound than I had expected, and threw up his hands, their shadows dancing behind him on the white wall, next to the rearing horse. "Besides, I'm the boss. "

Aetos and I looked at each other for a long moment. I nodded slowly.

"There's just one thing," I said.

He did not reply, and I felt my palms grow cold.

"I've had a personal . . . a death . . . in my family. In India."

Aetos's face was without emotion, his head angled at a slight tilt.

"I was going to take a break—my first in three years—for two weeks. But because of my grandfather's death . . . and some personal . . . some family matters around inheritance, I might need more time away."

I realized I was drumming my fingers again and stopped myself. Aetos had tilted his head to the other side.

"I could work remotely," I said in a rush of breath. "And because of my planned vacation, I had already made plans for Gil and my team to handle some of the season. Nothing would be disrupted at all." I exhaled as Aetos touched the paperweight with the tips of his fingers.

"How long?" he asked, lifting the paperweight into the air.

I felt the desire to laugh. It was almost a relief that he had asked no questions around my state of mind and only the logistics of my travel.

"Eight, maybe ten weeks. I need to settle some legal affairs."

Aetos looked up at me. "What if I said no?"

For a few moments, I stared at the white wall in front of me. "I think I have to go," I said slowly.

Aetos looked reflective, as if weighing the trouble of losing my institutional knowledge versus having a senior employee on another continent for two months. Suddenly brisk, he set the paperweight down with a thud, startling me.

"Eight weeks remote. Not a day more. You're lucky we are still in the process of transitioning Wyndham into Phenom, so it's good timing for you as the administrative processes get sorted out. You can complete trainings remotely. I'll expect weekly progress reports on the work you do while you're away."

I LAY ON the grass in the little park that I crossed daily to reach work. Subway commuters rushed past me, a blur in the glare of the white sun. The sun felt good on my face, antibacterial and hot. I wondered if it could give me cancer.

My phone lay next to me on the grass, and I thought about calling my father and Iva.

"Lila, what the fuck?" Molly, palm over her eyes, shading her face from the glare, was standing over me.

"Oh god. I forgot I said I would call you right after."

"I thought you were a goner," she said, dropping to the grass next to me.

"You and me both."

"I screeched into Gil's office to find out, and there he was, his face like that Munch painting," said Molly as she let all of her features sag, her mouth opened in a silent scream.

I laughed, despite myself. She reached into her bag and produced two plastic cups and a mini bottle of wine.

"I thought we should celebrate. You would be the boss of me, right?"

"No one could be the boss of you, Mol." I took the cup.

"Gil knows you deserve it." She fell silent, caught in her lie—we both knew that Gil, at fifty-six, did not think that I deserved to be his professional equal at twenty-nine. "He wants it for you, but he's worried they'll push him out." Her voice softened—we both loved Gil for what he had done for our lives, black and brown girls who might have spent years we could not have afforded as assistants but for our trailblazing, insistent mentor.

I brushed crumbs off my pants. "Gil will continue to lead editorial."

"With you," said Molly.

I struggled to find the right words, because with Molly, I wanted them to be the truth.

"Gil and I work well together," I said. "We always have."

She nodded. "Do you think it was optics, them promoting the two of us?"

I heard the edge in her voice, the reflection of my own impostor syndrome.

"Who cares?" I said. "I think they're fucking lucky to have us because we're crazy good at the job."

"Better to promote us before we're poached—I mean, who doesn't want a diverse face in senior management. Do you know how hard we are to come by?" said Molly as we laughed.

As a child in Kolkata, I was pale, overprotected, and kept out of the fierce Indian sun. We went from air-conditioned cars with tinted windows to cool classrooms to curtained homes. I kept my pale color, and my relatives made happy comments on my fair skin—inherited from my mother. "European, almost," I once heard my grandaunt say in hushed, awed tones.

But in New York, there was no escaping the sun, and I had turned the dark brown that defined my identity. At Columbia, I once overheard a professor, trying to remember my name, refer to me as "that dark girl," and it had felt both shocking and natural. As a woman in India, I was not Indian enough—a foreign look to my skin, words, ears, and now my face too dark for husbands. In Brooklyn, I was a creature from elsewhere, like everyone, except the literary canon who occupied their brownstones as one might a kingdom. It seemed crazy that my color might deny me husbands one week, get me promoted in another, and mean mysterious things across geographies.

Guilt flooded me even as Molly and I brought our cups together, the dull thud of plastic against itself anticlimactic. But slowly the sun-warmed rosé worked its way into my veins, and the thought entered my head that I had permission to be powerful now.

BY FOUR, THE wine had worn off. I had unhappy family to reunite with, a boss with outsize expectations as I was about to go on leave, and the loss of my grandfather felt like a continuous thrum in my chest. Had he declined so rapidly that he had remembered his grandchild in America one morning and changed his will suddenly, before he had had a second chance to be rational? Had he mistakenly left his ancestral home to his memory of the seven-year-old child he had once known, the nineteen-year-old he had last met? And how would I pretend to know anything about being management? I made an insurmountable list of things to do.

Almost everyone had left the office—the publishing industry took summer Fridays off, to start their weekends early, and it was the last Friday of August. I joined Gil on the Wyndham patio, the Williamsburg Bridge stretching in front of us like a silver arc over the sunlit water. Gil looked tired, with none of the fury I had steeled myself for. As he wiped his glasses with the end of his linen jacket, he seemed older than he was.

"God, when did the furniture here get so comfortable?" he asked, leaning back in the neon lounge chair.

"The minute we stopped paying for it ourselves."

We smiled together. Gil closed his eyes against the bright blue of the sky.

"Molly and you celebrated at lunch?"

"She brought wine."

He shook his head, smiling, eyes still closed.

"I'm sorry, Gil," I said.

Gil's chest rose and fell.

"You saw it firsthand, I guess," he said. "How much I wanted to be king."

He swept his hand in a flourish across the terrace, the boardroom behind us, attempting humor.

"It's your kingdom," I said.

"Yeah." He deflated. "Do you think you'll take it?"

"Take what?" I said, realizing immediately what he meant. "The promotion? What do you mean?"

Gil opened his eyes and sat up slowly, elongating his back as he chose his words with care.

"You could be anywhere you want, doing the thing you love best—finding great books, great stories. Publishing them. Somewhere that will let you do that."

I laughed. "You're not trying to get rid of me, are you?"

"No," he said, serious. "I don't like that Malcolm is pitting us against each other, but if I'm here, I want you here. You're part of the reason I do my job well. If it were up to me, I would say 'Let's build this thing together.' But is that what you want?"

I felt sweat prick at my eyelids even though the terrace air was cool, gusts of East River wind blowing my hair around my face.

"You're not suggesting that I can't have a seat at the big-boy board table, are you? I mean, why wouldn't I want this—I've earned it as much as you and Molly."

"Of course you have," said Gil. He paused. "I'm saying that it'll be more money than we've ever had. You'll get prestige. But, Lila, it won't be the same kind of book business. And I don't mind that, but I have a feeling you might.

You always loved the books. You wanted to get each one right. You wanted to stay small, curated. You like writers, Lila, not the business part of it."

I got to my feet, pushing the lounge chair back with my knees.

"You're not my teacher anymore," I said.

"Okay," he said with an easy shrug, lying back again, closing his eyes as I walked away.

4

IN THE EARLY 1980s, Mihir De, my father, had sold his parents' house in Shyambazar, the neighborhood in North Kolkata best known for its theater groups and populous markets. The old bungalow with its mix of colonial and Indian influences had been too painful to keep after Mihir's parents had both died, one after another, in a double whammy of cardiac failure. He moved to Ballygunge, a wealthy neighborhood in the south of the city—into the little apartment that his mother had bought in the '60s with savings from her job as a high court judge. Soon after, he met a girl who lived down the street in a five-story house—one of the many historical zamindar properties of Kolkata, a splendor of cement and stone—and had fallen headlong in love.

She was his first serious girlfriend, bony, with thick eyebrows and large eyes that filled her face, coarse hair curling around her shoulders, a fragility emanating from her at all times. (On the rare occasion my father talked about her, a mix of contempt and admiration would taint him, raising something inside me that felt the need to shield her—she who by then was thousands of miles away. When he would speak of her with hate, it would make me hate him, even while I agreed with him, and this shocking, complex burden was too large a secret to keep, but I did.)

My mother had been barely twenty when she had asked my father to marry her—a feminist proposal unheard of for the time, but she had no time to waste—she was too hungry to get out of the big house and to find some love. My father had agreed without reservation, wildly abandoning himself to the first love of his life (the biggest, he once told me after two martinis, another secret we would both keep for good). They had moved into his apartment, only a short walk—barely half a mile—from her mansion, but it had felt like light-years of blessed distance for my mother.

TWO YEARS INTO an unhappy marriage with my mother, my father had met my stepmother. Older than him by a couple of years, she had been a junior partner in the New York division of the legal firm where he worked. Iva Lechner had arrived in Kolkata to consult on a case that my father had built, and together they ensured that a class action by workers at a mill against the Indian government succeeded. Each of the 416 workers of Maharajah Mills had received two thousand rupees, but my father's car had been set on fire in the middle of the night by local goons who worked for the corrupt party in power, the People's Left. In the pre-cell-phone year that followed, each time my father worked late, his parents and my mother lived in fear that he might have been beaten or killed in an alley. Everywhere we went, we looked over our shoulders, shadowy shapes terrorizing our subconscious or throwing rocks into our windows, one of which almost shattered the family terrier Rexy's skull. Eventually, we were forgotten, but my father never got that taste of India out of his mouth.

Quickly afterward, he fell intensely in love with Iva, who began to make frequent trips to Kolkata from the New York office. When my mother found out, my parents divorced in a public spectacle, screaming at each other on streets, once even yanking on either of my arms, she then escaping to the highest tower of the Lahiri castle, he retreating abroad, the bitterest of custody battles, a judge in an airless courtroom auto-awarding her my life, without a second glance at our papers and lives (surely, mothers were meant to mother—anything else an aberration to society), he finding refuge in the good, kind arms of his fair-maiden equal-pay savior-colleague, who led him into the suburbs of Connecticut, where screaming and feeling and passion and fear were whispers on the edges of the dark clouds my father exorcised in therapy.

I, too, was welcome, but inside me lived my mother's demons, and so I had never found any peace. At sixteen, I had moved to America to live with my father and stepmother, in the cocoon they had built with two dogs and two children, in an updated three-story brick-and-stone Queen Anne Victorian. There were four bedrooms, and I had my own, the first real privacy of my life. As I wandered through the halls, into the spacious kitchen with its granite island, past the maple cabinets and double oven, past the tiled Victorian mantels, onto the porch, it was with the feeling of a forest person who had moved in with a pedigreed family. To me, it was an otherworld. Even as my half siblings tried to share their things and their feelings with me, and my stepmother cooked for us, it felt like I had somehow intruded on a private family moment and had sat down at the table when nobody was looking.

I FELL INTO a thick fog of sleep on the train to Hartford. The house usually smelled of the tea cakes that my stepmother baked for my visits. It should have filled me with warmth, the cozy existence of it. Instead, a low jealousy hummed inside me every time I saw my stepmother tuck a strand of my half sister Robin's hair behind her ear or when my father took my half brother, Avi, to a game, their half-brown, half-white skin (even my father felt caramel within those walls) the perfect contrast to the red-brick home they belonged so entirely in.

My phone buzzed, insistent. I jerked awake as the train pulled into its stop, the fabric of an anxious dream slipping away, a news alert for Obama's weekly address gleaming up at me, outlining the furor of candidates who were trying to unseat the Democrats in the next election.

It was a short walk from the Hartford station to my father's house. The exterior was exactly as it always had been—inviting, the glow of yellow lamplight soft against the midnight-blue evening sky. I had grown from teenager to adult in this house, returning from college like my half siblings, for holidays and laundry, and yet I had always been looking in from the outside.

"Li."

Robin came barreling out of the house. Robin had been five years old when I had first met her. She had shadowed me for a year and a half until I gave in and loved her back. She smelled like a Yankee Candle, of strong cinnamon and apples, as she hugged me.

"What are you doing standing out here? We've been waiting for you. Cake's almost done."

"How's college, button? You staying away from those frat boys?"

"I love the library. It's huge." Robin dragged me across the grass by the hand, into the house. "When can you visit? You can stay in my dorm. We drink vodka in transparent plastic bottles, and the professors think it's water." She giggled. "Don't tell Daddy, or he'll lecture me on how much tuition he's paying again."

Inside, my father was in an armchair, drinking tea and spilling shortbread crumbs into the pages of the book he was reading.

"Lila," he said, rising with pleasure, as he set the John Grisham face down on the ottoman at his feet, crumbs sprinkling everywhere.

"Hi, Baba."

My siblings were regularly hugged by my father, but he and I had the language of nods and unspoken affections that passed between Indian children born in the '80s and their fathers. I dreamed of crossing over into the land of effortless holding and kissing that my siblings were citizens of. My father and I smiled at each other instead, and for the moment, it was enough.

"Is that Lila?"

Iva, my stepmother, came in from the kitchen, her blond-gray curls in a pile on top of her head, her face red from the heat of the oven. She smelled like Robin, and she kissed me on my cheek with easy warmth, the kind she had always extended. Through the windowpanes in the garden, Avi, flanked by rosemary bushes, laughed at something on his phone as he raised his hand in a wave to me.

AT DINNER, MY father and Iva sat at opposite ends of the table, flanked by Avi and me and Robin. Hartford was cooler than Brooklyn, and the midsummer evening temperature felt like a relief. A chicken, golden brown, in a pool of citrus slices and white wine, sat at the center of the table—Iva's specialty, which I had hated for its blandness as a teenager but loved now.

"How's the book business, Li?" asked Avi.

Avi and I had only warmed to each other as adults; in our childhood, we were warriors for my father's distracted attention, and Avi resented the sudden split of his mother's attention three ways instead of two, the bulk of which was heaped onto me, the brooding new entrant whom Iva was careful to never scold or ground. Avi had longed for the freedom to be me, who apparently could curse (testing out teenspeak to fit into my American private school), steal (money from my dad's wallet), and smoke (out of my bedroom window) without punishment. Instead, they took me to therapy and, in Avi's eyes, coddled me with more love (the kind that was too unfamiliar for me to know what to do with). Avi did not know that I longed to be scolded and loved in the same way that Iva mothered her own children, whom she was never careful around.

Years later, one summer, a premed Avi came home from college with his roommate, Akiko. Iva had made up the guest room and asked me to put towels in the adjoining bathroom for Akiko. When I entered the room, Avi and Akiko had their arms around each other, their naked passion for each other so powerful that I gasped before hurrying away. As I disappeared down the hallway, I knew Avi had seen me, but I never mentioned it to him or anyone else, and when he finally came out to our family two years later, it was with a transformation of our relationship from wary housemates to real friends.

"Aetos has installed expensive armchairs in all the lobbies, and we have a coffee machine worth twenty thousand dollars in the kitchen now," I said.

"He's a smart man, worth twenty-seven billion dollars," said my father.

"He lives on electrolytes," I said to my father.

"A self-made visionary," my father, reproachful, informed me.

"That must be why he made me co–editorial director today," I said, my tone light.

My parents were stunned, I could tell. I wondered if they, too, thought it might be a diversity promotion. But their pleasure was genuine.

Iva clapped her hands together. "What? Lila, that's wonderful."

"All of my professors want to pitch you their book ideas," Robin said. "I'm going to tell Professor Belleti immediately so he kisses my ass a little more in class."

My father pulled out his phone, putting on his glasses. "I'll send a Whatsup to the family."

"WhatsApp," corrected Avi.

"Does this mean I can use nepotism to get a job at Phenom?" asked Robin.

"I thought you wanted to become a lawyer," I said.

"To Lila," said Avi, raising his glass of wine as they toasted me, the family that had accepted me into their fold.

We ate the chicken, Avi and Robin fighting over the dark meat, as they always had, my parents resigned to eating the breast. I discovered a cinnamon stick on my plate.

"I didn't realize there was cinnamon in this," I said. "That's why mine doesn't taste the same."

Iva's face suffused with happiness. "Have you been trying to make it?" she asked.

It was her mother's trademark recipe, and she was pleased that I wanted to inherit it. This was how we had built our bridge, Iva and I, with little bricks of polite kindness extended to each other over the years, each one reassuring the other on loop that we might belong together, failing and achieving, my father happy with me for trying, the whole thing forming a shaky terrain beneath my feet.

"Avi, stop hogging the potatoes," said Robin, gesturing impatiently.

"I'm going to India," I said. I had planned to tell my father in an email, but the sentence rushed out of me, taking me by as much surprise as my family.

My father frowned. "It's August. The monsoon must have arrived in Kolkata."

"Dadu died," I said.

The Labrador—with its warm, golden fur—shifted on my feet. Everything in the house was golden. My eyes stung beneath the hum of the wine that I had sipped on an empty stomach. There was a silence as my family grappled to understand what to say.

"He was a good man," murmured my father, a sadness floating onto his face.

"I know how much you loved him, Lila," said Iva, her sympathy requiring nothing of me.

I nodded at her, grateful.

"What happened to him?" asked Robin, cautious, as she was when asking about a family she knew nothing about, a Wild West of her father's past life.

"He had trouble with his kidneys. They tried dialysis, but it didn't work."

"I'm sorry, Li," said Avi quietly. I imagined him trying to conjure my grandfather, a man he had never met, in a country he had traveled to only twice.

"He left me the house," I said.

There was a stillness to their shock, and the Labrador tensed beneath my toes, alerting to the shift.

"Wow," said Avi, shaking his head. "You're full of surprises today."

"Is it a big house? It's a big house, isn't it?" asked Robin. "Do you have a picture, Li?"

"Robin," admonished Iva, instantly rendering me the guest whom her children were gaping at.

I smiled. "Yeah, it's big. Ma's whole family lives in it." My feet were beginning to sweat. I slid them out from under the dog. "Including her," I added.

"I didn't know you were that close to Tejen Babu," said my father. "When did you talk to him last?"

"We talked on the phone—he would call on Sundays," I said, guilt sticking to my ribs.

I had missed far too many of my grandfather's calls, and had not noticed when he hadn't called last week.

My father looked puzzled as he tugged on his earlobe. "But why would he leave it to you, darling?" he asked. "And not his brothers, or your mother?"

I felt something crumple inside me. I shook my head.

"I don't know," I said to my father.

Iva leaned over and touched my hand. We ate in silence for a few minutes, the tinkle of our forks and knives polite against our plates. I thought of my large, messy family in India, mouths and fingers and silverware and opinions, all chaotic and clattering against each other at dinnertime.

"What are you going to do, Lila?" asked my father quietly.

Dr. Laramie had asked me the same question. I could see that my father wanted to know.

"I don't know. I have to go there, see what's going on, probably get a lawyer."

My father looked at me for a long moment. "Are you sure? You don't have to. We could handle it from here."

"I'm sure," I said.

My father shook his head, in the exact stubborn tilt I recognized as my own. "I don't like it. Why would Tejen Babu throw a young girl in the middle of all this? That family won't like it either."

"I'm not a young girl, Baba," I said hotly. "I was his family too. We were"—I choked on the word—"close. I don't see what's so crazy about a grandfather leaving a house to his granddaughter."

We looked at each other, both of our chins jutting and mutinous. My father sighed, relenting, and stood up.

"I'm going to get you in touch with Palekar at my firm," he said.

My father had not worked at that firm in Kolkata in almost thirty years, but he considered it his, a dot on a map in a country that was indelibly ours. I nodded. Introducing me to his old friend and former colleague, a lawyer who knew the ways of Kolkata, was my father's way of rescuing me.

"Can I stay at your apartment?" I asked my father.

"But the big house is yours now, isn't it?" said Robin. "You're not going to stay there?"

"The apartment is yours," said my father as Iva frowned at Robin. "I'll tell Palekar to send someone to get it ready for you."

"It's wonderful that you're going to spend some time in it. We've been saying how it's a waste sitting there empty, waiting for one of our visits," said Iva as she put more chicken, more potatoes on my plate.

"When will you come back?" asked Robin. "You're coming back, right?"

Something thudded in my chest, and for a moment, I was out of breath.

"Of course I'm coming back," I said lightly. "I mean, I just got promoted, didn't I?"

The last time I'd been in Kolkata, ten years ago, I was nineteen, my first and only visit since moving to the US. I was with my father and stepmother and my siblings—the trip was their pilgrimage to an unfamiliar country that was an enigmatic part of their DNA. We traveled like tourists, visiting relatives, taking trips on boats at the ghat, eating in iconic Park Street restaurants, shopping at Fabindia. I had left the country only three short years before, and to be a tourist felt akin to a perpetual state of make-believe.

LATER, THERE WAS the cake that Iva and Robin had baked, and vermouth, and my father and Avi played Scrabble in the living room. It was a game they had started without me, and so I watched from the outside, their tiles coming to life in my mind, the words beautiful objects to focus on: *silky, teat, tenuous, limbic, snarl.*

"Dad, 'potrero' isn't a word," said Avi. "It's a hill in San Francisco."

"You're trying to be a doctor, not a police officer, Avi," said my father, grim.

"Baba, he's right," I said, laughing.

"Quiet. You are not even playing," said my father.

"I'm playing by proxy," I said, leaning over Avi's shoulder.

"No playing by proxy," said my father, irritated.

Robin came into the living room, strapped to a backpack larger than her torso, a full trash bag in either hand.

"Darling, I wish you would use the suitcases I sent you. They have chargers built into them," said Iva, from the chair where she was drinking wine and reading.

"Mom, they're too pretty to put my sweaty stuff into," said Robin. "This is fine. See you later, alligators."

"What time is your bus?" asked my father. "Do you need a ride?"

"Nine thirty," said Robin.

"I got it," said Avi, rising to stretch. "Thanks for dinner, Mom. Baba, I'll beat you next time."

"A fantasy," said my father, grim.

"I'll head out too," I said, laughing as I reached for my handbag.

"I'll call you an Uber," said my father.

"No way. The station is such a short walk."

"It's late," said my father. "You're not taking the train." He tapped his phone vigorously. "It is done. Jaspreet will be here in ten minutes."

I exhaled as my siblings snickered. Iva patted me on the arm.

"It'll make me feel better too," she said.

WE GATHERED ON the porch, Avi's white compact gleaming in the moonlight.

"Call me if you need anything," said my father as he handed me my thin jacket, the concern in his voice transparent. We had not talked about what it might mean for me to be confronted by my mother, but it had to have been uppermost in his mind.

Iva handed me a Tupperware of cake. "Bring the box with you next time," she said as we hugged, their worry hanging over me. I knew that they would stay up talking about me after we were gone.

"And call Palekar as soon as you land," said my father, arms folded across his chest. "Property and inheritance can be a complex matter. Lots of people in that house. They can't be happy about this."

Outside on the porch, I held Robin close. "Don't drink too much, okay? It makes you stupid."

"Text me from India," she said. "C'mon, dada, I'm gonna miss the bus."

Avi kissed my cheek. "Call if you need anything," he said, exactly like my father.

I watched them drive away, the wheels of Avi's Jetta silent in the night, escaping from suburbia, as I climbed into my waiting cab.

IT WAS ALMOST midnight when I reached my building in Brooklyn, bag, jacket, and Tupperware in one hand as I fumbled for my keys with the other hand. A drunk man pushing a supermarket trolley ambled by.

"Mornin', hotcakes." He winked at me.

I closed my fist around the keys, deep inside my purse, one eye on my admirer, who had stopped to watch me as he put one hand into his trousers and pulled out his penis.

"Put that away, or I'm going to have to call the officer again, Charley," I said, turning the key into the rusted lock, which needed a thousand turns before it would give.

I pushed open the door and pulled my phone from my bag. The phone rang, once, twice, three times—before the fourth ring, it abruptly went to voicemail.

As I took it away from my ear, it lit up.

Hey, you good?

Yeah, I typed back.

If Seth didn't answer my call, it meant he was with someone else. We had an unspoken code—one that even allowed for emergencies, the emoji of a lemon. I wondered if this qualified as an emergency.

You up? I asked.

He began to type, then stopped, then began to type again. The three dots appeared and disappeared until they swam, my eyes watering against the brightness of the screen in the darkness of the hall.

Nvm. I added an *X,* a casual kiss belonging firmly in the genre of booty calls, a light throwaway that would reassure Seth. *Next time.*

The dots bubbled again. As I walked up the stairs, Seth was still typing.

Go back to ur night, I said, then added an exclamation mark.

U good? asked Seth again.

I sent back a brown thumbs-up, and the dots disappeared. I kicked off my shoes even before I was fully inside my apartment, shedding clothes, bag, scarf, bracelet like skin, locking the door behind me.

5

IT HAD BEEN an hour and seventy-nine dollars from Brooklyn to JFK, then three hours of waiting, followed by seventeen hours from JFK to Dubai, four mini bottles of wine while I answered every frantic email in my inbox, and two bad movies followed by a transcendent second season of something, so that what little sleep I might have slipped into was erased. I spent my three-hour layover in Dubai with coffee and a Danish, sugaring my exhausted mind. Then, there was nowhere to go but the final leg—to Kolkata—five hours away from occupying the same air and ground as my mother did, my hands and feet turned to ice at the prospect.

Dada was brother, *didi* was sister, and I was now on familiar turf. A stranger had caught hold of my bag and was yelling to another man standing by him to help, while an elderly woman gave them advice on the best angle to slide it off the belt. Suddenly, a throng was lifting my bag off the conveyor, my uniformed porters had produced a cart out of nowhere, and my bag was on the cart as they fought over who might push it.

"Thank you," I said to the crowd of passengers, who grinned at me as I clutched my purse, trying to keep up with the arguing porters as they made their way to the exit.

OUTSIDE, IT WAS a sauna—I stood near the doors of the airport, beads of sweat rising on my scalp, as the porters whistled for a taxi. They had taken charge, and even if it was for a price, I felt relieved. A taxi careened out of its fifth or sixth place in line, and this partnership, I could tell, was preplanned.

My bags were placed in the trunk and my porter friends smiled wide as I handed them each a hundred-rupee note. They folded their hands above their heads, like my yoga teacher in Bed-Stuy, divine in their pleasure at good business.

Whenever my father returned to India, he breathed it in as if he had had no air in years, but the truth was that he had found his home in Connecticut. The smell and sight of the country he had been born in was born of the safety of nostalgia. For me, India was an assault on my senses, as if I had been dragged back into the most dangerous place on Earth, only to discover that it was the one place I might belong. But there had been enough years in the anodyne safety of Connecticut and Brooklyn, and I too breathed it in this time—a sharp pleasure in my veins, at the highway, the green fields next to the airport, the rivers, the countryside melting into city, clatter, chaos, cows, Marutis, autos jostling for space on roads that had no lanes, the taxi-seat velvet under my skin, the driver whistling, humidity, sweat, trucks, mosques, schoolkids with oiled braids and uniforms, a man eating mishti outside a shop where I had bought a thousand sweets, the temple, the alley where I had once kissed Adil, the streets that had housed my friends—and, suddenly, I was home.

The taxi pulled up in front of my father's apartment building, frightening the sleeping mongrels on the curb. The green gates and white cement walls had received fresh coats of paint since the last time I had been there, but that was the only difference. Ram Bhai, caretaker and security guard for the building since before I was born, emerged, his hands folded in greeting. He had thick glasses now, and as he smiled up at me, I felt a rush of wanting to hug him. But hugging was not a part of Ram Bhai's universe. It was not as if Ram had been particularly fond of me as a child—he had looked the other way when boys pulled my hair or when I was left out of games or when, as a three-year-old, I had climbed the wall behind the garden, unable to climb back down for hours. Ram Bhai had been staunch in his belief that children needed discipline, even when my father would rescue me in the late evening, showering curses at Ram, and envelop me in his arms with his cologne smell. But Ram was testimony to a time I had existed in, the first years of my life, spent in this apartment with my father and mother, and the last time I would see them together in the same room.

The apartment was physically the same—three bedrooms and a living room, centered by my grandmother's long dinner table, carved from mango wood. But everything else had changed. The floor was tiled now in modern cream squares. The sofa was cream too, with pale-rose cushions. Dark, low tables with coffee-table books on them studded the room, fabric lampshades with little bowls under them, to catch keys and earrings and odds and ends that a family might leave around, the unmistakable whiff of Iva everywhere. As I showered, I was glad for the modern plumbing, the hot water geyser, the electric kettle.

I made tea and toast and wandered through the rooms. Some of the art had belonged to my father's parents—Jamini Roy paintings, with female bodies in motion, trademark doe eyes painted over, moving sightless. What was it about men who painted women with grace and pattern and the absence of sight? My childhood nursery was lined with shelves of my father's books: legal texts and thrillers, Perry Mason, Grisham, Nehru. A photograph of my grandparents in an Irani café, my baby father in their arms, hung in my mother and father's once-tumultuous bedroom, now cream and rose as well. The bedroom was outfitted with a new air conditioner, which I turned on gratefully. The linen sheets against my skin, wet hair, wet pillow, fake peonies in cream vases, so real they could be the real thing, the air cold and the duvet warm, I sank into sleep.

EVEN THOUGH I had slept through the night, I woke up in a state, a slow burn spreading in my chest, fear trickling into my stomach. I wondered if I was ill as I drank from a glass on the bedside, too disoriented to decipher if it was day or dusk. I looked at Iva's quartz clock by me—I had slept seventeen hours, and the light was not fading. It was dawn, and the day of my grandfather's funeral.

There was no reason to be afraid—I was removed from deadlines (though I had checked my emails thrice). But fear was born of the unknown: A plane could crash into you as you made tea behind a bolted door. Your mother could be less than one mile from where you stood.

A SCHOOL BUS stopped across the street as I left the apartment. Ram Bhai, cleaning his glasses, followed me through the gates.

"Your grandfather was a good man, Lila Madam," he said in Hindi, trying to focus on my face.

I nodded, feeling a constriction in my throat. A group of schoolchildren stared out the bus windows. Immediately, I was self-conscious, as if at one of my college friends' all-white upstate New York weddings where the photographers would follow me around—I was exotic there and, somehow, here as well, where my skin did not stand out, but something inside me did, and children were the most clear-sighted of us.

I had managed to put together the customary all-white clothing for the funeral—a shirt and slacks—with my brown saddlebag across my chest, leather sandals on my feet, an umbrella, in case it rained. I wished I had remembered to pack one of the kurtas or saris from the box in my closet in Brooklyn marked INDIAN, which I pulled out for Indian weddings or when my parents took me to a Durga Pujo festival in New Jersey. It was the second week of August, and at six in the morning, I was already sweating, wondering if I had underestimated the transparency of my linen shirt.

BALLYGUNGE PLACE ROUSED fierce pleasure in me: the old town houses, painted green and blue and pink, standing shoulder to shoulder, weather-beaten but regal; the sweetshop and the temple; neem and chhatim and debdaru trees blanketing the neighborhood in familiar green; telephone wires and a plethora of crows and sparrows overhead; mongrels asleep at every corner. There were changes, like tall buildings where old houses had once stood and restaurants that had replaced corner stores. The pharmacist's wife, once my geography tutor, did not recognize me as I passed by her window. This was a street where everyone had known me once. Maids rushed past in fluid motion, on their way to the first of the many homes they would clean or cook for during the day, saris wrapped so expertly around themselves that they might have been in yoga pants. Schoolchildren, a mix of chatter and resignation at the early hour, waited at the bus stand. Fruit sellers set up outposts for the day, under the banyan tree, for respite from the sun. The rickshaws were positioned exactly where they had remained through my childhood—and I realized that some were the same men who had been here for forty, fifty years, pulling carriages, some barefoot, all of them lean, muscled, leathered by the sun.

I had lived the first sixteen years of my life on this street, the first eight months in my father's apartment, and then fifteen years in my grandfather's house with my mother, on the fifth floor, after her marriage ended, and where her entire family, spread across five stories, weighed in on the matters of her heart. I had gone to school and returned home, and rushed to math tutors and art classes and friends' homes, on this street.

At the tea stall, cardplayers were already congregating to drink tea, talk about revolution, frown at the paper, and begin to play. I stopped on the street. About thirty feet in front of me was the Lahiri house, and it took my breath away. Weathered by rain and neglect, covered in ivy, brick exposed (purposeful in Brooklyn, decay here), the wide balconies unlit, as if housing darkness inside. And yet, even ruined, it was still magnificent, like a once-wealthy aristocrat, struggling to stay upright, stay relevant, even in poverty.

There was a narrow driveway to the left of the house, wide enough for a single car, but drivers needed to go all the way in, into the expansive courtyard, to turn the car around. The courtyard was meant for family weddings, festivals, religious ceremonies, and funerals. Today, it was draped in white flowers, and a priest sat in the center, chanting in front of a large photo of my grandfather. Even though I entered noiselessly, my grandmother noticed immediately.

"Mummy," I said, taking in her small, grieving face.

I had always called her what my mother had, despite my mother's protests that I would give anyone else a maternal title and dump the short, curt Ma unjustly on her. It did not matter that I called all the other members of the Lahiri household what my mother called them, mirroring her since childhood, using for her young twin uncles the same *kaka* moniker that she did. My mother and grandmother had never been able to love each other in any simple way, and since that was also true of my mother and me, my grandmother and I had a reservoir of leftover love for each other, united by our lack of comprehension of my mother's ways.

There was a slowing of the chatter in the courtyard as my family turned around as if they had been waiting for me, and I realized that they had. And then it dissolved, and there was pandemonium, and my grandmother's thin arms were wrapped around me.

"My God, Lila, it really is you," she said, her frame birdlike against me, as if shrunken since the last time I saw her.

My grandfather's brother Hari strode across the room.

"Lila," he said, his silvery, musical voice echoing through the courtyard. "Why didn't you tell us what time you were coming? I would have sent the car."

"Hari, don't shout at her," said my grandmother, affectionate, still in my arms. She looked up at me. "He went so quickly," she said in disbelief.

I noticed the white of her sari, the absence of her signature burgundy lipstick. My grandmother was a widow now, and the color had left her.

"Hari's been fighting with the priest again," she whispered into my ear. "Apparently, thakurmoshai raised his rates for funerals and spirit sendoffs, and Hari isn't happy."

"Geeta, let the girl go," said Hari. "Let's have a look at her. What a foreigner you have turned into, Lila Ma," he said, inspecting me.

My grandmother, reluctant, let go of me as Hari enveloped me in a cloud of sweet temple smoke and nicotine. His stomach was a balloon between us, distended by beer and sloth, according to my mother. I leaned into his wide shoulders, feeling unexpected emotion for this family of mine.

"Your mother and grandmother's hearts are broken," said Hari. "All of our hearts are broken. But we've been taking care of each other." Hari brushed my hair out of my face. "You're home, Lila Ma."

Hari's skin was sunburned and dark brown, a coarse, thick mustache on his upper lip. He was a chunky, loud man, given to perpetual song and belly laughs, like his older brother, my grandfather. But unlike his brothers, Hari was prone to bursts of temper, and it did not pay to argue for long with him.

"Lila, you're so tall," my uncle Rana said softly behind us, even though I was exactly the same height I had been since sixteen, an inch below my mother, at five foot six.

Rana was the mildest Lahiri, kind and pale, with almost-translucent skin, like his mother's, blue veins forming a map across his throat and neck and knuckles.

"Hari, let the poor girl breathe," said Rana's wife, Gina, pleasure in her crisp voice. "When did you get here, Lila?" she asked.

"Last night," I said.

My aunt Rinki smiled at me. She was only a handful of years older than me, because, like her uncles, Hari and Rana, their sister—her mother, Bela—had been born late in life to their mother. Her soft hair and dimpled cheeks framing her face, her forehead knitted into parallel lines, she exuded the same mix of happiness and concentration as she had as a teenager.

A tall man with gentle eyes and a wan, scholarly face stood next to her. I gave him the once-over and winked approvingly at Rinki. His eyes widened, and she laughed. We were girls again, Rinki and I, immediately.

"This is Bashudeb," she said, smiling up at him.

I nodded to Bashudeb as Hari's wife, Mishti, squeezed my hand, her gentle, large eyes alive with pleasure.

"Lila, you were just a girl when you left, and look at you now," she said.

"Lila," screamed Hari's daughter, Biddy, from across the room as she entered it. Thirteen when I last saw her, she was a lithe gazelle of a woman now.

It was a maelstrom of affection and exclamation and hugging. The young priest turned around from his chanting.

"Shanti," he said, firm, and the room quieted.

"Thief," said Hari, but under his breath.

We had known the priest his whole life, from when his father was the family priest, and even Hari would not risk upsetting him.

"He's not that cute anymore," whispered Rinki.

I laughed, turning to examine the priest, our old flame, and it was then that I understood that it was not the priest whom my family kept looking toward in anticipation; it was my mother, who sat next to the photo of my grandfather, half-hidden by the large wooden frame, watching me. Her face had not changed, the curls still cut to a stern bounce around her collarbone, the compact frame of an elegant, unhappy woman, arms wrapped around her knees, her eyes almost too large for her face. There were new lines on her face, crinkles around her eyes, but you could not tell that a decade had passed.

"Hi, Lila," she said, polite, rising.

For a moment, we assessed each other, uncertain. Then, she came closer, reaching for me, and I was in her arms, feeling myself fall into her body, as an unrestrained, frightening joy spilled from her, the past once again erased.

BY THE TIME the priest finished with his mantras, the woodsmoke and incense had permeated my skin. My grandfather seemed to be laughing at the ceremony of it all, in the portrait they had chosen of him that would later be hung over my grandmother's desk. The funeral's guests had begun to leave, and Biddy, funeral-fabulous in a white eyelet kurta and pink lipstick, sat with me on the steps of the courtyard, snipping marigold garlands in half and sliding the flowers into wicker baskets, to be repurposed later. I had been standing alone as the family cleaned up around me, and Biddy had asked me to help with the flowers—a one-person job, but I possibly gave off the air of a house pet out in the wild.

My mother and Rinki were distributing prasad to the line of beggars waiting outside. I watched as my mother talked to a woman, pressing sweets and flowers into her outstretched palms. The woman smiled as my mother gave her shoulder a reassuring squeeze.

"I have a fiancé now," announced Biddy.

"Oh," I said, taken aback. "How wonderful."

"I was so jealous of your boyfriend when I was little," she said. "You would sneak off to kiss Adil behind the jamun tree, and Rinki Didi would talk for hours to some boy on Rana Kaka's phone after he would go to work. But now I have a fiancé. He's cute."

She giggled at this last piece of information, suddenly six again.

"I bet he's cute," I said, wondering how Biddy had been able to spy on us so thoroughly back then.

"Do you have a boyfriend?" she asked.

"Well, it's . . . complicated. No, no, I don't really."

"Sounds like a Facebook status." She laughed again. "Boys are complicated. But Arjun proposed, and now I'm going to marry him."

I did the math on how old she could be—twenty-three—as Biddy stretched out an arm. Sunlight caught the ruby on her finger.

"The first week of October," she said. "Lila Didi, you can dance at the wedding."

There was so much that had happened without me. As I touched the ring, I felt a flash of anger—my mother had not told me, assuming I would not want to come.

"And he's cute." She looked at me, to make sure I had understood this clearly.

"And he's cute," I said, shaking my head.

"Here, look—" She thrust her phone at me. "Look at my YouTube."

Biddy and a shirtless boy with a sharp nose and jaw, thick eyebrows, all chisel and biceps, danced in front of me in perfect sync to a Macklemore song.

"Wow," I said.

"I know," she said. "Though not out of my league?" Biddy frowned.

"He's very handsome, and you're too cool for him."

"It's true," she said with pleasure.

I tried to think of what to say. "Biddy, you're . . . you're happy?"

"So happy. He's, like, a dream." She looked at me. "What? Do you think I'm too young?"

I took a breath—my neck hurt from sleeping in a plane seat. "Well, are you ready to be married?"

"So ready," she said. "Man, I can't wait to get out of here and travel with Arjun. Here, look," she said, thrusting her phone at me again. "I have twenty lakh followers on YouTube total."

I examined Biddy's little universe, filled with likes and comments and bright videos that saturated the screen. At Wyndham, we had been trying to get writers to up their social game, and so far it seemed hopeless. Seth, with his twenty-four followers and his pictures of rare-book covers and the occasional capture of an esoteric Brooklyn diner or bar, was an example. The thought of Seth made me smile.

"What are you smiling at? One of Biddy's obscene videos?" asked my mother.

Rinki and my mother had finished the distribution of sweets in the neighborhood. I realized that she would want me to come upstairs with her now, alone.

"Maya Didi, you're so old-fashioned," laughed Biddy, a note of spite in her tone.

"Lila, lunch will be ready in about half an hour," said my mother.

I had not said that I would have lunch with her. Still, I nodded, struck by the way in which Rinki smiled at my mother with real affection. My mother knitted her eyebrows together, a familiar purse to her lips.

"Biddy, wearing almost nothing and shaking your body for the general public does not make you modern. Education might help with that," she said.

"It shocks me that I agree with Maya," called Hari from the corner of the courtyard, where he was counting money to pay the florist.

Biddy let out an impatient noise. "I make more from YouTube than any of you. Leave me alone, please. College courses aren't going to give me some sudden enlightenment. All I want is to get out of Kolkata. And this house," she added under her breath.

A familiar heat spread through my mother; I knew it by the muscles in her jaw, the tendons of her neck raised, the frisson of a tremble in them, the way her shoulders tightened.

"Will you be here tomorrow?" asked Rinki in an attempt to defuse the tension.

If the family was predictable in any way, it was that they would always attempt to change the subject in conflict.

I nodded. Brooklyn felt light-years away.

Rinki brightened, hugged me, and kissed the top of Biddy's head. Her husband appeared, car keys in hand, and placed a palm on Rinki's back.

"Ready?" he asked as my mother disappeared up the stairs.

"Ready," said Rinki.

Biddy stood up as Rinki left, her skin taut across her brooding, lovely face. "Sometimes, I hate this house. You should kick them all out, Lila."

6

AS I WALKED up the stairs to my mother's studio, I could hear the priest laugh at Hari's reenactment of the florist's disbelief that the marigolds had been any less than perfect. I felt my shoulders release—Hari's spirit ran through the house like veins of lightness, breaking the pall of my grandfather's death. As a child, I had heard stories of Hari being the prankster of the Lahiri siblings, leaping out from corners at my mother and Bela, leaving insects on their pillows and nightstands. Hari had always been his sister-in-law Geeta's favorite, even as his own mother preferred Rana. When Geeta had arrived as a young, lonely bride in the Lahiri house, ten-year-old Hari had climbed the plumeria tree in the courtyard, nearly breaking his leg in trying to get her a fistful of the yellow flowers.

Unlike my mother, Hari was easy to love. Even she basked in Hari's glow on occasion, as did I. It was something to experience—you had to be there to feel special in the way only Hari could make you feel. When my mother returned to the house with me, freshly divorced, Hari had made a joke about the chickens in the backyard that had made me forget, for a minute, leaving my father. Then, he had hoisted me onto his shoulders and carried our suitcases to the fifth floor.

My mother had stayed there, on the fifth floor, in the studio with the little kitchenette. If you opened the door, you were on the expanse of the terrace and could see almost all of the city without traffic or smog or cars or people to obscure its specific beauty.

I knocked on the door. The paint smelled fresh, a recent coat, but she had kept the color the same—stark white, modern against the old-fashioned latched wooden panels. Something knotted and balled up in my stomach. It felt incredible that I had lived there once, with her. I pushed the door open— she never locked it, and I knew the map of easy-give latches on the other side by heart.

"Lila?" called my mother. She was in the kitchen and sounded faraway.

Nothing had changed in the little studio that her father had hastily constructed on the terrace after the divorce—my mother to be temporarily hidden away as the neighborhood forgot. Her bed still occupied most of it, shelves mounted on the walls on either side, books everywhere. There was a new table in the patio dining area and new yellow fabric-bound chairs that looked out onto the terrace. I remembered the fifth-floor terrace as a vast open space, from which you could plot an escape for hours on end.

My mother's kitchen was tiny in comparison to my sunlit, open kitchen in Brooklyn, but its carved wooden cabinets and the century-old pale-green marble countertops, which ran through all of the floors, gave the space an eerie luminescence. Nothing here had felt tiny to me as a child—everything had been larger than life, as if it could swallow me whole.

My mother smelled of my grandmother's chicken curry as she stirred the steel korai, the familiar yellow gravy bubbling up from its sides.

"Hi, Ma. Are you making Mummy's recipe?"

"It's my recipe," she said, sharp. Then, as quickly as it had arrived, her anger, streaking across her face, was gone. "I'm glad you're here. Sit. Do you want tea?"

I nodded. I wanted tea and the Marie biscuits that I knew would come with it, that my mother had in a little chipped, red china jar, on the second shelf of her pantry cabinet. The chip was from the time when she had had too much lotion on her hands and it had fallen to the floor. She had been relieved that the jar had not broken, and I, that it had not been my fault.

I wandered back into the bedroom, trying to unclench my shoulders in the quiet of the studio. There were plants on the bookshelves and the side table and the dresser, some trailing out of wine bottles, a clump of lilies grow-ing out of a glazed mud bowl. I sat down in the wicker chair that faced the bed. The bed and chair were the only two places to sit inside the studio. As a teenager, I would fall asleep after dinner, after homework, tucked in on my side, while my mother sat in the chair, reading late into the night, the lamp a fireball framing her head, wrapped in the knitted red shawl that still hung neatly on its back.

Art and literature were the only two things my parents had in common—there was a Jamini Roy on the wall, smaller than the one in my father's apartment, and a framed 1922 cover of the *New Yorker*, a doorman staring into the many familiar windows of a Manhattan brownstone. A sudden anxiety spliced through me—surely, this image that had hung here through my haunted childhood had not been the reason I had chosen New York. A set of pigeon cartoons by the avant-garde Goan artist Mario Miranda hung alongside a Dalí print of an impossible elephant, thin and tall, under a ray of light. On the other wall was a green Charlie Parker record cover, with a thin gold frame around the edges.

The walls were covered in my mother's jumble of tastes, and as I looked around the neat lines of this space that I had once inhabited, at the Turkish rug and the teetering stacks of magazines, it was hard to bear that it looked just like Brooklyn, like the inside of my own home.

She stepped into the studio, two large mugs of tea in her hands. As a teenager, I would want the adult cup of tea she drank. We would fight over the amount of milk she'd add in my mug. For her, she who had considered me a child then—and likely now—caffeine was off-limits. But I had developed an early taste for the strong tea, almost the color of caramel, ginger-spiced, that my grandmother drank, and demanded it. My mother condemned both my grandmother and her tea and forced me to drink the pale liquid she served instead.

"Thanks, Ma." I accepted the mug, inspecting the tea.

It was thin and watery and beige. I took a sip. It was bitter but drinkable. She had brewed it too long.

"Good?" she asked.

"Yes," I said.

Maybe my mother had just never known how to make tea for all of those years that she had tortured me with the milked-up version. Once, I had thrown it up, and she had made me drink the rest of the tea after cleaning me up. Discipline, she had called it.

"Tell me how you are, Lila," she said, settling into the cushions.

A bookshelf was built into the headboard of her bed. Classics—like *Emma, Pride and Prejudice, Silas Marner, Jane Eyre*, some Shakespeare—lined the shelf. It was where I had learned to love books. Anxiety rode through my veins again.

"You're so thin," she said as she took a sip of her tea.

"The studio looks great," I said. "The plants are thriving."

She lit up. "Do you remember how we would put the cuttings into wine bottles? These are the same ones."

She touched the vines of a trail of pothos.

"I've missed you," she said.

I felt a quick sear of longing in my chest. "Why didn't you tell me Biddy was getting married?"

She looked surprised. "Oh . . . I thought I did. Didn't I?"

"No." I drank the tea, letting it scald my throat as I swallowed. "You haven't called in a while."

"Yes. You're so busy. But that's good. You work hard, just like me." She beamed, a proud mother, who had forgotten that she had hung up the phone on me one offended day and had not called me back for fourteen months. Even so, a peculiar pleasure passed through me.

"They promoted me," I said.

"Really? Excellent, excellent." Her eyes widened.

"It's a really big job—a whole team to manage. And I'll work directly with Malcolm Aetos. Here, I'll show you a picture of the new office," I said, rummaging through my bag for my phone.

I scrolled through; I had taken dozens of pictures of the larger, sunnier office before I had left, incredulous that it was mine.

"Here," I said, handing her the phone. "You can see Manhattan across the East River from the window."

She inspected it, peering.

"That's Harriet, my assistant, on the side. She's very smart. They should pay her more."

She swiped to the next photo, continuing to swipe quickly. I leaped up.

"Ma, c'mon. You can't just go through my phone."

I snatched it back.

"What?" she said, amused. "I'm your mother. Don't I deserve to know what's going on in your life?"

I shook my head at her, scanning quickly to check what she might have seen. Nothing personal.

"Oh, here. Here's a good sunset from the window," I said, holding it up, out of reach.

"Very nice." She smiled at me. "What is it you do exactly?" she asked. "Tell me again?"

For a second, I drew a blank myself.

"I . . . Come on, Ma. I'm an editor."

"Yes, yes, I know it's something to do with publishing books. I tell my friends all the time—Lila, she's done it, made it into the big league. Did I tell you I was made head of the Literature Department?" she asked, trailing her hand over the pothos.

"Oh, that's great," I said, still holding up the phone. "Did you . . . Did you still want to see pictures? I have one of my apartment."

"They demand a lot of me—fifty-six undergraduates in a single class, and then meetings to fix the messes the dean makes." A pleasure suffused her face.

I put down the phone. "Sounds like a lot to handle."

She launched into a tirade about the dean. The afternoon sun bounced off her hair, gleaming, like her eyes. I realized that my mother had not aged. Everything here was untouched by time.

FOR LUNCH, SHE had made my three favorite dishes—chicken, gravy dried out the way I liked it, okra fried to a crisp, and raita.

"This is good, Ma," I said, my mouth full.

"You're sure you don't want another roti?"

"No, I'm full."

She put a roti on my plate. "You're too thin. Do you want a glass of wine?" There was the delight of scandal in her eyes, like a kid suggesting a cigarette to a friend.

"You're a grown-up now." She shrugged.

"Do you drink wine?" I asked.

My mother had been largely disapproving of anything that brought anyone pleasure through my childhood.

"Now and then."

I wondered if the rest of the family's judgments on pleasures pursued by a young divorced woman had mellowed with time. I laughed.

"I'll have a glass if you will."

"I can't today. Dadu's thirteen days."

The thought of my grandfather silenced us. Hindu custom involved a thirteen-day mourning period—no meat, no alcohol, and if a man had sons, they would shave their heads.

"Does that mean you won't eat any of the chicken?"

"No. I made it for you," she said.

I was suddenly overcome with feeling for what it might mean to lose a parent.

"I miss him," I said.

She looked away. My mother had never known what to do with the emotions of others.

"Did he. . . suffer?" I asked.

My mother nodded, her jaw set. She did not lie to spare me this time. "But he went quickly, thank god. It was best, this way. He was in so much pain, and not . . . in his right mind at the end."

As our eyes met, we both knew that she meant the house. Her house, that was now mine.

She rose quickly, beginning to clear the table. "Did you want some shondesh?"

"No. Thanks."

"It's not too sweet. I'll get you a piece."

It had been a long time since I had eaten an entire meal with my hands. I washed my hands in the bathroom, trying to get the turmeric of the curry out of my nails. The bathroom was on the other side of the studio, and you had to cross the breadth of the terrace to get to it. There had been a drizzle during lunch, a sign of the delayed monsoon. But the brief shower had evaporated as quickly as it had appeared, leaving behind the smell of wet earth as the afternoon sun blazed onto my bare legs. I felt a burst of hope that perhaps my mother and I might reunite in a shaky peace after all.

WHEN I RETURNED, she was sitting at the patio table, a piece of the sweet, milky shondesh for me in front of her. There was the familiar bitterness to the set of her lips, and her eyes had slid sideways as they did when she was upset, as if inspecting something out of their corners but, really, remembering some grave injustice. It was a look I knew by heart, and as I picked up a piece of the sweet, my heart beat faster, the soft milky taste dissolving into fear at the back of my throat.

"He didn't leave it to me because he wanted me to know that he didn't love me," she said.

"He would never do that," I said, a dull prickle beginning to stab the sides of my ribs, as if deflating tiny balloons of my breath.

"He had gone mad. The pain had made him mad. The pills were giving him headaches and changing his brain. He was not himself." Her eyes were glittering. "He'd left it to Hari and changed his mind all of a sudden. The lawyer told me."

She looked triumphant, because this, she knew, might dismantle me.

"I need a Pepcid or something," I said, looking around. "A digestive. I think I've got acid reflux." The stabs were intensifying with each exhale. If my grandfather had wanted to leave their house to his brother before he had fallen sick, then my windfall was ill-gotten gains, from a fevered mind that had altered a tradition of rightful inheritance.

"The person who inherits the house takes care of the family," I said, trying to breathe. "You don't even like them, Ma."

"They're my family," she hissed at me.

I nodded. "Yes. And I'm going to try to do what's best for them. I promise." I got up and looked through her kitchen drawer, the one where the medicines used to be kept. No Pepcid.

She shook her head. "The madness of it. Leaving it to a child. Just to make a point to me. When I've taken care of everything for years and years on end."

"Maybe he thought I was an adult. Do you have any Sprite or antacid?" I asked, my voice shrill to my own ears, looking through her fridge.

She rose from the chair, as if registering my pain at last.

"What is it, Lila Ma?" she asked, concern softening her features.

"Acid reflux. Do you have something for it?"

I gulped cold milk from the fridge, a trick that Iva had taught me when I had been in pain postmeal. I felt a longing for the safety of Iva, who always kept a jar of Pepto-Bismol on the counter for me. My mother rushed back into her studio. I could hear her rummaging as I leaned against the refrigerator. She reemerged and handed me a strip of pink pills. I gulped two down, with more of the milk. Slowly, I let out a ragged breath.

"Better?" she asked, pulling a chair close to me.

"It will be. It's probably just because I'm underslept, and ate a big meal."

"I have a good doctor. Dr. Sanyal. We should take you for a full checkup. You're too thin."

"I'm fine, Ma."

There was an edge to my voice. I did not want her maternity. She drew back as I took a long breath, finally able to.

"I'm sorry Dadu didn't leave the house to you," I said. "He should have."

She looked away. "He would have if I were his son." She got up from the patio table and went back into the studio. "What do young girls listen to these days? What about Brubeck? Or are you in the mood for some Geeta Dutt, now that you're home after so long?"

"Sure," I said, following her inside.

I sat down and leaned back into the cushions of the bed, closing my eyes. Geeta Dutt floated over me. *"Ei mayabi tithi,"* she sang. A powerful sadness settled into me.

"Ma, why didn't you just leave this house?" I asked, eyes still closed. There was a long silence. "You could have had your own life, somewhere else."

"This is my home."

I opened my eyes. She was in the wicker chair, the red shawl over her shoulders.

"But you could have lived without . . . without all of them hanging over you every second of the day," I said.

For a minute, something haunted passed through my mother's face, but like quicksilver it was lost and she smiled at me.

"This is my home. It is my duty to take care of it," she said, calm, Geeta Dutt singing to us. Dutt had died a raging alcoholic. In her lifetime, she had transformed loneliness into music that inhabited your bones.

"Duty isn't everything, Ma."

"I'm glad he left it to you. I know you'll do the right thing," she said, watching me.

I closed my eyes again. I wanted to go home, back to my father's apartment, but the music had wrapped itself around us.

"Maybe we can go to Trincas and listen to music there on Saturday? They have wine," said my mother, hopeful.

A thousand years had passed since we were mother and daughter, and yet there was no escaping it.

"That sounds nice, Ma."

My mother asked me several times to stay the night. Refusing her was a matter of appetite for repetition, because she could ask you the same question, over and over again, as if it were the first time. It was designed to be a slow chipping away at your resolve. But there were some things I could not bodily handle, and spending the night next to my mother in her bed was one of them. She stood at the top of the stairs, watching as I made my way down.

"Bye, Ma," I said.

"Will I see you tomorrow?" she asked.

"I think so—I'll call you," I said, slipping down the dark staircase, eager to get away from her.

The lights were turned off on the fourth floor. Since Krishna Lahiri's sudden death, the floor had remained dark, to preserve electricity costs. I felt my way through the landing, lit only by a dim bulb that flickered, my great-grandfather's shadows leaping at me in every corner. I hurried down the stairs, clutching the stone banister.

The third-floor landing, where my grandmother's rooms were, was bright—the flood of tube-lit fluorescence harsh to my eyes. Disoriented, I walked past my grandmother's kitchen, through her dining area and the narrow hallway that led to her bedroom. The tiles of the floor were hexagons of cream and emerald, painted into the stone, there since the beginning of the house, over two hundred years ago, unique to Bengal's zamindari ancestral houses.

I shivered—it was always colder inside, the stone and cement dropping the temperature by a few degrees. The pillars, with their carved dancing creatures and deep webs of thin cracks, felt like a presence, bearing grim witness over the years that my ancestors, the landowning Bengali zamindars, had terrorized their tenants, impoverished peasants and farmers, into paying steep taxes that had empowered colonial rule. When India had achieved independence from the British in 1947, one of the first few reforms had been the abolition of the zamindars, stripping my great-grandfather and his ilk of their status and ill-gotten riches, reducing them to ordinary citizens.

From my grandmother's bedroom window, I saw her standing, bent over Mishti, Hari's wife, who was sitting on a chair. Relieved at the sight of them and the warm lamplight inside the bedroom, I knocked on the loosely latched wooden door, identical to my mother's but without the bright white paint—my grandmother preferred the natural mahogany of the worn wood. The noise startled them—my grandmother sprang back from Mishti, almost guiltily.

"Lila, it's you." She put her hand over her heart. "You gave me a scare."

Mishti giggled. "Geeta Didi is always seeing her mother-in-law's ghost."

"My mother-in-law would probably be haunting the halls with her loud music and scolding me for wearing white as a widow. 'Put some makeup on, Geeta,'" said my grandmother, mimicking the formidable Katyayani.

For a second, we were silent as my grandmother looked into the distance.

I knew that widowhood and all that she had given up, including a cabinet full of maroon lipsticks, was still a new cross for her to bear.

"Come on, come inside, then," said my grandmother, leaning over Mishti, who obediently reclined on what I recognized as my grandfather's old office chair. "Lila, would you turn the lamp toward us?"

"Sure. What's wrong with your eye, Mishti Kaki?" I asked as I swiveled the neck of the old-fashioned lamp.

My grandmother had white gauze and tape in her hands.

"Here. Hold this, Lila," she said, handing me the tape and then measuring the patch of gauze over Mishti's left eye. My grandmother shook her head. "Too small," she said, and took it off.

I gasped. It looked as if the whites of Mishti's eye had exploded into hundreds of tiny red shards, her pupil oddly stretched out, glowing in the light.

"Jesus," I said. I swallowed. "Sorry, I just—"

"Oh, it's fine," said Mishti, cheerful. "I went to work for an hour after lunch, and one of the toddlers at the crèche had a toy in his hand while I was putting him down for naptime. And, well, he gave me one right in the eye."

"Some toddler. Is he training to be a boxer?" I looked away from her eye, enormous and bloody in her small, fragile face.

"You should complain to the parents," said my grandmother, stern. "A lawsuit," she added, taping the gauze in place, above Mishti's distended eye. "Do you know the doctor thinks it might have detached her retina? A lawsuit," said my grandmother again. "That's what we need."

"He's just a baby. It was an accident," said Mishti.

"Hold still," said my grandmother. "Lila, are you cold? You're shivering."

"I should have worn jeans," I said. "You should get a heater in here."

"If I made a list of everything this house needs, I would be at my desk till morning," said Geeta. "There, you're done," she said to Mishti.

Mishti's eye was a perfect little square of gauze now, all its bloodied batter hidden from sight.

"Come on, Lila," said Mishti, jumping up. "I'll give you one of Biddy's sweaters—very glam." She winked at me with her other eye.

"Oh, it's fine. I was on my way out anyway. Just came to say good night to Mummy."

"What about dinner?" protested my grandmother.

"I ate upstairs," I said, after the smallest fraction of a pause.

I could see the annoyance flash in my grandmother's brief nod.

"Of course," she said. "What did your mother make?"

I exhaled, knowing what lay ahead. "Just . . . a whole bunch of things . . . You know, the stuff I like . . . my favorite things."

"What kind of favorite things?"

"Chicken curry, bhindi," I said.

"Dry chicken curry?"

"Yes."

"What else?"

Mishti giggled at my grandmother's interrogation.

"Bhindi fry," I said.

Outrage creased through my grandmother's wrinkled, beautiful face. "And raita?" she asked.

"And raita," I said, resigned.

"That girl," said my grandmother, breathing hard. "That girl," she said again, shaking her head in outrage.

Mishti frowned, not following. "What's wrong with that menu? It sounds good to me."

"They're *my* specialties," said my grandmother. "My specialties that Lila loves. She didn't want to let me make them for Lila."

"Mummy, you can make me other stuff . . . What about your prawns?"

"Yes," said Geeta, heated. "And keema. You like my keema-stuffed capsicum, don't you? And peeyaj kolir chochori. Yes, tomorrow," she said, determined, asserting the statement more to herself than me. "Lila, be here at noon sharp. We will have lunch, *together.*"

Mishti stifled another giggle.

"Yes, Mummy," I said, kissing her cheek as I hugged her. She felt tiny in my arms, and I loved her love for me. "Good night, now—go to bed. Will you be okay?"

"Yes. I'll go shopping in the morning to get all the ingredients. What fun, I haven't been outside in weeks. I had planned on your favorites, but no matter, we'll make new favorites," she said, cheerful again. "Mishti, remember that that bandage needs changing daily."

RANA AND HIS wife were at their son Vik's apartment for dinner, and so the second floor was dark too, but it was a friendlier darkness than that of Krishna Lahiri's floor. Mishti and I went down the stairs in companionable silence—something in her personality felt effortless to be around.

"Can you see, with one eye covered?" I asked.

She laughed. "I know this house by heart. I could take these stairs with my eyes closed."

"Why hasn't my grandmother been outside in weeks?" I asked Mishti.

"It's the stairs. All of the older family members suffered when they were alive—their knees can't take it, each step is too high, and we have too many floors."

"Why don't we build an elevator?"

Mishti laughed. "A lift? What a thought. Where would we put it?"

We reached the ground floor, where she and Hari lived.

"Your grandmother and mother love you so much," she said.

"It's an Olympic sport for them."

She laughed. "You're always making people laugh, Lila. You were like that as a child too."

"Really? I always thought of myself as a serious kind of kid. Hari Kaka is the real family joker."

Mishti smiled. We stood in front of the door to her apartment.

"We're never short on invitations, it's true," she said. She glanced at the door. "But you know, after all these years, I sometimes wish we had a little more quiet." She laughed. "The grass is always greener."

I nodded. Marriage universally seemed to me a territory of striving to appreciate one's own grass, whether in Brooklyn or Kolkata.

"We're all so happy you're back, Lila."

"Are they? I mean, it's so awkward, isn't it? Ma thinks Dadu lost his mind."

Your dadu was a good man, Lila." She leaned closer, almost whispering now. "But he was naive about a lot of things, Lila. Be careful. Remember that this house is the only precious thing that this family has left. They are not going to give it up so easily."

A latch rattled, startling us both. Hari flung the wooden panels of his bedroom door open.

"What's all the chatter outside my door? Is that you, Lila? That's what I thought, a little American bird chattering outside."

"Sorry, Hari Kaka," I said. "I was just going home."

"This is your home," he said, his voice high and pure.

I wondered what might have been the result of either of the Lahiri twins pursuing music as a profession.

"It's late," he said, looking at his watch. "I will drive you back."

"No, I want to walk. I've missed the neighborhood."

Hari looked at Mishti, uncertain.

"It's only a ten-minute walk," I said, a little desperate now.

"She's grown up now, Hari," said Mishti, an affectionate palm on his back, gently steering him away. "And you've had a glass of whiskey."

"No need to advertise my sins. Send us a text when you're inside your father's house," he said.

As Mishti closed the doors behind them, I began to walk down to the courtyard and toward the entrance. As I stepped into the street, I heard Mishti call my name behind me. I turned. She had come out without her slippers, slightly out of breath.

"There's a board meeting tomorrow—to discuss Biddy's wedding," she said. "You should come."

"Really?" I asked, uncertain. Neither my mother nor my grandmother had mentioned it to me. "It's not a private family thing?"

"It's your house now. How could you not be on the board?"

I smiled, despite myself. "Okay."

"Eleven thirty," she said, disappearing back into the hallway. "Half an hour before your big lunch."

THE NEIGHBORHOOD WAS still by night, white light from the streetlamps mixing with moonlight, everything bathed in the glow, the effect like an old Bengali movie. I felt safe; the city ate dinner late, at nine or ten, and windows were still lit with families around tables. The sweetshop owner was closing his gates, pulling down the noisy metal shutters, his wife loading a large rect-angular metal pan of leftover rabri into a waiting rickshaw. She smiled as I walked by, and I smiled back, but I wasn't sure that she remembered that I was Maya and Mihir De's daughter. The strays wagged their tails at me, and I resolved to put a pack of Maries in my bag in the morning.

I was almost home, a block away from my father's apartment. An elderly man, a lungi tied around his waist, a toothpick in his hand, stabbed at his teeth as he stared, pointedly, at my breasts and bare legs as I walked past. It did not feel unsafe, but I remembered how to look him in the eye as I approached. It took a full few seconds, but he looked away, as I had known he would. That skill, learned at eleven or twelve in Kolkata, was like swimming or riding a bicycle, which once learned by heart always lurked at the back of your skull, that special place of instinct.

Ram Bhai had locked the gates of the building, and I rang the buzzer on the wall, harsh in the silence of the night. My purse vibrated against my side—it was probably Gil with work questions. There were launches and deadlines and authors that remained undeterred by my altered time zone. Seth, for instance, was due to submit his manuscript in a little over three weeks, but I suspected that he was far from accomplishing that end. I needed his book; it could be a big title for the next season. I resolved to call him as soon as I was inside.

Ram Bhai pulled open the gates, a roti in one hand.

"I'm so sorry—you were eating dinner, Ram Bhai," I said.

"Oh, that's fine, Lila Madam," he replied. "I like it when you or the family come—always a little more excitement around here."

He put the roti between his teeth as he struggled to pull the gates shut again. I reached to help him, pulling the left gate as he tugged on the right one, but he stopped, holding up a palm in outrage.

"Lila Madam, good night. I'll see you tomorrow."

"Are you sure?"

The look on his face was enough answer for me, and I retreated up the stairs.

INSIDE THE APARTMENT, I switched on the lights and got a cold beer from the refrigerator. I pulled out the phone from my handbag and connected to the Wi-Fi. Immediately, an avalanche of email poured in—there were thirty-seven unread ones and the top four were from Gil. The phone began to vibrate again—it was Seth.

"Seth, hi," I answered with pleasure. It was good to hear his voice. "I was going to call you."

There was silence on the other end.

"Seth?"

I looked at the phone to see if the Wi-Fi had wavered. There were four bars.

"Hello? Lila?" said Seth, tight and clipped.

"What's wrong?"

Seth was never unfriendly—the tone of his voice gave me anxiety, and I felt a twinge through my gut. I distractedly wondered if I had remembered to pack any Pepcid.

"Is it the eighth chapter? You want to talk through it?" I took the beer and put it against my sticky forehead, settling back against Iva's rose cushions. "Seth?" I asked into the void.

"Lila, how could you just leave like that?" He paused, terse. "Without any explanation. Not even a text."

Taken aback, I fumbled. "I . . . I'm sorry. It was sudden."

"You told Molly."

I took a swig of beer. It had not occurred to me that he would mind that I was on the other side of the Atlantic Ocean for a few weeks, but it should have. He was in the final throes of his book, certain he would never find the light, even though I knew he would.

"I'm sorry, Seth. It was a tough couple of days, and I didn't think. I'm sorry."

The silence on the other end seemed to soften.

"How are you?" he asked.

"Fine, fine. It's hot here. Look, I'm still available—you can call or email me anytime you get stuck, and we can talk it through. Does that sound good? And Gil is going to check in with you too—we're all here for you."

"You're here for me," said Seth slowly.

"Yes. Completely."

"Goddamn it, Lila."

"What?" I was getting annoyed with him. I had already apologized.

"You just left. You didn't even write a text. Not a word. You didn't answer the phone when I called. You didn't tell me."

A flutter of recognition went through the part of my body that recognized Seth as my lover.

"You don't care," said Seth. "It's just staggering that you truly do not give a fuck. Even as a courtesy."

He had never raised his voice at me before, I realized.

"Seth, my grandfather died." I raised my voice back at him.

"Yeah, and, you know, I'm just the guy you fuck sometimes, right? I don't need to know."

"You're . . . one of my authors."

"Fine. I'm an author. I don't matter. No need to tell the author you fuck sometimes on a Tuesday if you're bored that something awful happened to you and you left the country."

I began to laugh. "We've never fucked on a Tuesday. Well, maybe once."

"Great. Please laugh at me. Please make a witty little joke of my feelings."

"Seth," I said, my voice firming. "We decided this was casual. Stop shouting at me."

"We are casual. Doesn't mean . . . It doesn't mean . . . we're not . . . human."

Fighting the urge to laugh again, I imagined Seth's pale skin turning a mottled red, as it did when he was upset.

"And you left the country. Indefinitely," he said, furious through the line.

A frisson of unknown pleasure went through me. "It's not indefinite," I said.

I heard a click and a rush of breath on the other end.

"Did you just light a cigarette?"

"So you're coming back?"

"So much for quitting—you're an idiot. Yes, I'm coming back."

"How long?" I heard an anxiety in Seth's tone, and a surge of longing for my apartment shot through me.

"Eight weeks," I said.

"Why didn't you just say that?"

"You didn't ask," I said, flirtatious. "I'll expect dinner the night I'm back, after all this fuss."

"Okay," he said quietly.

"And let's plan to talk once in a while, in my nights, an update at least—what the day's been like, what you wrote—so we stay on track."

I could hear him smoking on the other end.

"Put the cigarette out and go back to work, Seth. I'll see you soon. Probably on a Tuesday."

He laughed. "See you, Lila. Sooner than later, I hope."

7

THE NEXT MORNING, I jerked awake from a dream where I had lost most of my teeth and had been searching in my mother's drawer for my Brooklyn dentist's phone number. Iva's clock beeped insistently, and I realized it was eleven, and that the Lahiri board meeting was in thirty minutes. I rushed out of the building ten minutes later, Ram Bhai trailing in my wake, ever investigating where I might be going, ever suspicious of women who lived in apartments alone and returned home past ten. Half running, I wondered what Gil, Molly, Seth, Harriet—any of them—were doing right at that moment.

Outside the house, I stopped to catch my breath and admire the old Contessa parked on the street outside: vintage maroon, regal, despite a layer of mud splattered all over its sides. The car honked at me, the sound like a trumpet over the traffic cacophony of Ballygunge Place. A small, muscular man, who had been hunched over the leather-clad steering wheel, his sharp nose (the Lahiri nose) a shadow against the sunlight, stuck his head out the car's window.

"Lila," he shouted, patting the seat next to him, as curious maids and drivers, clustered around the paan shop on their breaks, stared at us.

I climbed into the car, beaming. "Hi, Vik."

He leaned over to hug me. "Little Lila," he said.

He wore a delicate cream muslin shirt rolled up to his sleeves and linen slacks the color of the Contessa—it was like looking at a magazine ad.

"Nice car," I said, hugging him back.

Vik smelled of cigarettes and expensive, faint cologne. Like my grandfather, he had gone to Oxford—rare Lahiri men, to have gone to college. He was a senior staff writer at the prestigious, if poor, *New Statesman*, a local English-language newspaper that made its left-leaning opinions clear across its pages.

Vik laughed. "It's actually a really great machine."

"Krishna Dadu would have had a heart attack if he saw his Conti covered in mud."

"Good thing he isn't around, then . . . I'm joking," he said at the look on my face. "I tolerated the old man, despite the asshole he was."

Krishna's bullying of Vik's father, Rana, had left a permanent strain between the patriarch and his only grandson. After Krishna's death, my grandfather had assumed the reins and given new freedom to the Lahiri men. But it was too late for Vik by then; unlike the others, he had moved out and rented an apartment on Shakespeare Sarani.

Vik lit a cigarette. "So I hear you're the queen of the manor now," he said.

"Hardly the queen. I don't think anyone really takes the inheritance seriously."

"You think they don't take you seriously?"

I swallowed. "Well, it's not like I really know what I'm doing here."

"They don't know that. They're waiting to see your next move. They're terrified."

He offered me the cigarette. I paused for a second and then took it from him.

"What do you think I should do with it?"

"The house? I don't know. It's got a lot of history, and a lot of people in it. You're not thinking of selling or anything, are you?" he said.

Vik and Rana both should have inherited a piece of the house that I had been given in its entirety. I took a drag, inhaling deeply.

"I don't know what I'm thinking," I said.

"You know what you should do?" asked Vik.

I returned the cigarette. "What?"

"Fix it. Fresh coat of paint, repairs, geysers in the bathrooms, better lights, maybe even a generator for the blackouts. It'll raise the price of the property, and at least the Lahiris won't look like they're flat broke."

"Where would I get the money to do that?"

Vik stared at me. "You really don't have a clue, do you?"

"Where exactly would I get my clues from?"

Vik laughed. "You didn't just inherit the house—you inherited the estate fund. It's a trust, set up by Jagannath Lahiri when he built the house in 1822. He wanted to re-create his father-in-law's Murshidabad Rajbari. It's a small fortune, but the family only has access to the monthly interest. The owner of the property, though, has access to the whole fund." Vik took a dramatic pause as he smoked. "They're waiting for you to decide what you're going to do with it. None of the Lahiris in the last few decades have actually used the money to repair or restore the house. They use it to . . . survive. Groceries, medical bills, and so on. You know, because none of the men work." Vik's forehead crinkle. "Did Maya Di not explain any of it to you? Or Tejen Kaka at some point? He must have. He left it all to you."

"I know the history, Vik," I snapped, furious with myself for not expecting that my mother had to have hidden things from me.

"Sorry." He looked surprised. "I know how much you loved Tejen Kaka."

I shook my head. "It's all . . . a bit much."

"Yeah." He threw his cigarette into the street. A stray dog got up to investigate. "I hear you're a hotshot editor in Manhattan now."

"Brooklyn. You should see what I get paid. Poor and shot is more like it. Come visit sometime."

"Yeah? Maybe I will. Your brother Avi and I hung out once when the family was here. Seems like a great guy."

"Half brother," I said automatically, looking at him, surprised. "Yeah, he's great. Are you guys friends?"

"Twitter friends. Same politics. That's all you need these days." Vik seemed uncomfortable as he said the words.

"How did you guys meet when Avi visited? Did he reach out?"

Vik looked out the window. "We have friends in common," he said.

I decided to let it drop. "I can imagine you two bonding over torching the far right on Twitter."

Vik laughed. "Easier on Twitter than at work these days."

"I heard you were promoted. You're the hotshot these days."

"All glory, no power. This central government has us in a muzzle. If we so much as make a sound, our offices will be set on fire, stoned. I wrote an op-ed on a Muslim scientist's strides in gene editing last week, and a group of thugs threw buckets of mud at me as I drove out of the parking lot."

"Why on earth would they do that?"

Vik shrugged. "The article lauded a Muslim. Sometimes, just saying that is enough to be considered unpatriotic."

"The thugs work for the central government?"

My shock must have been transparent on my face, because Vik laughed as he nodded.

"The National Popular Front," he said. "Right-wing hoodlums elected on the promise of an all-Hindu India." He shrugged again. "I'm used to it. You don't become a political reporter because you're looking for a soft couch. But we try to keep the fire alive, best we can. Democracy dies in darkness, so said Bob Woodward."

The fishmonger passed us by, screaming his singsong chant: "Lobster, katla, bhetki, parshe."

"Lobster, katla, bhetki, parshe," mimicked Vik. "Bet you don't hear that in Brooklyn. Now watch as Bhola Bagchi's wife, Lata, tries to get a large bhetki for the price of a small prawn."

Lata Bagchi walked toward the fishmonger, her jaw set, her sari pallu wrapped in front of her, the body language of a warrior stepping into a ring.

"You remind me of Krishna Dadu when he would talk politics," I said to Vik.

My great-grandfather had been a freedom fighter in the Indian struggle for independence. We had a picture of him with Nehru, both of them with tea roses pinned to their waistcoats.

"God, don't say that—the man was a tyrant," said Vik.

A series of thumps on the windshield startled us both. Hari, his fist against the glass, grinned at us. Vik rolled the window down, reluctant.

"What are you kids doing here?" asked Hari.

"Just catching up, Hari Kaka. Coming in a minute," I said.

Hari sniffed the air inside the car, sticking his head in, inches from Vik's face. He grinned. "Up to no good as usual, Bikram?"

Vik stiffened. There was a silence as Hari's smile receded, and I realized that there was a tension between the men that I was not privy to.

"Has the board meeting started, Hari Kaka?" I asked hurriedly.

"We're waiting for you," roared Hari, as if announcing the punch line of a joke. He retracted his head and clapped his hands. "Come inside, quickly."

Vik watched Hari as his uncle went into the house.

"They treat me like a kid too—it's infuriating," I said with sympathy.

When Vik did not reply, I touched his shoulder.

"Should we go in?" I asked.

"You go. I just need a minute," said Vik, popping open his pack of cigarettes again. He took a deep breath.

I felt a burst of affection for him—he had always been an outsider too.

"Let's hang out soon? Wherever people hang out in Kolkata?"

Vik's forehead relaxed. "You should come see my friend sing on Thursday night. At Trincas. The owners opened a second floor upstairs—it's fantastic. Come. My friends Adil and Silky will be there too."

I looked at him for a long second. "Adil Sarkar?"

"Yeah," said Vik. And then memory dawned on him. "Oh, right, you and he, you used to go out."

"I was fifteen. That's not going out, so much as hiding out."

Vik laughed. "Well, it'll be a trip down memory lane, then. Adil is one of our lawyers at the *New Statesman*."

I nodded. "He had always wanted to become a lawyer," I said.

Vik was distracted, looking at his phone, which seemed to have a thousand alerts going off simultaneously.

"Sorry. Bloody news cycle," he said, putting it away. "So you'll come?"

"Yeah, I'll come," I said, my heart thudding.

Adil. Long skinny body, quiet eyes, an elegant string bean behind wire-rimmed glasses. The serious lines of an already-crinkled forehead as he read, as he ate, even as he slept. The way his breath felt on my face, the first boy whose breath I had ever felt on my face.

I closed the car door behind me, specks of crusted mud dispersing into the air. It was going to rain, and the sun, behind clouds, felt silken on my skin, the traffic a rising orchestra, this city a home for familiar, sweet secrets.

INSIDE, THE FAMILY was congregated in the courtyard. The maids had laid down woven straw mats, each brighter in color than the next, and the board members sat cross-legged or leaned against large cushions propped against the courtyard's stone pillars. Rana and his wife, Gina, sat together, chatting with Mishti, the latter's bandage eclipsing a quarter of her sunny face. Biddy, her long limbs sprawled over cushions, appeared to be filming the meeting on her iPhone. My mother, grandmother, and Rinki sat on the floor, facing Hari, who was the only one on a chair. I felt a jolt of memory, reminded of all the meetings I had been too young to attend as a child. And here I was now, a family member the others waited for, in order to start.

Bari, the live-in maid, replenished teacups and carried in platters of biscuits and sour-sweet chanachur. A silent toddler followed Bari around, sucking on a thumb, holding the empty teacups that Bari handed to her periodically. When I was a child, I remembered, the house had a staff of ten or twelve—a combination of maids and jamadars and drivers. Now there was only Bari.

Hari, regal, read from a lined school notebook. "The pigeons have been defecating in the ground-floor storage room, behind the boxes of newspaper cuttings and important diaries, as well as on the upper-level cabinets of the old insurance office. Malta's ledge is covered in shit, which she claims is from our pigeons and poisonous and giving her a disease called"—here Hari stopped to consult his notes—"histoplasmosis, which she claims is the reason behind her seeing the ghost of her father-in-law at night and subsequent breathing problems."

My grandmother and Rinki snickered. Vik walked in, scanning the courtyard, and then came and stood next to me.

"Who's Malta?" I whispered to Vik.

"The neighbor," said Vik, his nostrils flaring in amusement, the sunlight catching the piercing in his right ear, a tiny green stone set in gold.

"She's got a temper," he said. "And a husband with political connections. Can't mess with them."

My mother looked furious. "Malta is an old bat, and we're not paying to have her ledge cleaned," she said. "The terrace needs repairs—my kitchen cabinets are going to come crashing down if you don't fix the broken wall behind it."

Rana spoke up, pleasant and mild, a dreamlike quality to his face, as if we were discussing a poem. "We should fix the pigeon problem soon, though. They're laying eggs everywhere."

"Big white gobs of shit everywhere," said Hari, using his fingers to illustrate.

"Bad for our lungs," said Gina, standing up, her stance commanding, as if she were teaching one of her classes at the university. "I read a piece about a woman dying because the pigeons left feces in her air conditioner."

"I wish we had air conditioners," sighed my grandmother, propping her chin on her delicate fingers.

"Ma, can we eat pigeon eggs?" the toddler asked Bari in Bengali, loud.

I realized the child was at least six, but thinner and smaller than she should have been.

"Quiet, Ami," said Bari, shushing her. "Employers are talking."

"Why can't Malta pay for cleaning the ledge?" asked my mother. "Her husband wanted us to put up that ledge for privacy, so nobody could see the NPF thugs they have over for dinner."

"Yes, but apparently it's our pigeons defecating on them," said my grandmother. "Bari, give Ami a biscuit or something."

Hari's mustache glistened in the sun, his skin darker than usual, as he wiped sweat from between the folds of his neck with a cream handkerchief.

"Those damned birds are not ours," he said.

"Geeta's right," said Gina with authority as Rana looked on with admiration. "If we let Malta pay for the cleaning, there's no telling what she could say tomorrow. She could claim that the land the ledge stands on is hers."

"That land is ours," said my grandmother angrily.

"Biddy, no filming," said Hari, his voice raised. "How many times do I have to tell you that this is a private matter, not for your YouTube."

As the family quarreled, I slipped past Ami, who stared at me as I sat down next to Rinki.

"Glad you could make it to the show," whispered Rinki, her dimples ravines of mirth in her soft cheeks.

"Guess what? Vik invited me to some show at Trincas, and he's going to bring Adil."

Her eyes widened. "Adil Sarkar? Wow, I haven't seen him since . . . since . . . since that last movie we all saw together on Tejen Mama's VCR, before you left. What was it—*Schindler's List*? I wonder if he became a scientist or something."

"A lawyer. At the *New Statesman*. He works with Vik."

"No, really? Of course. He was so smart. All the Xavier's boys became the biggest lawyers and doctors and journalists in Kolkata."

"And so cute."

Rinki giggled. "You were a foooool for him."

"Mm-hmm," I said as my mother looked at us, suspicious.

"Bashudeb says the *New Statesman* is the only paper that tells the truth anymore in Kolkata," said Rinki with a sigh.

I lowered my voice, uninterested in the merits of the *New Statesman*. "Well, can you come?"

"Come where?" asked Rinki.

"To Trincas," I said, impatient.

"Oh, I . . . I don't think so. It's at night, isn't it. Bashudeb will be home."

"Can't you take one night off from making his dinner?" I regretted the words as I said them. "Sorry, sorry. I just thought it would be nice, like old times."

Rinki smiled, gentle. "You don't know how much I miss going out with you."

Hari had moved on to an issue about the fruit seller having a romance with one of the teenage maids that came in the afternoons to help Bari. The Lahiri family did not want to be seen as the facilitator of romances originating under their roof or, worse still, any unplanned pregnancies that might occur. The maid's arrival time would have to change to after Babulnath the fruit seller had delivered his watermelons.

"So, you don't have a boyfriend, Lila?" asked Rinki.

I thought of Seth. "No," I said.

Rinki nodded. "Is it hard living alone? I couldn't imagine it."

"It's lonely sometimes, but I like it."

"Do you still like Adil?"

I laughed. "C'mon, Rinks, I haven't seen him in thirteen years."

"Let's look at his Facebook," whispered Rinki, pulling out her phone.

Mishti leaned over, her bandage white against her skin. I noticed a tinge of mucus and blood on its edge and drew back, revulsed, despite myself.

"What are you girls gossiping about?" she asked.

"Nothing," I said, immediately covering Rinki's phone and pushing it back into her handbag.

Mishti took a deep breath, her usually smiling face serious, the sharp edges of her jaw determined, as she stood up.

"I'd like to discuss Biddy's wedding next," she said. "We've had a lot of changes during this time, and I want my only daughter's wedding to take place in the house she was born in."

"But we would have to make repairs and fix the staircase. The house hasn't seen a festival or a wedding in years," said Rana. "I thought we agreed to do it at the Park."

"Why does it have to be so soon?" demanded my mother. "The boy just proposed. Why can't we plan it for next year, like normal weddings?"

"We're in a hurry, Maya Didi—I've told you." Biddy laughed as she said the words, but something in her voice made me turn to look at her.

"We can't let people come in and see the house like this," said my grandmother, looking around. Suddenly, she focused on me, a question in her eyes. "It's a broken mess. Isn't that right, Lila?"

The idea that they might look to me for an opinion felt incredulous. Flustered, I set my cup down. A little of the hot liquid splashed onto my wrist, but I clenched against flinching.

Vik touched my shoulder. "Don't worry," he said in my ear, so quiet that I had to strain to hear him. "They *should* be worried about what you think."

I had forgotten he was there. He made a good journalist, I realized. He was quiet, observing fatal flaws even when we were on guard.

Biddy stretched out, like a bored, yawning cat. "Geeta Kaki, people see us 'like this' on my YouTube every day."

"But what if we made the repairs?" asked Mishti. "Why can't we use the trust money? Tejen Da had said he would consider it."

"I vote we use the trust too," said Hari, a tenor in the courtyard. "You know, Biddy is a celebrity now. A YouTube viral celebrity. It would bring honor to the family. Imagine if the press came and took pictures. It would be like the old days."

Biddy arched an eyebrow. "Oh, now I'm a celebrity," she said.

"But that's outrageous," said Gina. "We can't spend all of the annual budget on one wedding. Each household has repairs to make in the kitchens and bathrooms. We can't fix the staircase and balconies and paint the exteriors to show off, and have our lives be a daily hell. I want a geyser this winter."

"I want a new kitchen wall," said my mother, brittle.

"Chill. We can just have the wedding at the Park," said Biddy as she peeled off crusts from the pink polish on her left toe.

"Quiet," said Hari to her. "You will get married in this house. I am president of the board, and you will do as I say. "

"My father was the president. I am his legal heir," said my mother.

"But you're not," said my grandmother.

The silence was abrupt, like a blanket over us. Ami giggled; immediately, Bari covered her daughter's face with her hand.

Vik poked me in the side. "Your turn," he whispered.

"Lila isn't interested in the affairs of this household," said my mother.

"No, I am."

My mother looked at me, something white-hot in her eyes, all permission to be powerful drained from me. I floated away from my body, my heart and lungs removing themselves from the mouth and feet and arms that were going to battle with her.

"That's absurd, Lila," she said. "You're a child, and you have no idea what to do here."

"Tejen Da left it to her," said Mishti, who, I could see, wanted Biddy's wedding in the house above all else.

"My father's brain had softened with all the drugs he was given," spat out my mother.

"When I was a child, Dadu used to tell me that he would leave me this house," I said as I floated over them, over myself, seeing and hearing this pantomime of fractures below me, the pigeons and dark corners of dust mites and ceiling fans, my refuge overhead. "I'm not sure why he did, but I want to do what is best for the house."

My grandmother began to cry in a corner, twisting the thin end of her white cotton sari between her fingers. "It's true." She hiccuped. "He would say it to her. I can't fathom why, but he would. I thought it was one of his jokes."

I felt the loss of my grandfather, enormous, with a presence of its own, fill the room.

"Does this mean you're moving in?" asked Gina. But all that I could focus on was the silent rage of my mother as she stood up, a block of dark ice, her hair on fire, backlit by the sun.

"Or selling it?" asked Rana, fearful.

Biddy pointed her iPhone at my face and zoomed in as she breathed carefully to steady the camera, understanding that here, finally, was a moment of real drama for her fans.

"Nonsense. Nobody is selling our house," said Hari. "You wouldn't do that, would you, Lila Ma?" he asked, sudden tears in his beautiful voice. "Where would we go?"

Hari looked at his palms, as if to examine how much money or work they might be worth. I could feel the family stiffen, their pride and fear rippling through the room, at having to ask this question of an outsider. Even Biddy took her eyes away from her screen, looking at me.

"Nobody is going anywhere," I said, the soles of my feet cold against the courtyard floor, the summer air cooled to its lowest possible point, made drafty by the stone pillars. "I haven't made any decisions yet, but when I do, I will make sure it is in the best interests of everyone here. Biddy, we should have your wedding here. Mishti Kaki is right—my grandfather would have wanted you to."

"Cooool," said Biddy, relaxing into her usual bounce. "Is the meeting over? Can I go now? I'm meeting Arjun at the cinema."

Gina looked outraged. "What about my geys—"

I held up both my hands. "Look, we've got to make repairs and updates, both inside and outside the house. And that's regardless of the wedding. You can't keep living like this, without central heating or hot water—and who knows what structural damage there is."

"What do you mean there's no hot water? What do you think my immersion rod is for?" said my grandmother.

"You're going to electrocute yourself using that one day, Geeta," said Gina, stern.

"Houses in Kolkata never needed heating before," said Rana. "The weather gods have turned things upside down. They are not pleased with us. Look at how late the rains are this year."

Biddy let out a little giggle.

"All I'm saying is that I'm going to take a look at the trust tomorrow and make a budget," I said. "At our next meeting, we will need a list of items—an elevator, geysers, ceiling fans, bathroom repairs, and, yes, a fresh coat of paint—and then we will see what we can allocate immediately to each family. The wedding may not be as grand as the old Lahiri affairs, but we'll make sure the house is ready in time to receive Biddy's guests."

As I said the words, I prayed that Vik was right, and that there was enough in the coffers to cover the promises I had dared to make.

"What is an elevator?" asked my grandmother.

"A lift," said my mother, irritable.

"A lift will destroy this house, the foundation. All these old beams. No chance," protested Hari, shaking his head.

"Let's just have a contractor come in and take a look at the structure," I said, a stranger to my own ears.

"I would never have to take the stairs again," speculated my grandmother.

"No," I said. "You wouldn't."

"It would ruin the house, the traditions of the architecture," said Rana, as if reflecting on the idea of dessert after dinner. "In the long run, it is a bad idea."

"We could try to use the back wall of the house—that whole yard space is overrun with weeds," I said. "It could be one of those glass-walled elevators, and you step out into the garden in front of the back entrance. The structural underpinnings of old houses are usually strong—they were built to withstand modern improvements."

There was a silence. I did not look in the direction of my mother. In texts with my father, and nights of search-engine questions, I had hypothesized enough to sound as if I knew these things. My grandmother smiled at me.

"Well, if someone is actually looking at the budget and making informed cuts and allocations, that's a good thing, in my opinion," said Gina at last.

"I don't suppose we have much choice," said Hari.

"That's not true," I said. "But we should choose what's best for everyone. We're all getting older, and Mummy is in her seventies. These stairs are no joke. And you can't be heating buckets of water in the hallways with electric rods and carrying them to the bathroom."

"You're going to leave the design as it is, right, Lila?" asked Mishti, worried. "This is a historic building."

"The property valuation depends on it," said Hari.

"Ballygunge Place would never be the same if you tore it down and made it into apartments," said Rana dreamily, as if trying to imagine a skyscraper emerging from the debris of the Lahiri house.

"Jesus, Rana Kaka. Who said anything about apartment buildings?" I said, my voice rising.

"If you do tear it down, can I get my own apartment?" asked Vik with a glint in his eye.

Rinki laughed, nervous. My grandmother looked horrified. I saw Biddy push the gate open and disappear into the street.

"Shut up, Vik. I'm not going to do anything to the house," I said. "All I'm suggesting is that we put in a few geysers and other amenities that'll make life easier. Maybe a dishwasher or something."

"Now you want to take Bari's job? What's wrong with the way she washes dishes?" asked my grandmother, now outraged.

Bari's eyes widened as she looked at me.

"Mummy, you just said that you thought the elevator was a good idea."

"Listen, Lila Ma, if you want to get some work done, I have a guy who can do it," said Hari, putting a friendly arm around my shoulders. "Very cheap," he added.

My mother picked up her teacup and, without looking at any of us, walked in the direction of the staircase, into the house.

"Tejen should have made Maya a part of it," said my grandmother with a sigh. "It's natural she feels left out."

"Lila, you won't want to run the meetings now, will you?" asked Hari. "I do them in a certain way, like Tejen Da or Baba used to."

"Please do everything the way you're all used to. I'm only here to help," I said. "I'm not making any changes without taking everyone into consideration."

"Let me know, Lila Ma," said Hari. "I'm going to go play cards now, but you know my cell phone number, yes?" He held up a battered phone with a piece of tape wrapped around its bottom.

"Is lunch ready?" asked Rana, hopeful.

Gina rolled her eyes. "Bari, make Rana a plate, please, if you've finished cooking."

"Ma, I'm hungry," said Ami to Bari, tearful.

"Shh," scolded Bari, scooping up the child in her arms.

I felt dizzy, as if the family and the house were closing in on me. "Can I join lunch?" I asked Bari.

"I've made your lunch, remember?" my grandmother said to me. "All your favorites. Bari, there are a lot of leftovers in the fridge. Please feed the child as well."

I wondered if my grandmother had made a lunch identical to the one my mother had made the day before in order to permanently prove that she made them better. It would not be unpleasant, but then I would have to comment on my favorite of the favorites, and there was always the possibility of war and debris in these conversations between my mother and grandmother.

"Why can't Ami eat some of what you or Bari have made today?" I asked my grandmother as Bari hurried out, her daughter staring at me again, over her mother's shoulder, as though I had shouted at her. An obedient Rana followed them up the stairs.

"Lila, really," said Geeta, exasperated. "You've been here a day. Could you just let us live the way we know how. Please come up for lunch in ten minutes."

I PILED KEEMA, cooked in cinnamon and mustard oil, onto little pieces of the soft white roti my grandmother had made, spooning onion and tomato salad on top.

"I'm starving, Mummy," I said, my appetite suddenly enormous.

"Good. Keema, pui shak, chingri, and malai kofta for you. Have another roti," said my grandmother.

"There's no way," I protested as she tore one in half and tossed it onto the mustard-coated shrimp on my plate.

"Half for you and half for me," she said.

"How on earth am I supposed to eat all this?"

She spooned some of the mutton keema onto her plate.

"I'll help you," she said. "Yes. I'll be damned if they turn me into the poor old vegetarian widow in white. I'm going to live, even if he went and died." She put the spoon down, her elbow landing on the table with a thud. "Lila, he's left me all alone."

"No, he hasn't. I'm here. He wanted me to be here."

I reached out for her veined, thin fingers. She clasped them, resting my fingers on her cheek, her gray hair in a little braid, her build so slight that from a distance she might be mistaken for a girl.

"Promise me, Lila, that you'll take care of us, the way he did."

I nodded, but I felt real fear, because I did not know how to take care of anyone.

She briskly let go of my fingers and began to eat.

"So, do you have a husband yet or not?"

"Yes, he's in my bag. I forgot him on the way over here."

"Is he tall, sharp features, a good strong nose like the Lahiris, high cheekbones, eats rice?"

"Rich, don't forget rich."

"Listen, Lila, you must find someone and have some children. I won't live forever, now, will I? How can you let me die without a grandchild?"

I laughed. "I'm not letting you die anytime soon. Can I have some more shak?"

"Of course," she said, spooning the fried spinach onto my plate. "What do you think of Biddy's boy? Handsome, no?"

"She's such a darling. What does he do?"

"His father owns Ghoshal Gold, the jewelry shop." She leaned over, whispering. "But he's a model."

"No," I said, my eyes widening.

"Yes, loaded with money and looks. He wakes up at eleven, goes to the gym, makes his muscles"—she clapped her hand to her upper arm for emphasis—"and then, around two, goes to Ghoshal Gold for a few hours and charms all the ladies into buying bangles. Then, he comes around here, on his motorbike, *vroom-vroom*, for Biddy"—she mimicked riding, presumably the motorbike—"to take her for a spin. It's all fantastic," she said, sighing with pleasure. "Hurry up, Lila. I want to dance at your wedding. I'll be the only widow who does."

"Oh, yes, you will," I said.

Before we heard her footsteps, the slap of her rubber flip-flops urgent against the tiles, I knew my mother was near, the back of my neck prickling against the cool sweat of the hot afternoon.

She stood in the doorway, blank with what I knew to be anger, but if you looked at her, you would see only the long lashes and thin nose, the jut of her determined chin, a vivid woman, perpetually on the serious side. Every once in a while in my teenage years, I would discover photographs of a beautiful woman—large eyes, small face, all youth and loveliness, holding an infant, or a toddler—and I was always taken aback that it was my mother holding me. For years, all I remembered was a spiteful, wizened face, attached to the bony arms that I feared. Now, she held three large steel containers—one in each hand and a third cradled in the crook of her arm, like the expert waitresses in Brooklyn. She stared at us, as if making a discovery.

"Maya Ma . . . come and sit . . . I've cooked," said my grandmother, fear in her frail voice. "I . . . I should have asked you . . ."

My mother marched in, silent, setting the containers in her hands in front of my plate, between the roti casserole and the salad. The third, she slid to her palm and banged down in front of Geeta's face. I flinched, but my grandmother simply looked at her as if she had done this a thousand times.

"Come and sit," my grandmother repeated tiredly.

"Shut up," said my mother, vicious.

Turning to me, she smiled, bright cheer painting itself over her eyes and nose and mouth, the tendons on her neck raised and angular.

"Hi, love. Did you know I had cooked for you? I thought I said I would," she exclaimed, each consonant and vowel landing sharp and hard, filled with the white blaze of my mother's madness.

"I'm eating with Mummy today. You cooked for me just yesterday."

"Of course," she said, taking the lids off her containers—one filled with potatoes fried with onions, a second with a salad, a third with what looked like chicken stew—each uncovering an act of hate, lifting up, showing me, banging down, more hate. "I just made a few things, hoping you would come," she continued.

My mother's love had always been hate, and I was filled with it, inescapably.

"Thank you," I said.

She stared at me as I looked away, and I could tell she saw the horror in my eyes even as I struggled to hide it. In these moments, my mother had always seemed childlike, frightened by her own debris.

"Come up sometime," she said, her voice now tiny, faraway.

"Sit, Maya," said my grandmother, pushing a chair outward, her voice in the distance, as I left once again, removing myself from my mother, flying into the golden afternoon sky, the pigeons trailing behind me, defecating, searching for scraps in the air, the smog coating us all.

When I looked behind me at last, my mother was gone, and all that we were left with was the feast and my grandmother's sadness.

8

IN THE LATE 1920s, when the Anglo-Indians of Kolkata had held court on Park Street and Ripon Street, two Swiss gentlemen, a Mr. Flury and a Mr. Trinca, decided to open up a bakery and a tearoom, respectively. Under the patronage of the British Raj, the two establishments became crown jewels of Park Street. The Bengalis and Anglo-Indians would order cream puffs and mutton sandwiches at Flurys and wear their best silks to afternoon tea at Trincas.

By the late 1950s, the British had left, but their appetite for a proper English breakfast and live music had reshaped Kolkata's culture. But then, Trincas had been taken over by a pair of friends in the hospitality industry who decided that the live music that the British troops had enjoyed had permeated the middle and upper classes enough to revamp the tearoom into a restaurant, with a bar license and bands playing every night of the week. Over the decades, the carpeted floor had grown battered and worn, the gilded ceilings had been replaced by affordable, modern white painted beams, and the predominantly Anglo-Indian patronage had been replaced by Kolkata's melting pot of Hindus, Muslims, and Christians.

Later, even after Trincas had wilted under the Maoist insurgency of the 1970s, when capitalism and dancing were strictly frowned upon, what had survived, which had made Trincas impossibly glamorous to me growing up, was the music; booking avant-garde bands of all ethnicities, from Sufi music to Usha Uthup's disco to a surprise appearance from Mick Jagger one winter, Trincas was the embodiment of a Kolkata that felt like a sexy, fearless classic.

I had promised Vik that I would meet him at Trincas at seven thirty. My hair had turned perpetually damp and curling, my keratin treatment and straightener no match against the humidity. But outside, there was a rare, cool breeze as I stood in front of the building, trying to wave a cab down.

Every time one of the black-and-yellow Ambassador taxis would stop, I would say, "Park Street?" Without a word, the cab would whisk off, leaving me still on the street, muttering "Motherfucker" under my breath.

Ram Bhai watched me as he chewed on a stick of sugarcane, perched on his stool positioned outside the gate, presumably guarding the building while chatting with the steady stream of his friends who visited him through the day.

"Where are you going, Lila Madam?" he asked loudly.

"Park Street," I said.

A passing teenage boy slowed his pace to inspect my outfit. Ram Bhai stood up and walked toward me as I glared at the boy, who hurried past us.

"They'll never take you if you keep telling them where you're going," he said, waving down a passing cab. "No sane man wants to sit in traffic from Ballygunge to Park Street at the hour that the babus leave their offices."

As another cab stopped in front of us, Ram Bhai yanked open the door.

"Inside, Lila Madam, inside," he said to me, impatient.

I clambered in, grateful to get my heels off the uneven sidewalk.

Ram clapped the door closed with a finality as the driver turned around and began to ask, "Madam, where are you goi—"

"Park Street," roared Ram Bhai, with two swift claps to the side of the cab. He locked eyes with the driver, whose eyes widened in horror, then resignation, as his shoulders deflated and he turned back to the wheel in certain defeat.

IT WAS ALMOST eight when we finally rolled up outside Trincas. The trip had been silent the whole time, and as I handed the driver a fifty-rupee tip (less than a dollar), he turned around, surprised.

"Thank you, madam," he said.

The tiny amount was generous to him, I knew, and as he drove away, I felt a specific shame in my ribs at not having given him more. But doing so would have been considered foreigner behavior, and my grandmother and Ram Bhai would have berated me, saying I was setting a bad precedent and flaunting my dollars.

Inside, Trincas was dim—soft chandelier light spilling over patrons at white-clothed tables studded with little roses in vases. The large old-fashioned windows still had their signature red-velvet curtains tied together with gold rope, giving the place its theatrical quality. If you didn't look too closely, the floor wasn't scuffed from years of neglect and the velvet was plush, its wear and tear masked by the shadows of incandescent bulbs overhead. Everything about Trincas felt like you shouldn't look too close—the man in the white suit, impeccable sophisticate, was bound to disappoint as he turned lecherous in gaze, as the whiskeys hit his bloodstream, his wife looking at her watch, eager to get away as the crowd grew more drunken. The band, set up on the worn little stage that had existed since the beginning of postcolonial Trincas, was dressed in suits—a guitarist, a bassist, a saxophonist, a drummer—all men but one, a single female vocalist in a cocktail dress.

I spotted Vik immediately, his spry frame in a lavender paisley shirt hunched over a table, in earnest conversation with Adil, who must have felt me staring as he lifted his gaze to turn and look at me.

"Hi, Li," said Vik, rising to give me a hug. "Wow, you clean up nice."

"Thanks." I was annoyed at Vik for drawing attention to the fact that I had spent an hour deciding on the blouse and jeans and heels that now felt like a siren.

"Hi, Lila," said Adil.

"Hi, Adil," I said, turning to him.

For a second, we stood looking at each other, making note of the ways in which thirteen years had altered us. He was even taller than I remembered him, still skinny, his angular jaw still made of the same lines. He had the same serious, kind, brown-flecked eyes, still hard to look away from but framed by beautiful jade-green glasses now, but there were also filled-out shoulders, a grown man's arms and wrists, and rolled-up shirt cuffs on the boy I had once loved.

"You grew taller," I said, smiling at him.

"Six one and counting."

"I stayed the same, as you can see."

He laughed, reaching to hug me. I did not remember what he smelled like before (it could not have been this male scent of cologne and a day's work and bourbon), but his body had always felt safe against mine, his arms a circle that had protected me. I felt sixteen, a girl again, heady, at home.

A waiter appeared at my elbow as we sat down.

"Mishraji, you only appear when the lady arrives. I've been trying to get another whiskey for thirty minutes," said Vik in Hindi. "Here, meet my cousin Lila. She's from America."

"Stop telling people I'm American," I snapped at Vik.

But Mishraji looked impressed, as Vik had known he would, and he folded his arms in a namaste. "What can I get you, madam?" he asked.

"Ek glass red wine?" I said in Hindi, eager to assert my nonforeigner status.

"Sure, sure," said Mishraji. "Any snacks? Chilli chicken fry, french fries, chicken 65, Gobi 65, pigs in a blanket?"

"Ek chicken 65," said Vik.

"Whiskey, two cubes of ice," said Adil.

It was impossible to believe that the boy who had helped me with my geography homework, who had been obsessed with biographies of Gandhi and Nehru when I left, was ordering whiskey, two cubes of ice, the faintest trace of stubble on his cheeks—all man, no boyhood left in him except when he laughed and his face broke open with easy happiness.

"Do they still serve pot roast?" I asked.

"Yeah, and masala papad, kulfi, and Manchurian chicken," said Adil. "The Queen could eat here, and so could the common man. Have you missed it?"

"Yeah. I've missed it."

It was true. I hadn't thought about Trincas or Park Street or any of it in years, and suddenly it felt like I had been away too long. A fierce sense of belonging burned my throat.

"It's still Trincas," said Vik. "A little seedy after hours. You can't get too romantic about it."

Vik liked to come to Trincas on Thursday nights because at ten, his friend, Nina of the Night came on. When Nina strode onstage, we recognized that she was a star, the kind that narrows your focus because someone with aura has walked in. She wore her hair in a waterfall, red lipstick, a smattering of gold makeup around her large eyes, and a sequined sheath and heels—it wasn't an expensive dress, and a label peeped through the scoop of her lower back, but there was something rare about her.

She sang an old Hindi song—a classic, overplayed hit—but it was new in her warm, rich voice. Once it was finished, Nina looked around the dark room and flirted with us for a bit—a few jokes here, an observation on the weather there, a little wit directed at the man and his bored wife at table five—it didn't matter; we couldn't take our eyes off her.

Later she sang a Nina Simone song. It felt like fingers of sorrow had made their way deep inside me. Vik, Adil, and I were suspended in the mellow dream-haze of the room, the music floating through us.

I remembered how Adil and I had gone to school music festivals with each other, how he would be entirely absorbed in a song one moment and look up at me the next, shy, to hold my sweaty palm. Nothing had ever felt as breathless or sweet since, and I told myself it was because he had been the first. Adil turned to look at me, and I smiled, embarrassed to have been caught midstare.

"What?" he asked, smiling.

I shrugged, smiling back, both of us lit out of our minds. Vik's back was facing us, and it felt like we had a secret, the same one we'd always had. Vik turned his chair around, flushed by the hot room and the alcohol, and took a long drink from the cold bottle of Bisleri mineral water on the table.

"You're drinking all of Li's water," said Adil.

"Oh shit," said Vik midswig, looking around for Mishraji. "Where's the commoner water?"

"Just drink it," I said, laughing.

"Might be too much for my pedestrian constitution," said Vik. "Best to let it flow to the foreigners," he said with a sweep of his palm at me.

"Lila's no foreigner," said Adil. "Is it true that you own the house now?"

"Yep," said Vik. "She's the memsahib malkin. You should have seen her go at the board meeting on Tuesday."

I giggled, the wine and Adil's sweetness unraveling the knot I'd felt when the house came up.

"Who would have thought it?" said Adil.

"Nobody ever knew what went on in Tejen Kaka's mind," said Vik. "Least of all his daughter."

I looked at him, sharp.

"Just saying." Vik raised his palms in defense. "Your mom was as surprised as the rest of us. Lucky it wasn't me he left it to—I would have been terrified of her."

I wondered if Vik had had the same thought that I did—that he would have been the far more appropriate choice. I turned to Adil, desperate to change the subject.

"So you're the boss of Vik now?" I asked him.

Adil laughed. "I'm just a common lawyer at the paper, who he doesn't like taking advice from."

"So you tell him what words he can or can't put in print," I said. "That sounds like the boss of him."

"He's not my boss," protested Vik. "The government is the boss. My boss, his boss, all our bosses. Hail, National Popular Front." Vik raised a drunken fist.

"Be quiet," said Adil, looking around, the faintest trace of alarm shadowing his face.

"See. He's scared of them too," said Vik. "Our esteemed senior legal counsel, who's supposed to protect the journalists. You protect me, right, Adil?" said Vik, a little defiant.

"Yes," said Adil. "Speaking of which, it might be time to get you home."

"What? No. Nina just came on," said Vik.

"Let's stay a little longer," I said, touching Adil's arm. I didn't want this time, this nearness to Adil, Nina, any of it, to end yet.

Adil leaned back in his chair, my palm still on his elbow. Had he always been this tender man, simultaneously light and deep, and had my skin always risen in bumps near him, as if touched by cold air?

"Try not to get us arrested, Vik," said Adil softly, a warning in his voice.

Mishraji, a solicitous six feet away, was examining the cuff of his uniform, leaning in our direction. Vik looked up, and immediately the elderly waiter straightened.

"Drink, sir?" asked Mishraji.

Unlike them, I lived in a country where I could say what I liked, without having mud or stones hurled at me. I did not say it aloud.

Vik shook his head, resigned. "Better let the boss of me take you home while I'm still a free man, Lila. God, I've had too much whiskey."

Nina, luminous, was singing a cover of Rupa's disco-jazz number "Aaj Shanibar," the music washing over us, lifting Trincas into an effervescence.

"We can stay longer if you want," said Adil, looking at me for a second longer than necessary.

A thrill passed through my chest as I nodded.

"How do you know Nina?" I asked Vik.

"Nina is a fucking star. A gem. A gem star if you will. Queen of my heart," said Vik, resting his head between his knees below the table. "My best friend in the world."

"I thought I was your best friend," said Adil, nodding at Mishraji.

"I have two best friends," said Vik, frowning, his head rising from between his knees, phoenixlike, two fingers held up, swaying.

As Adil and I laughed, Mishraji hurried over.

"Another whiskey, sir?"

LATER, VIK AND I stood at the back entrance of Trincas, waiting for Adil, who had left to extricate his car from the valet. Vik pulled out a cigarette and offered me one. I shook my head, and he lit up, sliding the box back into his pocket.

"Are you coming back with us?" I asked.

Vik shook his head, newly sobered. "I'll hang out here for a bit. Nina—his name is Pedro—is an old friend."

"It's like when I was twelve, and you'd pack me and Rinks off before going to meet your cool friends," I said.

Vik laughed. "You want to come hang out with Nina of the Night?"

"Just invite me next time," I said.

"Sure thing. Although we'll have to be careful. Word can't get back that a Lahiri was hanging out with a drag queen."

"I can hang out with anyone I like. And you're the Lahiri, not me," I said.

Vik put an arm around me, good-natured. "You're such an outraged American. And more of a Lahiri than I ever will be."

I snatched his cigarette from him, taking a drag.

Vik laughed. "There are local cops interested in arresting people just to make a buck. It's still illegal to be gay here. With the election coming and the Right poised to win, they're more interested than ever in upholding the nation's moral character."

Vik winked at me. I felt a shame settle into my cheeks.

"I'm sorry. I should have realized."

"How could you have?" said Vik. "You're not from here."

"Vik, I'm from here as much as you are."

"Fair enough," he said. "I'm glad you're back, Li."

AFTER VIK HUGGED me goodbye and left, Adil held open the passenger door of his seven-seater SUV. "You'll have to give me your number," he said. "Or I'll be texting Vik every time I want to reach you."

I climbed inside. "Four-four-zero-seven-zero-zero-four," I said.

He laughed. "Oh, I remember."

We had had a landline phone in my mother's studio when I was fourteen, and, to her fury, it would ring primarily for me. Adil and I would talk for hours on end, using our science projects as an excuse.

"What's with the soccer-mom car?" I asked.

"I'm in touch with my feminine side." He turned on the radio and grinned at me.

"You're a grown-up version of the same Adil I knew," I said. "Except you drive now."

"I'm the same. Are you the same, Lila? You seem glamorous, out of all our leagues."

"You don't really mean that," I said.

"No, I don't. You feel exactly the same."

We bumped over the many potholes and bumps of the winding inner lanes of Kolkata.

"Did you ever think about leaving?" I asked.

"After university, I thought I would stay in London. Even got a job at a firm. My life is here, though. I want to live here, help build whatever this country becomes."

He had always had a quiet conviction that had fueled him—everything that he read and understood and loved was born of that certain knowledge.

"I wish I felt like I belonged somewhere, like that," I said.

"You belong here, Lila. Obama isn't *your* president." He laughed.

"What? What brought that on?"

"C'mon, I could see it on your face, when Vik was talking about the party goons. The relief of an American in these Obama years, the assurance of democracy no matter what."

I felt a sharp anger. "Well, first of all, Obama *is* my president—I've lived in New York my whole adult life. And of course I care about what goes on in India. Of course I worry about free speech and dictatorship . . . and . . . and everything you guys were talking about."

"Yes, but it's worrying in the way the UN worries. It's not real, or going to change anything," said Adil.

"Wow, glad to see you're still rude as fuck."

He laughed, reaching over to touch my hand. "I'm just saying, you can belong here, Lila, in case you ever wanted to belong anywhere."

"Pay attention to the road," I said, my heart beating in my throat.

He smiled and put both hands back on the wheel. We rode along in the kind of silence that lets you change a radio channel, listen to music, and be entirely in the company of the other person. We entered the sweep of Ballygunge Circular Road, the massive marble Birla temple glistening in the night, devotees on its steps even at midnight.

"When I was a kid," I said, "I thought the Birla temple was going to be the eighth Wonder of the World."

Adil nodded. "We all did. It was the most beautiful thing we had ever seen."

I wished the streets were longer, the detours more. The fear of having this moment end slithered between my ribs.

"Can I ask you a question? It's a silly one, and I feel like I should know, but I don't, and I can't ask anyone else," I said.

"Always."

"Is Vik gay? I don't know why I don't know," I said again, feeling like an idiot.

Adil laughed. "What? Because he's friends with Nina?"

"Well? Is he?"

"He had a girlfriend once, a long time ago." Adil rubbed his neck—I wondered if the thought had ever occurred to him. "He would have said something, at least to me," said Adil, a flicker of uncertainty crossing his face. "No, I don't think so. I'm his best friend, despite what he said to Mishraji."

I laughed as Adil looked ahead, smiling. We rode along in silence.

"Li, what's it like . . . being back?"

I looked out the window.

"You don't have to talk about it," he said, gentle.

"She's still the same," I said.

Adil nodded.

"I own the house she lives in now, and it should give me some power, but she still has all the power. All of it."

"You have power, Li."

I desperately wanted to sleep with him, merge my pain with his, erase the years that had reduced us to a memory.

We pulled up in front of my father's apartment building. Ram Bhai was sleeping inside, and the lights were off. I would have to wake him or his wife to get in. If I leaned over to kiss Adil, who would know? (Everyone would know—some maid, some mother. Someone was always watching on our little street.)

Adil turned off the car. "Li, I've thought about this so many times over the years—tried to wrap my brain around it. Maya Aunty . . ."

In my mind I flinched—*No, no,* I thought. *Don't call her that, or anything else.* I wanted no part of his kindness to touch my mother.

"She has these extremes of emotion and anger because she thinks she's a victim. So many Bengali women do, because there're so many rules this town expects them to follow."

"Don't defend her," I said.

"I would never," he said with certainty.

I took in a sharp breath, relieved that he had not forgiven her either, or abandoned the small plot of land that was my side, my defense, against my mother.

"But I know that she's had a hard time. Especially after you left," he said, quiet.

I opened the car door, bitter at my mother for having robbed me of this moment with Adil.

"Li, I know lawyers I trust who could help with matters of the house. Just in case you had any questions or wanted to think things through with someone."

"My dad put me in touch with someone, a real estate lawyer friend of his. I'm seeing him next week."

"I'll come with you," said Adil immediately.

"Okay."

We looked at each other for a long moment, and then I closed the door of the car. "Good night," I said into the window.

I knew he would wait until I rang the bell, until Ram opened the gates, and until I turned on the bedroom light, our long-ago language of codes still alive, our secrets still between us. Upstairs, I waved at him from my bedroom window, my heart lifting in the way that it had forgotten to for so long, as Adil waved back. Then, with a soft roar, the black SUV disappeared into the night.

9

IT HAD BECOME customary for me to wake in the middle of the night and spend a few hours reading emails and editing manuscript drafts. An odd email from Seth, with no subject, said: *Went to RedFarm and ordered our duck dumplings/can you send me your address?* I hoped it was to send me a completed draft of his manuscript, though I knew that he could not have made enough progress and would look askance at what shipping a hard copy to India might cost. Perhaps he wanted to send me some form of an apology for yelling at me—a grand gesture of frozen duck dumplings that would be intercepted by customs before they left JFK.

At some stage of early dawn, I fell asleep again, my hands still on my keyboard, enveloped in Iva's voluminous pillows. In the center of a haze of a dream, Molly and I were trying to swim in an ocean, but she kept passing me, stronger and faster, her golden-bronze skin rippling in the warm blue-green water. Exhausted, I kept trying to keep pace and catch up, tiny ripples of jealousy coursing through me, as Molly laughed, flitting through the waters, eternally at home in the waves, calling to me, "Lila, Lila, Lila"—until I finally caught up, and it was my mother instead.

I woke to an insistent ringing in my ears. It was my laptop, still open in front of me. I reached for the glass of water on the nightstand, swallowing as I pressed answer on FaceTime.

"Hi, Mol."

"Lila, I've been calling and calling. Where were you?"

"Sorry," I said, weary, rubbing my eyes.

"Did you just wake up?" she asked, peering at the screen.

"It's seven a.m. here," I said. "How are the Carnival books coming? Ready for the announcement?"

"It's been crazy, just trying to coordinate between all of these departments for the announcement. Phenom has so much paperwork and protocol, for every little thing. I miss how small we used to be—is that crazy?"

"It's not crazy. I miss it too. But we have more resources, right? More nice things?"

"Yeah." Molly sounded glum. "A lot of trainings, though."

"And a Booker nomination. That's got to be making Aetos pretty happy, right?" I tried to muster false cheer, even as I felt anxious, so far away from a rapidly evolving workplace that everyone but me was learning how to navigate. Phenom was an alien mothership that had absorbed Wyndham whole, and I worried about not being able to recognize my beloved company by the time I returned to Brooklyn.

"Yeah, yeah," Molly said, distracted. "Nadine Emecheta called out of the blue with a fucking fever dream of a series about immigrant kids in a Kentucky high school, with superpowers born of their traumas. Aetos and Gil were over the moon."

Molly ran her hands through her hair, a halo around her face, backlit by a lamp. I raised a hand self-consciously to my own curls, untamable in the Indian humidity.

"But the Phenom people have already started asking about things like 'commercial viability' and 'PR potential,'" said Molly. "All talk, no taste."

I laughed at Molly's perfect sinister imitation of the marketing department at Phenom. "All that tasteless money you'll soon be going to the Hamptons with," I said.

"Anyway, do you miss us?" asked Molly, impatient. "I can't wait for you to come back and be the boss."

"I do," I said, feeling a stab in my chest. "So much. It's like living on another planet."

"Hurry up and come back, then. We miss you. Seth asks about you, you know. I saw him at a book party the other night. We went out and got beers."

"I wish he'd email and ask me, and maybe even answer my questions about the draft he was supposed to have finished two weeks ago."

Molly laughed. "Ah, Li, that mind of yours, never too far from business. He's into you, you know."

I fidgeted, as I did when Molly or Gil, the only two people who knew, brought up Seth as my lover.

"He's into sleeping with me," I said. "Just like he's into sleeping with half of New York City. I'm like his regular-order martini. Doesn't mean he's not drinking everything else on the menu."

Molly laughed, her head thrown back, magnificent. "You're such an idiot sometimes. Okay, I just wanted to make sure you were good. I have to go—it's Gil's fifty-seventh tonight."

"Right," I said, desolate. Time had ceased to exist in the same way for me that it had in New York. "Call me tomorrow, then?" I asked, hopeful. "I want to hear about everything that's going on."

"Can't. I have a date, a second date, tomorrow. Guy I met at Henry Public. He was reading Austen. I offered him my fries. He said yes."

"What? No. I have to know everything."

"He's cute. A real dork. Funny glasses, nice sweater. I want to do unspeakable things."

"Mm. Sounds like a dream."

"Li, I miss you," said Molly, suddenly serious. "Without you here, it isn't the same."

I nodded. In the way that many in our generation did, Molly and I had appointed each other chosen family. Without her, my life felt as if it lacked a central yoke.

"I talked to Harriet yesterday," I said. "I know you've been covering for me with Gil and Aetos, checking in on my submissions and making it seem like I'm on top of things at the weekly meetings. Harriet told me."

Molly shrugged. "You'd do it if I flew halfway across the world to clean up some funny business."

I laughed. "God, that's accurate. And if only you could see how I keep making it a bigger mess on the reg."

Molly leaned forward. "Lila, you're the most calm, organized person I know. It's ridiculous, and we know it comes from your need to control, but, babe, there never was a better time to have some confidence in your abilities."

"You know, it might have something to do with you," I said, rueful. "Maybe I just need you to be myself."

She shook her head. "You don't, but I want you to keep thinking that, because it's really me that needs you. This is the longest we've gone since college without talking every day. I can't make sense of men or my sister or Gil's damn guest list without you."

"Have we ever been this nice to each other? We should say these things aloud more often."

"Yes, we have. And, yes, we should." She blew a kiss at me. "I really do have to go now," she said. "I'm in charge of Gil's cake."

"Tell him I say happy birthday," I said unhappily.

"I'll call you this weekend. Love you."

"I love you, Mol."

"Bye."

She was gone before the computer could end the call. I huddled back into the pillows. It was only natural, that eight thousand miles away, things would change, even in the space of the few days I had been gone, that events would occur without me in them and the gap of my existence would shorten and fill with the existence of new stories, none of which I would understand fully, having not been there. I felt silly and melodramatic as I blinked back tears, wondering what it was about the Lahiri family that had made me leave my life in Brooklyn so far behind.

Eventually, I padded to the kitchen for toast, wrapped in a robe that could only have belonged to Iva. My doorbell rang, a musical birdsong, unlike the outsize single jangle of the buzzer attached to the main entrance of my mother's house.

Ram Bhai stood outside, serious, holding a small piece of paper. "Six hundred rupees," he said.

"What is it for?" I asked in Bengali, taking the note. It was a white scrap of a notebook sheet with a hasty *600* scrawled on it.

"Newspaper," he said in Hindi, solemn as he examined the pink flamingos on my green robe.

"Six hundred? That's"—I calculated—"twenty rupees a day. For one paper?"

He nodded.

"But the paper costs four rupees."

"Delivery charge," he said.

"But that's outrageous. Delivery can't be four times the cost of the paper. Can you negotiate?"

"Yes," he said, taking the note back. "How much?"

"I don't know. What does he charge you?"

"I read the Bengali newspaper, so it's only two rupees extra for delivery. Yours is English."

"That's ridiculous. He can't charge me higher delivery fees for language," I said, heated.

Ram Bhai nodded again. "How much?"

"Four rupees for paper, four for delivery. Two hundred and forty for the month."

Ram Bhai looked impressed. "Difficult," he said, "but let me try." Bargaining was a prized skill in the city, and while it bordered on criminal when my grandmother asked the farmers to sell her their fruit at cost, I wasn't willing to be advertised as the American who paid three times what the neighbors did for her English paper.

Ram Bhai turned to leave.

"And your mother is downstairs," he said.

MY MOTHER WAS, in fact, downstairs, waiting in her pointed way, in front of the gates. Flamingos still wrapped around me, I stepped into the street.

"What's wrong?" I asked.

"Hi, Lila," she said. "Nothing's wrong. What would be wrong? Can't a mother come to see her only child?"

"Ma, what are you doing here?"

"I wanted to make sure you were okay, since you have not been answering my calls," she said, virtuous.

"Ma, we talked yesterday afternoon." It had been a drawn-out conversation to assure me that she was not crazy to have made the scene at my grandmother's lunch and, in fact, that my grandmother was a devious manipulator, hell-bent on coming between her and me, did I know that? "And I was out last night."

"Out where? Lata said you came home at twelve thirty with a man."

"Who?"

"Lata. From across the street. You picked limes off her tree when you were a child. She saw you with a man."

"That's not Lata's business or anyone else's."

"Who is he?" she asked.

"Ma. I was out with Vik."

She did not look satisfied. "Vik is usually up to many dangerous things," she said. "Be aware, Lila, this is India, not America."

"I happen to have lived in India for the first sixteen years of my life."

She pursed her lips. "I brought you tea bags. Since you refuse to stay with us, I thought you might need tea."

"I didn't *refuse*. I can't live in a house that barricades its front door at nine p.m."

I took the tea bags from her.

"Thank you," I said.

"That rule is to prevent crime. You can always call me, and I will open the gate."

"Coming home after midnight is going to be considered the real crime by the family."

We stood on the street, my mother's arms crossed in front of her. Both of us knew the real reason I did not stay with her. I sighed.

"Would you like to come up?"

"Yes," she said, brightening. "I can make tea."

"I'll make the tea," I said, frowning at a passing schoolgirl who had stopped to stare at my flamingos.

In New York, I had made a habit of averting my eyes like the rest of the city; in Kolkata, I found myself in perpetual collision, head-on.

MY MOTHER HAD not been inside my father's apartment since they had divorced. When I was a child, I would catch her looking at the shuttered windows as we passed the building, with a fleeting look on her face that seemed to morph from rage to sorrow to curiosity. He was long gone to America by then, but I had still yearned for my father in those everyday passings-by, even as she yanked on my arm, walking quicker.

"That's quite a bathrobe," my mother said as I marched up the stairs.

"It's Iva's," I said, not turning to look back at the pain I knew she would feel at the idea of Iva's things.

I had forgotten that I had left a beer bottle on the windowsill and my suitcase open on the living floor. I zipped the suitcase shut and dragged it into the bedroom. When I came back into the living room, my mother stood in the center, suddenly small in the open space of my father's apartment.

"Ma, do you want to make tea?" I asked.

She was looking at the rose cushions, the fabric of the couch, the photograph on the low table of Avi, Robin, and me, our arms around each other. I felt an intense sorrow.

"Or have a seat, get comfortable," I said. "I'll make the tea."

She nodded and sat down, clutching her purse.

I CAME BACK with two mugs of tea and a packet of chocolate cookies.

She took her mug and sipped at it.

"Nice," she said. "Those biscuits are rich. You shouldn't be eating them regularly. Does your father eat them regularly?"

Irritated, I shook my head.

"He eats pretty healthy."

There was no need to spring to my father's defense, but in her presence, it was a constant habit.

"Do you drink too much, Lila?"

"Ma," I said, exasperated. "Could you just relax for a minute? Stop playing detective. I like *one* beer after a long day."

I put a whole cookie in my mouth, crushing into it, chased by a sip of the scalding-hot tea.

"I was just asking," she said, her voice small.

There it was again, the sadness that threatened to swallow me, the steady rhythm of enormous sorrow, enormous rage, more sorrow, more rage.

"I know," I said. "How's work?"

"Wonderful," she said happily. "I got Badal Sircar approved for the syllabus. The first time we've had an Indian playwright in there. Otherwise, it's all Shakespeare, Shaw, and Neil Simon."

"*Evam Indrajit?*" I asked.

"Yes," she said in pleasure. "My favorite of Sircar's plays. You know it?"

"Of course. It's one of my favorite plays too. Round and round they go, the four men. Amal, Vimal, Kamal . . ."

"And Indrajit," she completed. "The cyclical futility of life, as interpreted by undergraduates. God help me."

I laughed. "Better them than us. I feel like a cog in a wheel constantly these days. Round and round I go, like Sircar's characters."

"You're not a cog," she said, sharp. "You live in America, and you are an important editor in New York."

"Hardly important. I'm not saving any lives."

"We would have nothing without books. Or art, or music, or poetry." She stared at the paintings on the wall as if trying to comprehend them. "The painting of the paddy field. Is that a local artist?"

I smiled, even though it was a betrayal to Iva—the painting was her one artistic contribution to my father's apartment—but Iva would have allowed herself to be the butt of a thousand jokes to mend some fraction of my soul.

"I think it's from the Victoria Memorial souvenir shop," I said. "Supposed to give you Bengal vibes."

"The vibe is very . . . hotel room."

"Ma, that's mean," I said, amused.

"But the flat is nice," she said softly, looking around. "They are happy."

I got up to bring out the teapot. We drank more tea. We bantered about literature and the Laxman drawings she had in the studio (I could have them all, after she died), about the saris she had bought me for my wedding (Not a groom in sight, she noted), the Amrita Pritam art exhibit at Nandan, the music at Trincas (Had there been Mishraji? We speculated about the possible lives of Mishraji—headwaiter, government spy, long-term bachelor, maybe gay?). We discussed Biddy and YouTube, and would I like to go to Tangra and eat Mrs. Ling's momos on Sunday for breakfast? I felt as if I might have a mother, after all, as we talked about the things that mattered to us, even though we were both suddenly desperate to please each other, like strangers who had hit it off in a rare manner. She could be funny and wise and charming, and had a way of turning my head, like the way you meet someone for the first time and feel the thrill and hope that a new spark with a new person could lead to something eternal and wipe your slate clean.

"What do you have planned for the day?" she asked.

"Nothing. I was going to maybe go to College Street, to the bookshops. Do you want to come with me?" I asked, excited.

In this new mother manna, anything was possible, even the quick, unfamiliar rushes of love I felt for this stranger, the enormous wrongs forgotten for now .

"I have to be at the university," she said.

"That's okay," I said, drinking from my cup so she would not see my disappointment.

I wanted to be easy and light and effervescent, wonderful company that she would maybe want to spend more time with like this. My heart felt doubled and airy, infused by the connection between us, which I trusted with newborn certainty.

"There is a lot of pink and beige everywhere," she remarked.

I wanted to say something wicked and funny back, but I could not do that twice to Iva—so I said nothing, and my mother watched me in that way of hers, knowing why I did not join in the joke. We were bound by the fact that I had come from her body (a fact I could not imagine—I knew nothing of her body, what she felt or smelled like, what her fingers or toes were like, this nonmother of mine), and yet I could not ever look at her and not see some part of myself.

"What happened to that physics PhD student you had all those pictures with on Facebook?" she asked, as if struck by the memory of something she could not have had knowledge of.

I laughed, wiping my sweaty palms on the flamingos. "You've been stalking me, Ma."

"You tell me nothing about your life. How else would I know?"

She had spent fourteen months in silence but had taken the trouble to go online to know more about the daughter she would not talk to.

"We broke up," I said, pulling a towel out of the drawer.

"Was it very hard for you?"

I had not talked about Manolo to anyone but Dr. Laramie and Molly, but it felt surprisingly easy to say to my mother, "No. It was time. He was my college boyfriend."

She looked shocked. "You left him?"

"We . . . left each other. We were too young. It was slow, over time," I said. "I'm going to take a shower."

She followed me into the bedroom. "You didn't want to make it work? He seemed like such a nice boy."

"Ma, you've never met him. How do you know I was to blame?"

"I'm not blaming you." She shrugged. "Relationships need work. He seemed like a nice boy. . . on Facebook."

"He was a nice boy. And I'm a nice girl. We're still friends."

"How modern," she said with bitterness.

My mother had been excommunicated and singled out, a pariah born of divorcing a nice boy, in an era and city that did not believe in divorce. She had weathered the storm by retreating into the highest recesses of her childhood home, into the studio room that my grandfather had had specially built for her. It had been her decision to leave my father, and they had spoken only in courtrooms after, on matters relating to my custody.

I wondered if she ever regretted leaving him, if she went online and searched for photos of Iva, Baba, Avi, Robin, and me. I shrugged out of the robe. I wore a negligee underneath, and she looked at it with interest as I coiled my hair into a topknot.

"That's a pretty slip."

"Do you want one? I can send you a few."

She giggled.

"Imagine me in that. Imagine if I opened the door and one of the maids or the gardener or Hari or Rana saw me."

"Good—give them something to talk about for years."

I turned around to take off the negligee and pulled a towel around myself before turning back around.

"You have a good body," she said, staring at me. "You must give me some exercise tips."

"All bodies are good bodies, Ma."

"Not mine," she said dissatisfied. "It's because you're young."

"Don't be weird," I said. "I'm going to take a shower."

"I have to go now anyway," she said. "To the pharmacy, before my classes start. Your grandmother needs her medicines tonight."

My mother lived in hatred of her mother, performing daughterly duties stripped of affection, banging pills down wordlessly in front of Geeta, acts of service that only served as a bitter reminder to both that they needed each other.

"Be kind to her, Ma. It would be so nice to spend time together, the three of us."

"I am very good to her, Lila," she said, straightening the pleats of her sari. "When will I see you?"

"I'll come by for dinner," I said.

"Good. And listen, Lila. Don't tell people about your breakup."

"What? My college breakup? Why not?"

"Here, women don't have many boyfriends. They marry one man. They won't understand."

"Yes, well, I plan to marry six, so I guess I'm not a good girl."

"I'm just explaining how Kolkata is, Lila. I think you have a wonderful life. I wish I were free, like you."

I take a deep breath. "See you later, Ma."

"I'm going. Eat something. By the way, Janani came over this morning," said my mother. "She's helping to design the invites for Biddy's wedding. You know what a good eye she has. She said you and Adil had met?"

Adil's mother was an effusive, exuberant woman who had loved me as a girl and who had suspected that Adil and I might have been more than friends when we grew into teenagers but, knowing my mother well, had kept our secret. Suddenly, I felt as I had as a teen in front of my mother, afraid of what she knew: she knew that it was not Vik who had dropped me home and had wanted to see if I would lie.

"That's nice," I said, holding the towel tight around my body. "I'm going to shower now, Ma."

"Yes, yes, I'm leaving. Janani said Adil got home quite late that night, when all of you met."

I stopped on my way to the bathroom, unable to help myself.

"So Adil still lives at home?" I asked.

"Yes. A very good boy," she said, pointed.

I laughed, despite myself.

"Nothing to laugh at. Adil and his wife live with Janani and take care of her, like good, responsible Indian children." She picked up her purse, cheerful, on her way out. "Bye, Lila. Draw the curtains so people don't see you after your bath."

THE SHOWER STAYED hot for longer than I expected, thick steam billowing through the remodeled bathroom, white and cream tiles, the spray like rain. I tried to empty my mind—of my grandfather's house, of the Lahiris, of Molly and Adil and my mother—and focus instead on the water against my skin. Why had my mother not brought up the house at all? Surely, she was curious to know what I would do with it.

I padded out of the shower and reached for my phone and dialed.

Adil picked up on the second ring. "Hello."

"Hi. It's Lila."

"I know. I don't get too many calls from New York. We should get you a local sim."

We.

"It's not a big deal," I said. "I can afford it." I immediately regretted saying the words.

He laughed, easy, at my belligerence.

"Where can I get a sim?" I asked.

"Any local electronics, phone, repair shop. I'll grab you one on my way back home tonight."

I could hear the busy newsroom behind him, people yelling in a mix of Hindi, Bengali, and English, screens ablaze with angry TV journalists, a tea seller yelling, "Chai, chai."

"Ek chai," said Adil. "Hold on a sec, Lila."

I imagined him taking the cup. Hot, sweet afternoon tea. Suddenly, there was only silence on the other end.

"I'm in my office now—all yours," he said.

"Busy day saving democracy?" I asked.

"I wish. I'm in meetings all day," he said. "The legal team's job feels like managing the expectations of dozens of journalists furious with the right, like Vik. Just trying to keep us going, you know."

"I can tell you love it." I could hear him smile.

"I do," he said. "But sometimes I want to escape it all."

I wondered if his office had a window with a blue skyline, like mine, that he looked at as I did. *Sometimes I want to escape it all.*

"Ma came by," I said. "We spent the morning together."

"Oh," he said, careful, as if handling broken glass. "How was it?"

"Good. We had a nice time. Didn't kill each other."

"That's nice," he said, quiet.

In the moments of my childhood that I would readily forgive my mother in return for her brief bursts of motherhood, Adil had been my silent, predictable safety net, allowing me to soar into her love without comment, ready for the inevitable, crushing fall from grace.

"I called because I'm going to see Palekar next Friday," I said.

"Palekar?"

"My dad's friend. The estate-planning lawyer. He said he would help me . . . figure things out."

"Can we go after two? My last meeting is at one."

"You don't have to come," I said quickly. "If you've got advice, you could give it to me now . . . on the phone."

"Li, this is serious business. You own a giant property on Ballygunge Place that has belonged to the Lahiris for years. Your last name is De. You need a full picture of what your rights are, and a plan for whatever it is you want to do."

I bristled. "I don't need to be rescued," I said. "I run a company too, you know." (This was not the only lie I was prepared to tell.)

"Right. But this is Kolkata."

"I wish everyone would stop saying that to me. I was born here."

"Lila, just let me come. I will, in fact, be silent the whole time. A fly on the wall."

"Flies aren't six feet tall, with your opinions. I can take care of myself."

"Yes, you can. Please let me come?"

I shook my head, trying to clear it of thrill, of sorrow, of a heavy doom. I wanted to escape it all too—this thick fog of Kolkata that threatened me at every corner.

"Fine. Friday at three."

"See you then," he said, faint triumph in his voice.

He waited, eager I knew, to close the conversation, as he always liked to do after a win.

"Ma said she ran into Janani Aunty," I said.

I pictured him leaning back, processing in his solid, serious way. "Did she?"

"Yes."

He was silent, and I listened to the soft rise and fall of his steady breath.

"I should have said something yesterday, Lila. I don't know why I didn't."

I wondered if he was sitting or leaning or standing or pacing.

"Congratulations. You would think I'd have seen it on Facebook or something."

"I don't have Facebook."

"That's idiotic," I said, as light as air. "How else are your childhood friends and enemies supposed to gloat over what you look like at forty? What's her name?"

"Silky," he said. "My wife's name is Silky."

"Silky?" I asked.

"Be nice."

"She sounds . . . fun."

I pictured smooth skin, shiny hair, an eternal lightness of spirit.

"I think you'll like her, actually."

He said it in a resigned way that inflamed me. He had not told me he had a wife because like me, he had wanted to be the version of ourselves that we had long left behind.

"Well, I'll see you Friday," I said. "You can tell me the details then."

"Lila . . ."

"Yes?"

He paused. "I'll see you Friday."

There was nothing to be done about the past—no way to forget or revive, no way out of its erasure—except to reach back in, fall into it, touch and spill and search memory, drink it in, and, in the end, to know that it was dead but we were not.

10

SLOWLY, MY BODY recalibrated itself to Kolkata. I began to eat dinner later, at nine, even ten. After lunch, I felt sleepy, often joining in the citywide siesta. The shopkeepers began to recognize me, the sweetshop throwing an extra jilipi in my order and the grocer knowing that I wanted skim milk, the kind in Tetra Paks. I would wake early—before the bell on the newspaperman's cycle rang below my bedroom window as he threw the rolled-up *New Statesman* onto my balcony, before the school buses rumbled through, before Ram Bhai's transistor began playing Hindu bhajans.

The early mornings were cool against my skin, before the blaze of the late morning sun, the stillness of the hour allowing me to work in peace. Seth had sent a full draft, and Harriet had been emailing me the most promising submissions—we had to grow the list immediately and needed a glut of titles. Wyndham, it seemed, had ballooned in the little time that I had been gone. Soon, we would need two of me, two of Gil, two of us all.

Seth's draft was really good—something had possessed him lately. He wrote with an abandon for grammar and syntax, spiraling into a dizzying fiction of his own truths. I called to congratulate him, but there was no answer. Disappointed, I speculated that he had written himself into a frenzy of no outside contact, and bursts of sleep or food when the desire took him.

I missed the sound of his voice, his wicked humor, his knowledge of my American self, our banter. Seth and I were good friends, with an easy connection I had taken for granted, buried in the recesses of a professional relationship and booty calls. When I returned to Brooklyn, we would have a frank discussion about dispensing with the convenience of sex to focus on a less transactional friendship. This would be hard; Seth and I had an inevitable chemistry, especially after a back-and-forth on his work or the work of others we liked. *Epilogue sex*, we called it, made funnier because he knew that if I dreaded much in fiction, it was the presence of a waiting, self-satisfied epilogue.

ONE MORNING, AFTER a dawn installment of work, I showered and dressed to meet Rinki at the local wet market. I remembered holding my grandfather's hand as a child, going to buy pieces of fish from the same fisherwomen whom his father had bought fish from over the years. My mother had been too exhausted from teaching, translating, and trying to parent a child who had developed a passion for climbing trees (specifically guavas, to be able to throw the hard fruit at unsuspecting pedestrians) and a hatred for every one of her rules. In the years that I had lived with my mother, it was always my grandparents or the maids who took me on expeditions to the wet market, so that I could touch the ice-cold silver bhetki and pronounce it fresh.

Rinki wanted to spend more time with me, but her schedule of breakfast and dinner planning, mill luncheons, mill parties, and the mill-theater association and book club did not afford her the same ease as Vik's unannounced visits. We had planned to meet at eight at the wet market, where she would do her week's worth of shopping. Ten minutes before I was going to leave to walk to the market, I heard an insistent honking below my bedroom window. I went onto the bedroom balcony and saw a Maruti van the size of a small school bus, its driver in white uniform, his palm against the horn. My neighbors stood on their balconies, grim.

Mrs. Chatterjee, in a floral daytime nightie, from the window across from mine screamed, "Chup!"—covering her ears with her hands.

Rinki, peering out the window of the van, waved at me.

"Jabbar, Jabbar, ruko," she said to the driver in the front seat.

When he went on honking, she reached over and tapped his shoulder, at which he stopped and the world had silence again.

I went downstairs and slid into the van, next to Rinki.

"Well. You'll be paying for Mrs. Chatterjee's next set of hearing aids."

"That old witch is always terrorizing us," said Rinki. "We would play music on our Walkmans on the way home from school, and she insisted she could hear it from her flat, when she was already deaf."

"I can imagine you cool, with a Walkman," I said.

"I was cool," she said with a sigh.

I had missed out on the cool years, and here we were now, Rinki in her green sari, with a full life, ensconced in her community.

A young woman, in her early twenties or so, hair in a neat bun, sat in the front passenger seat next to Jabbar. She turned to smile at me.

"Namaste, madam. I'm Lily."

"Namaste, Lily. I'm Lila," I said, to which Lily giggled and turned back to the front.

"I thought I was meeting you at the market," I said to Rinki. "And what are you, Michelle Obama, with this full staff of people? What, is your man the president of the mill?"

She giggled. "Senior general manager. But I'm president of the mill ladies' club. It's such fun, Li. You should come to one of our boat parties sometime with Biddy. All the mill men will be thrilled. Who knows, you might find a husband, and then what fun—we can be mill ladies together."

"Dreamy," I said.

"I'm starving. Let's get some Tasty Corner first," said Rinki.

"WHAT SORT OF a name is Silky, anyway?" I asked, tearing into a kochuri, the salty-sweet dal inside crumbling over my cotton dress.

"Marwari or Punjabi," said Rinki matter-of-factly while chewing. "Here, have some alu," she said passing the potato curry, in its sal-leaf bowl, to me.

I scooped up some of the potato, the thin gravy clinging to the waxy potatoes, the whole thing a familiar explosion in my mouth—ginger, tamarind, cumin, hing—everything at once, like the city.

Rinki inspected her phone with one hand, a kochuri in the other. "At least she's ugly."

"Jesus," I said, grabbing her phone.

The woman staring up at me on Rinki's extra-large phone screen, with an arm around Adil, was serious, her straight hair in a bob, angular and fragile and lovely.

"He married fucking Posh Spice," I said.

"Bengali men don't like scrawny women," said Rinki.

"Ugh, Rinks."

Rinki laughed. "You're so American, god. People are fat, people are thin—what's the big deal?"

"He looks plenty like he likes her," I said. "Where did you find this? I thought Adil didn't do Facebook."

"She's Vik's friend on Facebook."

"Yeah," I said, jealous. I didn't want her to be Vik's friend.

"Jabbar, bring us some jilipis—for dessert," shouted Rinki to her driver, who was washing his hands at the Tasty Corner tap, fitted on the wall, no sink below. The water was meant for a postmeal rinse of one's hands and mouth, and flowed directly into the gutter under the sidewalk.

"And get some for yourself and Lily too," added Rinki.

The car was parked a few feet from the crowded sweetshop, which provided kochuri, shinghara, and jilipi breakfasts to the entire neighborhood, so cheaply that everyone could eat it, so delicious that people traveled neighborhoods for it. Jabbar brought us the thin orange crystalline jilipi. The syrup ran down my hands as I ate, blissed-out by the tart-honey-crisp sensation.

"Are you heartbroken about Adil?" asked Rinki, gossipy now that she had eaten.

She handed me a wet wipe from a large tote.

"What? No," I said with a laugh. "I hadn't seen him in years, before last week at Trincas. We never even slept together—we were kids. I was sixteen when I left. I just feel . . . sort of sad. Like I've lost that part of myself."

"Do you sleep with a lot of men?" asked Rinki, her eyes widening a fraction.

I paused. I hadn't expected her to focus on that, though I should have. But Rinki wasn't Molly, and I didn't want to be judged a harlot by my family.

"Well, I'm not seeing anyone exclusively right now."

"What does that mean? What is 'exclusive'? Like, special? Like an exclusive designer dress?"

I laughed, uncomfortable. "When you just see one person, that's exclusive. I'm just doing casual . . . dating. Nothing special."

"So dating isn't special?"

"Rinks," I protested, laughing.

"You have such an interesting life. I've only ever had sex with Bashudeb. Is sex more interesting when you have it with a lot of people?" Rinki seemed despondent even as her eyes glittered with curiosity.

I looked away. I would have a lot to explain to my mother and grandmother if two Lahiri women were overheard discussing sexual conquests outside Tasty Corner.

"Honestly, if we never had sex again, I wouldn't care," continued Rinki. "I just don't want him to feel like I'm a bad wife."

"Yeah," I said after a pause. "I was in a long-term thing for a while. It got . . . Well, we had to reinvent things."

"Oh god, you have to tell me everything," said Rinki.

The intense sugar of the jilipi had begun to give me a slight buzz.

"I mean, you could try . . . role-play, or toys, or just new, fun stuff, maybe."

Rinki's large eyes widened, enormous over her round cheeks. "Toys?" She leaned forward, conspiratorial. "You know, my friend Bindi, her husband once bought her a nurse costume."

I nodded. "As long as it's fun for both of you, anything goes."

"Could you imagine Bashudeb's face? What about his mother? Imagine my mother-law finding my stethoscope? Or opening the door and finding me dressed like a nurse. I mean, she never even knocks to come into our bedroom."

"That's one way to make sure she does," I said.

Lily climbed back into the car, curious at our uncontrollable laughter. "Ready, madam?"

Rinki looked annoyed.

"The best fish usually sell out by noon, madam," said Jabbar through the window, a toothpick between his teeth.

"Fine, let's go," said Rinki. "Lila, we have to spend more time together."

"Just so you know, I'm no expert," I said. "That particular long-term relationship didn't work out."

"I have to make it work out, Lila. I'm married."

AT THE WET market, Rinki lifted her sari above her ankles as we splashed through the lanes. The fishmongers shouted their wares at us—"Pomfret, rui, katla, magur, golda chingri, kakra"—a rising crescendo in which the most prized items, the shrimp and crab at the end, were sung the loudest. Rinki's entourage followed us, Lily stepping in to bargain and examine the fish, and Jabbar holding our bags.

"My grandmother always wore nylon or polyester saris to the fish market," said Rinki. "So the smell wouldn't seep into the fabric. Here, smell me—see?"

I sniffed the end of Rinki's sari's pallu. It smelled faintly of lavender.

"Impressive," I said. "I guess I'm going to be slightly shrimpy the rest of the day."

"The crabs are very sweet this time of the year. Did you want to buy any for Maya Didi or Geeta Mami?" asked Rinki, as we watched Lily, with Poonam the fisherwoman, inspect the live creatures scuttling around the wicker basket.

"God, no. They'll both want to make it for me, and I'll have to eat two crab lunches on the same day."

"Come on. Let's go get some ilish," said Rinki, taking my arm. "Lily, we're going to Bhagavan's stall—come after you're done. Poonam, must you try to rob us each week?"

"Must you rob the rice out of my child's mouth, didi?" said Poonam with a cheerful shake of her head.

We left Lily and Poonam to their negotiations and walked through the market. There were yellow lightbulbs overhead, and the warm light sparkled off fish scales and cleavers and the steep walls of the market. I pulled out my phone to take a picture.

"It's funny," said Rinki, "you're taking photos of our wet, smelly, dirty fish market, and some foreigner will look at it and decide it's the most fantastic thing he's ever seen."

I put away the phone, embarrassed. "I hated the market as a kid, but it feels so beautiful and historical now."

"Yes, welcome to our hundred-and-forty-year-old landmark—the pigeon shit and the stone walls are both historic," said Rinki with a flourish. "And Bhagavan, who cheats me daily, charging me hundreds of extra rupees for his worthless ilish."

Bhagavan grinned up at Rinki from his cushion, slabs of fish gleaming in front of him. They clearly had a bit.

"The finest ilish that the River Padma has seen, Rinki Madam—my son catches it with his own hands."

I watched as Rinki and Bhagavan went through the motions of bargaining, before settling on seven hundred rupees for a whole fish sliced into fillets.

"At Whole Foods, they charge extra for filleting and deboning," I said to Rinki in Bengali.

Bhagavan looked up with interest.

"Quiet. Don't give him any ideas," said Rinki to me in Bengali. "She doesn't know anything," said Rinki to Bhagavan in Hindi. "She's from America."

"America," said Bhagavan, pleased, stripping away scales, removing pin bones, and slicing up perfect disks of fish.

I wanted to express my admiration for his expertise, but I worried that Rinki would laugh at me again. The fierceness with which I wanted to belong rivaled the constant throb of my longing for Brooklyn.

"I'll take half a kilo for Mummy," I said.

OUTSIDE THE WET market, I breathed in the damp air; it felt like the smell of fish had reached the insides of my brain. The monsoon had yet to descend, but dark-gray clouds hung over the city, as if to signal an impending apocalypse.

"Didi looks like she enjoyed our market," said Lily.

"Lila, look how crowded the Costa Coffee is," said Rinki. "No place to sit.

Jabbar and Lily are going to have tea at the stand. Should we just ask them to bring two cups to the car for us?"

I nodded. Costa Coffee was packed with a medley of the next-door temple's upper-class devotees, trendy teenagers and mothers who were waiting for their children to finish school over three-hundred-rupee coffee frappés. Rinki and I clambered into her van, the silence and air-conditioning inside a relief.

Rinki exhaled. "Thank goodness the fish is off my list. The rest of the shopping I can do at HyperCity."

"The new mall?" I asked.

"Yes, it's delightful. Organic fruit, veggies, meat, milk, Bashudeb's whiskey—all under one roof. Clean plastic trays, low-calorie chips, even American Oreos."

"They don't let you bargain there, I assume?"

"No chance." She laughed.

Lily brought over two little bhars of tea, the tiny clay cups filled to the brim.

"Lily, I'm going to need about fifteen more of these," I said to her in Bengali.

"Mohan Bhai will be happy if you do," said Lily. "He's been losing too much business to the big café."

"One look at Lila, and Mohan will charge three times the price of a bhar," said Rinki.

Lily went off to chat with the maids and nannies holding their charges and drinking tea at the stand. Traffic honked and whizzed past us, flinging an occasional curse in the direction of our van, which took up a quarter of the narrow lane. (*Did your father pay for the road? Move this fucking car. Who do you think you are, the prime minister? Behenchod.*) A small team of goats marched by, the animals attuned to the crack of the thin whip in their owner's hand. I sipped the tea—it was strong and sweet, and meant to be drunk in small doses.

"It's hard to see the point of haggling over the price of fish with fisherwomen," I said.

Rinki looked at me, surprised, and then laughed.

"Oh, Lila, you've been holding that in for the last hour, haven't you? You haven't changed a bit—still bottling away everything until you have to blurt it out."

"We pay twice the price at malls but make sure the bajar fishermen make the bare minimum on their fish."

Rinki touched my shoulder, gentle. "It's part of the culture," she said. "The way things are done here. They quote a price that's triple what it should be, we bring it down to below acceptable, we threaten to walk away, they quote a final price, we turn away, shaking our heads sadly, they throw us another final price, we start walking, and this time, it's the final, final price, usually at least twenty percent above cost price, and then it's time to pay. It's a dance as old as time. Our mothers did it, our grandmothers. You should try it—it's fun."

Jabbar returned to the car. "Ready, madam?"

Rinki nodded. "Lila, you'll come home with me, right? Or did you want to go back to your father's flat?"

"I'll come with you," I said, though I felt a stab of anger at Rinki, at Vik, at my mother, at the sweetshop owner. So what if I lived in another country. So what if I had a twang. So what if I had to reach into my memories to excavate forgotten words of Bengali that had blurred in meaning, so that when I said a sentence, I sounded like a toddler and everyone laughed. This pit in my stomach was their fault, from constantly having to defend and explain and contextualize and smooth over the amorphous edges of my identity.

Jabbar had his palm pressed flat against the horn again, a steady stream of a high-pitched protest against the unmoving sea of traffic and pedestrians in front of us, an incessant siren inside the air-conditioned car.

"Rinks, is this really necessary?" I asked. "It's not like honking's going to make traffic move any faster."

At my sharpness, Rinki shot me a look of concern. I felt the beginnings of a headache.

"Jabbar, my goodness, must you behave like a maniac? Stop that honking at once," she said.

Lily giggled, and Jabbar, sheepish, removed his hands from the horn.

"They weren't moving, madam," he said, defensive.

"And now they are?" asked Rinki, even her endless patience waning, in the heat and noise of the afternoon.

"Look, madam, isn't that Hari Sir?" asked Lily, excited.

"Where?" asked Rinki. She sounded tired.

I felt regret at having sulked. I put a strand of her hair behind her right ear. "You okay, Rinks?"

"Yes, just a little warm." She opened the window and extended her head out of it. "Ah, that breeze feels good. Oh, you're right, Lily, there's Hari Mama."

Lily began to fan Rinki from the front seat, with an old-fashioned bamboo fan. Rinki, grateful, leaned back. Hari was standing at the tea stall.

"Should we offer him a ride?" I asked.

"Who, Hari? No, he's probably busy arguing with his cronies and drinking tea."

"Hari Dada," yelled Lily, above the cacophony of the traffic, in the direction of the stall.

"Lily, please," said Rinki. "It's not like we won't see him at the house later. Let the man be. Here, give me the fan."

She took the fan from Lily and waved it in front of her face as we watched Hari accept two bhars of tea. Hari sipped from both—the cups were overflowing—and then turned to cross the street, weaving his way through the standstill traffic, right across from where we sat in Rinki's van.

"Oh, look, he's coming to this side," said Lily.

"Lily, must you get excitable over everything?" asked Rinki, amused.

The color had returned to her cheeks. I handed her a bottle of water.

"It's as if Hari Mama were Shah Rukh Khan," said Rinki. "The other day, Bashudeb's mother had a vacuum delivered, and Lily was so excited she couldn't sleep."

"That vacuum has a ghost inside it," said Lily.

"A ghost," sneered Jabbar, delighted.

"Where do you live, Lily?" I asked.

She turned around. "I used to do just the cooking and shopping at Rinki Madam's house and go home to my parents, but the last two years, it became easier to just live with her and Bashudeb Sir and do all the household work too. They're nicer to me, and I have friends in the neighborhood."

"Lily is the mill's Miss Popularity," said Rinki, affectionate.

Hari had crossed the street and stood about six cars in front of us.

"Oh, that's his car. They must be on their way back from lunch at Mishti Mami's parents' house," said Rinki.

The rickshaw in front of us moved an inch, and we could now see Mishti's profile in the window of their car as she accepted one of the bhars from Hari. Hari was frowning and stood with his hands on his hips, glaring at the traffic.

"Hari Dada looks angry with the traffic," said Jabbar with a snicker.

"You don't see him honking from here to heaven, do you?" asked Rinki.

Jabbar scratched his jaw, nonchalant.

Suddenly—so quickly that it felt like a misleading blur of the harsh after-noon light—Hari turned back to Mishti, and as I watched his lips moving, I realized that his face was contorted in rage. Mishti's head bobbed out of the window, her eyebrows raised, arguing back even as Hari took his bhar (*Was there tea in it?* I wondered) and smashed it against the gravel of the street, grinding it to dust under his feet. I felt Rinki still next to me, her breathing quicken, as Hari took the bhar in his wife's hand next and, in one motion, crumpled it against the side of his car, the sweet, thick tea and its strands of milk skin trickling to form a pattern against the red of the passenger door. Mishti held her hands up to her ears as Hari yanked open her car door and then slammed it back shut, inches away from her small body. The motion seemed to reverberate into the stillness of our car, even though Jabbar had rolled up the windows again and we could only hear the faint hum of the air conditioner, my imagination doing the rest of the work. Hari went back around to the driver's side and pulled open the door. As he entered the car, I held my breath, but he shut the door, blank-faced, with an ordinary click, as if the last few seconds had not happened, as the unrelenting traffic finally gave way, groaning open, and we began to move forward.

ON THE WAY to the Lahiri house, the van was silent—even Lily ceasing her chatter. Jabbar turned on the radio, and an old Mohammad Rafi love song began to play, its loveliness haunting.

"Jabbar, turn it off please," said Rinki, staring out the window.

As we turned into the driveway, Hari's car stood in the sole parking spot. Lily, Rinki, and I got out and walked into the courtyard, where Mishti was unloading the shopping bags from the trunk of the car.

"Hello, ladies," she said, her face lighting up in pleasure.

Her bandage was gone, only a slight tinge of red to her eye now. It felt surreal to see her completely her normal self.

"Here, Lily, give me a hand with these bags," said Mishti. "Could you make sure Bari puts them straight into the fridge?"

"I took Lila to the fish market," said Rinki.

"Really?" Mishti came closer and sniffed my shoulder. "There it is—you're a proper Bengali now, Lila, the perfume of fish always somewhere on your skin."

"Bhagavan even added in a bit of the special ilish eggs for Lila to taste," Rinki said. "We're going to have to take her along every time to get what we want."

At Mishti's laughter, Hari came out, smiling. "What's all this about?"

"Apparently, the fishermen are all in love with Lila now," said Mishti. "They won't give us the best pieces unless we take our American."

"Excellent. Tell that rascal Bhagavan we want the belly, and not the tail, of the bhetki—he's always trying to cheat us," said Hari. "Lila Ma, stay for dinner."

"Sorry, Hari Kaka, I have to head home. Maybe next time."

"Nonsense. This is your home," said Hari as he strolled out of the compound.

Mishti smiled. "Sure you won't join us? Bari is going to make begunis."

"Save me a few for tomorrow."

"What about the ilish for Geeta Pishi?" asked Rinki.

"You give it to her," I implored. But it was too late.

"Lila, is that you?" My grandmother, delighted, hung over the third-floor balcony ledge.

"Be careful, Mummy," I said.

Within seconds, my mother's head appeared from the fifth floor.

"Lila, is that you?" she asked.

As my mother and grandmother narrowed their eyes at each other, I turned to Mishti.

"I guess I'm staying," I said.

"Excellent," she said. "I'll send up some begunis."

"Where's the ilish?" I asked Rinki as Mishti went inside, in the direction of her kitchen.

"Lily will bring it up," Rinki said, linking her arm through mine, as we would as girls. But we were not girls anymore.

"Rinks, what was that?" I asked, my voice low.

"What was what?" she said, turning to look at me.

I felt my head throb in confusion. "Hari Kaka . . . The way he slammed the door. The fight."

Her face fell immediately. It felt like for everyone but me, there had been a seamless transition from before the incident into this postuniverse, where Hari and Mishti had descended back into ordinary marital concerns of shopping and mealtime.

Rinki shrugged. "They had a fight," she said, her voice lowered. "Couples fight. Married people fight. It's normal."

"That was not normal. Married people don't fight like that. If they do, they shouldn't be married," I hissed.

She looked at the upper floors of the house, alarmed. "Lila, be quiet."

My mother felt miles away, on the fifth-floor balcony—but even from a distance I could feel her gaze in the center of my shoulder blades.

"That was awful, what he did, Rinki. She could have had the door slam on a finger or her side—she could have been really hurt."

"I . . . I really don't think so. It was just a fight. They argued, and he slammed the door. It happens."

Had it been a paranoid illusion born of my own red alert to conflict? I ran through the incident in my head. *No, it wasn't just a normal fight.*

Mishti passed by the third-floor hallway, above us. She waved as she called out: "I'm leaving the begunis in Geeta Didi's room, Lila. Eat them before they're soggy."

"See, she looks fine," said Rinki in a small voice as my mother's eyes burned into the back of my neck, my skull, the top of my arms.

"Rinks, I'm sorry. I don't want to upset you. It was just . . . It was . . ."

Rinki looked relieved at my retreat. "It was nothing. Husbands and wives squabble here. Bashudeb and I do too sometimes. It's like haggling in a market. It's silly Bengali culture. Nothing more to it."

She took my arm again and led me into the house.

"It's the way things are, Lila. Now tell me when you're coming to the mill to visit so I can treat you to a proper mill ladies' day out."

I WASHED MY face in my grandmother's bathroom, the water's iciness a reprieve for my aching head. Lily had delivered the ilish, and my grandmother stood in her kitchen, marinating the pink fish steaks in turmeric and salt. Rinki, one hand on her hip, leaned against the heavy wooden frame of the kitchen doorway, chewing on a paan, half of it still in her hand.

"There you are, Lila. I was just telling Geeta Mami all about our fish-market adventure."

"I hear you're quite the talk of the town," said my grandmother. "And that you're going to meet some mill men to audition as future husbands?"

At this, Geeta and Rinki burst into laughter.

"Well, I'm off to my own husband. Lila, I'll call you soon," said Rinki, kissing my cheek.

My grandmother smiled at me as Rinki left. "Thank you for the fish, Lila. They're from the river Padma, sweetest in this season. Stay, and I'll fry you a piece."

"Not today, Mummy. I'll come by later."

"But it's just one piece," she protested.

"Not today."

She looked up at me. "Oh, okay."

In that moment, I knew that Rinki had told her of my outrage at the incident with Hari and Mishti. The bubble of unbelonging inflated again in my chest—a De in the Lahiri world, looking in, no right to judge or jury.

"Here, take some nimki with you. I made you some this morning," she said, wiping her hands on a cloth.

She strained to reach for a tin on a shelf above her. I took it down for her and she pressed it back into my palms.

"Lila, my love," she said, pausing, "families are complicated. All of them. Your family is complicated in its own way. Ours is complicated in its own way."

"I'm part of this family too, Mummy."

"No, of course you are," she said in a rush. "But I mean, this side of your family has its own history, and it is different from that side, and we should just accept that people are different. What seems like rudeness in one culture is often commonplace in another."

"I have to go, Mummy. Thank you for the nimki," I said, turning away.

I took the stairs, two at a time, just as I had as a child, and was outside in minutes, walking quickly through the courtyard, out the enormous gates, and down the street I knew so well, toward the direction of my father's house, my mother's stare still embedded in my back, following me ceaselessly as it had through all the years we had been apart. Had I had misunderstood a simple spat between a husband and a wife, a private affair for their eyes only? If so, it was because of her—she who raised me on edge, on the precipice of suspicion and fear perpetually, on the certainty that the worst was unfolding for us at all times.

11

THE FOLLOWING DAY, I woke to pouring rain, the kind you could not see through. The monsoon had arrived, and the balcony had flooded. I hurried to shut the windows before Iva's cushions and chairs were soaked. A lone elderly man hurried through the streets, an enormous black umbrella and his white dhoti billowing after him. I made tea, comforted by the storm. I had always loved rain, the way it soaked and soothed the earth, the sense of drama and longing it brought with it.

I texted Adil. *It's raining.*

In your part of the world as well? he shot back immediately.

I wondered if he woke early every morning. I sent back an emoji, a happy yellow circle, rolling its eyes. *So I guess I cancel with Palekar?*

He sent back a circle, the one that laughed sideways at you, a tear spilling from one eye.

But it says it'll storm all day. It's a kalboishakhi!

It's just rain. You won't melt, Lila Madam.

A few seconds later: *I'll hold an umbrella over you.*

I imagined the light catching his eye, teasing me.

In Brooklyn, we would have to evacuate.

Here, we go back to bed and pray to the rain gods to spare us.

Okay, wise guy.

Did you just wake up?

Yes.

Do you still wear silly pajamas?

??

Smurfs, dragons, the ice-cream set?

It was true that at fifteen I had gone to bed in matching sets that my father and Iva would send me, wholesome and all-American. I looked down at my silk slip. *I can't believe you remember.* A beat later. *I'm in grown-up clothes, unfortunately.*

I saw him typing. And then he stopped. He started again. I leaned back into my pillows.

Seven minutes later: *I'll see you at 2.*

Kk.

The storm rumbled outside, lightning cracking through the gray sky. Maybe there would be a rainbow later, the kind that split its way across neighborhoods and children flew their kites against.

AT 8 A.M., I had a Skype call scheduled with Seth; in the past two weeks, I had stayed up every night, well beyond 2 a.m., so that I could send him edits. I had hit send very late the night before. Harriet had put weekly editorial check-ins on my calendar and had invited him to them in her no-nonsense manner, but I did not think he would pay attention to things like calendar invites. Yet he appeared on my screen as another bout of thunder rumbled above.

He was rumpled, his hair messy, in little tufts, as if he had slept in the sweatshirt he wore, handsome in the sleepy, intellectual way of Brooklyn's Jewish writers. It felt like he was even more attractive than when I had last seen him—I made a mental note to get a new author photo for his book—he would have more than a few extra fans for it. It was good to see him, this familiar person from home.

"Hi, you," I said. "Did you see what I sent last night?"

"God, what is that sound? Are you in a war?"

"Yep. Bombs flying overhead."

He looked alarmed, and I laughed. "It's just a storm."

"Sounds like an evacuation is in order."

"That's what I said," I exclaimed. "But apparently these houses have stood for years and hurricanes have come and gone, and I'm just a silly American."

"Well, hello from another silly American," he said, grinning at me.

"The draft is so good. Seth, can you believe how close you're getting?"

He ran his fingers through his hair.

"Do you like it, really? You're not just saying that?" He put his glasses on and focused in my direction. "I can't be sure of anything these days."

"When have I ever said anything to be polite?"

"God, Lila, I miss you," he laughed. "I've been in such a hole, just trying to dig this fucking book out of myself. I have no perspective on anything anymore. When do you get back again?"

"I . . . I don't know yet."

I realized I didn't. This felt like new information. I had thought I would know by now.

"What about your job?" he said, frowning into the screen.

"I have six weeks left of the leave they gave me. After that, I don't know. I'm seeing the lawyer later today, though. Maybe I'll know more after."

He looked as surprised as I felt. The idea that I might have to stay for many more weeks, until the matter of the house resolved itself and I knew what was to be done had not risen into the realm of definite thought, and it felt like my chest was deflated. What if Aetos decided I was dispensable? *Lila, you're the heart of this division,* he had said once, smoother than a new spoon, but what if he thought that senior management, in fact, managed better when not in remote locations of the earth?

"How is your mother, Li?" asked Seth, as my lover now, or perhaps my friend—I couldn't tell between our blurred edges.

For the most part, he was absorbed in himself, his mind overheated with the affairs of an academic and a writer, almost to the edge of narcissism. There were moments, however, mostly postcoital, where he had said something that looked right into my core and confronted it in the way only writers might, casual to the point of indifference. *What a little Heathcliff you were,* stroking my face before kissing me. *Love must be awful for you, Li,* mumbled into my neck seconds before falling asleep. *You won't really let any of us know you,* suddenly, middrink. *Give whipped cream a chance—you can't run from everything in your childhood,* laughing as I scraped off a sundae. *If your nose and hands are just like your father's, where do the rest of the parts come from? You're whiter than I am, Li,* as I mailed off my Hartford Tennis Club member renewal fee. *It's a lot, to survive our parents.*

"She's exactly as I last left her," I said. "No surprises." I had never talked to Seth about my mother, so in his mind, she was any mother, every mother.

He nodded, serious. "Have you spent time with her?"

"Sure," I said through my immediate discomfort.

Seth held me trapped in his clear gaze. "Is there any chance you might not come back?" he asked.

We paused as I swallowed.

"No," I said, relieved at what Seth had chanced upon, this discovery of certainty. "I'm coming back."

He nodded again, relief in his smile.

"Will you water my plants?" I asked.

"Yeah. I'll pop by tonight."

"Okay. And look over my edits, try to be fast? They're really not too bad, and we can make the list if we can move it along in the next two weeks. If the apartment gets too claustrophobic, take yourself on walks, breathe, do what you have to. Just get this thing done. You're so close."

"It's actually really good, isn't it?" he asked, a glimmer in his eyes.

"Yes," I said. "Better than either of us could have hoped."

I was rare with praise, and Seth shone visibly.

"The important thing is for you to fix the section where he returns to the village. That's the biggest part that needs rethinking."

"You know, that's a good idea, to go away somewhere to do the revisions," he said slowly. "Give my brain some space to think."

I had suggested a walk, not a vacation. It was important he did not lose momentum. I needed Aetos to see me birth a bestseller before the end of next year.

"It's the hardest part now to get through," said Seth. "The scenes where he returns to his birthplace, to the scene of the crime where his friend drowned. Hard to write that kind of thing without becoming maudlin. A new setting sometimes unsettles me into delivering the truth better, sharper."

"Maine?" I suggested. "Or your mom's place?"

His mother, after divorcing his father, had received their summer home in the Hamptons in a settlement. Seth and I rarely argued, but once, when I had described his point of view as "privileged" at a party, he had been incensed.

Seth looked reflective.

"Do you want to talk again in a week or so?" I asked. "After you've had time to work on the revisions?"

I could see from the way he nodded again that he was absorbed in whatever he had begun to formulate. Seth had a way of letting go of you in the deep end of the ocean.

"Okay." I laughed. "Keep me posted on where you end up."

THE STORM ABRUPTLY stopped at noon, the air filled with the ripeness of the debris it had left behind—trash and leaves and the gutters overflowing into the street as the muddy, knee-deep water began to recede. Vik had called to see if I had electricity. I did, but the Lahiris' power had been out for six hours.

"Don't they have generators?" I asked Vik, frowning into the phone.

"Old ones, from when electricity was first discovered."

"Very funny. Don't they want them replaced? I could include it in the renovation."

"Many years ago, my father bought them new ones, because he saw a sale somewhere, and ended up paying market price for a pile of junk."

"Poor Rana Kaka," I said.

Rana had been kind to me through my teens, many times proving a refuge from the attentions of my mother.

"It's fine," said Vik. "He wrote a poem about it, like a good Bengali man. Channeled his rage with etiquette."

AT ONE FORTY-FIVE, I was outside Amlan Palekar's office. My father had called with plenty of advice: *Ask Palekar if they can fight you on ownership. Ask him what identity documents you need—will your PIO card suffice? Ask him if I need to be present for any proceedings.* (In India, a father or husband could add much gravitas in a courtroom situation, even render a single woman in a more favorable light.) *Don't say anything to Maya or Geeta yet.*

At all this, I had been calm, separating useful logic from worry, and pleased that he was, in fact, worried about me.

I typed a note to Adil: *Here early. Going in. Join whenever you get here. No rush.*

Turn around, he texted back.

He was parking his family-size car in the adjacent lot. He leaped out, grasshopper legs the same as they were at fifteen, now sheathed in stylish trousers hemmed a little above his ankles, his loafers muddied by the puddles everywhere.

"I just knew you would try to do this alone," he said.

"Nice to see you too."

"C'mon, Li," he said, and he took my hand as if it were the most natural thing to do, swinging it between us, a damned rainbow stretching itself across the sky overhead.

PALEKAR WAS BESIDE himself with delight to see me. For the third time, shaking his head, he said that I looked all grown up.

"It's nice to see you too, uncle," I said. "You haven't changed." This was a lie—Amlan Palekar had lost his hair and gained what looked like a beer belly and a prosperous legal practice.

He guffawed, arching his neck. "Wait until I show you pictures of your father and me on the corner of Ballygunge Place, trying to look good for the ladies."

"Do you have photos?" I asked.

"Oh, yes. I might be a little chubby now, but back then, we wore bell-bottoms in shocking shades of blue or green. Wait, hold on a second." He rummaged in his drawer. "Ah, here we go."

Triumphant, he pulled out a yellowing photo. It was my father, his cheeks still full from boyhood, with a trimmed mustache, a big-buckled belt, a shirt so swirled in green-and-yellow patterns that it was vivid even in the aged photo. He looked intensely into the camera, one arm around an equally colorful Palekar.

Adil leaned over my shoulder; I could feel his breath on my right earlobe. "Wow," he said.

Palekar gleamed at us. "Oh, yes, we were the lions of Ballygunge."

I could feel Adil stifle a laugh as his elbow touched mine.

"This was right before Mihir met Maya . . ." At this, Palekar's voice trailed off as if a sudden thought had confused him.

Years later, my mother's divorce was still enough to make people look away, the tinge of scandal and acrimony like sour air over our heads.

"Your mother, of course," Palekar said. "Your eyes—just like hers, of course," he nodded again, clearing his throat.

The parts of me that were hers were visible immediately when we walked down the street together. But when in the arms of men who had never met her, or with people who knew me only as Lila De, I could appear without identity, seemingly inheritanceless—no mother in the slant of my jaw, the small bones of our wrists, the knuckles and lips and shoulders that gave me away.

Adil rested an arm around the back of my chair.

"Well, you can keep that photo, my dear," said Palekar, clearing his throat again. "I have many more. You must come over to my house one day, with your friend, for dinner. My wife would love to see you—she held you in her arms as a baby."

My forehead was beginning to prickle with sweat in the airless office.

"This is Adil Sarkar, uncle. He is a family friend and works for the *New Statesman*—he offered to help me with the property situation."

"A journalist," said Palekar, suspicious, over his rimless glasses. "For the left?"

"I'm senior counsel for the media group, sir," said Adil, rising to his feet to shake Palekar's hand.

There was a reassuring, respectful air to Adil—parents especially loved him for it.

Palekar softened, pressing a buzzer on his desk. "Sarita, please bring three teas, sugar separate—with milk." He looked at us, and Adil and I nodded. "With milk. And a plate of nankhatai."

Palekar took his finger off the buzzer. "Now, let's solve your little problem, my dear Lila."

SINCE I HAD no idea what my problem was, it took a full hour for Palekar to get to the bottom of the various scenarios around my inheritance.

"The good news is that India abolished inheritance tax back in 1985, before you were even born," said Palekar.

"The bad news is that they are probably gearing up to fight you on your claim, as we speak," said Adil.

"What?" I turned to him.

"He's right, my dear," said Palekar, removing his glasses. "They have probably already engaged the services of a firm to contest."

"Who? My family?"

Palekar looked uncomfortable as he reached for a nankhatai. "It isn't personal. The Lahiris have owned that house for decades. For all practical purposes, you are an outsider and have no idea how to manage the, quote, unquote, 'estate.'"

"Plus your grandfather was ill," said Adil. "If your grandmother or mother testify to his lack of mental clarity, they may be able to take the house away from you."

The idea of my mother and grandmother finally joining forces over taking me to court made me expel a frenzied giggle.

"Lila, you've got to understand," said Adil, as if urging a child to take the matter seriously. "That old ruin is still five stories tall and sitting in the center of the richest neighborhood in Kolkata. It's prime property, worth crores."

"Five point seven crores, to be exact, at last valuation," said Palekar over his glasses.

"Do you really think my . . . the family . . . would take this away from me if they could?" Inheriting the house had given me the first real sense of belonging I had had in a very long time—to India, the Lahiris, and even my mother, and I realized that I had little desire to give it up.

"Oh, yes, Li," said Palekar. "Decency is the first casualty of large inheritances. It is the norm. But there are things we can do. Let's first understand who might have a claim to the property, should they contest the will."

Palekar held up a finger at a time as he counted aloud: "Hari and Rana, as brothers of the last heir, Tejen Lahiri. Their sister, Bela, but because she had passed, her daughter, Rinki, would be next in line to inherit. Biddy Lahiri and Vik Lahiri, as the children of Hari and Rana, respectively. Maya De, as Tejen's daughter. And Geeta Lahiri, as his surviving widow. Eight total, including you, as Tejen Babu's granddaughter. But even if they win a combined suit, in the absence of a legal heir the ownership will be divided and you will get your fair share, one-eighth of the valuation."

The question of money or a sale had remained an arbitrary thought for me. The house felt like a symbol of the Lahiris, standing in the center of Ballygunge—decayed but sumptuous, a portrait of Kolkata through the century. When I walked through the hallways, touching pillars and breathing in the chill of the stone walls, each stairway a different legacy of the people who lived in it, I imagined my grandfather passing me some sort of grand, inexplicable baton.

"What if we all agreed to sell it and split the money?" I asked. "Six crores between eight people is still . . ."

Palekar calculated. "About seventy lakhs each. Say around ninety thousand US dollars."

Suddenly, it didn't feel like all that much. My share wouldn't even cover my student loan. I did not say it aloud, but Palekar nodded, as if he knew what I was thinking.

"Not that much, is it? The family would be out of a house, and with not enough money to buy new houses even close to the same neighborhood. And it's not like Rana or Hari have ever held down jobs to save their lives."

"I don't care about the money," I said. The idea of taking on my mother as her opponent in court sent a shiver down my spine.

"Are you cold?" asked Adil.

Palekar pressed the shrill buzzer again, the sound a version of Jabbar's horn. "Sarita, turn the air-con off."

"My dear Lila, everybody cares about money in the end. It is the norm."

IT TOOK ANOTHER two hours of sorting through my documents and taxes ("Just making sure you have a clean record," Palekar said) and going over the will, in which Tejen Lahiri had explicitly said, "To my granddaughter Lila De, I bequeath the sole ownership and management of my estate and trust." The words had made me feel powerful and frail at the same time, knowing he would never explain his reasons to me, knowing that I would never speak to my grandfather again. Palekar examined the will line by line, and pronounced it "watertight, unless a certificate of some sort of medical incapacity is produced."

To which Adil added that a certificate could easily be produced by paying either Dr. Sanyal, the family doctor (who had cured me of colds and acid refluxes and appendicitis in childhood), or some outsourced medical professional a hefty bribe.

With that in mind, Palekar had given me two tasks. One, I would have to get my grandmother or mother to say, on some kind of record, that my grandfather had been in full charge of his mental facilities. Two, I would have to add value to the property as soon as possible. The elevator, my braggadocious ambition from the committee meeting, would be a great example in court, Palekar assured me, of my desire to preserve the life of a historic property crucial to Kolkata's architecture. He was less interested in my categorical statement that my grandmother's knees had been my catalyst. Palekar didn't care about my need to see myself as a decent human, but he did care about my father, in an oddly deep manner, and saw himself as the custodian of my impending fortune, my sporadic moral compass an impediment at best.

Just as we were finally at the finish line of the meeting, a thin, sharp-nosed man, with the pronounced alertness of a hawk, entered the office.

"Good afternoon, sir," said the man.

"Ah, Bhaskar, welcome," said Palekar. "Lila, this is Bhaskar Gupta, from Chand and Sons, the law firm that your grandfather used. That actually all the Lahiris have used for years now. He is one of the lawyers who manages your grandfather's estate."

"Well, it's her estate now," said Bhaskar, his teeth polished to a gleam. "Good afternoon, Miss Lila. So sorry for your loss."

"Nice to meet you," I said, weary of all the paperwork and characters that had entered my life.

ADIL AND I drove back in silence. I was grateful he had accompanied me to Palekar's office.

"Do you think you'll sell?" asked Adil, lowering the volume of the radio, which swung between American '80s rock ballads and Bollywood hits.

"And then what? Have them all out on the street?"

"It's a historic property in a prime location—you could get a developer to add floors," he said. "They would all have flats in it, maybe four, no, three, per floor," he calculated. "And there would be extra floors to rent out. And once the older generation dies, you, Rinki, Biddy, and Vik could sell the whole thing." He paused. "I think the developer would appreciate the value that the architecture brings—you could easily preserve the structure—keep the pillars and courtyard and so on."

"Jesus, are you going to ask for a commission at the end?"

It sliced me, the way he rolled out the efficient blueprint of a plan that had me ripping up the Lahiris' legacy. He had not let me kill ants as a girl.

"Of course not," he said, looking hurt. "My job here is to make sure you have all the options."

"I'm not your job, Adil."

"What's your problem?" he asked, sharp, pulling onto the curb outside my father's building. The rain had begun to come down again, Adil's wipers working furiously against them. "You don't want my help, is that it?"

"I don't want whatever this is."

Ram Bhai under an umbrella, looked at us inside the car, interested.

"I'm just trying to help, Li. Why do you have to be such a pain in the ass about taking help when you need it? It's always the same story with you."

Hard anger bubbled up between us. When I was fifteen, Adil had suggested I might want to talk to the school therapist, to feel less bruised by life. When I had said I did not need it, he had insisted, and eventually I had gone. The therapist, a housewife without a medical degree (common practice in Catholic schools) had said that I needed to focus on my studies and that my hormones were raging, which explained why I might hate my mother. All teens hated their mothers, she assured me, and my mother was an ordinary mother, like her.

"You've always been great at giving unsolicited advice—you became a lawyer in order to get paid for it. I'm not fifteen anymore."

He brought a palm down on the steering wheel. It was in no way an aggressive motion, but I flinched.

"God, Lila, why can't you let a simple thing like friendship or affection exist? It's too basic for you, is that it? You've got to complicate it for it to be interesting?"

"Is that what you're doing here? Letting friendship and affection exist?" I asked, my voice cold.

A slow shock of recognition spread over him. I opened the car door and stepped out into the rain.

"There's an umbrella in—"

I shut the door behind me, hard, and walked into the building. I had not cried after my grandfather's death, but now it felt like all my losses had been consolidated into one throb in my chest, a constant encircling fist that reminded me of how little I had left in the world.

UPSTAIRS, I TURNED the shower on hot and stood under the water for as long as I could stand it. I got out and wrapped up in the flamingo robe. At my father's bar, I poured two fingers of brandy in a glass. I drank the brandy and poured another and took the glass back into the bedroom. My phone glinted up at me.

I'm sorry.

You were trying to help, I typed back.

Crossed a line.

Then, when I didn't say anything: *Are you going to sleep?*

I got up and went to the balcony window. The black SUV was where I had left it below. Adil raised his hand, in a silent, sorrowful wave.

HE WAS SOAKED from the few seconds it had taken him to get from his car to the main gate of my building. I held out my glass of brandy. He took it, finishing it in one swallow.

"I'll get you a towel," I said.

He stepped inside, closing the door behind him. Ram Bhai would have enough to regale the neighborhood with for weeks to come.

Lit by lamplight, Adil's shadow was giant, all angles against the cream walls. I brought back a towel and handed it to him.

"Nice robe," he said, taking off his glasses to wipe them.

"Thanks. I usually pair it with a cigar."

He laughed, putting his glasses back on. "Listen, Li, I just . . . I wanted to say that I don't see you as . . . my responsibility . . . or anything like that. I just . . . I want to be your friend."

I nodded. "Want another drink?"

"Sure."

He followed me into the kitchen. As I poured, he stood in the narrow doorway.

"The apartment's really different," he said.

"Yeah." I turned to him and held out the glass. "My stepmom has an eye for design."

He focused on my face in the bright kitchen light, on my swollen eyes, and exhaled. "Oh, Lila."

I swallowed. "I just showered."

He took the glass out of my hands and took me into his arms, where I let myself cry again, against his damp shirt. He held me tighter than was comfortable, but it felt natural.

When I had emptied myself of tears, it felt natural that he should hold my face in his palms, that he should kiss me, that we should submit to the version of ourselves that only we had known. And when he peeled off my flamingos, letting them slide to the floor, it felt natural too, the kind of rightness that we had been starved of for so long.

AFTERWARD, THE STREETLAMPS shone in through curtains that Adil had risen to draw. I lay naked in bed, unselfconscious even though we had only seen each other naked once before. Adil lay against me, his face against my collarbone, the sheets wound around our bodies, both of us silent.

"I should go," he said, quiet, into my skin.

I nodded, neither of us moving to unwind from the other.

"I can't explain it," I said. "But it's the same. I still feel the same way. It's pointless to say, but I do."

His breath was even against my erratic, unsteady heart. Slowly, he turned from me, toward the ceiling, breathing out deeply, without happiness.

"I do too," he said, resigned.

IN THE SUMMER of 2001, Adil had explained to me the legacy of Mohiner Ghoraguli, the trailblazing Bengali rock band of our youth, when we had gone to see them in concert. He had carried me, at fourteen, on his sixteen-year-old shoulders. I had held on to them and, to hear him better, put one sweaty cheek against his, to listen closely to his earnest, sincere paean to the band. It was my first concert and the first of many things I would experience in the next two years with Adil.

We read the same books, making lists for each other, our version of mix-tapes, kissed clumsily after school in secret hallways, using Vik as our excuse, and eventually ended up in his bedroom one afternoon, a first investigation of each other's bodies. It was my first experience of the heady thrill of romance, our sweaty hands intertwined at all times. For me, it was as if Adil had located my many parts and, quietly, without fuss, placed them back together in his careful way.

That was the way my father had found me at sixteen, on his annual visit to see the daughter he had left behind, both intensely fractured and oddly whole. On our way back from the police station on his last visit, my father had begged me to live with him and Iva, in tears, and immediately I had said yes.

As I watched Adil's SUV disappear into the night, I remembered the day that he had come to our secret spot in the garden behind my classroom, the day before I would leave, how he had said, "I wish I could come with you."

And so through the years that had followed, I had held on to a piece of him, the same one I had returned to.

12

THAT WEEKEND, I got an email.

My dear Lila,

Myself and your Gayatri Aunty, i.e., my dearest wife, are both eager to see you at our house for dinner. Gayatri has enquired if you like dhokla, which she is famous in the neighborhood for, once even accomplishing first position in the Alipore city cooking contest. I have many more photos and stories of dear Mihir and myself, and we promise that it will be a good dinner and that we are not too old yet to enjoy the company of humorous and lively youth. In addition, please bring my new dear friend, the lawyer Adil Sarkar. All up to you, however. The main thing is that you should be there.

Additionally, please find below some information from my property developer friend, Abhishek Das, who went to the Lahiri mansion (all very discreet—not to worry at all, my dear girl) and had his men put together the valuation. At this time, all figures are estimates, since they were not able to go inside the property without the family's knowledge. But Mr. Das is very knowledgeable on restorations and evaluations of old zamindari estates, so these are very good approximates. We can get actuals later, depending on your decision.

Current valuation: 5.9 crores, i.e., approximately $800,000 USD

Valuation with home improvements as discussed: 10 plus crores, i.e., $1,000,000 plus USD

If you did decide ever to sell (and, my dear Lila, I am not suggesting
you do), valuation after sale and development into an apartment
building: approximately 1 crore per flat, and you can get 3 flats per floor,
i.e., 15 crores.

Please phone my direct cell number if you need to talk about
anything further.

Looking forward to seeing you soon.
Your friend,
Palekar Uncle

THE FAMILY HAD either forgotten or pretended to forget that the subject of repairs and elevators had ever been broached. When Das and Sons
arrived on the premises in a van, my grandmother feigned horror, muttering, "What have we done to deserve this, Tejen Lahiri?" while Hari barked
instructions at them: "The pujo room is off-limits." "The pillars are old." "The
house is a landmark in Kolkata." Hari, upset that I had not taken him up
on his recommendation for his friend (an unregistered, no-website individual, simply called Ramesh, who had called me without warning at nine at
night and identified himself as "builder Ramesh"), stood around glaring at
Mr. Das as the latter instructed his team to measure and photograph and
make notes.

I tried to weave my way around their hostilities with a box of doughnuts
from Costa Coffee and anodyne pleasantries, while making sure the men
were not obstructed from their work. Gina and my mother were both at the
university, and Rana had not yet woken at ten, which meant that the outrage,
luckily for me, was limited to only a few family members.

At noon, Mr. Das wiped sweat off his forehead and neck with a pin-
striped, folded handkerchief.

"Miss Lila, give us a few days to make designs, and we will share the renovation plan with you," he said.

Hari, ominous, lurked behind him.

"With you *and* your family," added Mr. Das, smooth, clearly practiced in
the battlegrounds of property inheritance.

Bari came down the stairs, holding a tray of lemonade and a plate of sweet jam cookies.

"Have a glass of lebujol, Mr. Das," said Mishti.

"So kind," he said, reaching for a glass and a cookie.

"Bari, make sure all of Mr. Das's boys outside have some," said Mishti. "The sun is so strong today."

"Do you have a business card?" demanded Hari from behind us. "What is the guarantee that you are a legitimate company?"

"Hari Kaka, I've been to the Das and Sons office in Salt Lake," I said, annoyed.

Hari, sulky, frowned.

Mr. Das, jam on the left edge of his mouth, swallowed his mouthful. "Of course, what a reasonable question," he said, diving a palm into his pocket and taking out a dark-brown leather wallet. He produced two cards, thick and embossed, handing Hari and Mishti one each.

"Oh, you have two locations—one in Mumbai too," said Mishti.

"Yes, since 1996. My grandfather started the business, and I am proud to say Das and Sons has tripled in size since." Mr. Das beamed at me. "Well, Lila Madam, thank you for your time. We will be in touch shortly."

And with that, Mr. Das was gone, just as he had exited numerous families on the brink of an argument about the home that he was about to take apart.

"He seems like such a nice man and an expert, Lila. How did you find him?" asked Mishti.

"I hope it wasn't off a newspaper ad or some silly thing like that, Lila," said Hari.

"Yes, Lila. You must be careful here in Kolkata," said my grandmother, grim, shaking her head. "People aren't who they say they are."

I tried not to bristle. "Guys, relax. He comes very recommended. My dad's good friend, a lawyer from his old firm, said that Mr. Das was the best in the business."

I regretted the words even as I said them. Hari and my grandmother stilled, as if in unison.

"A lawyer," said Hari softly.

"Your father's friend," murmured my grandmother. "You must mean Amlan Palekar."

She turned away from me, toward Mishti and Hari. Their realization that I had legal help felt like an immediate wall erected between us, separating me once again from the Lahiris.

SLOWLY, THE FAMILY adjusted to the idea of the restoration, but not without grievances. My grandmother was certain that the elevator would shake the foundation of the house every time it moved up and down and that the geysers would heat the plumbing to the point where the pipes might explode over the waiting bodies of the family members. Gina was worried about the ability of the ancient electrical circuits of the house to withstand the new hallway lights and the six washing machines that were part of the remodel. (This was a legitimate concern, and I assured her that the remodel would include replacing the electrical wiring and adding electrical panels, although she still seemed doubtful.) Rana was certain that repairing the cracks in the floors would ruin the historic patterned tiles.

As Palekar and I tried to make sense of what I could spend from the trust, each family member made a list of their own demands, all of which were supposedly in service to Biddy's wedding (*Less than six weeks away, Lila!*).

My mother was upset that I had had Mr. Das review the building without her, and so she passed me in the hallways nearly without a word, icy as she responded to my "Hi, Ma" with a nod and a "How are you, Lila?"—to which there was no need for a response, we both knew. Sooner or later, she would come around, giving up fury in the face of the stony acceptance that I had had a lifetime to practice; it was only a matter of time. But there was one difference in our age-old ritual now. Being physically around her had made it easier for me to withstand the wax and wane of her rage. For the first time in our existence, there was something certain about her presence in my life, and I felt a sense of solid ground that was both unfamiliar and reassuring.

QUICKLY, RANA MADE friends with the construction crew and began to join them on their tea breaks, often offering up a round of cards that extended their break. The men enjoyed his mild, witty company and would often linger for an extra hour in the backyard, prompting admonishments from Mr. Das.

One morning, after the workers had gone back to the elevator installation, I discovered Rana sitting on the steps at the back of the house, watching them, unhappiness in his eyes.

"Don't worry, Rana Kaka," I said. "We're using the German design you liked so much. It's incredibly safe."

He nodded. "Lila, what you are doing is a good thing. All these things will make life easier for Geeta Boudi and, as we get older, all of us."

I had begun to see myself as a villain, disrupting their lives with my "improvements," and Rana's reassurance brought up sudden emotion for me. I looked away, but he was absorbed in his own thoughts.

"Their life is such fun, don't you think?" he said, so soft that I had to strain to hear him, a longing in his voice as he stared at the construction men, in their hard hats, going up and down the forklift, breaking down the back wall of the house to accommodate the new elevator. "They wake up and, every day, build new things. And when it's done, they can rest, and tomorrow there's something else to build again," said Rana.

"Rana Kaka, these men are manual laborers. It's hard, backbreaking work," I said. But I almost immediately wished I had said nothing.

"Yes," said Rana, gazing at them, his thick glasses so smudged that it must have obscured his vision. "But they have a reason to wake up in the morning."

He began to hum a soft tune.

"Soon it will be time for lunch," he said, picking up the deck of cards next to him, shuffling and reshuffling as he periodically looked at his watch.

For Rana, and so many Bengali men of his generation, no structure or purpose to their days and nights, time was infinite. They were the lost sons of Bengal, the once-wealthy zamindars, supported by decaying mansions and dwindling family money, and stripped of their corrupt colonial era privileges. They were no longer rich yet not so poor that they might have to think of an alternative solution while they pined for the old days of war, when they might at least have been freedom fighters, where their days might have amounted to more than the endless charade of tea and board games and hot debates and bitter cursing and genial brotherhood as they morphed into the well-fed, sloth-like selves that they secretly loathed.

It was supposed to have been enough to have lived lives of political rage and classical music, literature, and the theater and art. Instead, an entire generation had found themselves adrift when it was no longer vulgar to go to work and *earn*. Rana wandered in perpetual melancholy, caught between the legacy of a father who had been a feared and admired entrepreneur, and a brilliant journalist for a son.

ONE AFTERNOON, WHILE working on seasonal projections for Wyndham in my father's apartment, I received a call from Mr. Das.

"Hello, Lila Madam," he said, cheerful.

"Hi, Mr. Das. Is everything all right?"

In the past week alone, rain had halted construction for two days, leaving in its wake a mud-covered site and an enraged group of Lahiris. On Saturday, the local political party had come to inspect the "changes" being made to "their neighborhood" and the "historical landmark," and demanded to see a permit. I had explained that Mr. Das had obtained all the governmental permits necessary to make renovations to my private property (Hari had winced at the word *my*) but that I was only repainting the outer facade, with no changes to architecture or design. (I decided to leave out the matter of the elevator.) And would the gentlemen like a cup of tea and this (generous) token toward the party's welfare fund, as an appreciation of their vigilance? Yes, they had assured me, that would suffice.

"Nothing's wrong, Lila," said Mr. Das. "I just wanted to inform you about some phone calls I received. First, from the electricity department. They will be changing the wiring on the second and third floor—apparently just in time. Some of the old wiring was so ragged that it could have caused a fire at any moment. The new distribution system will be able to take on the load of the lift and the electrical appliances."

"What do you mean, could have caused a fire?"

"Oh, you know, old wiring is very dangerous. All sorts of things. What's important is that we fixed it."

"Did you tell the family? Make sure you tell them. Don't tell them I told you to."

"I made special mention to your grandmother, as well as your mother and Rana Babu," said Mr. Das quietly.

Either because I was the owner or because he felt sorry for me, so wildly out of my depth as I invaded my family's life, Mr. Das had placed himself on my side.

"Speaking of your mother, Lila Madam, I wanted to let you know that she phoned me." He paused and then added, "I assured her of my credentials, and that you have a great vision for restoring the Lahiri home to its earlier splendor."

The words made me cringe, and I knew my mother would have laughed a little at the implication that I was any kind of savior of the Lahiris.

"What did she want?"

"To look at the designs and plans. Everything that has been created so far and status updates on how long it will take to complete. She called after the party officials left the building."

"She thinks I'm a child, incapable of making adult decisions," I said, furious.

Mr. Das said nothing.

"Send her what she wants, but if she has any contributions or notes, tell her to come to me for approval, like everyone else."

I imagined Mr. Das on the other end, judging Maya and Lila De for being so far from the way mothers and daughters were supposed to be.

"Of course, Lila Madam."

I deflated in resignation. "Don't say that. Just send her whatever documents she wants, and you call me if she wants to change anything."

"Yes, Lila."

"Thank you, Mr. Das."

"There's one more thing."

"Yes?" I asked as I imagined my mother or one of the Lahiris finding a loophole in the will and taking the house, that was not mine, away from me.

"Hari Babu came by my office."

"Really? To check that you had an office?"

"Yes," said Das.

"What, did he walk around and conduct an inspection?" I asked, amused.

"Yes, and had some tea and shingharas and biscuits."

I felt embarrassed—Hari had possibly disrupted the Das and Sons office for a few hours with his specific brand of boundary overstepping.

"I'm sorry about that—he means well. I suppose he wanted to see the plans too?"

"Yes."

"Did he have any objections?" Had Hari flown into some sort of rage over the remodel?

"In fact, he wanted to be a big part of it. Asked if he could guide the team through the process, since he knows the house so well."

There was a brief pause. I heard the click of Das's pen as he tapped it on the table.

"Would it be mad to let him and Rana . . . help . . . sometimes? I don't know. Obviously, I want you to be able to do your job. What do you think?" I asked, slightly desperate.

"That's simple, then," said Das expertly. "We'll make sure to take Hari Babu's help when we need it. It will be useful, I'm sure."

"If you have any problems, just call me," I said, grateful. "They just need to . . . feel like they're in charge."

"Yes, of course." He cleared his throat. "One last thing. Hari Babu had forgotten his wallet at home. He wanted"—Das cleared his throat again—"to borrow some money. A personal loan."

"How much?"

"Eleven thousand rupees."

"What? For what? Was he taking a flight back to the house from your office?"

"He said he had to make a deposit for Miss Biddy Lahiri's wedding. He said that he would talk to you later and repay me out of the trust money. He asked me to keep it discreet. Of course, I was unable to extend the loan.

The safe was locked, and I did not have any cash on me. And then there was the matter of company policy."

"Mr. Das, thank you." I leaned against the wall.

"May I make a suggestion, Miss Lila?"

"Yes."

"I would be very careful with the finances. Especially with things like power of attorney and the trust's payment structure. The Lahiri trust is something the whole family depends on, to survive. You are using it well. If people who are less . . . financially sound begin to access it, even if they are family, it might not be used the way your grandfather intended."

"I'm the only one with access," I said, "and Palekar Uncle oversees all withdrawals."

Mr. Das sounded contrite. "Amlan Palekar is my friend, and so I feel you will forgive me for overstepping."

"It's not overstepping. Thank you, Mr. Das."

"Call me Abhishek Uncle."

"Thank you."

As Das hung up the phone, I made a mental note to do a thorough background check on him via Palekar—this was Kolkata and getting swindled was part of the experience—but I felt an intense gratitude to have him. There were a thousand unknowns at every turn, and who knew if my grandfather would have been horrified at all that I had set in motion, but at least there were a few people to clutch on to in the dark.

13

MISHTI HAD BEGUN planning Biddy's wedding in earnest, her usual cheer even more pronounced than usual. Collectively, the Lahiris seemed sunnier, as if the wedding had diffused the thick mourning in the air. I had not been given any responsibilities—I assumed Mishti thought that overseeing the renovation was contribution enough on my part—but a familiar feeling of being left out had begun to settle in my chest. My mother negotiated with musicians and priests, Hari and Rana auditioned caterers (oversampling their wares), and Gina and my grandmother made guest lists.

One day, Rinki arrived at the house just as the construction team was leaving. The house was bathed in the glimmer of the early afternoon Bengal sun; part of the facade had been repainted to its original cream and burnt-orange color, and the light bounced between pillars in soft shards. It reminded me of Brooklyn in the autumn, the rust and yellow leaves that would soon carpet the streets.

"Lila, I can't believe it," said Rinki, admiration in her soft voice. Her mouth rounded in surprise as she arrived at my grandmother's floor, where I was reading manuscripts. "The house looks like a palace."

"Hardly," I said, pleased. "But it's getting nicer by the day. All the construction covers will come off from the left side of the exterior next week, when the painting is complete, and I'm hoping the new lighting on each floor is up by then too."

"You look . . . happy," said Rinki, smiling at me. "Could it be that you're finally enjoying being here with us?"

"I've always loved this house," I said.

And the Lahiri mansion was starting to feel like something that I might consider my own in some part, as I became part of its transformation.

"Are you busy?" asked Rinki. "Biddy and I are trying to pick out her bridal outfits for the three days of the wedding events, and she might prefer your taste to mine. You want to come up to the Sixth and help us? I just went with the traditional classics, completely old-fashioned, for my wedding."

I kissed Rinki's cheek, grateful. "You are a classic," I said.

MY MOTHER'S STUDIO occupied less than a quarter of the fifth floor. On its far-left corner, my grandfather's grandfather, Ashoke Lahiri, had constructed a second terrace atop the first, a tiny "sixth floor" that stood on cement and granite legs—approximately three hundred square feet, with a panoramic view of Kolkata. That square of a second terrace was where members of the family came to exhale their secrets. It was where my mother had wept in bottomless rage after her divorce, where Vik smoked his cigarettes by night, where Hari drank stashed bottles of cheap whiskey, where Rinki and I had gossiped about the mysteries of sex, and where Bari, it was rumored, had conceived her daughter with Shakti, the neighborhood tailor. Rinki and I called it the Secret Sixth.

From my mother's studio, you could see upward into the Secret Sixth, unless it was a cloudy night. Out of breath from climbing floors of stairs, I stopped on the fifth floor to take a gulp of the warm air. My mother, loading her newly installed washing machine with laundry, her face in a mud mask, saw me from her studio window. My heart sank—I had hoped to climb straight to the Sixth. Still, I wondered if she might, because of the washing machine, feel fond enough to start talking to me again. A minute later, my mother opened the door, her mask splitting into a thousand angry creases.

"What are you doing here?" she asked.

I looked at her, outraged. "It's my house—I don't need a reason."

With my mother, my first instinct was to attack.

Her face slipped back to neutral, but the mask was broken into thin fissures. "You never come up to the fifth floor," she said.

This was true. I went out of my way to avoid it.

"Rinki and I are helping Biddy with her wedding outfits," I said, reluctant to part with the information. "She wants to pick something a little modern. They're on the Sixth, waiting for me."

"She must wear her grandmother's wedding sari," said my mother. "That girl has no respect for tradition. I'll tell Mishti immediately."

"Ma, please. Stop it. They invited me over for a nice thing, and I just want to hang out—please don't spoil it for me."

My mother glowered under her mask. "What do you mean, spoil it? Why should I spoil anything?"

"I'm going to spend an hour talking about saris and hair and makeup with them. Just, please, try not to get involved or create a problem," I said as I walked away.

"Lila," she called. "Come and have a cup of tea later." Her voice was tremulous, with a wavering defiance.

"Okay," I said.

My mother shut the door, but I knew that she would watch us from a distance, wishing she knew more about my conversations and friends and lovers and journals and secrets outside the house. It was my entire soul that my mother was in pursuit of, except in the moments when I offered it to her.

"CAREFUL, RINKS, DON'T fall over," I said as I climbed to the top of the thin metal staircase. She was sitting on the edge of the Secret Sixth's ledge.

"I'm too sturdy to fall over," she said with a laugh. "Getting married means you put on twenty kilos. Smart of you not to take the plunge."

"Why on earth would marriage mean that?" I asked.

Rinki looked surprised. "Well, there's no need to try anymore, is there? You're not going to be dieting to fit into anything perfect." At my silence, Rinki laughed. "Oh god, Lila, your face. Always aghast at the truth. It's marvelous," she continued. "No more diets—all the luchi I want. I can wake up in the morning and wear my nightie all the way to lunch, and he loves me anyway. It's good to be loved, Lila."

"I thought you just said I was smart to not take the plunge. Anyway, do we have to meet here all the time? We're not fifteen anymore, and Ballygunge has coffee shops now."

"But we love the Secret Sixth," exclaimed Rinki. "It's tradition to hide up here."

"It's tradition for all of you, because you can actually hide up here. I'm directly in my mother's line of sight."

"Oh, you're so funny when you're grumpy. Maya Didi's too busy with her work. She's not snooping on us."

"I would bet you a lot of money she's parked right at that spot at her table from which you can see directly in here."

Bari climbed up, precarious with a tray of tea, as Rinki giggled. I got up to take the tray from Bari.

"Where's Biddy?" Rinki asked Bari.

"YouTube," said Bari. "She said she would be here in five minutes."

"Do you have to go? Stay and help us choose her outfits," said Rinki.

Bari laughed. "Geeta Boudi needs to tell me what to make for dinner, and the beds need to be remade after everyone wakes up from their naps, and then Rana Dada needs his tea. And then after that, it'll be time for switching on the lights. Who's going to do all that if I sit here looking at saris with the two of you?"

Chastened, we watched as Bari climbed down the stairs. Bari was only a few years older than me, and when we were girls, she had seemed carefree as she helped her mother with the household's chores. She was also an insider to all of our secrets. She had watched Hindi and Bengali movies with us in Rinki's room, and we had learned to apply eyeshadow together. Inheriting her mother's job and the fact that Rinki and I now spoke to each other in English, a language she did not know, had resulted in a gulf between us, where our attempts to include her felt like performance, and Bari, eternally truthful, was quick to draw up any remnants of a bridge.

Rinki leaned forward. "Have you seen Adil since the night at Trincas? Tell me, tell me, before Biddy comes," she said, conspiratorial.

"Rinks, he's married."

"But surely there's something to tell? No electricity? No subtext?"

"Weren't you the one telling me marriage is for keeps?"

"Yes, but what's a little flirting, here and there?"

"He came to my meeting with Palekar Uncle," I said. "That's about it."

"That's very sad," said Rinki. "What else do I have to live for?"

HALF AN HOUR later, Biddy joined us on the terrace.

"If it isn't her highness, the queen of YouTube," said Rinki.

"Sorry, didi, I had five lakh people tuned in. So sorry."

"And they all want to talk to you and watch you sing and dance," I said with admiration.

"And rap," said Biddy. "Want me to show you?"

"Yes," I said, vehement.

"But we've got a thousand saris to look at, Biddy—the wedding is in less than a month," said Rinki.

"Oh, c'mon, Rinki Didi, let B2D out of the jailhouse. C'mon, c'mon. If Lila likes it, maybe she'll put me in a book."

"Who's B2D?" I asked.

"Her YouTube channel name," said Rinki, annoyed.

"Here, take my phone," Biddy said.

She handed it to me.

"Now press that side button . . . yes . . . and hit 'Record,'" she said.

"Is this a live session?" I asked.

"No, but can't miss a moment, in my line of work," said Biddy, patient.

She furrowed her brow, humming softly, rubbing her fingers together, as if in search of some secret texture.

"What's in New York, Lila?" she asked.

"Um . . . rats?"

Rinki burst out laughing. Biddy seemed delighted.

"Parks, leaves," I amended.

"What's in India?"

"Ma," I said.

"Love," said Rinki.

I looked at her in warning.

"Mm," said B2D.

"C'mon, Biddy, sweetie, let's get this done, or my mother's ghost will be upon us," said Rinki.

"Imagine if the spirits of your zamindari ancestors had to watch you marry your beau under a full moon, wearing an off-rack sari," I said.

"Yeah, yeah," began Biddy.

Rinki and I watched, amused, as Biddy moved to an inner rhythm.

"You know the deal
The real real
B2D talk dirty
Beats for my people
Faces, places, we take our places
Rats in our parks, in our hearts
The leaves have left us
Bodies on fire
The gutter beats faster
Like the filthy motherfucker
He tells you my story
No narrator
Orator, slaughter,
Out of my dungeons . . ."

I felt that prickle under my skin that came with an author I knew to be special. There was a lithe genius to Biddy's effortless, enraged performance, even for the most reluctant audience, her fury so potent you could feel a burn. I felt an involuntary shudder go through me.

"The moon drops kicks
So does my engine
I don't ride anymore
Pretend I'm fencing
The rats need their mother

Tell your mother
She gotta hustle
She gotta run
They're coming for her
The universe becomes her
You know the deal
Yeah
Beats for my people."

"Well," she demanded, snatching the phone out of my hands. "Did you get that?"

"Disgusting," said Rinki, mesmerized.

There was something about Biddy that I couldn't look away from, as if B2D had altered my understanding of her in a specific way.

"Biddy, that was incredible," I said.

Biddy rewatched the video, impatient.

"Don't encourage her," said Rinki. "She'll be a married woman soon."

Biddy looked up. "Good job, Lila—all I have to do is edit that," she said. "Okay, Rinki Didi, let's look at your damn saris."

SOON, WE WERE in the depths of Rinki's iPad, looking at jewelry, Kanjeevaram saris, and raw silk ghagras that Biddy would choose from for her various wedding events.

"What are you wearing on the wedding day?" I asked Biddy.

"Katyayani Lahiri's ancient sari—what else?" she said, rolling her eyes.

"Vintage," I said, feeling relief.

"Yes, but so dull. It's heavy and boring, and it'll take Arjun an hour to get it off me later."

"Biddy," exclaimed Rinki.

"What, didi? I'm a married woman now. And don't worry—we're going to be too beat that night for anything."

"You're not married yet," said Rinki, tapping on a picture of a gold nose ring, studded with emeralds, on her iPad. "Do you like this?"

"No nose rings—too much like I'm a cow he's leading to slaughter."

"Biddy," exclaimed Rinki again.

LULLED BY THE pleasant morning, I felt a warm sense of familial togetherness after Biddy and Rinki left the Secret Sixth. I decided to prolong happiness,
rather than risk it to my mother's mood, and drink tea with my grandmother
instead. My grandmother, thrilled, made a pot of strong tea and rolled out an
array of crackers, little salty squares of nimki, and slices of pound cake.

"You don't eat enough," she said. But with her, I felt a rush of affection
instead of hearing the recrimination I assumed from my mother.

As I ate a second slice of cake, she explained the Bengali soap she was
watching—who had cheated on whom, who was guilty of fraud or deception
or had a secret twin or a second family. I could see that my grandmother was
aging and lonely. I looked at the photograph of my grandfather above her
desk—strong and vital, a young father and successful executive—and felt a
sharp, now-familiar sorrow. She followed my eyes.

"I still can't believe he's gone," she said, looking up at the photograph as if
she had lost her way on a street.

"Bari told me today that he taught her how to read."

She nodded.

"What was he like, these past few years, after he got sick?" I asked after a
pause.

"He was tired of the way the children kept arguing at family meetings.
You couldn't make a single decision—everything took days—because they
were all auditioning to be in charge."

"Even Ma?"

"Especially her. She believes that she was entitled to the estate as his
daughter. Hari, I think, had assumed he would be the male heir. And maybe,
in a way, he was right to. After all, he was . . . is . . . like our son."

It was the first time my grandmother had admitted it, that she loved Hari
like a son—and thereby, more than any daughter could hope to be loved,
especially a hard-boiled daughter that spat love out like my mother.

"I told Bari I would pay for her daughter's school," I said.

My grandmother looked at me. "What? Why? Did she ask you for money?"

"No, it was my idea." I had not expected the statement to be received with anything but warmth—I was taken aback by her sharpness. "I'm going to pay for it with my own money," I said. "Not from the trust. It's barely more than a pittance at the government school anyway."

"Listen, Lila, you are just like your grandfather, with too many romantic ideas and an inability to see the ways of the world. Bari is a poor, young girl and she sees your money and wants it to benefit her and that child the tailor saddled her with."

"What's wrong with me using my own money to help her kid go to school?" I said, heated.

"Nothing's wrong," she sighed. "You have a good heart. But promise me," she said, turning the volume back up on her show, "that you'll make sure Bari is using the money for the child. Ask for receipts. In Kolkata, you must always ask for a receipt."

The sounds of the Lahiri household floated into my grandmother's airy room, with its cotton curtains and humming ceiling fan. The episode ended, and my grandmother sighed and turned off the TV.

"Well, Lila Ma, that's what happens when you have unsettled scores," she said. "I just knew his wife was not dead—that she would turn up one day. What is he going to do now?"

I put an arm around her. "Mummy, can I ask you something?"

"Of course," she said. "What is it? Do you want me to find you a suitable boy?"

I laughed. "No. But thank you."

She nodded. "Whenever you're ready." She opened her newspaper. "What did you want to ask me?"

"When Dadu died . . . before he died, the weeks just before, did he talk about me?"

My grandmother began to say something, and then her soft body curled imperceptibly inward for the briefest sliver of a second. She took a quick inhale and turned to me.

"It's difficult to say. He was in so much pain. So many unfinished things he wanted to do. But death came so suddenly." She shook her head. "It's hard to say if he even knew who I was, on some nights. Have another biscuit, Lila Ma. You don't eat enough."

We watched another show, and after a while, I excused myself to go to the bathroom. "Wear my slippers," said my grandmother without turning her head, wide-eyed in front of her screen. "It's slippery in the bathroom."

"Mr. Das is going to fix that before you break something," I said, sliding on the rubber slippers she'd kicked in my direction.

"Das needs to respect the Lahiri property, not mow down everything in sight," she muttered.

I passed by the bathroom at the far end of the third floor. The original paint on the walls had been pale mint, cream, and gold, with filigree work on the pillars. I had instructed Mr. Das to re-create the original, but he had complained that everyone in the family remembered the colors and patterns differently. Exasperated by their individual demands, each more insistent than the next, we had instead relied on a handful of black-and-white photographs and two color ones from the '80s, by which time the paint had already been crumbling off walls, bloated by weather, insidious cracks in a legacy. Repainted, the pillars gleamed in the dark, lovely, as I passed them by, and every Lahiri agreed that the new rendition, despite the modern sheen to the colors, was identical to their personal memory of the original.

"Palekar Uncle," I whispered into my cell phone as I entered the prayer room on Krishna Lahiri's haunted fourth floor.

It was the only place I knew to be fairly insulated. The goddess Durga stared at me as I covered my mouth to muffle the sound.

"Lila, how lovely to hear—"

"Uncle, I can't talk long. I'm in my mother's house."

"Oh, a secret phone call. How thrilling," he said, lowering his own voice.

"Nothing dramatic—I just don't want to upset my grandmother."

"What is it?" asked Palekar, voice still lowered to a theatrical level.

"I think you might be right. I think they might have hired a lawyer to contest the inheritance. It's probably the one thing they have all been able to agree on. I think they're going to claim my grandfather was out of his mind.

My grandmother certainly wants me to believe that. I think she might believe it herself."

"I see," said Palekar after a pause, his voice back to normal. "I'm sorry."

"It's fine," I said briskly. "It's their house. I never expected them to just hand it to a non-Lahiri."

"What is it you really want from them, Lila?" asked Palekar, gentle now.

I imagined him discussing it with my father. I felt embarrassed and angry at this friend of my father's, who like everyone else in this house, and in Kolkata, felt free to ask me anything they pleased, no matter how private. I did not know the answer to his question, but he had no right to ask it of me. Yet I knew that I needed his help.

"I don't think I've ever formally asked you to be my lawyer, Palekar Uncle," I said.

"Yes, of course," he said. "I'm your lawyer. And, Lila," he added, "should you need it, I am also your friend."

AFTERWARD, I FELL asleep on my grandmother's couch, drained by the sun and my early mornings and the endless secrets of the house and the love I felt despite them. When I woke, it was late afternoon and my grandmother's quilt was over me as she watched her television series, one hand on my sleeping body, patting me the way she would when I was a child, humming a slow, contented melody under her breath.

14

MY GRANDMOTHER, GEETA Karmakar, had been born in Kolkata in 1941, a few days after the death of Tagore, the nation's beloved Nobel laureate poet. Bengal went into a collective grief that pervaded every household, and Tagore's songs floated out of street corners, national gatherings, and the sorrowful humming of housewives, office goers, tradesmen, and executives alike. Everyone felt as if the one man who had understood their inner recesses had been ripped away. It seemed to Geeta that she had never shaken off this air of mourning at the hour of her birth. Then, when she was six, her mother, Jaya, died of pneumonia. The children had adored her—when joyous, Jaya had played with them for hours, almost a child herself, indulging them with noodles and kulfi at all hours. After their mother's death, Geeta and her ten-year-old brother, Ajoy, were left in the care of a sober father who had never learned to boil an egg.

In those years, Kolkata was the cultural capital of India, out of which rose distinguished bhadraloks, or Bengali men who aspired to be men of letters, music, and theater, equal parts emotional citizens of British and Bengali culture. The British Empire had created and absorbed this intellectual class to support and expand trade, making sure that English cultural influences permeated education, entertainment, sport, and aspiration. But Geeta's father, Lalon Karmakar, was not a bhadralok and had no time to consider becoming one. Lalon came from a long line of blacksmiths, and his father, a prominent blacksmith with his own shop, had left them a small family house and an even smaller inheritance, which Lalon used to buy a modest printing press.

Over time, the press printed thousands of books for Kolkata's educational institutions, and after Lalon became a widower, he put all of his energies into growing his business so that he might send his children to respectable schools, where they might become bhadraloks.

When Geeta was old enough to feel lesser in the homes of her school friends, who were sons and daughters of the landowning and mercantile class, whose parents were lawyers and doctors and bankers and, more often than not, Brahmin and Kshatriya, she felt a sadness that refused to leave her bones. She blamed Tagore, but it was the empire that had formally categorized her family as working-class, as part of the "Other Backward Class," who needed special help in order to be able to elevate as a community. This flagrant categorization of Geeta's family's *backwardness* seemed, too, part of an endless mourning. Helping out at her father's press after school, she would lie to her friends that she was in fact at music lessons and badminton practice and learning German for the winter break abroad. She was cold and hard at the end of long days.

Ajoy, inheriting his father's mild nature, was shocked by his sister's disgust at the smell of the press, the stacks of newly inked books. Father and son began to plan a future where Geeta would marry a man from a slightly higher caste than their own (Lalon had already begun to discuss the situation with his aunts and cousins, for their advice on prospective grooms) and Ajoy would work with his father at the press. To Geeta, the Karmakar men—indeed, all men—made their own decisions, leaving women's fates to be determined by them.

BY THE TIME Geeta turned nineteen, though, she seemed to have turned a new leaf, her edges prim and softened, the way young ladies of the era were supposed to be, her dark-rimmed cat-eye glasses a foil to her heart-shaped face (fair, a blessing) and muted pink lipstick, her salwar kameez always ironed, the folds modest and crisp along the lines of her slim legs. To her father's great relief, Geeta had blossomed into the kind of woman his mother had been, taking care of her father and brother's laundry and ironing, instructing the maid on what to cook for lunch, and running the household while the men went to work. She attended college for political science, a surefire stepping stone to getting an educated husband.

Still, at the advanced age of twenty, she remained without a fiancé, and Lalon worried that the romantic male heroes of the era, Uttam Kumar and Guru Dutt, had brainwashed his daughter. But given that the Karmakar caste had risen in status, even producing a new generation of engineers and inventors, and that Lalon's press had now evolved into a three-city operation headed by Ajoy, he felt confident she would attract a decent boy/family, for whom he had set aside a sizable dowry.

His biggest relief was that neither of his children had inherited the manic nature of his late wife: the wild sleepless swings of a high-energy, almost-terrifying euphoria, interspersed with listlessness, where she spoke of nothing but death for days and blamed destiny. Her joy had been entrancing, but when at rock bottom, Jaya would rage at life, bitter at her own failings, telling her babies that she was a demon, a ghost from another world, which would make them giggle or cry until Lalon would take them away. Lalon had taken Jaya to countless doctors, who had asked her to get more exercise and sunlight and prescribed drugs that left her in a haze. The rumors of madness followed the Karmakar family like a constant background score to their lives, and when Jaya died, Lalon had been both racked with guilt that her life had not been easier and relieved that it was no longer his lot to live with her.

Determined to live the life she'd experienced in the homes of others, Geeta wanted to find an upper-caste man who would unlock her from the shame of being a Karmakar. No amount of Lalon's professional success would buy Geeta the dignity and respect of the society she yearned for. She studied hard, passing her first year at Jadavpur University with flying colors.

Jadavpur, a bastion of leftist thinking, had been set up by affluent nationalists to protest against the empire's need to create a class of Indians whose tastes were British. It was here that Geeta first discovered dissent, and that she could be admired for her humble roots. This was a revelation, and she quickly morphed into a liberal feminist who would argue with men over literature and politics. Gloria Steinem had just entered the collective imagination of young Indian women at Jadavpur, and for those brief four years at university,

Geeta allowed herself to shake the branches of her deep-rooted beliefs: that women were as a class and a breed, less than men, that the British were in fact more cultured than her own kind, and that she, Geeta Karmakar, was always going to be considered part of the Other Backward Class. She argued with men and joined the debate club and the Jadavpur Economics Society and wrote a great many letters to the editor.

When Bela Lahiri of the economics society invited her home for lunch, Geeta visited the Lahiri mansion, then resplendent as a jewel of Ballygunge Place, for the first time. She ate with Krishna and Katyayani Lahiri, delighting them with her knowledge of music and Shakespeare and Supreme Court rulings, even as she exchanged glances with Bela's brother, the shy, chubby, sweet eldest Lahiri boy, Tejen, who, despite his dark skin and large nose, had marriage proposals from all over the country, his pedigree a heady combination of being Oxford-returned, a Brahmin, and the Lahiri heir.

It took three more chance meetings with his sister's new best friend for Tejen Lahiri to come to the conclusion that it would be in his interest to visit a meeting of the Jadavpur Economics Society. A whirlwind summer followed for Geeta and Tejen, filled with evening walks and spirited conversation and the occasional holding of hands behind mango trees, until the rumors became too much for the Lahiris and, despite their reservations, one afternoon, Krishna and Katyayani Lahiri asked their driver to take the forty-five-minute journey to CIT Road, where they rolled up in their Contessa in front of the modest two-story house of a bewildered Lalon Karmakar and asked for his daughter's hand in marriage for their eldest son.

IN MARRIAGE, GEETA blossomed as never before. Her classmates had been disappointed at the union, at her marrying a man of the old Bengali order, England returned. He was white inside, they complained. And yet, Tejen Lahiri's unassuming ways and learned responses won over his nationalist detractors. Here was a zamindar who felt embarrassed by his riches, ashamed of the history of landowning, who had married outside his caste and class—to Geeta's Jadavpur cohorts, he represented hope that the old order could be won over in the coming battles with the establishment.

What they could not have anticipated was that, despite herself, after the wedding, Geeta, once more, found herself in a pivot. She fell heavily, permanently, in love with the house: the engraved carvings on the staircases, the gold-and-green filigree of the pillars, the rich orange rust of the exterior, and the bedrooms that she counted, thirteen in all, of which she could now claim one for herself. Slowly, she adopted the ways and attitudes of her husband's ancestors, frowning upon too much modernism, instructing the maids to keep the silver polished, choosing silk saris over cotton kameezes—so much so that Katyayani Lahiri had raised an eyebrow to her husband and said that here was a true admirer of zamindars.

When Geeta and Tejen had their first child, a boy, Geeta felt a reckless, unconditional, wild love, the kind she had never experienced before, alongside the singular reassurance of having given birth to the scion of a grand family, of being mother to a king, and, finally, of being truly one of the Lahiris. So when the newborn died in his crib, rolling over and erasing his own breath one night, she made note to herself that the endless mourning would never leave her. Almost immediately, against the advice of Dr. Sanyal, she entreated her husband to try again, and in six weeks, Geeta was pregnant again. But when Maya Lahiri, a red-faced, angry, nine-pound girl-child, fought her way out of her mother's narrow hips, Geeta could not look her daughter in the eye for weeks, so desperately did she miss the son that she had lost, attributing her lack of milk and love for her newborn to her belief that motherhood, too, was going to be something to mourn.

But Geeta had emerged a butterfly from many a cocoon—she who had spent a lifetime triumphing in the face of adversity would not lie in bed endlessly now. Her mother-in-law, Katyayani, versed in the mental and physical aftermaths of pregnancy, herself a reluctant warmer to motherhood, made it clear to Geeta that she did not need to put up any facades. A full-time nurse would be hired while Geeta recuperated, or even went on holiday with Tejen, somewhere sunny, maybe Singapore? But Geeta stood straight, already dressed in her customary silk, and said that all she wanted was for her mother-in-law to host a (lavish) rice-eating ceremony for the firstborn of the next generation of Lahiris.

Maya Lahiri would still not take to Geeta's breast, but it was not for want of trying. Mother and daughter were locked in a perpetual cycle of trying to mimic other mothers and daughters—now a bedtime story, now a new toy, walks in the garden, matching bathrobes on holiday. Geeta launched an eighteen-year project to make sure her daughter was well fed, well educated, finished her homework much before it was due, dressed like a Lahiri, spoke different languages, knew her way around a room of Kolkata's politicians and intellectuals and socialites. In short, that she was equipped to be a lady, able to make her own destiny.

But Maya was not an obedient child and, having been born a Lahiri, like the rest of them, saw no greatness in the traditions of the past, instead shrugging off silver rattles for the plastic baubles that the maid's children would play with, developing an early dislike for anything her mother enjoyed and an apathy for her mother's rules, challenging their basis at every turn, until Geeta settled the matter with a powerful slap. In Maya, Geeta saw traces of her own mother, Jaya—the bitter railing and tantrums, followed by wild happiness at the arrival of her father, who would extend her bedtime or sneak a slice of cake into Maya's room.

When Maya turned into a defiant teenager, talking back, pushing back, screaming back, Geeta, haunted by her mother's madness, increased her scrutiny and guard, and only relented when her husband told her in no uncertain terms to soften, and to refrain from punishing his child daily, that she was in fact like any other daughter and needed love, not fear.

Slighted by her mother-in-law, her husband's recriminations of her parenting, and her daughter's rejection of her love, Geeta sought out her brother-in-law, young Hari Lahiri, only eight years older than her own child, who might have been her own son (how she wished it, in a way that felt like a stabbing ache in her stomach) in the easy way he loved her (no one had loved Geeta easily before). Katyayani and Krishna had considered Hari a reckless, wild offspring, entrusting his care to Tejen, their oldest son. But it was Geeta who parented him, making sure he had someone to confide in and play board games with when he was serving out his latest punishment (ten weeks at home after punching a boy at school, or two weeks without any pocket money for stealing out of Krishna Lahiri's wallet, or, once, a year sent away to boarding school, after having been involved in a disputed incident with a girl at school).

Unlike his twin, Rana, Hari seemed like he needed rescuing, a lone wolf trying to survive among the silver-spoon Lahiris, and in him, Geeta saw a piece of herself. Geeta kept the biggest piece of cake for Hari's lunch box, bought him new shirts, and gave him four rupees a week saved from her household allowance, so that he might go to the cinema with his friends.

When Hari chose to love her, above his mother, above his brother, without reason or need, never questioning her place in the Lahiri household, Geeta felt at peace, as if in all the things that had gone wrong, somehow her purpose (winding trajectory that it was) was finally being served. Just as Hari was misunderstood, so was she. When at seventy-four, her husband died, it was only natural that she assumed that Hari would take care of her and her beloved Lahiri home, in the way that only a son might. That her husband would will the house to me was a reckoning that threatened the ground beneath her feet.

15

I COULD NOT remember the exact moment that I realized that my mother hated Hari. Everything was so obscured by her hate for my grandmother that other, smaller, sporadic hates spread around the larger stain. She'd raged against Rana when he sent a mild barb in her direction, and pronounced Biddy a rogue child when she forgot to teach her how to update the software on her computer, and once had stopped speaking to Gina for months over a misunderstanding about an invitation to play cards (or the lack of it). The Lahiris were used to my mother—at her core fragile, still a child, imagined slights and monsters around every corner—and when she was funny or happy or kind, it was like a night sky that had found its star, a sudden parting of clouds.

After her marriage fell apart, the family and the neighborhood had come to the conclusion that Maya De was a furious divorcée, an eccentric working woman, capable of instant combustion. And so they compressed my beautiful, angry, ambitious mother, professor and academic, friend and lover, into the familiar tropes we knew.

In the weeks since we had reunited, she seemed mellowed with age, more tired than aggrieved at the maid, the weather, the country, the far right, her mother. One afternoon, on one of her good days, my mother, grandmother, and I sat in the fleeting sun on the third floor, and Geeta mixed shredded coconut, palm sugar, and ghee in a large bowl. My mother and I had been enlisted to shape it into orbs, which when roasted would turn into salty-sweet caramelized balls of nutty naru.

"If you take this," said my grandmother—she held up a ball—"and roll it around in your palms like so, so that the oils transfer to your palm, you can rub the oil under your armpits"—she raised an arm, setting the sweet down and slipping her hand inside her cotton blouse, rubbing with vigor—"and you'll never have to worry about armpit hair again."

"What?" I said, collapsing into laughter.

"Ma, that is a goddamn old wives' tale," said my mother.

"Look, just look," said my grandmother, wriggling out of one sleeve, raising the loose end of her sari, and showing off a smooth underarm. "Not a whisper of hair since 1964."

My mother, trying not to laugh, asked, "Because you've been rolling narus in there for fifty years?"

"Had you listened, you too would have silky underarms. And white ones, not black," added my grandmother.

"Does it specifically have to be leftover naru oil, or any coconut oil?" I asked, innocent.

"Ma, I can see your breast," said my mother.

"Quiet, both of you," said my grandmother, wriggling back into her blouse. "Who cares if you can see my breast—I'm an old lady. Lila, your mother never listens, but if you want white, smooth underarms, just listen to me."

"Mummy, women should grow their body hair if they want to—for centuries we've been shaving for men. Why not let it all out, you know?" I shrugged.

Geeta looked at me in horror. My mother burst out laughing.

"Enough," said my grandmother. "Roll your narus. Look how perfect your mother's narus are. It's because I taught her how to make them."

I watched my mother as she rolled out another naru. The sunlight was soft on her face—she was beautiful when happy.

"Here, Lila," said my mother, holding one out to me. "Take a bite."

"But it's raw," I protested.

"Just try it," said my grandmother. "Raw is good. Better for you, actually. You've gone to America and emptied your head."

Chewing, I remembered the wellness store two blocks from me in Williamsburg. A big board outside said raw, advertising that nothing inside—not the chocolate, the shakes, the protein bars—was cooked. The store claimed that it used the wisdom of ancient recipes to breathe new life into you. I looked at my mother and grandmother making the sweets in peace, the sun warm on our skin as we sat there. The naru was delicious, and maybe I had new life in my veins.

"Hello, ladies," said Hari, crouching beside my grandmother.

He had a quiet stealth—you never knew when he was coming, and this had allowed him to wreak havoc as a young prankster, especially on his unsuspecting twin. My grandmother, suffused with pleasure, put a naru in his mouth.

"Mm," said Hari, chewing. "I wait all season for these."

Just as my grandmother transformed around Hari, hanging on his every word, my mother became enveloped in something dark and viscous, a personal maelstrom that was terrifying to witness. She rose, wiping oil on her jeans in disgust.

"Why would you put so much oil in a coconut sweet, Ma? It's so uneducated, and bad for the heart."

"Aye, Maya, where are you going?" protested Hari as my mother gathered up her teacup and plate.

"I have a prior appointment," said my mother.

"You promised you would help me with Biddy's wedding invitations," said Hari.

"Maya, is chatting with some student really more important than a family responsibility? Biddy's cards need to go to Ajoy's press before the end of the week," said Geeta.

"Your brother behaves like we're not family—won't budge an inch on the deadline," said Hari to Geeta. "All the sweetness in the family went to you, Geeta Boudi."

My grandmother giggled.

My mother stared at her. "Just because you don't take my career seriously doesn't mean my work isn't important."

"Maya, must you always misunderstand me?" asked Geeta, impatient.

Hari leaped up. "Come on, Maya Ma, without your sweet words, how will we remind our richest guests that they must set aside some money and time to buy young Biddy Lahiri, daughter of Hari and Mishti Lahiri, YouTube celebrity, cousin of Maya, youngest of our clan, the biggest pain in our backsides, a *huge* present?"

He was ridiculous, dancing in circles around my mother, trapping her into standing still, sending my grandmother into paroxysms of delight, humming a playful melody, as he took Maya by the wrists and danced with her until even she smiled.

"Maya, we can't do without you," he said, taking knowing aim at my mother's Achilles'. "If I had to think of fine English words, I would be looking at a dictionary all day. 'Dear sir,'" said Hari, now in a British accent. "'Coh-dee-yal greetings from the Lah-hee-rees. What a mag-nee-fee-cent day eet is.'"

"Hari, stop it," said my mother, pushing him away. "Come up in ten minutes, and I'll write the message."

"Can't we just do it here?" wailed Hari. "Sun, Lila Ma, Geeta Boudi, naru, coffee—come on, Maya Ma, sit down with us," he said, tugging my unwilling mother down onto the woven mat.

And so it was, with Hari. The class clown, debonair despite his paunch, the life of the party, he could cry easily and forgive with speed, emotion always on his sleeve, something so utterly likable about him that none of us, least of all my mother, could compete. My grandmother must have also known he was an alcoholic, a gambler, slippery with money, haunted by nemeses I could not name, but she, like the rest of us, must have thought that we were all two sides of a coin, that we each had darknesses within us—it was easier to look at the light.

AS I WAS walking home that night, Hari slipped out of the shadows behind the main gate of the house.

"Hari Kaka," I said, my hand clutching my chest.

"Lila, I scared you," he said, laughing. "You should see when I leap out at Vik or Rana—they're such ninnies. Even Mishti sometimes. I'm a cat, did you know that?"

I smiled. "I did not know that," I said, looking past him.

The street was empty, as it often was at this time of the night, though there was no need for me to feel unsafe in this neighborhood that I had grown up in, or around this family member who had carried me in his arms since I had been a baby.

"Lila, the truth is, I've been meaning to talk to you."

"Hari Kaka, it's pretty late. Shall we talk tomorrow? I could come for l—"

"Tonight. Tonight," said Hari, urgent.

I could smell cheap liquor on his breath. He held my arm.

"Listen, Lila, I'm worried about everything. This house, the wedding, Biddy, our family . . ."

One of his eyes was a little bloodshot.

"What's the matter?" I asked, stepping back into the courtyard.

I checked to see if my mother was watching, but the lights were out, the Lahiris asleep.

"It's this fucking wedding. I cannot bear the burden alone. I feel all alone. I'm a failure, Lila." He began to cry under his breath. "No money to my name. All my savings gone. Just gone. I've made bad deals, bad investments, and now I have nothing."

"But Biddy has a wedding fund from the Lahiri house trust."

"Fund," said Hari as he spat a violent red stream of the paan he was chewing out into the street. "It's just a pittance, a pittance. As if she were not a Lahiri, but a maid. All of it has been swallowed up—the caterers, the decorator, the rented chairs, that motherfucker-of-crooks priest." Hari began to weep softly. "No one will help me. No one. Rana has no money, and even if he did, that wife of his would never let me have any. She earns, but would we ever get a paisa? No."

"She's a professor. Like Ma. They don't make much."

Hari wept harder at this.

"Uncle Hari, don't cry," I said. "I love Biddy. Of course I'll help."

He looked up.

"Not much," I said in haste. "I don't make much myself. And you have to promise to never go behind my back again to borrow from the trust."

Hari looked away. "That haramzada snitch, Das. What is the money for, if not to take care of the family?"

"The family has lost a lot of its money, Hari Kaka. All we have left is the house. The little money that the trust earns maintains the house so that the family can continue to live in it. We may not be the Lahiris of old, but if we're smart, we can rebuild."

Hari nodded. "We must rebuild. The Lahiris are one of the oldest families of Bengal."

"I can make a personal loan to you, for the wedding."

"You would do that, Lila Ma?"

"Yes. But it won't be a lot, because I don't have a lot. Let's look at what you need, and I'll make the payment directly to the shop."

He looked at me, sharp. Then, resigned, for he must have known that I could not have trusted a man known to make large afternoon gambles over cards at the tea shop, he muttered, "Flowers. The flowers are so expensive. And she still needs new things—clothes and household items—to take with her. It's so expensive to give a girl away in marriage. So much shame to not send her away in style. Especially a Lahiri girl."

I nodded. "We'll decide on a sum in the morning, okay?"

"Thank you, Lila Ma. We . . . I won't ever forget this."

I walked back home, relieved to be away from him. I could not have said why. Despite my initial shock at the car-door incident with Mishti (a fast-fading blur, so entirely had we dismissed it), I adored him like everyone else did. He made it easier to be in a room, especially if my mother and grandmother were there. He made us all laugh. And yet, I had wanted a light on, a familiar face—I had felt a sharp ripple of what was unmistakably fear.

16

ONE EVENING, NOT long after, Biddy and I were watching the sunset from the Secret Sixth. She had been making another of her videos, a kind of dance, something that took from her Odissi training and had a moonwalk to it. B2D had a way of making things effortless. I had watched her rehearse it from my mother's window. Biddy, who lived a life much watched on the internet, had turned around and waved to me afterward, as if she had known that I was an audience the whole time.

"Do you think I'm wasting my life?" Biddy asked as we sat on the ledge of the Sixth.

"God, no. I feel like you can do anything you want," I said. "Your whole life sprawling ahead of you. I'm jealous."

Biddy swung her legs to the other side of the ledge, the courtyard about eighty feet under her soles.

"Biddy, fuck. Turn back around," I said, my heartbeat thudding in my ears.

The slightest movement could plunge her six floors below. She looked back at me, surprised.

"Okay," she said, turning her whole body back around to safety, her feet touching the terrace floor again. "You know I've been doing that my whole life, right? I wouldn't fall—I've got great balance."

I nodded, my breathing shallow. "You do."

"I could catch myself in midair," said B2D. "I could catch you in midair."

I laughed. She was so serious.

"I would give a lot to have your powers," I said.

"Do you think Rinki's right? That I'm going to get married and then suddenly everything will go to shit and Arjun will become uncool and make me roll out his rotis? I mean, he's carb-free."

"Have you asked him?" I asked.

"Ya, he just wants us to get the hell out of here, as fast as we can," said Biddy with certainty. "Maybe live somewhere in Manali, or Shillong, or Ooty. But it'll probably just be Pune or Mumbai. I'm going to keep making my videos, maybe audition for some radio host jobs at the station my friend works at. And Arjun's going to open another branch of the family's jewelry shop—more modern designs or something."

"Won't you miss the house?"

"God," she said. "I can't wait to get out." I felt her body shudder next to mine.

I looked at her, but Biddy had returned to uploading her video. There was a silence. I had never asked her about the hatred she had expressed for the house on the day of my grandfather's funeral. It was unfathomable to discover that Biddy, who felt like a celebratory string of lights, adding cheer to any room, held some sort of acute loathing for a house that I had fallen in love with.

"You should come visit me sometime," I said as the sun began to sink into the evening.

"In America?" Her eyes were shining. "Really?"

"I'd love that."

"So you're not staying?"

"Staying? Here?"

"Oh, yeah," said Biddy, turning back to her screen.

The video had uploaded, a stream of likes and views pouring in immediately.

"They all think you're going to move into one of the floors, maybe Krishna Dadu's, on the fourth floor, and be the queen. Mental. I told them you were going back to America. You are, aren't you?"

I nodded.

"Cool. What's your Facebook?"

She did a quick search and had found me before I could respond. She clicked on my profile.

"Oh wow, you look sharp. Like a businesswoman."

"It's the only professional photo I have."

"Oh. Arjun takes good photos. He can take some of you. You look just like Maya Didi," she said, peering at my photo.

"Actually, I look like my grandmother, my father's mother," I said, trying to keep the bristle out of my voice.

"No, look—here's her profile."

Biddy pulled up my mother and clicked through a series of photos, dragging one into her desktop. My mother's image sat next to mine.

"See, you guys could be sisters," she said. "Same big eyes, chin jutting out, small faces. I like your photo—makes you look powerful."

I looked away from the photographs.

"By the way, all the guys in the neighborhood want to talk to you. Even my friends," said Biddy chattily. "The rumor mill is that you're having love affairs with all of them."

"Nice," I said, a warmth spreading into my ears and cheekbones as Biddy examined the photos on her phone. "I'll be the local cougar, chatting up your friends."

I wondered if she had heard anything that linked me to Adil.

"What's a 'cougar'?"

"American big cat. Show me that again." I pulled her screen toward me.

"Oooh. I can think of so many cougars in Ballygunge alone," said Biddy, reading on her phone.

"How on earth does Ma know my friends?"

I stared at my mother's Facebook on Biddy's screen, where Maya De and I had twenty-four friends in common. I scrolled through the list: Gil; Molly; Crystal, my Pilates trainer; Max, from college; Colby, from the first internship I had ever done.

"She's been adding all my friends on Facebook," I said slowly, horror spreading through me.

Biddy laughed. "Stalker much," she said.

"It's outrageous," I said. I could feel the fury rise in my ears, hot to the touch. "She has no boundaries, no respect for my privacy. God alone knows what she's been saying to them."

I felt real fear—had she sent messages to Seth, to Gil or Molly? Even Harriet was on the list. How much did she know about my life? What would she do with information about me, access to me? I took a breath. Molly would surely have told me—there were no secrets between us.

"She probably just wanted to get all up in your business. Nose around, figure out your life, who's in it. Regular mother shit."

I stared at her. "But it's a complete invasion. Who gave her permission to talk to the people in my life? These are close friends, colleagues. This is a violation."

Biddy looked uncomfortable. "Maybe it's just an Indian mom thing, and that's why it's weirder for you. My mom is an asshole about my YouTube. Monitors it like she's the government. Anyway, now you can watch my YouTube channel on your Facebook. Here, give me your phone—I'll approve my request."

Biddy took my phone from me as the last streaks of the sunset disappeared into the purple sky. Another storm was coming. I felt a cold fear in my lungs. Everything that I accused my mother of, that I harbored against her, that I incubated into little balls of tightly wound dislike, Biddy had dismissed in one breath. What were the mom things that seemed such an easy language for Biddy? What was the line that separated comedic nosing and overprotective love from a diabolical obsession? How did one know what things mothers did, without having had mothering? I felt small and embarrassed by my rage as I imagined my mother on Facebook, digging, unearthing, consuming the bones of my life.

17

PROGRESS ON THE installation of the elevator was going well, despite a small electrical fire at its base one afternoon, following which my grandmother and Rana had led a three-hour prayer to evict evil spirits that may have possessed the house in recent times, something I strove to not take personally. My days now consisted of waking up early and catching up on email, and then it was long hours with Mr. Das at the Lahiri house, fielding the many questions the construction team and the family members had. I was consulted solely on matters of the property at first, but as time passed, Biddy and Mishti would ask me for my opinion on things to do with the wedding, Rana would ask me if I wanted to listen to a new song he had heard on the radio, Gina would ask about the manuscripts I read, and my grandmother would braid my hair while lecturing me on the evils of drinking wine. I became a fixture in their lives, a new and chaotic one, much like the construction crew or the wedding vendors, but nevertheless, a part of them, so much so that if I delayed my arrival to the house, one or the other would call me to irritably inquire where I was. Even if they did not want me to own their house, they were beginning to take for granted the fact of my presence.

My phone and my computer were always on the brink of death in the Lahiri house. The sockets were ancient, the two-pin kind, and my converter plugs were no match for them. Every afternoon was a race against time, to finish my Wyndham to-do list before one or both died, brought back to life only at night, when I would return to my father's apartment. This, combined with inevitable demands from construction or wedding matters, or Bari's daughter's desire to show me a drawing she had made at school (Ami's new-found chattiness and vocabulary thrilling to me), would take precedence, and I lagged behind at work.

Even though Aetos had granted me eight weeks of leave, I felt as if I could not afford to fade in Wyndham's memory. I began to email more frequently, checking in with Gil, with agents, reading new submissions quickly, hoping to lock down new authors and keep the existing ones on track, while work-ers shouldered sheets of plywood up the temporary stairs, installing geysers in every bathroom. I sidestepped boxes of tile in the courtyard, ducts and wires everywhere, as sections of pillars were hoisted through windows on the fourth floor, the elevator workers welding metal into place, sending footlong sparks into the air.

But in Kolkata, all action was in slow motion—nothing felt urgent, not even my lists and deadlines. The men stopped to laugh at a common joke, or drink tea with Rana, who stopped to write a poem that suddenly took hold of him, or read a single paper for hours. Lulled by the sun, I fell asleep over a manuscript one afternoon. Like a slow ebb, the prickle and buzz of New York that had fueled my every waking minute and sense of self, began to fade as Kolkata seeped into my limbs.

One morning, I awoke to an email from Gil:

Lila, does India have you in thrall? It would, me. I'm wondering if you could join a couple of the meetings we're setting up with the larger teams at Phenom, so you're up to speed on all of the changes. Annoying protocols, but such is life as a big fish. I know you're technically off, but if you have a few hours to spare, I think it'll help a lot with catching you up on your new responsibilities when you're back. I noticed you've missed all the trainings so far.

Williamsburg Cinemas is showing True Romance. A few of us went after work—some of the new Phenoms too, as Molly likes to unsparingly call them (to their faces, on occasion). We missed you. We miss you.

Let me know. And how you are.

G

SINCE ADIL AND I had slept together, I had not heard from him, except for a text the evening after, to confirm that I was feeling okay. Since then, nothing had been exchanged. The silence and the memory were a dull ache somewhere in my chest, occasionally resurfacing as insistent between rib and collarbone, but I wanted to plow through and allow it to subside on its own, a military determination to not give in to what I did not understand. What had happened had felt momentous, but Adil's reaction, plain on his transparent face, had been the dawn of acute regret. My own moral syntax was a jumble of instinct and blurred cultural codes, but at least I could stay the hell out of someone's marriage, especially when I was a stranger, temporarily in town, no better than a pilfering dinner-party guest.

I alternated dinners between my grandmother and mother. My grandmother would make a feast, mostly Bengali specialties she had once cooked for my grandfather, invite guests (family members, friends of friends, potential husbands for me, neighbors, and so on), all of whom turned up, because she was delightful company in a crowd and needed frequent cheering up in the absence of my grandfather. Usually, there would be whiskey and dessert afterward, and Rana would play the harmonium or Hari would sing. It felt like the Lahiris had made some sort of comeback.

My grandmother and I grew even closer than before, enough for me to once ask if she loved Hari more than my mother.

She paused, frowning. "I love all my children equally. You, Hari, Maya, Rana, Biddy, Rinki, the unborn children who will follow."

This could not have been further from her truth, but I believe Geeta felt certain that she had acted correctly as a mother, focusing her attention with precision and care on her biological child, and accidentally reserving her love for another.

Dinner with my mother, on the fifth floor, was trickier. We were usually alone, in which case, I had to determine the weather of her mood. If good, we were going to eat experimental dishes, like Kerala stew or fried sausages, and she would order Australian wine and we would talk about Netflix shows and Henry James, my eccentricities as a baby, her students, and the many things she was always buying for me—from jewelry to T-shirts or the biscuits I liked.

Sometimes, Professor Roy, her colleague, would join. It was no secret that he was besotted with my mother, who, in front of me, always treated him as if it was the first time they were meeting.

"Why, hello, Professor," she would say, as if surprised to see him at the dinner hour on her front step.

To the shy, kind Mr. Roy, who I learned from my grandmother was a regular visitor and had been one for fifteen years now, I owed an enormous debt. Over time, I realized that he loved my mother. In her darkest hours, when she would slam plates down, when she would rage on about my uncles and my grandmother or the construction crew or the maids, all of whom were against her, so bitter it was like a machine gun of apoplexy—even on those nights, Mr. Roy would stay long after I had quickly disappeared down the stone stairs. And the next day, in the aftermath of his unconditional presence, my mother, at long last having been loved by someone wholly, looked slightly less the splintered woman that we had all lived with for so long. For my part, it was a piercing relief that I no longer had to try to love her—someone else, whose first name I did not know, had done the needful.

ONE NIGHT, AFTER a raucous dinner with Geeta, Vik, Biddy, Gina, and Rana, soporific from rasmalai and a late card game, I was on my way home when I realized that I had forgotten the keys to the front main gate, which meant that I would have to ring the bell and wake Ram Bhai. But as I approached, I noticed that the building's ground-floor lights were all on and Ram Bhai was making cheerful conversation with Adil, whose black SUV was parked at the curb.

Seeing me, Ram Bhai brightened.

"There she is," he said. "Adil Saab has been waiting for you for forty-five minutes. I told him you don't usually stay out this late."

Mrs. Chatterjee, glowing with the same subdued excitement as Ram, watched from her window across the street. Her maid lounged against their front gate with interest. The paan wallah, on the brink of closing shop, folded up his basket, one eye on us.

"I hope you know that this will be the headline of the Ballygunge rumor mill by morning," I said to Adil.

"I called you seven or eight times."

I blinked. "Oh. My phone dies all the time. The sockets at the Lahiri house don't accept my US-to-India converters."

Ram Bhai strained to understand us.

"Li, I'd like to talk," said Adil in a low voice. "Maybe we could sit in my car for a bit?"

"With the whole neighborhood watching?" I said, clipped, fumbling for my keys. "That's nice."

"I didn't mean—"

"You can come up if you like. And if that's too much for the bhadralok that you are, feel free to give me a call tomorrow," I said.

Ram Bhai was still scrutinizing us, hoping to understand from body language what words rendered impossible.

I smiled at him as I walked inside, my heartbeat drumming in my ears. As I climbed the stairs, I heard the quiet click of Adil's SUV door and his steady footsteps behind me.

INSIDE, I TURNED on the lights.

"Do you want a drink?" I asked, pouring myself one.

He stood near the front door, closed behind him, for what seemed like an eternity as I poured.

"Lila," he said finally, exhaustion in his voice, as he came up behind me, his arms sliding around my waist, his face burying in my neck.

We stood there like that, my eyes closed, the glass of wine in my left hand. Slowly, he turned my body to face his.

"Are you trying to get caught?" I asked, my face in his chest.

"I didn't know where you were," he said, ragged. "I called your mother. She said she didn't know either."

"I was downstairs with Mummy," I said, picturing my mother refusing to acknowledge the sound of the dinner party she had declined to join, the laughter that wafted up to her.

"I called a couple of times. Then I panicked, thinking that you never wanted to see me again."

I smiled, despite myself. "It would be hard to ghost you, given our families." After a pause, I asked, "Where did you think I was?"

"I don't know."

I unpeeled myself from him, but it was impossible to take my hands off his shoulders, to stop touching him, now that he was in front of me. We stood like that, my arms outstretched, as if holding him at arm's length.

"You haven't called," I said.

"No," he said, bowing his head.

His hair smelled of pine and cloves. I reached out, letting my fingers ripple through.

"Adil, you cannot ask me to draw lines in the sand. If you want to, you have to do it yourself." I let my arms fall to my sides and stepped closer to him.

"We ... I ... Silky and I ... we haven't been happy for a—"

I raised my palm in front of him, flinching, and shook my head. "No. I can't. I don't want to know. I don't want any part of it."

I picked up the glass of wine and took a drink. He stood, silent, in front of me. I handed him the glass. He took a sip.

"Whatever it is, I don't want to be part of it," I said. "What you do with it, that's your business. The morality of it, the difficulty, the confusion. That's all yours. I don't have anything to do with it. You and I ... we're just us."

There was a way that Adil looked at me when I was a girl, when I would place my palms in the air and push away the memory of my mother, when I would lie that, in fact, I was fine and would soldier on, believing I was okay. In those moments, Adil would look at me as he did now, with a mixture of compassion and sorrow and the ability to see through the skin I had convinced myself I lived in. I felt a surge of anger that he could dare look at me the same way when he now lived lies of his own.

"I've never stopped loving you, Lila," he said, taking a step forward, his arms folding around me, my body still prickling with rage at being seen, at the way things had turned out, but transforming into immediacy as he leaned down to kiss me, taking my face in his hands, as if to say that it might be okay to be so human, to permit myself the terrible things that came with it, if only for these few moments.

We made love like strangers, with a connection that shocked even ourselves. His body was not yet sexually familiar to me, a grown man replacing a boy, his nakedness intensely new, despite my having known him for so long. We knew the language of our desire, yet we were often as clumsy as fifteen-years-olds, trying not to hurt each other yet giving in to this furious union that we had kept alive in memory for so long.

AFTER THAT NIGHT, when Rinki would ask me about Adil (and she would ask often, in hope of some gossip), I lied easily: I had forgotten to text him back. He seemed busy and hadn't taken a call. We had, in fact, not seen each other since Palekar's office. I played up the character of Seth, elevating our casual relationship with the respectability of deep affection. Rinki thought my life was impossibly glamorous in a hedonistic way, and she lived for description—of Seth, of the office, of Brooklyn—and believed me with a goodness that came naturally to her.

Adil and I began to see each other in the very early morning, when Ram was still fast asleep and he could slip in past the maids or the newspaperman and use the spare key I had given him. Those were the sweetest mornings, when I would turn in my sleep and he would be there, freshly showered, fully dressed for work, lying on his side, an arm around me, the perfect scoop of my body against his as we held each other. He would then slip into my sheets, his clothes folded carefully on the reading chair next to the bed. We would pretend that he had been there all night.

I began to skip certain nights of dinner at the Lahiri household, my mother and Geeta each irritably assuming that I was eating with the other, and if he visited me at six or seven in the evening and did not park his car out front, it became easier to pretend he had left at some point and Ram had simply missed his departure, in the same way my grandmother kept a watchful eye for Professor Roy's departure from my mother's studio after 9 p.m. Adil's parents were family friends of the Lahiri clan—we never forgot this—and so submerged ourselves in each other only when we could.

One morning, he slipped into my bed before dawn had broken. As we lay watching the sun come up, I asked him why he had not told me that he was married right away.

"I don't know," he said simply, in his frank way, made immediately uncomfortable by the prospect of confronting something he had no access to. "I just . . . didn't want to tell you."

I stroked the line of his jaw—he was not what Rinki would call a handsome man, was more lanky than tall, wore glasses, without which he was blind, was serious and still his slightly awkward teenage self. But I felt the same fierce rush.

Adil never once asked me if I had someone in my own life, and this rankled under my skin. Either he assumed I was single or was cheating, like him (but, unlike him, I had apparently forgiven myself or was fine with it to the extent I never needed to bring it up). Both scenarios were thorns in my feet, during what was otherwise an idyll.

One late evening, the streetlamps filtered in through small cracks in the heavy drapes of Iva's curtains. Adil, propped up on one arm, watched as I ate chocolate from a bar balanced on my stomach, his other arm over my waist, both of us naked in the humid night.

"Do you ever think about your parents?" he asked.

"Think what about them?"

"Their divorce," he said, his palm behind my head as I turned to look up at his face, an inch away. "Do you think about what happened to them? To you?"

I placed a palm on his chest, pushing away lightly.

"You mean the scandal?"

"Yes."

"Sure," I shrugged. "It's not the kinda thing you forget."

"Kind of."

"Did you just correct my grammar?" I asked, incredulous.

"Technically, that did not have any grammar in it."

He laughed as I slapped him away, biting his ear softly. He sighed with pleasure.

"Are you asking if I worry about you, me—this being a scandal?" I asked.

"Yes," he said, breathing against my teeth, my hair, my ear.

"Do you ever think about what would have happened had I not left?"

"We would have been married," he said in his clear, sure way.

"Well, then, it's a good thing I did leave, isn't it?" I said with a little laugh. "It might have been me you were cheating on."

Adil never rose to my little cruelties, the kind of barbs I had inherited from the Lahiri women. It was not his way to engage in a fight that might have allowed me to expel some of the fear that hung over us.

History was playing its little joke on me. The world—specifically, Ballygunge Place—would connect my parents' histories with that of their daughter Lila De's, as she wrecked a beloved local's marriage and reintroduced the neighborhood to the rotting smell of divorce. This was the uneasy backdrop to my dizzying romance.

The scandal of Mihir and Maya's divorce that had enveloped the Des and Lahiris, every street corner buzzing with the news, a honeypot for everyone but the families, had had an ensemble cast: My mother, the tyrant wife, who screamed at my father so loud it woke the neighbors. My father, the cheating playboy, who had taken up with a white woman. White Iva, who was considered a slut before anyone had exchanged a single word with her. My teachers, who speculated that my father might have been cheating for years and that Iva had met him only six months before my parents' separation.

Being a child of divorce meant that I, too, was a participant in this Western travesty that threatened the morality of everyone we knew, the very fabric of society. At the time, the only other divorced people that we knew of were white, promiscuous, or movie stars (one and the same). Mothers were tremendously suspicious of us. Our biggest crime, though, was that we were deeply *Western*. The Des thought in English, ate ham, had money, got divorced/had affairs/had sex (one and the same), and made periodic disappearances abroad. This general consensus resulted in the mother squad keeping their kids quite far away from me. They had reached an agreement among themselves, and

I knew this by the way they looked at me. Even my academic achievements (the highest virtue in the mother-squad book) were not enough to let me near their kids.

A divorced woman in the '80s and '90s in Ballygunge was used goods, rejected goods, cast-off goods; she must have done something to deserve it. It was as good as being widowed. No amount of pedigree or money could erase the stain coloring her whole body. But surely, Kolkata had moved on. Surely, Silky Sarkar would not be subjected to the stain in the way my mother or I had. And surely, the sweetness of my first love, perhaps my only one, the truth of our innocent young selves, once more brought to life, could be spared the scourge.

18

DESPITE SETTLING INTO a routine with the family members, there was a new texture in the way the Lahiris interacted with me: an odd language of glances they exchanged with each other, the ceasing of murmurs when I walked into a room by chance, the hovering of secrets overhead. Whether this was my imagination or not, Palekar and I suspected that the Lahiris were building a case against me, and we had no insight into the facts or inventions that they might be threading together to challenge the will. I needed some sort of practical evidence, and Palekar had advised me to use the hour that my grandmother would be at the temple and my mother would be at the university to nose around. Describing the plan to Seth one morning via Skype, I painted an amusing caricature—my grandmother ringing the temple bell as I skulked through the Lahiri house, tiptoeing Pink Panther–esque and opening drawers.

Seth smiled at my antics. Then, in his earnest, anxious way, he said, "I'm so sorry. This is awful of them."

"It's just a formality, something they think they have to do," I said, irritable at once. "It doesn't mean they don't love me."

"But they're mounting a lawsuit. To take back something that your grandfather left you."

"It's not like that. Indian families are complicated . . ." My voice trailed off even as I realized it fully for the first time.

There was no way to explain that while my mother and grandmother had likely participated in legal discussions over the coup, they were also likely arguing over who would get to eat dinner with me. We were large and messy and chaotic, so different from the reasonable, loving Schwartzes, who had raised Seth to be fragile and concerned at what sounded like madness.

"I'm just worried there's one of you and a lot of them," he said.

"It'll be fine. It's no big deal."

"Do you have help? Or, as usual, are you fighting your wars alone?"

"I have my dad's friend who is my lawyer, and another lawyer . . . friend," I said.

Calling Adil a friend had taken an extra, sudden second. Seth frowned on my screen.

"How are the revisions coming along?" I asked as Seth stood to stretch.

I admired the flatness of his stomach, the slight ripple as his arms went overhead, remembering them taking my clothes off. I missed Seth my lover and Seth my friend, and felt guilty right away. There was so much that seemed to be at stake with Adil, and here I was enjoying the respite of a spark with an entirely different man.

"I'm going on a trip," said Seth. "Like you suggested. It'll be good for me—a change of scene."

I pictured him in a seaside cottage somewhere.

"That sounds nice," I said, wistful.

"Join me?" he asked, flirtatious.

I smiled back. "On my way."

ACTUAL DETECTIVE WORK in the Lahiri household proved much harder than Palekar or I had imagined. In a joint family, nobody had any privacy. People entered and exited rooms without knocks or announcements, and Adil had warned me about choosing the noon hour, when the traffic of maids, vendors, and construction crew peaked. But there was no other time in the week when my grandmother and mother would both be away, when Rana would be giving music lessons in his study, Hari would be playing cards at the tea stall, Biddy would be hosting her live YouTube show, and Mishti would be at the primary school where she taught.

My first obstacle was Hari, who I bumped into on the second-floor stairs. My skittish surprise must have shown, but he appeared distracted.

"Hi, Lila Ma," he said. "I told Das to paint the courtyard's second pillar—after they painted all the others, it didn't match anymore. Are you here to ask me about the extra cost?" He looked worried.

I shook my head. "No, Mr. Das let me know. I agreed that it should happen if you thought it was necessary."

He nodded, brightening. "Good, good."

"I didn't realize you'd be home at this hour. Is everything okay?" I regretted this immediately, but it was too late.

"Yes, well, Mishti's brother has started a catering company and offered me a job." He looked moody at this. "Obviously, I don't need a job. But I could consult. Or something." He stared off into the distance, vacant. "Times are difficult, Lila. What can I say? The Lahiris have fallen hard. My great-grandfather was once the richest man in Ballygunge. It's this economy."

It was always the economy's fault, in the Lahiri man's book.

"Anyway, you have a nice day," said Hari. "Tell Das to do his job and not faff around. And come to me if you need help. I'll be taking care of some business with Manu and the boys at the tea stall."

He thudded down the stairs, soaked in uncharacteristic melancholy.

I MADE MY way to my grandmother's rooms, on the third floor. The air was still, the smooth slate of the diamond-shaped green marble tiles cool beneath my feet. I looked over my shoulder before sliding the brass latch to the left. The Lahiris largely left their rooms unlocked, theft, privacy, and boundary neither an expectation nor a concern. The room was dark—it did not get as much sun as my mother's studio—but it was a respite from the summer day.

As I looked around, I felt an overwhelming shame. Everything here—the desk with its stacks of papers and the old, wound clock, the bookshelf, the mahogany carved cupboards, and the rocking chair in the corner—reminded me of my grandfather. What would he have made of this coup his family was staging? Or of the ways in which they had embraced me, so much so that I often felt like a Lahiri myself.

"You should have left me a letter or something to explain yourself," I muttered under my breath to the photograph of him on the wall: blue T-shirt, a smile that took up his whole face, a joyful, alive man only two years ago.

He would have told me to finish what he had started, I told myself.

The desk seemed like the place to start. My grandfather had died only five weeks ago, and for the most part, my grandmother and Bari had left his desk untouched. His soft evening shawl hung over the back of his chair, and I held it to my face, breathing him in. Then I pulled open drawers, looked inside notebooks, opened and closed files, feeling like a thief, but it was mostly financial records that I already had copies of, of the trust and the house— Tejen Lahiri orderly till the end, his neat notes in margins. I took pictures of the many prescriptions and bills from hospitals; if they were going to build a case that said he was made incompetent by medicine, Palekar wanted to know what my grandfather had been taking. There were letters from former colleagues, calendars that included phone calls to be made (*Call Lilama on USA time 7 a.m.,* said one devastating square—it was the call I had missed the week before he had died), and invitations to events that he would not attend. One letter that he had written to the editor of the *New Statesman* protested the censorship of Hollywood films by the Indian censor board, outlining how the films had been mutilated by the nonsensical cuts the conservative government had mandated (the dance scene in *Dirty Dancing* was key, he argued, to the film's axis). The letter made me smile, and I put it in my handbag, resolving to mail it later.

As I returned order to the stack, a sealed, unmarked envelope bulged from between the others, its middle bloated with folded paper inside. I looked at it for a while—the last thing I wanted was to find a private note to my grandfather—the wild thought crossed my mind that sealed letters were love letters.

Still, I teased the envelope's edges open. I examined what was a simple retainer with the firm my grandfather had engaged years ago to handle the affairs of the house and trust, including his will and the wills and affairs of all the Lahiris. It was not new information—I knew the lawyer, Bhaskar Gupta, the slick, informed, high-pitched man who I had met in Palekar's office, who was the liaison between the firm and me/Palekar. The retainer said that Bhaskar Gupta was the appointed lawyer from Chand and Sons who would handle the account on a daily basis, while a partner at the firm, Param Chand, also the founder's son, would oversee. Palekar would want the original retainer, I decided, and slid it alongside the *New Statesman* letter into my bag.

Suddenly, Bari burst into the room, a pail balanced on one hip and a rag in one hand.

I jumped, clutching my handbag to my heart. "Jesus Christ, Bari."

She screamed loudly, clutching the pail.

"Bari, Bari . . . Shh, quiet, it's me."

"Lila Didi. It's you. You looked like a murderer, coming out of the shadows." She burst into peals of laughter. "I didn't know you were here. Geeta Boudi isn't due back for another hour."

"I was looking for my grandmother. Thought I would wait here."

"Thank goodness I saw you in time, or I might have had a heart attack. Do you know Lipi Dasgupta's mother was murdered by a drunk man who broke in one night and ate their leftovers?" Bari set the pail down. "Are you hungry?" she asked.

I sank into my grandfather's old chair, still clutching the bag. "No, thank you."

Bari switched on the overhead fan, and the cool air rushed over my warm face. Bari began to dip the rag into the solution in the pail and wipe the floor free of dust, squatting expertly as she moved in circles across the tiles.

"How's school coming along for Ami?"

"Oh, she's learned to count already. Between you and me, I think she's smarter than most kids. You won't believe it, but she already knows all the words of poems and things like that. It makes me cry."

"I'm so glad, Bari. Do you think I could maybe come to school one day? See Ami in her little uniform?"

Bari was silent for a few seconds. "You mean, to see if I'm really sending her or spending your money on other things?" Her nostrils flared.

"No, no, of course not. I just wanted to see her in school. I'm happy she's going."

Bari's bottom lip trembled.

"Bari, forget it," I entreated. "Never mind. I don't want to do it if it upsets you. I'm sorry."

She softened. "It doesn't matter how long you've worked somewhere, or if they've known you since you were a little girl, or if your mother worked for them before that," she said, her voice lowered. "If a necklace goes missing or the milk looks watery, it's always the maid who probably did it."

"Bari, that's not how this family thinks of you." I shook my head, trying to dispel what she said, shame filling me.

She picked up her bucket and rag and tucked the end of her sari. "Let me know if you want some tea while you wait, didi," she said as she left.

After this, I decided to give up on the mission. I would keep my eyes and ears open the next time I visited my mother's studio, but riffling through her things, with a second chance at being discovered, felt out of the question. Even if they were planning to take the house from me, I wanted the Lahiris to trust me like one of their own. For them to learn to lock their doors because of me felt like too much to bear.

I lay back on my grandmother's bed, the hum of the fan overhead, in the exact spot that my grandfather must have lain when he decided to leave me the house. My ulcer throbbed, a painful flash that came and went as it pleased—I had not eaten all morning, but the last thing I wanted to do was run into Bari in the kitchen. I fell asleep, descending into dreams where my grandfather and Adil and Barack Obama and Nina of the Night swirled around me expectantly, each awaiting an answer, and all I felt was the growing panic of not having known the question.

At some point, I felt thin lips on my forehead and a cotton blanket over me—I held on to it, tighter, unwilling to leave the dreamscape until I found what I was supposed to be looking for.

"Lila, shona, wake up."

My grandmother's voice floated into the edges of my visions, her soft hand on my cheek. Or was it my mother's? A cold fear enveloped me as I woke up, my mouth dry.

"Mummy, Mummy, is that you?" I clutched at the air in front of me.

"Of course it's me," she said, placing her palm on my forehead. "Do you have a fever?"

"No." I sat up, slow. "I must have fallen asleep."

"It was wonderful to find you here, as if you were six again," she said, affectionate. "Here, drink some water, and eat this."

She held a plate in front of me with a slice of fruitcake. The rich, rum-soaked taste revived me right away, the sugar flowing into my veins.

"Bari, Bari," yelled my grandmother.

Bari appeared in the doorway, her lips pursed.

"A cup of tea for didi, and one for me as well."

Bari nodded and disappeared.

My grandmother frowned. "Another sulk day, I suppose. Her husband must have slapped her around again."

I looked up, shocked.

"Oh, never you mind," said my grandmother hurriedly. "It's just a turn of phrase. Poor people get drunk, and what they do in their own homes is none of our business. Want another slice of cake?"

My ears felt hot, as if blood were rushing into them—I had opened my mouth to respond when Bari appeared again.

"Ram Bhai left word downstairs for Lila Didi," she said, excitement in her voice, all traces of "sulk" gone. "He said he tried to call you many times on your phone, but it didn't connect. He says to go home immediately. There is a guest waiting for you, with a suitcase. He said it's . . . it's"—Bari's voice lowered in hushed awe—"a white man."

"MADAM, MADAM, LILA Madam," shouted Ram Bhai, waving to me from a distance as he saw me approach my father's apartment building, where he stood outside the gates.

Ram began to walk furiously toward me, breathless, as if I were not already halfway to him.

As he approached, he began to whisper loudly. "Well, madam, I've been phoning you for the past two hours, on your local number, the American number, even. Then I went to the big house to leave word. And now, finally, here you are," said Ram, triumphant.

"Yes, thank you, Ram Bhai," I said, putting a hand on his shoulder.

This unexpected contact threw off the suspense he'd been building; for a second, Ram looked at me, blank. I removed my hand, and he pointed inside the building, seemingly confused as to how a great story had had its ending snatched from him.

"A man—a shaheb—came," said Ram. "Two hours ago."

As I looked up at the gates, Seth Schwartz, relief on his face, emerged, a large, sleek suitcase rolling silently, like a panther, behind him.

It took me a full few minutes to grasp that Seth could be standing in front of me, on the street that I had grown up in, in India.

"Surprise," said Seth.

I had not known what to think when Bari said that there was a white man waiting for me. It might have been a friend of Palekar's or my father's. Someone who lived in Kolkata—maybe someone Kashmiri—who looked white but wasn't. The wild thought of even Gil, escaping from . . . what exactly? Anyone but Seth had crossed my mind, except that in the back of my brain, some niggling alarm had gone off, because before we know things, our bodies arrive ahead of time.

"Hi," I said, blinking at him.

"Hi," he said.

It felt like the world was still. I imagined every eye and ear on the street trained on us like snipers.

"Didi, should I call Mihir Saab?" asked Ram Bhai, worried.

"Ram Bhai, this is my friend Seth."

"A seth?" asked Ram, puzzled.

The word *seth* in Hindi means "merchant." I giggled, feeling faint.

"His name is Seth," I said in Bengali, emphasizing the *th*. "He's my friend from America, a writer. We'll put him up at the guesthouse in Mandeville Gardens this evening. I'm going to take him upstairs for a cup of tea. We have business to discuss."

Ram Bhai nodded, approving.

"Business," he repeated. "A writer. Mihir Saab told me your business is to make books. Namaste, Seth Ji."

He folded his hands and hoisted Seth's suitcase off the street.

"Oh, I can take that," began Seth.

"You run the risk of serious offense," I said, shaking my head.

"It has wheels," said Seth.

But Ram had disappeared into the house. I took a breath. Seth looked like he might melt from the afternoon heat, his eyebrows crinkled in worry.

"Good surprise?" he asked, tentative.

I began to laugh. "Seth, you fucking madman. What are you doing here?"

I put my arms around him, and as I imagined Ballygunge Place abuzz in uproar, we hugged, unexpected happiness pouring out of both of us.

AFTER A TOTAL of twenty hours in the air, a mysterious country filled with unfamiliar color and language at every bend, and two hours of waiting for me on Ram Bhai's charpoy, Seth had been too exhausted to protest when I informed him that he was staying at the guesthouse down the street, a ten-minute walk from my father's house.

"Why can't I stay here, with you?" he asked hazily, reaching for my neck as we curled into each other on Iva's couch. I leaned into the kiss, melting into the familiar smell of Seth.

"This is India," I said into his lips. "You can't be shacking up with me and not be even a boyfriend or a fiancé. The news has probably traveled neighborhoods by now."

"I can be your boyfriend."

He nuzzled my neck, slipping his hand under my shirt, tugging on the waistband of my jeans so expertly that I slid into his lap. Unbidden, I thought of Adil.

"Why do they care so much? Are you some sort of celebrity here?" Seth asked.

"Seth, stop," I said, pushing his face away from my collarbone. "We've got to get you to the guesthouse before it closes."

He put an arm around my waist, holding me in place as he sat up. "Li, I'm here. In India. Isn't that great?"

I laughed. "This was your relaxing getaway to do the revisions?"

"Yes. I figured I'd work best close to my editor."

"Seth, I . . ." I shook my head. "How did you even get my address?"

He laughed. "Come on. Your address wasn't the hard part. Trying to get a cab, now that's a different story." He kissed me again. "I've missed you, Li."

I had missed him too. The witty delight of Seth— the minute ways in which he described Kolkata Airport and the biography he had read on the plane, the familiarity of his presence—was bigger and more profound than I could have imagined. I wondered if I just missed home, except that it was unclear where I belonged anymore.

"So you're here to finish the revisions?" I asked again, trying to imagine how I might juggle the Lahiris with Seth.

"Yes," he said, sliding his head into the crook of my neck again.

"And you didn't think to maybe ask me if I thought it was a good idea?"

Seth looked stricken.

I shook my head, laughing, despite my incredulity, as I pushed him away, deciding to postpone any questions.

"Let's get you to a hot shower and bed," I said.

MALATI AUNTY, WHO ran the Mandeville Gardens guesthouse, had red lipstick on, her pale Punjabi cheeks pink with rouge, rings adorning each of her fingers, as she paged through her registration book, chiffon sari periodically sliding off one shoulder.

"Well, Lila, you've come just in time. I have one room left for the week, and of course as soon as Ginger told me this morning that you had a guest, I knew that I had to get it ready. Is your friend a vegetarian?" she asked as she examined Seth with admiration, the folds under her eyes creasing in delight.

Ginger, Malati's sixteen-year-old daughter, lounged on a bench nearby, taking indiscreet photos of Seth.

"I'm not," said Seth, with the same smile that was on the jacket of his novels.

Malati blinked, and an interested Ginger looked up from her phone for a few photography-free seconds.

"Thank you for having me," said Seth.

"Of course, of course," said Malati, sparkling. "It's not often we have such a charming guest from overseas. Lila, you can be sure he is in safe hands."

"Raju," she shouted. "Come take the shaheb's bags."

Seth turned to me. "I guess I'll see you later, Li. I'm in good hands."

I rolled my eyes. "I'll pick you up for dinner around eight."

Raju, the guesthouse manager, folded his hands in a namaste. "Welcome, sir. Can I take your suitcase?"

Ginger stood up. "I'll take you to your room," she said to Seth. "Would you mind taking a selfie with me first? It's something we ask all our guests to do."

WHEN I WENT to see if he wanted to go out to Kwality, where I had eaten all of my birthday dinners growing up, Seth would not wake up.

"I've tried waking him twice, Lila, and Ginger has texted him on iPhone as well as Facebook, but he didn't respond," said Malati as I came out of Seth's room.

"He's just jet-lagged," I said with a laugh. "He barely knew where he was when I shook him. Maybe you could leave a snack outside his door in case he wakes up hungry?"

"Raju," shouted Malati. "Prepare some chicken sandwiches with the good butter."

"So you're Facebook friends already?" I asked Ginger.

"He's fine," she said with a laconic shrug.

"That he is," I nodded as I left.

I FELT ODDLY desolate as I walked back home. I had looked forward to an evening discussing books and our friends. I missed my old life fiercely and longed for the solace of my apartment, the clamor of the office, Molly's indispensable presence in my life, and even the bar downstairs. I resolved to call Molly when I got home, and together we would decide what to make of Seth's bizarre arrival, as we had made sense of the most inexplicable things in our lives. Indian-Chinese takeout and a glass of wine would help.

But as I walked up to my father's building, my mother stood outside, her arms folded across her chest, a tote bag slung on one arm, her face concentrated on the street in front of her as if entering battle.

"Hi, Ma," I said from behind her.

"Lila," she said, surprised, turning around. "I thought you were coming from that side of the street. Weren't you at Mandeville Gardens?"

"I took a different route back. I see the information networks have been in overdrive today."

My mother did not look embarrassed. "I brought dinner," she said, holding up the tote. "Enough for three."

I sent a prayer of thanks to the god that had decided to let Seth sleep through the evening, as I imagined him accosted by my mother, whom I had barely ever mentioned, before I had a plan to explain his presence.

UPSTAIRS, MY MOTHER set down her tote impatiently. "Well, where is he? Your mystery guest. Malati said you told him dinner was at eight."

I narrowed my eyes at her. "I told him dinner was at eight, with me."

"I just thought he should know your mother. I mean, he's come all this way ... for you?"

"Ma, leave him alone. He's a writer. Here to finish revising his book. It's a job. Please don't spread any rumors."

She looked flustered at my explosion. "I just ... I just wanted to know ..."

"I know. He's not a boyfriend. Happy? Thanks for dinner."

"Lila, why are you being so rude? I just wanted to say hello to your friend. I was going to leave after I said hello and dropped off the food. Why are you acting like I have some sort of poisonous agenda?" She was tearful now. "You're always blaming me for everything, but have you ever thought that you judge me without giving me any benefit of the doubt?"

I let out a long breath. "I'm sorry. I just—it's been a long day. Thank you for making dinner. I'm going to have a glass of wine. Would you like one?"

She did not respond, belligerent tears rolling down her cheeks.

"And, please, join me for dinner."

At this she sniffed, brightening. "It's okay. What time will your friend get here? How will he find his own way? You should ask Ginger to walk him here, but tell her to not flirt with him. Do you at least have three dinner plates? Didn't you tell him eight o'clock?"

MY MOTHER'S DISAPPOINTMENT at having dinner alone with me was not mild.

"I don't see why we can't just go wake him up," she complained, spooning dal into a piece of roti. "A young man needs to eat, after all."

I drank a long glug of wine.

"Do doctors advise against drinking every day these days?" my mother asked.

"You sound like you definitely have an opinion on it."

"I wish you would be kinder, Lila. You remind me of Bela sometimes. God rest her soul, but such a sharp tongue, that woman—thank god Rinki is such a sweet child. But I think it came sideways, and you've inherited it." She sighed.

I drank more of the wine.

Rinki's mother, Bela, had been only ten years older than my mother, and my memory of her was at her beloved mill, where she would make evening snacks for me and Rinki when I went to visit. I felt a pang of loss. So much had happened without me to this family that made up half my history.

"What kind of cancer did she die of?"

My mother frowned. "Why do you want to talk about that?"

"I'm just curious. You can't be the one with all the questions all the time, you know."

"If you must know, it was . . ." She touched her chest.

"A heart attack? I thought it was cancer."

"No, no." She lowered her voice. "Breast cancer."

"What? Oh god. That's terrible."

"Yes. They say it was because she had such a sharp and unkind nature."

"That's the most ridiculous thing you could say," I said. "It could be genetic. Didn't Katyayani die of breast cancer too? What if Rinki has the gene too—or any of us?"

I felt anger at myself at never having asked Rinki about her mother's illness, but even if I had, in Kolkata, bodies were private and breasts were secret things, to be kept hidden.

"Shh. Quiet, Lila. Stop saying that word. There's no such thing in any of us."

I didn't know if she meant *gene* or *cancer*, but I was furious.

"You're actually blaming your aunt for creating her own cancer?"

"Why are you so angry all the time? It really isn't good for you." My mother looked worried as she made a little triangle of roti and placed a few pieces of fried okra into it. "Here, open your mouth."

I did, and she deposited the food into it, fiercely intimate without trying.

I swallowed. "Can I ask you something, Ma?"

"You ask too many questions."

"You cannot be serious," I exclaimed. "From the nosiest woman I've ever met."

She pursed her lips. "What is it?"

"When people get divorced now, is it different? You know . . . from when you had to."

Her eyes widened in shock. It wasn't just the unexpected quality of my question but that I was asking it at all. It was the most painful part of her, to my knowledge. To bring it up so easily was to yank off the skin covering her wounds. She pushed her plate away and took a drink of water.

"I think times have changed. They won't ruin a young girl's life or blame her entirely if the marriage falls apart. Will they still pick over the remains of the woman and the story like scavengers? Yes. To get divorced in Kolkata is still the biggest scandal you can choose. And like anything else, men fare better than women. Just look at the film stars."

"I hate that they blamed you, Ma."

"They didn't just blame me. I was a dirty secret, meant to be hidden away. The shamed divorcée on the fifth floor of the big house. Like Rapunzel." She laughed, bitter.

"I'm so sorry, Ma."

"For what?" She bristled. "I'm fine."

"But you're not. I can see. And it's okay to be angry. They were awful to you."

"Oh, Lila, stop with your American ways. I've had enough to eat—what about you?" She got up and carried both our plates into the kitchen. When she returned, she sat down and asked without preamble, "So there's nothing between you and this boy, then? What? It's my turn to ask questions."

"He's a writer on a deadline, and as his editor, I thought it was wise for me to read the last few chapters as he revised them," I said. "It's a big book for us."

"And it is usual, yes, for a writer to be so . . . close to an editor?" asked my mother, her face arranged into innocence. "To fly so many kilometers," she reflected.

I laughed. "We're actually very good friends. He needed a break and decided to come. It's the kind of thing Seth does."

"I see," said my mother.

"Don't add fuel to the fire, Ma."

She smiled, as if in knowledge of a secret. "I will actually have a glass of wine now."

WHEN I BROUGHT out the glass for her, she was staring at the piano, gleaming in the soft lamplight. She reached out to touch it.

"Here," I said, handing her the glass. "It's beautiful, isn't it?"

"Yes, I remember your father playing. And your grandmother. They were both fine players."

The words jarred me. Imagining my mother occupying my father's universe so intimately felt painful and out of whack with the order of things, the order that Iva and Avi and Robin occupied.

"Didn't the piano used to be black?"

"Yes," I said after a pause. "I . . . They painted it."

She looked up at me sharply. Then, nodding, she looked at the piano again. "You will inherit it, I'm sure. Mihir knows that it, this house, is part of your history. You can always paint it back to black."

IT IS A cruel joke played by genes that allows one's mother to know one's secrets. I had never permitted her anywhere near them, never divulged how deeply I hated the white gleam of the once-classic black Steinway that made music in my troubled childhood. I would rather die than reveal to my mother what powerful hurt I felt at Iva's alterations to the pieces of my history: a sofa here, a painting there, shiny ivory instead of the dull-black gleam that I had held so dear. I felt deep shame to be so seen by a woman who hated Iva—Iva, who had rescued me and taken me into her home, loving me and protecting me from the storm. But see me, my mother did, like a mirror held up on the sly to look at one's own reflection, one's own betraying blood.

That night, I dreamed of large breasts filled with milk and tumors. In my dream, my mother was telling me a story, describing in detail how beautiful a baby Lila was, down to the details of my skin and nose and dress and boots. And somewhere in my dream bones, I knew that she was lying—about the details, about it all.

Our bodies are fragile, dismantled easily by accidents and objects and illness; they remember hurt in swift, canny ways, alerting us, saving our lives. Our traumas are more mysterious, lodged in strange places, knee jerks of the brain, immovable and insurmountable unless we yield to them. My mother railed against her own wounds, hiding them away. I recognized this because I had inherited the same deceptions. We who were hurt had to believe that the relief of being in secrecy was greater than the freedom of pain.

19

I HAD LEFT Brooklyn at the beginning of August. Five weeks later, I could see the leaves begin to change color behind Gil on my screen. One morning, I awoke to an email from Aetos. Things were ready to "accelerate," an exciting segue into the volume business that was the future of Wyndham. From a tiny thumbprint to a great wave, he boomed into the email. What was the date of my return again, just so he could set the wheels in motion, for the strategy meetings we were going to have for the new year? More wellness and definitely more romance—did I know his wife was a novelist? *Love and light, Malcolm.* PS—I should feel free to fly first class on Pacific Air on my way back. He had just bought the airline (*Top secret!!!*) last week.

MY GRANDMOTHER HAD instructed me to bring Seth to the bridal shower that the Lahiris were having for Biddy. Delighted, he had accepted my reluctant invitation, despite my urging that should he want to stay home and revise the book that was due very soon, he was more than welcome to.

It was almost noon on the Sunday that the shower was supposed to take place, and I pushed my laptop away and rubbed my eyes. Molly and I kept missing each other's calls, time zones stretching between us. I wanted her advice on telling Adil that Seth was in Kolkata and the complexities of booking a return date when it felt like Kolkata had swallowed me whole. It was Molly, more than anyone, who knew instinctively what I needed to let go of or hold on to. Without her, I felt unmoored, worried that I was making choices to please the world.

I'm sorry I missed you, Mol, I texted, but it would have to wait until the sun rose in Molly's world.

SETH WAS DRESSED in a cream linen shirt that set off his green eyes, his dark hair brushed back in waves. He sat on the couch in the reception area of Malati's guesthouse, a magazine in one hand and a cold drink in the other, legs crossed in the elegant way of New York's male publishing class, as if on the cover of *Town & Country*, yet somehow at home here in Kolkata. I entered to Malati's laughter ringing through the room.

"Li," he said, sipping. "You must try this drink that Malati made me—it's the most incredible thing I've ever had."

"It's just a simple shikanji," said Malati, dimpling. "Lila, I must say your friend has such a good sense of humor."

It occurred to me that I knew Seth well as author, lover, and friend, but Seth charming the parents and aunts and the gossipy aunties of Bengal was a foreign experience.

Seth rose and handed me the drink. "Here. Try it, and you'll see what I mean."

I took a sip from the same straw that Seth's mouth had touched moments ago, regretting it even as the salty-sour-sweet liquid flooded my mouth and Seth leaned over to kiss my cheek. I stepped back as Seth looked confused and Malati vibrated with delight.

"It's great," I said, short, setting the drink down. "We should get going."

OUTSIDE, WE WALKED in silence in the September sun, the air humid on our skin. Vendors with baskets of seasonal vegetables—peas, amaranth, and methi leaves crowning small white cauliflower—shouted out their wares. People stared at Seth as we waited to cross the street. He was handsome, but most of all, he was white, and men and women alike seemed to be filled with admiration at this.

"You're upset," said Seth, quiet.

I shook my head. "No, it's just unusual. Walking with you . . . here."

"I love it. The city, the streets, you, being here. All of it."

I could see that he meant it.

"It's only been two days. Give it time—especially when you get pickpocketed," I said as we crossed the road.

A teenager whizzed by on a bike, inches from Seth's face.

"Hello, sir," screamed the blissed-out boy as he disappeared into the stream of cars, a cow, rickshaws, autos, and trucks.

"Good god, he's going in the opposite direction from traffic," said Seth.

"That's Chintan, my mother's friend's son. He's been flying through these streets since he was four."

As we approached the Lahiri house, I heard Seth gasp under his breath. The house, freshly painted, gleamed in the sun, an imposing aberration in the apartment building and town-house landscape of Ballygunge Place, five stories of gold and orange, the carved pillars and green Roman windows dazzling, despite construction ladders and scaffolding like vines all over it. I felt a stab of pride.

"Jesus, what is that, a consulate or something?"

"That would be the house my grandfather left to me."

Seth began to laugh. "Are you a princess, Li? Princess Lila? Is that what I should call you?"

"More like the black sheep come to cause trouble." I tugged on him before we could go in. "Seth, listen. I . . . You can't kiss me like that, in front of them."

"I didn't," he said.

I looked down at my shoes, dusty from walking.

"Oh, you mean your cheek."

"Yes. My cheek. The touching. The inside jokes. They're not stupid—they'll be able to tell."

"Tell what?" he asked with a gleam.

"Seth," I said, shaking my head. "This isn't Brooklyn. I . . . The family . . . I don't want them to think we're something we're not."

"What did you say I was doing here?"

"Revising your book. The truth."

He rubbed his neck, stretching it out. After a pause, he nodded. "I'll be careful."

"They . . . My mom . . . There's no boundaries or privacy," I said, my pitch rising. "They're not going to get that we're casual. Things are different here. They don't know what that is."

He nodded again, silent.

"I'm sorry if this is weird."

"I'm the one who landed here without so much as a text as warning. For some crazy reason, I thought you might be happy to have a familiar face from Brooklyn."

"I am. Seth, I'm ridiculously pleased to see you." It was the truth. Even though I still could not imagine what I would say about him to Adil or my mother or anybody else, I was happy to have him as I fought unknown ghosts and battles. "And it's going to be great for the book," I added. I did not know this for sure, only that proximity might inspire him, but I had the great desire to say it.

Seth smiled. "Do I get to see the inside of your castle, or what?"

WHEN THE BRITISH left India, they left behind a permanent taste for whiteness, combined with a simultaneous revulsion. This was still pronounced in Kolkata, but especially in the Lahiri household, whose ancestors had been the first results of the British desire to mold men who drank tea, played cricket, spoke English, were often Oxford-educated, and, despite their brown skin, embodied the essence of Blighty. In Mumbai and Bangalore, however, globalization was acute (Zara! Starbucks! Tabloids!), and expatriates filled the entertainment industry and financial markets, while tourists lounged on the beaches of Goa in bikinis. Whiteness, more ordinary in these cities, was not held in the same exotic esteem (though still in esteem).

In the capital city of Delhi, the government had proclaimed Hinduism to be superior to all other religions (especially Islam, but also Christianity and Sikhism). But for all that, a perpetual colonial hangover lurked in the country, and made itself clear in, say, Agra, where if you were white, you could get in the front of the line to see the Taj Mahal, ahead of the fifteen hundred Indians behind you, but you had to pay approximately thirteen times the Indian price, and they would try their best to grab your butt (regardless of color) on the way out.

Seth might have been a movie star, so special was the treatment extended to him. In the periphery of his dazzle, I, too, had chairs pulled up for me at the house, a steady stream of tea and champagne proffered, and the usual gruffness of the family replaced with sparkling wit and manner.

Despite it being in Biddy's honor, Seth was the focus of the lunch. He went from delight to bewilderment to discomfort quickly, especially when my grandmother served him the largest piece of fish in the curry and asked Bari to go out to buy more mineral water.

"And what do you do, Seth?" asked my mother, a lilt of England in her words, rounding her *o*'s as she did when on the phone with foreign professors from her university.

"I'm a writer," he said.

My mother raised her eyebrows as if I had never said this to her. "Oh, that's very interesting. Anything I might have read?"

Seth swallowed. "A book . . . A novel called *Reminders*."

My grandmother frowned. "A novelist," she repeated.

Biddy raised her cell phone. "Is your last name Schwartz? Look, Geeta Kaki, his book is going to be a TV show. Maybe we'll see it on Star TV."

"A TV show. How wonderful," said Gina.

Rinki let out a small laugh from across the table. I frowned at her.

"Is there money in TV?" asked Hari from the other end of the table.

"Hari!" said Mishti.

"What? I'm just asking if he made any money from it. Here, writers are paupers, Mister Schwartz Babu."

"Correct," said my grandmother.

"It is a wonderful thing to have written an entire novel," said Rana dreamily. "You must tell me how you did it."

"He's finishing his second one now," I said with pride.

My grandmother looked at me, sharp, as the others clamored over Seth. "Lila, help me bring out dessert, please," she said.

Seth looked stricken.

"I'll be back," I said to him.

On my way to the kitchen, I stopped at the far end of the table to whisper in Rinki's ear. "Rescue him, please."

I FOLLOWED GEETA into her bedroom; we both knew she did not suddenly want to be involved in duties long delegated to the maids. With a quick burn of shame, I remembered the last time I had been in it.

"Sit, Lila," she said, patting the bed as she went to her wardrobe.

The carved panels opened into shelves that had held silks and cottons for generations of Lahiri women. Taking the large ring of keys around her waist, she slid the smallest key into a drawer built into the bottom shelf. From it, she took a velvet pouch and returned to sit next to me.

"I wanted you to have this," she said.

I pulled at the little gold rope around the pouch, and immediately a large ring slid into my lap. I picked it up, the ruby in the center catching the light, the thick gold band heavy in my palm.

"It's your grandfather's wedding ring. He would have wanted you to have it."

I felt a wave of laughter at the idea of Seth walking around Brooklyn with a large ruby-studded gold ring on his finger.

"We had a long and, for the most part, happy marriage," said my grandmother. "I once gave this ring to Maya for your father, and when they . . . did that divorce . . . he returned it. I want you to give it to the man you choose."

"But, Mummy . . ."

She shook her head. "I know it's an old-fashioned ring. You can do whatever you like with it. Melt it down, make it yours. Maybe make two rings with it. Whatever it is, I want you to share it with someone you think will be good to you."

I found myself blinking back tears. "Mummy, Seth is just my friend."

To this, my grandmother picked up the ring and held it in her palm, turning it over. "Your wheels are spinning too fast, Lila. I don't like it."

I felt an indescribable sorrow, like she was telling me some large and incomprehensible truth.

"I just don't want to see you make the same mistakes your mother has. Don't throw love away. It's so hard to find."

She began to cry softly. I held her in my arms. The ring dropped onto the bed.

"Careful," she said into my collarbone. "It'll roll away."

I put a palm over the ring, catching the cool metal midmotion.

"Bari said you were looking for something in my room the other day."

I stiffened. She did not pull away from me.

"Just an earring I was missing."

She nodded into my shoulder. "I'll tell her to look for it when she sweeps the floor tomorrow."

Music and laughter floated up from downstairs.

"Seth is probably in a panic," I said. "I should go."

"You know we love you dearly, Lila." She looked up at me. "You do know that, don't you?"

"Yes," I said.

Whatever secrets my grandmother had, whatever plots the Lahiris were orchestrating, what I did know was that they loved me. I felt a gripping desire to tell her the truth of what I had been doing in her bedroom.

"Can't you marry a nice Bengali boy?" she asked. "Someone like Malati's nephew Sopan maybe? Sopan Guhathakurta. I mean, think of how beautiful your wedding would be." After a pause, she asked, hopeful, "Should I just float the subject to Sopan's mother, just to see what he says?"

I began to laugh. "What has poor Sopan ever done to you, Mummy? You don't want to saddle him with me."

"Nonsense," she said, smoothing out her sari. "Nice girl like you, smart— if you gain some weight, you're a catch. You have too many opinions, but marriage will cure you of fighting every battle. Marriage is about winning the war." She stood up. "Can I ask you something, Lila Ma?"

"What is it?" I asked, wary.

"Is it . . ." She lowered her voice. "Is it true that white people don't wash their bottoms?" She looked horrified, as if in preparation for what I might confirm.

"Really, Mummy," I said. "They use toilet paper. It's perfectly hygienic. I"—I faltered, despite myself—"use it myself. It's very . . . clean."

My grandmother's eyes closed as she turned to leave the room, the familiar words of a Hindu prayer under her breath.

AFTER LUNCH, THERE was garland making for the wedding, for which Rinki had enlisted Seth, thereby sparing him from more interrogation. Then Biddy asked him to assist her in making a playlist for the reception. Finally, as the sun began to dip and all the sweets had been eaten, the Lahiris began to look tired.

"This is our chance," I said to Seth.

"I'm having a good time," he said, but he got to his feet immediately, brushing petals off his slacks.

"Put on your shoes," I whispered. "We'll never leave if you start saying goodbyes. One of them will ask us to stay for dinner, and then it's over."

Seth slid on his shoes. "An Irish goodbye," he whispered, too close, into my ear.

As we snuck out, the evening sky providing dim cover, I felt my mother's eyes bore into me—I did not have to turn around to know that she was watching us leave.

SETH CAME BACK with me to my father's apartment, neither of us questioning that he would. It felt natural, and even Ram Bhai nodded at us as we went upstairs. I switched on the lights and made Seth a cup of coffee.

Seth breathed in the liquid as he held the cup in both hands. "I've missed coffee. I realize now that Indians only drink tea. I just thought that was a Lila thing."

"It's most Indians. The South drinks a lot of really good coffee."

"This is a beautiful apartment. Iva's done a great job."

I felt a pang slice through me. "It was always beautiful," I said. "But, yeah, Iva's really fixed it up. When I was growing up, you had to shower in six and a half minutes or the hot water would turn to ice."

Seth looked at me. "You seem at home here. In this apartment, I mean."

I laughed. "And not in the Lahiri house?"

"No. You're at home there too. But it's different. Less . . . easy. Here, you're the Lila I know." Seth had the transparency of a boy who had known love and simplicity as he grew up.

It was true, in the apartment, I could be the Lila I had adopted for adulthood. In the territory of the Lahiris, love and hate were intense, complex beasts that you had to nurture and ride and buckle under, feeling everything under the sun, packed together like sardines on the New York L train, never escaping, with the promise of inevitable pain or togetherness beckoning at every turn.

I knew the look in his eye. Our chemistry had never been any one thing when we were alone—business colleagues to friends to lovers in seconds—everything was easy, the opposite of the Lahiris and Adil and my mother and all that was hard and impossible to let go.

"Seth, what are you doing here?" I whispered, our bodies suddenly electric in their nearness.

"I told you," he murmured into my neck, lifting me to my feet, his fingers in my hair, one palm on my buttock, securing me to him.

"Seth," I murmured. Despite myself, I asked again. "What are you doing here?"

He was disoriented with desire, my palm still behind his neck, his body reacting to mine. He took in a breath, dragging his palm through my hair, his arm still holding us conjoined.

"I wanted to make sure you were okay," he said. "You can call me a New Yorker or whatever, but it seemed crazy to me that you should want to go millions of miles away and do this crazy thing in a place you haven't been to since you were a teenager." He let go of me and took a step back. "I couldn't just let you do it alone."

After a pause, Seth sat down on the couch as I stood in the center of my father's living room, an unfamiliar current between us. "I want more," he said. "This is my grand gesture." He held out his palms. "In Brooklyn, you would have sent me home. We're a long way from home here, Li."

We stayed like that, in silence, neither knowing what to do. Finally, I sat on the couch, next to him. "Seth, I . . . I've met someone."

He regarded me, uncomprehending. "What are you talking about?"

I said nothing.

"When? You left so quickly, and you called me that week before you left. I would have heard—"

"Not in Brooklyn. Here."

Seth looked away in disbelief. "You've been here five weeks," he said, dismissive.

"He's someone I used to know," I said.

"Used to date?" Seth asked, quieter now.

I nodded.

He laughed. "Let me guess, your one true love."

I shook my head. "I don't know about any of that. He was the first boy I had ever felt that way about, and he knew . . . he helped me through a lot of things when we were kids."

Seth put his face in his hands, weary.

"I'm sorry. I didn't know," I said.

"But you did know, Lila. You've always known how I felt. You always know the things you tell yourself you don't know. Life is much easier for you that way." He stood up. "Would have been nice if you'd said something on the phone." His voice was flat now, the Seth who could cut you to the quick with words. Almost immediately, he shook his head, remorseful. "I didn't mean any of that."

I leaned my head against the edge of the sofa. "Yes, you did."

I held out my hand to him. He took it and sat back down on the couch, turning over my cold palm in his smooth hands, the way astrologers did when my grandmother would invite them home to tell her how many sons or degrees I might have.

"Is it a done deal?" he asked, his thumb stroking the center of my palm. "This guy and you," he said. "Like an Indian wedding I have to be prepared for?"

"It's . . . it's its own thing."

Seth looked at me with interest. "Complicated?"

"I don't want to lead you on. And the timing of . . . this past relationship, and then you turning up here while I figure things out with my mother and the house, feels like everything all at once."

"Okay," he said, tucking a strand of his hair behind his ear, in his careful, deliberate way.

"Okay?" I asked slowly.

Seth shrugged. "Look, something's going on with this guy you've rekindled things with. But you and I—we have a history too. You can't just send me packing. Well, you can. But I'm asking that you don't. Let me finish the revisions here—you know you're the best person to help me cross the finish line. And if by then, you and this guy become . . . a thing—"

"We are a thing."

"A bigger thing."

Seth waited for me to object.

When I did not, he continued. "If you and this guy become a bigger thing and he decides to move back with you to Brooklyn and live happily ever after, I'm happy to take a hike. No harm, no foul. Okay?" He held up his hands, like a mediator at a high school table. "Plus, I do have to finish the book—both our careers are riding on it, as I understand from Gil."

I rubbed my temples, feeling a throb behind them. "You're insane. This is what writers practice. Insanity."

"Yes, I see that now." Seth pulled me to him and kissed me. "You never know, Lila. You never know how insane people can be."

20

THE MONTH OF September usually saw the monsoon rains slowing, making way for sunny October, when Bengalis could finally find the first pomegranates and oranges in the markets and begin shopping for new clothes for the festive Durga Pujo season. But this September was a confusing mix of dropping temperatures, along with thunderstorms that left an oppressive humidity in their wake, transforming the hours after sunset into ice-cold nights. Old homes like the Lahiri mansion, made of stone and cement, became unbearably cold. My grandmother suffered new chills and aches, and I bought her both an air conditioner and a heater. After protesting at the evils of modernization, she admitted that the sun was not as reliable as it had always been, that the world was changing too quickly for her knees, and, to my relief, she began to turn on the heat at night.

My emotions felt rogue, like the weather. Fear lurked everywhere: Fear that Adil would leave me (Could I be left? Did you have to have something in order to lose it?). Fear that Seth would abandon our friendship or his book when he found out about Adil. Fear that when Adil found out about Seth, he would see me differently. Fear of my dreams in which monsters roamed the streets with me in daylight. And yet I was also exhilarated by the maelstrom of feelings that now suffused me, when once my days had been even-tempered, with easy rationale.

ONE EARLY MORNING, I woke up with a start. Adil, dressed for work, was on the side of my bed, just as he often had before Seth had arrived four days ago. "Jesus, Adil," I said, my hand on my chest.

"Sorry," he said, palms raised. He looked confused. "Sorry. I wanted to talk. We haven't talked . . . in a few days."

My breathing slowed back to normal. I wondered distractedly what I might I have been dreaming of, remembering that I had been afraid.

"You're scared," he said. "I didn't mean—"

"No, it's fine. I just wasn't expecting you."

"Lila, what's changed?"

I said nothing.

"You haven't replied to texts, or if you have, you've barely said anything."

I nodded. "I'm sorry. So much has been going on."

Adil looked at me as only he could, taking my hand. "I've missed you."

"I have too," I said, looking at our hands.

After a pause, he said gently, unbearably slowly, "Malati has been saying you have a boyfriend in town and that he's very handsome." Adil, too, examined the union of our hands as he said this. "My mother told me," he added.

I nodded, imagining how he had felt when beloved Janani Aunty said, *I hear Lila has a white boy courting her at Malati's.*

"He's not my boyfriend," I said.

Adil looked up, relief in his eyes.

I shook my head. "But we are not just friends."

I had intended to say that we were just friends, but somehow in the complexities of grand gestures and first loves, all I could be was truthful with the married man who sat in front of me, who I might be with if we could be transported back in time into a universe that permitted us to become again what we had once been.

"He's one of my writers," I said. "I'm working on his second book. We're close to deadline, and he thought it would be a good idea to come here."

"To work on his book?" asked Adil.

"Yes. And he was worried about me. We're friends. And on occasion . . . we have had sex." I faltered at this.

Adil released my hand. "And so he is here," he said, "to work on his book and be friends and have sex with you."

"He wants more. It turns out he has for a while."

With a very slight nod, Adil said, "You don't take a plane halfway around the world to finish a book or have a little sex."

I desperately wanted some assurance that he wasn't done with us, but I said nothing. The sun started to rise, and soft light framed his jaw as Adil stared out the window. It reminded me of his teenage self thinking through complex physics equations.

We heard the clanging of the gates—Ram Bhai was ready to begin his day. The milkman's cycle bell rang. Someone's car purred out of the driveway—likely the upstairs neighbor's daughter who was a flight attendant for Air India. Adil turned to me, reading what was plain on my face—I could not have hidden how I felt about him if I had tried. We sat like that, locked in things that we could not change.

"Lila," he whispered, shaking his head, his body toward me. His head sank into my shoulder, both of us sinking back into the bed.

I held on to him, rocking us back and forth.

"Your hair," he murmured, breathing in.

My hair had once again reverted to the tendrils and volume of tropical humidity, free from the keratin shine that my Brooklyn salon had locked it into for years.

"I don't know what I am supposed to do," he whispered.

"What do you want to do?"

He took in a breath. "Don't make it that simple."

"I know. I just want to know, for you and me. I'm not asking you for anything."

He sat up, miserable. "I can't just go to New York, can I? Leave my life behind. I'm not . . . twenty."

I stilled. "I didn't ask you to."

"I know you didn't. But for a minute, put yourself in my shoes."

"Adil, I'm not asking anything of you. Stop talking as if I am."

"Do you have feelings . . . for this man?"

"What does it matter?"

He got off the bed. "I don't understand how you can think it's irrelevant that you have a man in your life, just when—"

"Just when what?"

"My wife has been in my life, in my family, for ten years." His shoulders sagged.

"I don't think you get to shame me for you being married."

He shook his head. "No. I'm not ashamed of us."

I looked at his back, with its familiar bony shoulder blades, the clench of his muscle, his thin, graceful arms crossed over his chest, as he studied the street below. He was built like a poet or a teenager who did not get out much, lovely to look at, to be around.

"You love her," I said.

He did not need to agree. He turned around. "You do not love him?"

"Who? Seth?" I paused. "I've never considered it."

He nodded. "I'm so sorry, Lila. I've dragged you into my mess."

My vision blurred. "Don't say that," I whispered.

At some point, he must have left, because then I was alone, unable to emerge from the fog of the past.

THE NEXT DAY, I made lists. I checked on Seth to make sure he was in a routine. I knew that I needed to reply to Aetos, but instead I sent Gil an email outlining all the progress I had made, and copied Aetos on it. I called Palekar, and we went over the impending visit to my grandfather's lawyer's office. I checked on Das, to see when the elevator's sliding door, the final piece of its completion, might be installed. Furiously, I organized my desk, arranging manuscripts, notepads, and pens in neat rows. I vacuumed, even though Iva had arranged for a maid to clean the apartment each day at three. The one material thing I could not gain control over was my hair. No matter how much conditioner I put in it or how straight I blew it dry, it refused to lie flat.

In the evening, I was to accompany my mother to a soirée. There was no getting out of it—she had called to confirm a week in advance, a day in advance, and the morning of. It was a gathering of her university colleagues and a chance for her to show me off to her peers and friends. When

I was younger, my mother would do this right after an excellent report card or an extracurricular award or, once, after my baby weight had slid off me.

In my tenth-grade exams, my percentile average had been ninety-three. A group of her mom friends had organized a celebration for their children, all of whom had done well. She had worn a new sari and bought me a hip silk skirt for the party. Just as we were leaving, she had turned to me and said, "Let's tell them it was ninety-five. Just to round it off." I had nodded immediately, knowing that this version of motherhood and daughterhood would bring her happiness unlike anything else. I remembered the evening as one of the happiest I had ever spent with my mother.

"YOU LOOK TIRED," she said as she met me outside the Lahiri house. She was radiant, in a turquoise silk sari and a black full-sleeve blouse, my grandmother's diamonds in her ears, her hair curling around her shoulders, the style magnificent on her. Her beauty, as always, took me aback when I was not blind to it.

"Taxi!"

The black-and-yellow Ambassador meandering down the street paused in front of us. My mother ushered me in and climbed in after me, tucking the folds of her sari bottom into the car.

"God, Lila. Look at the shadows under your eyes. A young girl like you. Here, take my compact." She reached into her purse.

I accepted it and patted the powder into the sponge, then smoothed it under my eyes.

"To the left," she instructed. "Now rub it in. You should go to bed earlier. Is it stress over the restructure, with Phenom taking over?"

I felt a jab of pleasure that she had enough interest to invest in the details of my life. "Yes," I nodded. "Sometimes I think I might get lost in their vastness."

"Well, they're smart to hold on to you," said my mother, taking her compact back, satisfied. "Your face looks nice now."

"Thank you."

"You should smile more. If you go around with that frown, you'll get wrinkles before you're forty."

PARTIES WITH MY mother were confusing on many counts. She seemed to morph into a butterfly, monarch wings gliding through a room. I found myself drawn under her spell—her laughter ringing through the crowd as she held court, her eyes brighter than I thought normal, her whole being vibrating with a glamorous happiness. She told little anecdotes that men and women laughed at, and exchanged serious conversations with heads of departments. I could see a young male professor tilt his head toward her as she discussed the merits of his teaching style.

"Marvin Sir, you must meet my daughter," my mother said. "She's from America. Lila, come here."

I crossed over the room, from where she knew I had been watching her, to the balcony. Marvin Sir, possibly a decade older than me, nodded.

"Hello, Lila. I've heard so much about you from your mother."

My mother laughed at the look on my face, cruel. "She does not like it when I introduce her like that," she said. "But it's true, she is from America."

"My dear Lila," exclaimed Padma Mishra, striding up to us, a silver cigarette holder in one of her hands, between two fingers. "All grown up. Time to find a nice boy."

"Well, good luck to you, Padma," my mother said. "She certainly isn't going to entertain any boy I present to her. Daughters do not like to listen to their mothers."

Padma winked at Marvin, as if he, too, were in on this secret where my mother was an ordinary mother whose cautionary wisdom went unheeded by an ordinary daughter. "For example, our dear Marvin here," said Padma.

She nodded at Marvin, as if urging him to participate.

Devoted Marvin smiled at my mother.

"Dear Marvin, a PhD doctorate and on tenure track. Now there's a good boy," said my goddess mother.

Behind her, Lali Mukhopadhay joined our little circle.

"Now, Maya, are you trying to marry Lila off to Marvin again?" said Lali, bursting into peals of giggles.

"I think she might be trying to exchange him in place of me, for a son," I said.

Padma let out her throaty guffaw. "Funny girl. Your mother wouldn't exchange you for a million bucks. She cannot stop talking about you, your job, your life. You are her world."

I wondered if it had occurred to my mother that she had been talking about me to these people for the fourteen months that she had not spoken a word to me before I arrived in India, or the many periods in our lives that had passed in silences she had imposed on us. But perhaps the daughter Lila of her conversations was softer and kinder, at once erudite and sparkling and pretty, as my mother was in this alternate existence.

"Padma, I wish you would give up that dirty habit. You're stinking up my clothes," said my mother.

"Oh, come on, Maya, don't get your panties in a twist," said Padma, rolling her eyes, to my delight.

Familiar rage swept across my mother's face, even as she pressed her lips together, smiling tightly. "Really, Padma. Sometimes that mouth of yours belongs in the gutter."

"Now, Lila, tell me all about your fancy life in New York," said Lali, linking her arm around mine. "Your mother is always telling us how little you sleep."

"It keeps me busy," I smiled.

"What does it take to get published in America?" inquired Marvin politely.

"I'm in the fiction division, so I mainly look for stories that feel like they haven't been told," I said. "Are you a writer?"

Marvin looked shy. "Not really. I've written a few short stories here and there."

"Everyone's got a book in them in this room, Lila," said Lali. "You've got to be careful, trapped in a room of professors. What's that old saying—those who don't write teach?"

"Or edit," said my mother.

No one said anything for a few moments; even Padma smoked quietly.

"What?" My mother shrugged. "Lila was a wonderful writer as a child. I'm just saying she should write one of those books she stacks her shelves with."

"Do you like to write, Lila?" asked Marvin.

"I've considered it," I said. "But I really like bringing other people's books to life."

Lali nodded. "Yes, there's a beauty to that."

"Dinner is served," called out Priya Ravi, the dean of the university, clapping her hands in the center of her living room.

"We better go in before Dean Dinner Party gives us a mouthful for being late," said Padma.

My mother snickered, sweet again at the emergence of a separate villain. It was a cool night, and on the balcony I shivered in the thin cotton dress I was wearing.

"Are you cold, darling?" she asked, putting an arm around me.

"I'll be fine once we go inside," I said, the small, warm happiness I felt when she touched me in that way spreading through my stomach, even though I had been wounded in precisely that spot moments ago.

THE LARGE DINING room was fitted with a long wooden table, a centerpiece of marigolds in the middle, a crystal chandelier suspended overhead. My mother and I sat between Dean Ravi's husband and a professor of classics, Barun Thakur. As we waited to be served dinner, Professor Thakur and my mother argued about the real reasons why the right-wing Hindu party might come to power in Bengal.

"A lazy urban class of nonvoting millennials," said my mother. "They think that being apolitical is fashionable."

"Nonsense. It is because the poor people of Bengal are fed up with the left's elitist ways."

Dean Ravi's husband, like me, a silent bystander to the spectacle of the room, leaned closer to me. "Are you the new historian?"

"No, I'm not at the university," I said. "My mother—she's a professor. Maya De." I tilted my head to my left, where my mother was growing more heated by the minute.

"Of course. I should have seen the resemblance. I watched her give a public lecture once, on literatures born of colonization—she's a brilliant woman. You look like her."

"Actually, I look like my father. I'm wearing my hair curly these days, so it just feels like I look like her."

"You must be very proud of her."

As servers appeared out of nowhere in livery, serving up cream of mushroom soup and whitefish meunière, Dean Ravi raised her glass of champagne.

"Thank you all for coming tonight. I know the Puja break is near and we are all gearing up for the holiday, but I cannot tell you how happy it makes me to have you all under one roof."

"She's going to talk about London in just a second," said my mother under her breath.

"As I prepare to leave for the United Kingdom this week, I must reflect on the academic term that has passed, one in which all of you have contributed only excellence."

I stifled laughter, basking in our inside joke, as my mother squeezed my elbow. She tucked a wild curl behind my ear.

"Let's get you a haircut on Monday."

"What's wrong with my hair?"

"Lila, stop snapping at me. I didn't say anything was wrong with it. I just suggested a stylist. She's very good."

ON THE WAY home, my mother leaned back in the cab, fanning the cold night air over her face with one of the paperbacks she always kept in her bag.

"Red wine makes me so warm," she said.

My mother put a hand over mine.

"You look sad," she said.

I looked out the window at Ripon Street and Entally speeding by, sweetshops and biriyani houses closing for the night.

"I miss home," I said. I felt something ball up in my throat. "My friend Molly—she and I would talk every day, figure out work and life together. It's hard being so far apart from her—she was, is, like my family."

I fought back tears. In India, my body seemed to fill constantly with tears and anger at little things, leaving behind the even-keeled existence of being Lila De on another continent.

"Sometimes, we see people as we want them to be," said my mother. "Who they really are is another matter altogether. Take, for instance, Gina. She's a colleague, but she's Rana's wife and my family too. She was supposed to be there tonight. But just to prove a point and make me look bad to the dean— she knows I'm up for tenure—she skipped the dinner. 'Oh, I have a fever,' she said. All lies. I know when it's a load of hot gas," said my mother angrily. "She knows it reflects badly on me."

In a way, I was glad that she had forgotten about me. "Molly's not like that," I said. "And for what it's worth, Gina said she had a cold yesterday."

My mother's lips thinned and twisted at this disregard of her theory.

"Let it go, Ma."

"No need to give me advice," she snapped. "And Lila?"

"Yes, Ma." I leaned back, exhausted.

"*We* are your family."

It was in the vein of a demand, a hostile conquistador staking a claim, planting a flag, but it gave me no small measure of happiness.

21

EXCEPT FOR THE elevator, construction was complete on the house. Mr. Das had done such an excellent job that five separate members of the family had invited him to the wedding. He had restored the decaying mansion to some former glory, even throwing in two Maharaja-style glass chandeliers at half price—a gift for Biddy, who Das viewed as somewhat of a celebrity client, after her M*nsion R*novation videos had starred him in a lead role. As Das pulled the cord of one chandelier, the courtyard filled with light.

The elevator was a different story; it had been plagued by the building's lack of infrastructure, the erratic monsoon, old wiring, and hazardous roofing, resulting in three aborted attempts to launch. Still, we lived in hope, viewing it as the symbol of a new era for the house.

One night, on my way to the Secret Sixth, I passed by my mother's studio, taking care to be noiseless, in the hope that she would not hear me. As I neared the bottom of the Sixth's winding staircase, I realized that Gina and Rana were sitting on the bottom rungs, talking softly, about me.

"Tejen Da was right," said Rana as I stilled. "We needed a younger person, someone with energy and dreams to help with the house."

"He knew that you and I would have sold it and left," said Gina.

Rana sighed. "We needed fresh eyes to see it."

"You know it's not just that," said Gina, lowering her voice to a sharp whisper. "He would have made our lives hell if we became the owners. With her, Hari feels in charge. Lila's no fool. She won't threaten monsters—the girl has had a lifetime of handling them."

Rana sighed again, a long, soft breath. After a pause, in which I panicked that they might have sensed my presence, he said, "Is there any moon like the moon in Bengal? Shelley would have written a thousand more poems had he witnessed it."

"Not all of us are lucky enough to pine after the moon, Rana," said Gina. "Let's go downstairs—Bari's laid out dinner, and I have fourteen papers to grade, likely filled with nonsense about moons."

THE BROTHERS LAHIRI argued ceaselessly over guest lists, lighting, seating plans. It always ended with Hari saying something so vicious to his twin (in his silver voice, so musical, usually accompanied by laughter, that I had to replay to understand the barb) that it would shrink Rana into silence.

No member of the house, despite having lived with Hari for decades, was used to his sporadic rage. It was mercurial, like my mother's, but seemed especially to arise if Rana was gaining ground. Hari would deliver a one-two into Rana's gut—mocking his brother's teeth or lack of income, his wife's masculine ability to earn, his good-for-nothing communist son—insults so petty that they might have been laughable coming from anyone else but that were certain poison, as if a physical blow, from Hari to Rana. Rana would then sulk for hours, until Hari, slinging an arm around his brother, would affectionately bring him back into the fold, begging his forgiveness.

But the brothers took real pleasure in planning Biddy's wedding, almost delirious to finally be regarded as men of the house by vendors and visitors alike.

ON ONE OF these afternoons, I was to help with final choices on catering and floral issues. Mishti, Rinki, and Biddy had invited me to sit on mats in the courtyard at teatime and eat jhalmuri, from the street seller on the corner of Ballygunge Station. He had been mixing mustard oil, cilantro, salty nuts, chopped onions, and green chilies into seasoned puffed rice since he was a boy. The snack made tears stream from my eyes as I ate, but it was like coming alive, all of my senses on fire.

"Let's go with marigolds for the entrance—they're traditional," said Rinki.

Bari handed me a cup of tea. "Oh, they'll match Biddy Didi's golden sari perfectly," she said.

"I don't want the house to look like a temple. How about something cute, like lilies?" asked Biddy.

"But lilies are white," said Bari, horrified.

"Lilies are for funerals, Biddy," snapped Mishti. "Sorry," she said after a pause. "I just want it to be perfect. Most people have three, four, five children, I have just the one."

"Maybe I'll have three, four, five weddings to make up for it," said Biddy.

"Biddy!" said Rinki.

"How about the tiny pink roses that the flower market has right now?" I asked, laughing.

The women looked surprised.

"I love that," said Biddy. "Those things are so pretty and vintage-y. That's perfect. We should get, like, a million of them. Here, Bari Didi, look—these are what they look like."

Biddy, as usual, had found an exact match on the internet in under a minute and she lifted the phone for Bari to see.

"Beautiful," said Bari, admiring. "We could do bunches of the roses everywhere, on every floor, and even have them in the malas."

"Tea roses," said Biddy. "Boom. That's what they're called."

Mishti looked at me, awkward, then shot a look at Biddy. "Well, they're expensive. And we've already spent so much. I don't know, Lila—what do you think? I don't want to dip into the trust too much this year. We have so many years in front of us, and the interest is all gone."

Biddy looked at her mother. "What do you mean it's all gone? I thought Baba was managing the finances while Tejen Kaka was sick. Did we spend it all on the renovations?" She looked at me, accusing.

"No. It's not Lila's fault. The only thing she's touched is this year's fund," said Mishti. "Look, Biddy, we've never worried you with these matters—"

"I'm not a child, Ma," exploded Biddy. "You think I am. You think I don't see things, that I never know what's going on." She stood up, breathing hard.

In that moment, I recognized where B2D came from.

Bari gathered up the cups on the floor. "I'll go make more tea," she said, quickly leaving the room.

"Biddy," I said. "The house is fine. If you want, come with me to Palekar's office next week, and you can take a look at where we are. You should know anyway." I turned to Mishti. "Mishti Kaki, Biddy's wedding isn't eating into anything—we've planned for it. And if the roses are a little more than we thought, don't worry about it. I was wondering what I could give Biddy, and this would be a nice present from me. It would have no impact on the trust."

Biddy looked uncertain.

"We're not your charity case, Lila," said Mishti, cold. She began to put the marigolds back in the basket. "I really appreciate all the work you've put into the house, but let's be clear: the family would have been fine, one way or the other."

I faltered. "I didn't mean—"

"Yes, you did. You walk around here thinking you're better than the rest of us, looking at how weak and stupid we must seem, and you think, 'That's fine. I'll just use my dollars to pay for the silly little flowers they can't afford.'"

"Ma," said Biddy softly.

"Quiet," hissed Mishti.

I stared at her. Mishti, who never had an unkind word for anyone, inflamed with hate for me.

"We can take care of our daughter's wedding, Lila," she spat out. "You don't need to be the hero every day."

"Ma, you're bleeding," said Biddy with a cry.

Bari rushed in. Biddy screamed again, the sound ringing in my ears.

"What the hell is going on down there?" shouted Hari from the third-floor balcony. My grandmother appeared next to him.

"Biddy, darling, what's wrong?" she called out.

Mishti's mouth seemed overflowing, as if her anger for me had turned to blood. It soaked the ends of Bari's sari as she tried to stop the bleeding.

"What is going on?" shouted Hari again from above.

Biddy looked at him, her eyes bitter. "Call Dr. Sanyal," she screamed at her father. *Do you hear me? Call the doctor.*

As Hari's eyes bulged, his face white, and my grandmother began to pray loudly, two of Mishti's teeth fell to the floor, landing with a quiet double tinkle, then rolling across the uneven stone floor, absurd in their minute contrast to the pandemonium around me.

EVERY FAMILY MEMBER had some sort of role to play in taking care of Mishti, and I felt useless in the way an overstaying guest might. At one point, I found Dettol and a mop in Bari's kitchen and cleaned up some of the blood. It was the kind of blood you imagined at a crime scene, the kind a reporter photographed for a story or an investigation. I took out my phone and took a picture, looking up to see if anyone had seen me. Only Ami, equally alone, stared at me from behind a pillar on the second floor. She had an alphabet book with her.

"'A' for 'apple,'" she said to me under her breath, staring at the blood.

My mother was still at work, and I imagined her coming home to find me cleaning blood off the tiles. Before the sun set, Dr. Sanyal arrived, driven by Hari, who had gone to the family doctor's house and begged him to make a house call. The doctor had hurried past me, Hari in his trail.

When he left the house, it was almost dark, and Hari and he drove off without noticing me in the shadows.

"Lila Didi, what are you sitting in the dark like this?" asked Bari, turning on the lights.

The new chandeliers came on, as did the rest of the lights, slowly, over the floors.

"Stay for dinner. I've made begun bhaja and luchi," she said, bustling around me.

I felt grateful for Bari's existence in my life. "Where is my mother, Bari? Shouldn't she be home by now?"

"Apparently, she's having dinner with Mr. Roy tonight," said Bari, lowering her voice, with a little giggle. "Malati's maid saw them entering China Garden at seven."

"Well, that's nice. Having dinner with a friend is a good thing."

Bari must have heard the sharpness in my voice. She pursed her lips and wrapped the end of her sari around her waist.

"How is Mishti Kaki?" I asked.

Bari shook her head. "I've never seen so much blood, not in this lifetime. It's not good to have blood fall like that—it curses the floor. I'm going to ask the priest to bathe the goddess with milk and water tomorrow and sprinkle a little Gangajal in the corners. If so much blood spreads over the floor, can death be far behind?" She shuddered, waving her arms in the air, as if to dispel the curse.

"Really, Bari, what nonsense. You'll give yourself a nightmare."

"Don't laugh, didi," she said over her shoulder. "Blood and pain live on forever, unless you do something about it."

IN HER BEDROOM, Mishti was lying down, an ice pack on one cheek. Biddy was next to her, bored and scrolling, all traces of B2D gone. I knocked on the open door.

"Hi, Lila," said Biddy, bright. She smiled.

Mishti struggled to sit up. "Oh god, Lila, come in please."

"Ma, you're supposed to keep your head down," said Biddy, annoyed. "He said the bleeding could start back up if the stitches rupture."

"Don't get up, kaki," I said, sitting next to her on the bed.

Mishti sank back down, clutching at the ice. "God, Lila, the way I talked to you. I really don't know what came over me."

"Please don't apologize."

"You must know I didn't mean it. I was overcome, and . . . Tell her, Biddy."

Biddy raised her eyebrows. "What am I saying?"

"Look, kaki, it's okay." I pressed my fingertips to my temple. "Coming here, thinking I could just do things, was . . . You were right to say what you did."

"Oh, Lila, don't say that—you've made such a difference. Tejen Da had such dreams for this house, but between managing Hari and Rana and your mother and all of us, and his illness, he just couldn't," she said, her voice cracking a little.

"Ma mouths off once every decade, and you were just standing in front of her for this one," said Biddy.

"Be quiet," said Mishti, affectionate.

I swallowed, a bright burning at the back of my throat.

"How are you feeling now?" I asked.

"Oh, just fine. Just a little bruise," said Mishti.

Biddy went back to scrolling.

"Did you have a cavity, or a root canal or something?" I asked.

"Oh, no, oh, no." She laughed softly. "Just a little bruise. From when I slipped and fell in the bathroom. The moss builds up on the floor, and Bari can be so lazy in the cold—she doesn't want to wash it off because the water is icy. This is the result."

"But your teeth—"

"Yes, when I slipped and fell, I must have dislodged a few. Dr. Sanyal said that tissues in the sockets and gums are so vascular, plus I've been pushing them around with my tongue and fingers. I probably ruptured too many vessels. That's why there was so much blood. But it's almost stopped now. See, here's the bruise," she said, triumphant, lifting her hair away from her shoulders, the purpling along the folds of her neck and above her collarbone stark against her skin.

Biddy looked up at me from her phone with her steady hazel eyes. Something in them sent a chill through me.

"Do you want a drink, Lila Didi?" she asked. "We have beer or vodka if you like."

"Yes," I said.

"Which?"

"Either."

She nodded and got up to go to the kitchen.

"I really am sorry, Lila," said Mishti, awkward.

"We both know I have some things to learn."

"Your gift. It was really generous and kind of you. I . . . I hope you'll consider still giving Biddy the flowers."

I felt the overwhelming urge to cry.

"Yes, of course," I said. I looked over my shoulder.

I could hear Biddy in the kitchen, shaking ice into glasses.

"Kaki," I whispered, covering her free hand with mine. I shook my head, unable to get the words out. "Tell me what I can do."

Something passed between us as she clutched my hand. When she lifted her head, seconds later, only a distant melancholy remained in her eyes.

"You're such a sweet girl. You have so much love inside you to give. Maybe next year, we can allocate some money to the bathroom repairs."

Biddy came in, cheerful. "We didn't have orange juice, so I just added ice and water—is that okay?" she asked, handing me a glass of vodka as she took a sip out of her own.

I took a long sip.

Mishti, watching me, said, "Both of you shouldn't drink too much. It'll give you bags under your eyes, like Malati."

"Ma," said Biddy, rolling her eyes. "Malati's the happiest human we both know. Lila, I'll be sleeping in Ma's bedroom from now on. With the eye and the teeth"—Biddy took in a short breath—"she needs help."

A heavy silence descended over us.

"I guess it's got to do with the ventilation," I announced suddenly. "The bathroom. The moss is because there's only one tiny window and it's high up, so it's always humid and the vegetation is growing through the cracks in the floor."

"Yes. That's it," said Mishti quietly.

"We'll get it fixed this week," I said. "Put another window in."

The three of us sat as the ice melted from Mishti's pack, thin rivulets that spilled over the side of the bed, reaching Biddy's feet, crossing over to mine, bursting with little water vessels, like blood cells, I imagined, busy and over-loaded, a neural network of the secrets and lies that we took daily refuge in, hiding the truths that were too terrible to allow.

22

THE NEXT DAY, I called Seth impromptu at 9 a.m. and asked if he wanted to see a matinee that was part of the Nandan Film Festival. It was a Saturday, and a movie with Seth at beloved Nandan felt like escaping into light. I listened to my father's Bing Crosby records, moving to the music through the apartment as I got ready.

At ten, my mother rang the doorbell. She must have seen the pall pass over my face, because she raised her eyebrows.

"Not who you were expecting?" she asked.

"I wasn't expecting anyone. I'm getting ready to go out."

"Lila, please don't be rude."

"Sorry," I said. "I just can't be late."

"I just needed a few minutes . . . to talk."

I felt a sinking in my heart. There would be no dissuading her, and opening the door was the only route to getting the conversation over with. She followed me into the living room.

"Where are you going?" she asked, curious. "That's a pretty top. Maybe a little low-cut for India."

I looked down at the scoop-necked blouse I was wearing over jeans.

"You can't see cleavage," I said.

"That's because you don't have any, darling. But see how it shows the top of your tiny breasts?" she said, helpful, as she pointed to my chest.

"Was there something you needed?"

An unfamiliar hesitation settled over my mother.

"Is this about the house? Do you want them to repair something?" I asked.

"I wish you thought better of your own mother. I don't always have an agenda."

I sighed as I picked up a hairbrush. "Sorry, Ma."

"I heard you saw . . . that you were there when Mishti . . . when she fell down."

My heartbeat began to quicken. "No," I said, curt. "I was there when the bleeding . . . her tooth . . . teeth—"

"Yes," my mother nodded again, too quickly. "The doctor says she's fine now."

"I was there when he left," I said as a part of me longed to make a dig about her dinner with Mr. Roy.

My mother looked at me. "I just want to make sure you're not going to do anything . . . without thinking."

"What do you mean?" I asked, my voice hard in my own ears.

"This is Kolkata," said my mother, from light-years away from my body. "People don't want their private lives public. I just wanted to make sure you didn't tell anyone anything that . . . that simply may not be true."

"What do you mean?" I asked again.

"You know what I mean," my mother said, traces of anger in her voice.

"You want me to keep my mouth shut. Is that correct?" I felt an airlessness in my chest. I got up to push open a window.

"Don't be melodramatic," said my mother.

The sunlight and the unseasonal chill rushed in together, the balcony rail cool beneath my fingers.

"Lila, if people think the family has some sort of . . . another scandal, we will not be able to hold our heads up in this community that we have to exist in, long after you've gone back to America."

I closed my eyes. Through all of their strife and secrets, it was their certainty that I would go back—that I would remain an outsider—that held them together with tape and scissors and some sort of indelible glue, as a family.

"Mishti asked me to come," my mother said. "She begged me."

In the distance, as if a mirage, I saw Seth crossing at the Ballygunge Phari light, his lavender shirt a bright dot against the color of the city. I turned around.

"I have not said anything to anyone," I said. "Not ever."

My mother held my gaze, as we took in the shape of each other, strangers who had been thrust into frightening roles. *This, here, is your mother, and this, now, is your daughter, and no paperwork or extended silence can ever dissolve that, so you must both play the part.*

The doorbell rang.

"Seth is here," I said.

She nodded. "It's time for me to go anyway."

BUT WHEN SETH came in, my mother did not go. Instead, she developed that slight British accent again, asking him questions about the part of Manhattan he had been raised in (*The Upp-ah West Side!*) and the ending of his last book (*Whot did it feel like, when you were wroiting that scene when he grows up and finally confronts his kidnap-ah?*), shaking her head excitably. To my knowledge, my mother had never been to Manhattan or read Seth's book, though the last reprint had resulted in a Wikipedia page that summarized the plot.

Seth, polite and happy, answered dutifully as I applied lipstick in the bathroom. I listened as he asked her how her classes were going (he had taken the trouble to know the courses she taught) and what I had been like as a child.

"Very serious, with that same little frown plastered between her eyes, even when she was four or five," I heard my mother say. Her voice grew softer, wistful. "But she could turn in seconds, naughty, almost wicked, and if you played a game, she hated to lose. She was always in her own head, living in books and making up poems and stories. That girl should have become a writer."

"Well, she's very good at what she does," said loyal, kind Seth, firmly on my side.

"Yes, of course, *ohf* course. Here. Just look at that pho-toh—isn't her face like a heart?"

In the living room, Seth was admiring pictures of me, a toddler with unruly curls (the truth of my hair was revealed) frowning into the camera, an infant in a woman's arms.

As she saw me, my mother began putting the pictures back into the Coach wallet I had saved up and bought her as a birthday present at twenty, paying nearly double in international shipping almost a decade ago, its edges frayed, the leather scuffed. Pictures made sense, tucked into the recesses of a wallet that one held close every day, to practice a version of love and motherhood and daughterhood that was without the grief and pain of the real thing.

"You changed," said Seth, standing up. "Now I feel underdressed. Is this movie theater fancy?"

I shook my head.

"What a beautiful shirt, Lila," said my mother softly, touching my elbow hidden beneath the full-sleeve silk shirt I had changed into, buttoned up from my wrists, against my torso, all the way into the hollow of my neck. "You look wonderful."

NANDAN CINEMA HAD been born a year before me, a government-sponsored cultural center that took pride in screening art-house films and turned quickly into a meeting ground of the cultural, intellectual elite. The building was an extension of Kolkata's passionate cinephile movement, spearheaded by Satyajit Ray, whose *Pather Panchali* had by then won at Cannes. When Ray designed the Nandan logo himself, it was taken by every Bengali to seal Kolkata as the cultured capital of India. Ray and the city's thinkers and artists had been fiercely liberal, and Nandan stood as a bastion of sorts, frequented by the leftist chief ministers and other government officials. For me, growing up, Nandan was the place you went to be cool. To be associated with even a whiff of Nandan was to be a free and smart citizen of Kolkata, learning all sorts of things about sex and queerness and art and history.

But in the last decade, a former railways minister had come to power who considered herself a person of the people. Sreela Banerjee was queen of a new populist left, which had no patience for the men who had poured investment into art-house cinema that denounced the melodrama of commercial Bengali cinema, and who refused even to recognize the average Bengali citizen's idol, Uttam Kumar. Banerjee revived Kumar as a cultural talisman, creating a twenty-acre film city in Howrah and an archive of his films, and it paid off handsomely in her voter base. Her new liberal party was called Grassroots Power of Bengal, and she portrayed herself as one with the rural masses, averse to the luxury haunts and what she deemed the pseudo-intellectual conversations of her former bosses.

Art-house films began to have trouble finding their way into the screening lists at Nandan, and more commercial Bollywood films secured show times. Yet Bengal remained one of the last few liberal states left in India, and Kolkata continued to be a liberal haven for Muslims and Christians and Hindus alike, all of whom adored and were united by Sreela.

Then in 2013, the central conservative government descended upon the state. The right-wing National Popular Front installed a censor board chair who, though a suave advertising professional, seemed distinctly Hindu in his taste. He had been quick to include a few new clauses to the restrictions that the board made on films, notably including "No promotion of sectarian, obscurantist, antiscientific and antinational attitudes" and "No national symbols or emblems, except in accordance with the Emblems and Names (Prevention of Improper Use) Act, 1950."

Despite this, Nandan and Kolkata had stayed seemingly—obstinately—liberal, foiling the NPF each election cycle, the cinema's programming board proudly denouncing the right wing in its press. Sreela, outraged, even allowed the resurgence of experimental film and art-house classics at Nandan. The right wing, ironically, had finally united all the factions of the left, because they threatened not just Sreela Banerjee, but the deeply liberal spirit of Bengal.

I TRIED TO explain Nandan to Seth. "It's a bit like Lincoln Center but, really, more like Williamsburg Cinemas."

He nodded, staring at the geese in the artificial lake next to the theater. We were early and had ordered masala tea and a packet of Parle-G biscuits from the canteen and taken it out onto the lawn that cordoned off Nandan from the rest of traffic-fueled Kolkata.

"That kid is going to fall into the water," said Seth, as a very young boy doubled over the rail to inspect a goose up close.

"Ki hotocchara chele," a woman screamed, running toward the boy, a fluid flying human, an expert in her sari.

The boy, grinning, leaped away from the rail, covering his head with his hands, in certain knowledge of what was to come. The instant his mother reached him, she planted a resounding slap across one ear, to which the boy promptly burst into tears.

A man sauntered toward them, eating peanuts out of a paper cone. The boy ran to him, climbing him like a squirrel on a tree, tucking his face into his father's shoulder.

As the woman berated her son, the husband nodded along.

The boy, looking up, widened his eyes at Seth, then winked and gave us a little wave.

Seth, visibly shaken, waved back at him as, peace restored, the family walked in the direction of the theater entrance.

"What did she say to him, before she, er . . . slapped him?" asked Seth.

I shrugged. "She called him a name," I said. "Wretch of a boy. Standard. She was worried he'd fall in."

"That was . . . quite the smack she gave him." Seth raised his eyebrows up and down in rapid succession, the little wiggle of concern he did when trying to frame something correctly with words.

"It's just Bengali mothers," I said. "Their love is all slapping and barking at their kids to study. That little guy knows it."

Seth looked at me, curious. "Your mother isn't like that."

It was part question, part statement. The goose was savagely picking at the little boy's crusts, now floating in the algae. I imagined myself floating underwater in thick algae, trying to find a boy.

"And what is she like?" I asked Seth with a laugh.

"Poised. A lot like you. She's eager to make a good impression."

"Also like me," I said, trying to block the goose out.

"When I first met you, there was something there—like a mystery. And of course, it's part of your charm—I was mad for you immediately. But she has it too, in a different way," said Seth. "There's something so secret, so private, about the both of you. And in a room, it's like you're both part of that, and everyone else, or, well, just me . . . I'm not in it, you know?"

People were staring at us. Seth could have been a model in the Bollywood music videos that were partial to white, aquiline men.

"You have fans," I said, stretching my legs.

Seth looked uncomfortable. "Someone asked to take a picture with me when you were buying tea."

I laughed. "Did you take it?"

"Of course not." Seth looked shocked. "I apologized, though. I mean, it's weird, isn't it?"

"Yeah." I shrugged. "But the Lahiris treat you like a king too, and that's fine by you."

"It's different," said Seth, wounded. "They like me, as a person."

"They sure do. Should we go in? I like watching the trailers."

"Sure," said Seth, quiet.

"I didn't know you were mad for me when we met."

I slipped my fingers into his hand. The ticket attendant stared at us as I handed him our tickets with my left hand.

"Real mad," said Seth.

I HAD BOUGHT two tickets to *Charulata*, my favorite Ray film, about a lonely and rich housewife unable to repress her attraction to her husband's visiting cousin; I loved how it turned morality and the idea of heroes and villains on its head. By the time we settled into our seats, Seth was mesmerized by Kolkata's finest, decked out in block printed saris and kurta pajamas.

"I'm underdressed," he whispered in my ear.

I shook my head. "The Bengalis just take the film festival really seriously. You're fine."

"But look at you," he said, tugging on my silk collar, his fingers resting briefly on my collarbone. "You smell and look good enough to eat."

"You could almost pass off as Bengali, in those glasses, by the way," I whispered back. I inhaled his cologne, the easy sexual familiarity of lovers between us.

"Shh," hissed an elderly voice behind us, as a presenter came on to introduce the film.

Seth, suddenly doubtful, whispered, "There are going to be subtitles, right?"

"No," I said, cheerful, as the lights began to dim and Seth's eyes widened in horror. "But it is such a beautiful film—every frame is gorgeous. You're going to be fine."

THERE WERE SUBTITLES, to Seth's relief, and I could see that he forgot me after a while and disappeared into the film. It gave me special happiness when his face, so full of sorrow in the last few minutes, burst into incredulous laughter at the startling final freeze-frame.

"What was that?" he said as the credits rolled and people began to leave. "God, I never wanted it to end."

We were among the last few to leave. Seth held my hand and didn't say much, and I felt a shift between us—as if he saw me as more special than I had been an hour ago. Outside, I went to the bathroom and we agreed to meet in the lobby.

"Drink at Trincas?" I asked him, a look in my eyes he knew well, all but forgotten since I had left Brooklyn.

"Yes," he said. "I'll be waiting."

BUT WHEN I returned to the lobby, police officers with guns and batons were everywhere. Panicked moviegoers crowded into corners or clutched children, looking for the people they had come with. The cops screamed instructions to the crowd, slamming their batons against the walls of Nandan. They had locked and barricaded the glass front doors and stood in a single layered phalanx behind them. Outside, two TV trucks were parked, as journalists and crews filmed an army of protesters, who held up signs, chanting and screaming, a muffled roar behind the glass.

Afraid, I looked around for Seth. I pushed my way through the mass of people, the goose boy crying in his mother's arms now, past groups of frightened older citizens. Finally, I found him, talking to a young couple, likely in their twenties, Seth's brow knitted in concentration.

"Seth," I said, clutching at his arm. He turned from his conversation as if nothing were wrong.

"Oh, Lila. Here, look. This is Deepa and . . . I'm . . . man, I'm so bad with names—remind me again."

"Ismail." The man in the blue shirt smiled, relaxed in the frenzy around him.

I smiled back, my heart slowing to a thud. "Hi. What's going on? Why are there so many cops here?"

"That's what we were talking about," said Seth. "It's a protest, against Nandan."

"It was started by friends of ours, from our college film society," said Deepa, her voice lowered to a whisper. "Nandan refused to screen Shubho Rai's latest film at the festival, because it showed a gay couple having sex—"

"A love story," corrected Ismail with a laugh.

"Yes, a love story, but about gay men, so it caused a huge furor when Nandan refused to screen it. All the intellectuals of Kolkata say that Sreela Banerjee . . . and Nandan are becoming more and more aligned with the National Popular Front."

"I hardly think that's true, though," said Ismail. "Sreela left a protest. Doesn't make her a right-wing fanatic."

"Stop interrupting me, Ismail," said Deepa, exasperated.

Deepa reminded me of Molly, and I felt a piercing of longing for my friend.

"Sorry, sorry," said Ismail, holding up his hands.

My phone beeped as messages trickled in. *U ok?* asked Vik. Seconds later, from Adil: *Where r u?*

"The film people are protesting against censorship, but it's also brought the queer community here today, protesting Section 377," said Deepa.

"What's 377?" asked Seth.

"It isn't legal to be gay in India. The Supreme Court is reviewing the law," said Deepa before I could. A memory of Avi, joyful and easy, the freedom with which he lived his life, flashed in my head.

"The buggery bill," said Ismail. "That's what the British called it. A remnant of a colonial law, but it looks unlikely to find removal."

"We're going to join them," said Deepa.

"The crowd?" I asked, shocked.

"Yes," Ismail said. "You should come."

"But the police are all over the entrance. You'll get arrested," I said.

"We're going out the back," said Ismail, texting. "Our friends are guarding it."

"Bye! It was nice meeting you," Deepa yelled.

Seth grabbed my arm. "Lila, let's join them."

"What? No. It could be dangerous. NPF men could be out there."

"But they're homophobes and fascists," said Seth, pulling me along as he followed Deepa and Ismail.

"Seth, for god's sake. Suddenly, you're an expert on India? What if you get arrested?" I hissed in his ear.

The door opened, and cheers greeted Deepa and Ismail as they disappeared into the protest. I held Seth back. It was raining outside, and spray and wind gushed in as the door closed, Seth and I left standing in the shadows of the lobby. We could hear chants outside—"Azadi, azadi, azadi!"—a lilt of violence in the air. A few feet from us, at the main entrance, a police officer began to shove and handcuff a protester, the scuffle turning ugly and dangerous in front of us.

Seth looked uncertain and horrified. "Lila, I'm such a fucking zhlob. What if you got hurt or arrested. Jesus, I don't know what I was thinking, behaving like we were protesting in Brooklyn."

"What's a 'zhlob'?" I asked.

"An idiot," he said, miserable, his dark hair curling around his perfect face in the damp, cool air that smelled of rain and earth.

I kissed Seth, the chants reverberating through us, his hands going around my waist as he drew me in immediately.

"Do you know what 'azadi' means?" I asked, murmuring against his warm breath. He tasted of the sweet sugar biscuits of my childhood.

"No," he said hungrily, pulling me closer.

"Freedom." I stepped back from him and took his hand again and opened the back door of Nandan. "C'mon, my zhlob. Let's go pretend this is Brooklyn."

OUTSIDE IN THE rain, which simultaneously felt freezing and warm, bubbling over in the frenzy, I felt myself soar over the crowd, as if on a fuel of their adrenaline. What did it mean to use your lungs and heart and body and say "No," again and again, repeating it until it was a force so powerful that no baton or gun could slam it to the ground?

The crowd had grown large, a local celebrity had joined to lend her support, and the TV crews stood waiting like patient hawks, ready to snap up the slightest scent of atrocity from the police, who, resigned, slid into their vans as protesters screamed curses at their retreating backs.

But you could tell that the police didn't like being chastised, that there would be a next time. You could tell in the way their eyes glittered and their biceps trembled, as if to contain their rage at having to restrain themselves.

IN THE CAB home, Seth pulled me into his side. I curled against him, our bodies making a familiar shape against the velvet seat. The driver made note of us in the rearview. A fog of sleep was descending on me. The rain had started up again, a lulling drum against the windows.

"Dada, could you turn it up, please, just a little?" I asked in Bengali.

The driver turned the music a notch up—it was a Kishore Kumar romantic classic. "I love it too, didi," he said in Hindi.

"You know, I swear I saw Vik for a second in the crowd," said Seth.

I yawned, nuzzling into his collar. "Really? Why didn't you say something?"

"I . . . well . . . He was with someone."

I struggled awake, raising my head. "Who?"

"Well, it looked like he was with a . . . someone in drag. A queen. She was . . . beautiful." Seth kept tilting his head, trying to formulate his words.

"Nina of the Night," I said before I could stop myself.

"What's that?" asked Seth, straining to hear me.

"Were they . . . together?" I asked, even in knowing the truth.

"It looked like it."

I felt a sharpness in my chest as I thought of Avi again, who existed with such ease in New York, and Vik, who had taken such great pains to keep secrets from us in Kolkata. Even Adil, whom Vik trusted with his life, did not seem to know. *One day, our secrets will be the end of us all,* I thought.

Seth and I were silent as we listened to the rain and the music.

"You okay?" I asked.

He turned his body toward me, rearranging.

"I want you, Lila. I want this, here. Us. You." He shook his head. "I want the whole thing. Learning who you are, where you come from, marriage, babies, a car, a cottage somewhere—"

"Your father's house in Maine," I said automatically.

He laughed. "Or your grandfather's house in Kolkata, if that's where you want to be," said Seth. He swallowed. "I don't know what exists between you and this other guy, but I've never loved someone like this. I've never wanted to end the whole women thing like this. I've never wanted to just be with one person. It's like a part of me is gone when you're gone."

He ran out of breath at the last sentence, as if flailing just seconds before finishing a marathon. Wife, baby, mother, man, house, life. The rain and Kishore Kumar rose and fell. I reached out and touched Seth's ear, the line of his jaw, the back of his neck, mesmerized by the vision of an uncomplicated life.

"Okay," I whispered.

His brow knitted. "Okay?"

"Okay. Let's be everything you said."

"Are you sure?" he asked.

"Yes," I said as Seth bent to kiss me, the smell of rain and taxi and velvet and sweat and fear and joy, rising up, engulfing us.

I WAS BARELY awake by the time we reached my father's apartment. Ram Bhai made note as we both went upstairs. Seth deposited me in bed tenderly, a Seth I had never fully met before, drawing the bedspread up as I slid in between the sheets, covering me with the comforter, his lips against my cheek, turning the light off, the door clicking softly as he left me safe.

I rose to watch from behind my window curtain as he crossed the street, lit by moonlight and streetlamps. I went into the kitchen and poured a glass of water as my phone glowed in the darkness.

After four rings, Adil answered, his voice low.

"Lila, goddamn it. I was worried."

"I texted you. I'm fine."

"Vik said you were at Nandan. Inside when it happened."

"Outside, protesting, actually," I said.

"Are you insane?" he said, his voice thick with restrained anger. "You sound proud of it, like Vik."

"Do I?" I was surprised to hear it, but if I felt any pride, Adil was the person who might know it.

He took a long breath. "I'm glad you're okay." After a pause: "What were you doing there?"

"*Charulata*," I said. Without notice, my eyes filled with tears, an overwhelming choking in my throat.

Adil was silent for a long time. *Charulata*, beloved Nandan, beloved childhood, beloved history that had somehow faltered in strength and honor, living on only as the past.

"Adil," I whispered. "This is where it ends."

I felt him breathing. I pictured him at home, someone else's home: Did it have cushions and flowers and settees and armchairs and art? And if so, what did they look like, in this world he occupied outside of mine?

"I'm so sorry, Lila."

"I know."

"You can't know how much I wish I didn't . . . that I could—"

"I know."

"I love you."

I know. I'm going to go to sleep now."

"Bye, Lila," he said, so softly that I could barely hear him.

Then he was gone, and the only thing left was the phone, burning hot and neon against my ear, until it, too, disappeared into the dark.

23

THE NEXT MORNING, I was on a Skype call with my parents and siblings. They were together, at dinner, a train ride away from Brooklyn, nine and a half hours behind Kolkata. Iva and my father sat in front of the screen, with Robin milling about. Avi, fixing himself a drink offscreen, asked me questions about my life thousands of miles away.

It was an odd reversal. At their home, I blended into the messy, bustling landscape of family dinnertime—watching, rather than being watched. Now, they were crowded around me. I felt profoundly homesick, jealous as my father bopped Robin on the head, as Iva took the drink that Avi offered her, at the description of dinner—roast chicken, nothing special, my father's masala potatoes—but it was all special.

"When will you come home?" asked Iva.

"What about the job?" asked my worried father. "Are you able to manage, so far away from the office? Make sure you stay in contact with the new boss."

I was managing, I reassured him.

Could I buy Robin a kurta? Was the house finished? Did the elevator pass city inspection? (My father.) Was Hari behaving himself? (Also my father.) Was the house okay? Was Ram Bhai taking care of me? Was I comfortable? Was I well? Was I coming home soon? Their questions filled me with an obscure happiness and anxiety.

Robin had been in a minor car accident, and for a brief respite, the attention shifted to her as we examined her bruised wrist, the result of a thud against the dashboard, and my father held a mini lecture on the perils of speeding in New Haven's misleadingly suburban streets filled with the care-lessness of Yale's finest, as we held back our amusement.

My doorbell rang—it was early, six thirty in the morning—so I assumed it was the newspaperman, come to collect his month-end payment.

"I'll be right back," I said to my family.

I opened the door, purse in hand. It was my mother, dressed in what I called her "professor look"—a kurta, jeans, a leather tote, oxfords, and con-tact lenses instead of her glasses, her hair pulled back from her smooth face, into a short ponytail. She could have been my sister, only two decades older than me.

She held up a plastic bag—"I had some extra of the murukku you like."

It was a peace offering. I took the bag, my hearing heightened, suddenly acutely aware of my family in the background.

"Thank you."

My mother's smile was dazzling. You wanted to bask in it.

She waited, and after a few seconds, I said, reluctant, "Do you have time to come in for tea?"

"Yes," she exclaimed. "I made sure to wake up an hour earlier than usual."

She followed me inside as I hurried to my desk.

"I'm on a call," I said. "Make yourself comfortable—I'll be done in a minute."

The desk was a few feet from the couch, where she settled in, and opened the Barbara Comyns that I had been reading. I turned the volume back on, a cold pit taking shape in my stomach. Immediately, the clamor of my father's household filled the room, and I did not have to turn my head to see my mother look up.

"Is the toaster doing okay?" asked Iva.

"It's still a little temperamental—the toast comes out between a bit spotty and fully burned," I said.

Iva shook her head, the lamp lighting her curls in a golden glow. "I'm just going to get a new one shipped to you."

"Guys, I have to go now. I'll call again next week," I said.

"Say hi to Vik from me," said Avi.

"I will."

"Your father and I will be in Manhattan on Tuesday," said Iva. "Did you need anything taken care of in Brooklyn?"

"No, thank you," I said, desperate to end the call.

"They're going to see the scandalous new *Madame Bovary* at Lincoln Center," said Avi.

"What about your plants?" asked Iva. "You said Harriet was supposed to be watering them, but there's a lot going on at the office. We could check on them."

"Okay. Thank you. I'll see you guys next week."

"Excellent, darling," said Iva happily.

"We'll pick up your mail too," said my father.

"Bye, Baba," I said.

They chorused their endless goodbyes, and my apartment was silent again, with only my mother's presence filling the vacuum. I shut the screen of my laptop.

"Sorry, I'll make the tea now," I said.

My mother looked up from the book.

"Of course," she said, polite, her brilliance faded, replaced by the winter we both knew so well.

WHEN I BROUGHT out the tea, she was still reading.

"I thought this was going to be a lovely little book about the English countryside, but it's filled with bleeding pigs and dying hens and all these horrible things."

"Yeah," I nodded. "It's pretty good, though—she's a real original—sharp, funny. It's still the English countryside, just in savage freewheel."

"She certainly is very original."

I nodded. My mother's love for art and literature always took me aback. Even though it was ever-present, it was a side that slipped my mind constantly.

My mother sipped at the tea. "Was that your family?" she asked pointlessly.

"Yes," I said. I looked at the clock. It was almost seven, and her bus would stop at the bus stand at seven twenty.

"Your father sounds happy," she said.

I felt the vast sorrow that only she could fill me with.

"Does he? He was cranky about a car accident that Robin got herself into."

"Robin is your sister," said my mother, vacant as she stated it.

"Yes."

"How is she?" asked my mother. Her tone had taken on the quality of an interrogation, and I began to chafe, as I did when conversations about relatives who did not call my mother anymore (who had not "bothered to stay in touch") came up.

"Yeah, just a scrape," I said, sharper than I would have liked.

"How old is she?"

"Nineteen," I said.

"You laugh a lot when you are with them. Why don't you laugh with me? Everything I say, you take personally. Look at you now—I ask a small question, and you behave as if I'm the enemy."

"You're not the enemy, Ma. But you do ask a lot of questions, and then you get upset. And I just want to have a nice morning."

"What's wrong with asking questions?" she demanded.

"Ma, please. I really don't have the energy to do this now."

"With them, you are happy because it is easy to be happy with them. They have gone through nothing, the way I have." She was furious now, tears forming. "I have nothing in my life, no one. My own daughter treats me like an enemy."

A wave of sorrow submerged me, cascading above anger and resentment, drowning my body.

"That's not true," I said, even though it was. I hated her for this familiar drowning, which I had felt in her presence since before I could speak full sentences—a cloying sadness at the bone-deep grief that my mother carried with her every day, that made it impossible to submit to the freedom that hatred could give me.

She wiped away her tears, defiant. "I will buy you a toaster," she announced.

I shook my head. "The one we have—the one here—it's fine. I just need to figure out the heat."

"I will buy it for you," she said again, her breathing coming in swift, sharp bursts. "Why won't you let me do anything for you?"

The sorrow that cloaked us froze and melted, froze again, melted again.

"Okay, Ma," I said. I tried to smile at her, she who could go from fearsome dragon to child in seconds. "I'd like that."

She nodded and stood up, purposeful. "Tonight. You'll have it tonight." At the door, she turned. "Do you remember, Lila, how you would eat toasted peanut butter sandwiches, your nose in a book, as the rain washed the grime of the day away?"

It sounded like a line from a bad book to me. I had no memory of eating peanut butter sandwiches while left alone to read in peace around my mother. But she did this often—resorting to belief in constructed memory, fiction that, repurposed long enough, could take the place of reality. Our reality, therefore, had slipped her mind entirely.

I smiled and shook my head.

She sighed. "See how you never remember the good?"

AFTER SHE LEFT, it took me an hour to focus on all of the emails that had streamed in. Aetos had begun to email me directly, regularly. I had signed two new authors, Paloma Okinawa, a former Harper editor who had a remarkable proposal for a three-part romance set in Tokyo and Austin, both cities equally her own. The second, Saima Eisenhower, a Pakistani-Jewish journalist, was writing a novel about a young German journalist who had discovered that her father was a former Nazi official. Aetos was delighted with both and called me his truffle hunter.

By the time I looked up, it was evening and Champa, the maid in the house opposite my father's apartment, was rolling out rotis. Every night, like clockwork, the lights would click on in the kitchen at seven, and she would come in to knead and shape dough into dinner. My living room window looked directly into the kitchen where Champa worked, and in my first few weeks, she had looked at me disapprovingly as I drank beer or when I wore shorts. Over time, with familiarity, she forgave me my bare legs.

As we waved to each other tonight, the doorbell rang, and my heart immediately accelerated at the thought of another interrogation from my mother. Champa, curious, stopped mid–vigorous knead as the bell rang again. In Kolkata and New York, homes were built in a manner that allowed your neighbors to hear your doorbell as clear as their own. I got up to answer it on the third ring, and Champa went back to her dough.

It was not my mother.

Ram Bhai stood outside, a large box in his hands. "Madam, your mother sent this for you," he said in Hindi.

"Sent it for me? Where is she?" I asked in Bengali.

"She didn't want to come up—said to deliver to you. It's heavy," he said, in Hindi-inflected Bengali this time.

Ram held up the box. It was glossy cardboard, with a picture of a beautiful woman in a cocktail dress holding up a triumphant piece of golden toast. SIX SLICE SUPER TOASTING OVEN was lettered in shiny red above the woman's head.

I began to laugh.

Ram Bhai frowned. "Looks like a very good machine, madam," he said, reproachful.

"Yes," I said.

"She also said to give you this."

Carefully, he extracted a white envelope from his shirt pocket.

"Thank you, Ram Bhai," I said, taking the envelope from him. I imagined a greeting card, saying *Enjoy your new toaster. Love, Mamma* (spelled the European way she preferred, though I had called her Ma my whole adult life).

"Good night, Lila Madam," he said, making note of the glass of gin on the table. "Go to bed soon—it's late, and you have to get up to do your American job."

"How do you know what time I have to get up?" I asked, content to have Ram parent me.

AFTER HE HAD gone, I opened the envelope. A photograph slid out from between the thin white sheets. It was a picture of me eating what looked like two slices of toast, a sandwich of some sort, reading a book, frowning into it, intent and absent to my photographer. I could not have been more than ten or eleven, but here it was, her damning evidence that I was an unreliable narrator of our years together, my memory entirely obscured in the parts where she had in fact been mother enough to have toasted bread and put peanut butter in between slices, cherishing me enough to take a secret photo.

24

LESS THAN A week before the wedding, Biddy was having an engagement party. In true Lahiri style, she had wanted a party where she could celebrate with the family. Their need to do everything together was remarkable and absurd to me. But I was glad to have people invited to the house to admire it again, to serve my own incessant need for validation around the inheritance. For the party, we were going to use the largest room of the house, where the Lahiris stored the family's suitcases and unused furniture, on the second floor. From this cobwebbed room, Mr. Das had created a light and airy great room that would easily host thirty-five invitees.

On the day of the party, Rinki asked me if I wanted to get ready together, a tradition from when we were girls. As teenagers, we washed our hair with the imported bottles of Persimmon Passion, a heavily scented shampoo that my father and Iva would send me upon request, blow-dried the fragrant strands like we had seen on TV, and decided that persimmons were our favorite fruit, despite having never seen one in real life.

At one, as I was finishing edits on Seth's latest pages, Rinki rang the doorbell, with her maid, Lily, carrying a bottle of Sula Brut in one hand and a bottle of Persimmon Passion in the other.

I POURED THE brut into one of Iva's Swarovski flutes for Rinki and into my childhood steel tumbler for myself.

"Iva Aunty really did up this place," said Rinki, taking the flute from me.

"She sure did," I said.

"Wait, you don't like it?" exclaimed Rinki, following me into my bedroom. "Look at all this beautiful"—she waved her hands around—"stuff. She's got such pretty taste."

I turned on the air conditioner. It growled to life, flooding the room with cool air. "Sure, I like it."

"You *sure* don't," said Rinki, mimicking my accent.

I shrugged. "It's fine. I wish she hadn't changed everything. I mean, she broke the walls down."

Rinki nodded. "People do that all the time to old buildings. To let in more light and air, make the rooms look bigger."

"I thought it had plenty of light and air before. I had memories here."

"Oh, that's right. Maya Didi and Mihir Uncle lived here before . . . before . . . before the divorce?"

I laughed. "God, Rinki. Lots of people get divorced in Ballygunge Place now."

Rinki shook her head. "Not the way they did."

"Well, they were the first."

"And what a debut," said Rinki, turning to Lily. "Okay, Lily, go home now and get ready for the party. And make sure saheb wears the silver kurta I laid out. I'll go with Lila. Tell saheb to arrive by at least seven, or you'll both miss the rings and photographs."

I laughed as Lily exited dutifully. "Your majesty, Mrs. Rinki Bose."

"This is my lot in life," said Rinki, fluttering a hand over her eyes. "A bored housewife, subject only to her husband, queen of all else."

"Are you subject to Bashudeb?" I asked. "You seem happy."

"I am happy," said Rinki. "But this is Kolkata, and I live in Durgapur. Our men keep us happy, and, you know, we are their women." Rinki shrugged, content. "I'm not sure that if you went into the marriages of Manhattan, you wouldn't find some sort of compromise. We all compromise. You will too, when you get married."

I finished my champagne. "I wouldn't hold your breath."

"Don't you want a husband?" asked Rinki, lying back on the pillows. "They can be wonderful, you know."

"Tell me everything," I said, untying my bathrobe. "Seems to me like they're more trouble than they're worth. Except Bashudeb, of course."

AS I TURNED off the shower, I pushed aside the curtain to find Rinki sitting on the quartz toilet seat. She handed me the towel she had been holding.

"Is this what you're wearing?" she asked, running her fingers over my black jumpsuit, against the rack where I had hung it to steam. "I love the halter style—you have such nice collarbones. And with those glossy red nails, Mrs. Chatterjee is going to think you're a harlot in this outfit."

"I grew my collarbones myself."

Rinki giggled as I rubbed moisturizer into my skin. "Here, try this lipstick for tonight." She held up a tube, the color of my nails.

"You don't think it'll be a bit much?"

Rinki shrugged. "If you want to upset Mrs. Chatterjee properly, you have to commit. Do you want to borrow a bracelet for your dress . . . pants . . . pantsdress?"

"Jumpsuit. I was thinking I'd wear Katyayani's emerald ring and leave it at that."

"Oh." Rinki went quiet.

I turned to look at her. "What?"

"It'll look beautiful on you. I didn't realize she had left that to you."

"She left it to my grandfather. He left it to me," I said. Suddenly, the air was too cold, the bathroom too wet.

"I see. My mother had always loved that ring."

I swallowed. "I'm sorry, I didn't know." I wanted to tell her she could have it, but I wanted it myself and believed it was mine, and so the words extinguished in my throat. "Do you want to borrow it for tonight?" I asked, hopeful.

She smiled. "No, it's perfect. That ring was meant for the pantsdress."

We were both silent for a moment.

"Lila, there's something I have to tell you."

I leaned against the sink, towel-drying my hair. "What is it, Rinks?"

"I can't say it . . . say what it is. The thing is, I'm not supposed to." She looked at me in fear. "But I can't not tell you. I'm part of it."

I crouched next to her and put a hand over her hands, intertwined in her lap. "You can tell me anything."

She shook her head. "It feels like a betrayal to my mother. It's what she would have wanted me to do. I'm a Lahiri, Lila."

"Rinks, what on earth are you talking about? You're scaring me."

"It's the house. They . . . We . . . are going to try to take it back from you. We're talking to lawyers. They said we have a case." Tears began to fall from Rinki's face onto the bathroom tiles. "I'm so sorry, Lila."

I put my arms around her. "It doesn't matter."

"It really doesn't matter, Li. You know they, I—all of us—we love you. It's just the house. It's not about you." She raised her mascara-stained face to me. "We love you," she repeated.

"I know, Rinks," I said, stroking the back of her head.

She relaxed against me. "You promise? You don't hate me?"

"I promise. Rinks?"

"Yes?"

"I'm sorry I didn't call after Bela Pishi died. I didn't know what to say."

Rinki shook her head into my stomach. "I know you loved her. I knew you were thinking of us."

The truth was, I had meant to, and somewhere in the cracks of my existence, between the daily fabric of manuscripts and phone calls and dinners and dishes, I had forgotten to call Rinki and I had rationalized my feelings about my grandaunt's death as natural, as time passing, unsuspecting that all sorrow must be reckoned with ultimately.

AS RINKI SHOWERED and the smell of Persimmon Passion filled my father's apartment, I called Palekar.

"Rinki just confirmed it," I said into the phone. "Bela Lahiri's daughter. They want the house."

He sighed. "It is what is the norm."

"I'm a family member, who rightfully inherited the house. It's not the norm to respect that?"

"Property, inheritance, money—these are always contested," said Palekar, patient. "People fight over their own means of survival. Over the things they feel they were entitled to. A son who has felt he has not been loved properly by his father will always take the second wife to court over the house. It is the norm, dear Lila."

"You think they feel like my grandfather was unfair to them?"

"Correct. And since I expected them to feel such emotions, I have prepared, for when the time comes, to defend such an insinuation."

I swallowed. "Palekar Uncle, thank you."

"Do not thank me. Your dear father and I are brothers."

India was this country where my own family could come after me, and just as quickly, I would be adopted elsewhere, the currencies and barter of love, seamlessly transmitted at will.

"Lila?"

"I'm here," I said.

He cleared his throat. "It is not that they do not think of you as their family. This is a matter of property. It is just the norm. And after all, it is their house."

WHEN I WAS fifteen, the fragrance of Persimmon Passion shampoo gave us a heady power, magnifying the confidence with which we flipped our hair behind our shoulders. We felt invincible, all flaws and zits and pubescent problems dissolved into persimmon-scented fabulousness. At Biddy's party, in my jumpsuit, I felt persimmon power in my veins. Rinki shook her curtain of black hair across her shoulder blades, her sari catching the chandelier lights, as she sparkled up at her husband. Seth looked at me with a secret fire from across the great room, and my mother raised her eyebrows.

"Well," she said, "with a little effort, you can look so nice. Though aren't you cold with your whole back exposed like that?"

On the surface, the Lahiris did not treat me like the enemy. Instead, to extended family and friends, they extolled my commitment to the restoration of their house and their legacy, Hari going so far as to introduce me as Lila

Lahiri in a moment of drunkenness, and my grandmother tearfully telling her oldest friend that my return was the greatest gift that her husband could have given her. Despite the decay and mildew of the last decade, the Lahiris had not forgotten how to be hosts, their finest jewelry and manners out on display.

The photographer followed Seth around and took endless pictures of him until, exasperated, I reminded the man that it was Biddy's engagement. It was the first time that I had seen Biddy surrounded by her own flock, twenty-somethings posting and gesturing and glittering in their youth and beauty, filling and replenishing their inexhaustible joy as they took a thousand selfies and videos to crystallize the event online. Biddy's fiancé, Arjun, looked relaxed in a biceps-clinging silk kurta, leaning to touch his parents' feet for their blessing.

"I saw him on a billboard last week," I said to my grandmother.

"I think the parents want him to go into the family business. They're just letting him have his fun now, pleased he's marrying a Brahmin. Darling, are the threads on the back of this thing unraveling?"

Geeta was wearing her mother-in-law's heavy Banarasi Jamawar sari. I inspected the back.

"It's real gold thread," she said. "I'm worried the metal is too heavy for the old fabric now."

"It looks fine to me, but, Mummy, what if the whole thing unravels around you? Did you wear nice panties?"

"Quiet," said my grandmother as she arched her neck, looking at her behind.

Across the room, there was a loud crash. Hari, in dancing, had inadvertently spun Mishti too close to a flower arrangement on a side table and lost his balance, sending her backward into the table. Seth had caught Mishti before she fell, but the vase shattered into shards, water and petals everywhere.

In seconds, Bari had taken charge, and the catering team came in with mops and brooms. Mishti, laughing it off, took her husband by the hand and rejoined the dance floor even as Arjun's father, Mr. Ghoshal, narrowed his eyes at the father of his son's bride.

I watched Biddy, in the center of her chattering circle, search the room with her eyes until she found her father, and it was impossible to tell whether it was relief or anger in B2D's eyes, because she, like us all, had become an expert at concentrating, distilling, bottling thought and heat and fury and joy, such that we were generations of Lahiri women, perfumed with the barest trace of what we truly felt.

AFTER THE CHOREOGRAPHED performances by family and friends, the party began to descend into freewheeling dancing, fueled by the six cases of alcohol that had been delivered in the afternoon. Malati, enrobed in heavy jewelry, was helping Gina and my mother ready the little stage for the ring ceremony. It was unusual to see my mother take pleasure in anything involving the family; watching her arrange flowers and light candles was testimony of Biddy's effortless lovability. It gave me no small measure of happiness to see her this way.

"Can I help?" I asked them.

Malati, Gina, and my mother, whispering to each other, sprang apart a little when I came close.

"Oh, Lila, yes. Could you find Biddy, please? We've looked everywhere. Ginger even tried to text her, but she won't text her back," said Malati, breathless with excitement.

"Mala, don't make a dramatic thing of it," said my mother. "Lila, she's probably just taking a breather in one of the rooms and forgot her phone. Can you check?"

"What if she doesn't want to get married and has run off?" whispered Malati.

"Be quiet," said Gina. "Her in-laws are ten feet from your rumormongering. Lila, can you please try to find her now? We should have them exchange rings before Mrs. Chatterjee falls asleep and Hari gets any drunker."

BUT MALATI WAS right; Biddy was nowhere to be found. I searched all the bedrooms—even Rana and Gina's, which I had not entered before—each door unlocked, to my eternal amazement, each room a chamber of its own secrets. On Rana's bedstand, there was a copy of Rilke's *Letters to a Young Poet* and, below it, a folder. I picked up the book and flipped open the folder—it was a drawing of his empress-esque mother, Katyayani, whose ring now shone on my finger. I put the sketch back in and placed the book over it, turning off the lamp. There was no place to hide here, in this fortress of secrets with its unlocked doors. I knew where Biddy was.

Standing on my mother's studio's patio, the only place in the house from which you could see into the Secret Sixth, I watched Biddy smoking a cigarette ten feet above me on the ledge of the hidden terrace. As she exhaled a long stream of smoke, as if feeling my eyes, Biddy turned. I flipped on my mother's patio lights, and Biddy raised her hand in a wave, stubbing her cigarette out and rising. Even in heels and a ghagra, she slipped down the stairs easily.

"Hi," I said, walking toward her as she descended. I slung an arm around her shoulders. "You look pretty. And they've sent the cops to look for you."

"Thanks. You look so New York. Want some gum?"

"No, but you better spit that out before we go downstairs, unless you want to be chewing while you get engaged."

"It's for the smell of the smoke. I chew and swallow. Poof," she opened her mouth.

"Very good. That's going to come out of your butt in the morning, as is. Here, let me fix your dupatta." She stood obediently as I shifted it back over her shoulder.

"Sometimes I wish Baba would die, you know," she said into the night.

We both stilled. I reclipped the safety pin to her blouse.

"Bid," I said, stroking the round of her shoulder. "You shouldn't say things like that."

Even as I said the words, I wondered at how much of a Lahiri I had turned into, adopting their secret language of things unsaid.

"I don't really mean it, but if he was gone"—she closed her eyes—"can you imagine how much easier our life would be?"

She turned to look at me.

"I've felt that way about Ma," I said, unwilling.

We stood there, looking out into the view of Kolkata below us, the sound of a party wafting upward, like the smoke and perfume on Biddy's skin.

"Yes, but you don't love her the way I love him. He's the person I love most in the world, and I want him to disappear, just get away from us," she said, her anguish ripping through the night. Stricken, she looked at me. "I didn't mean—"

"It's true," I said. "I don't." My phone began to vibrate. "Yes, Ma?" I said into the phone. "Biddy and I are just fixing her dupatta. On the terrace. Yes. Okay, we'll be downstairs in five minutes."

I took the phone away from my ear and looked at Biddy. "Biddy, I want to help. We have to talk."

Biddy looked away from me. "Not tonight," she said.

I nodded. "You do want to get married, right?"

"God, yes. He's the best," she said, the eyeshadow over her eyes forming little sunrises, glowing like sequins. "We're going far away from here. Going to travel."

"You'll miss it when you're gone long enough," I said.

"Is that how you feel?"

I shrugged. "It feels good to be here. You ready?"

DOWNSTAIRS, AS IF reclaiming a prize jewel that had gone missing, Malati, Gina, and my mother whisked Biddy away from me the second we reentered the party, my mother glaring as if I had stolen the prize myself. Amused, I watched as my grandmother reigned supreme among the gaggle of glittering birds that were her friends—larks, my grandfather used to call them, the most reliable network of spreading information and rumors in Ballygunge Place.

"Lila," called my grandmother, imperious. "Come here."

"Turned out nice-looking, didn't she?" said a lark, inspecting me.

"Too thin, of course, but eyes just like yours, Geeta," said another.

"You must stay out of the sun, my dear," said a third. "India is very harsh on the skin. Can't get any darker now." There was a lilt in the lark's trill.

"No husband?" asked a fourth.

"Not yet, but I am hopeful," said my grandmother, raising her eyebrows with a meaningful nod in the direction of Seth.

"You'll have little caramels for grandchildren, Geeta."

The larks threw back their heads and laughed.

"Vik," I called, a little desperate as he walked in, resplendent in a floral kurta.

"Hi, Lila. What a dress."

"Jumpsuit," I said as the larks examined my outfit.

"Halter," whispered one to the others.

"I haven't seen you in so long," I said to Vik. "I've missed you."

"Had to go to Goa for a story," said Vik, smiling at each of the larks as he touched their feet. "Made a little vacation out of it."

I remembered Seth's description of Vik and Nina at the protest, even as I wondered if Vik was involved in the crusade to take the house from me.

"What a good boy, Bikram. So accomplished. Why not married yet?" asked a lark.

"Because you won't have me, aunty," said Vik, sending the larks into paroxysms of delight. "Now, I must introduce our American Lila to the delights of vodka phuchka."

Vik and I made our way toward the laden buffet table.

"One plate," said Vik to the caterer, who filled six crisp phuchkas with tamarind vodka water. "You needed rescuing," he said as he took the plate.

I nodded, grateful as I took a phuchka and put the whole thing into my mouth.

Vik popped a phuchka into his mouth, then looked up from his plate, chewing with pleasure. "Plus, Adil, Silks, and Seth are hanging on the verandah, and that's where we should go to have some fun."

25

ON THE OTHER end of the great room, a set of old teak doors, the slatted frames repainted in a gleaming olive color, opened out into a little balcony with engraved stone rails, overlooking the courtyard below. On it, Adil stood, talking to Seth as if they had known each other for years. A woman stood between them, throwing back her head in laughter, like one of the larks.

"Hey, cool kids," said Vik.

"Vik, it's good to see you," said Seth.

"Thank you, my man," said Vik. Then he hugged Adil and kissed the woman's cheek.

Adil turned around as I stood stupidly in the doorframe, my jumpsuit suddenly too tight, too revealing, my lipstick a scream for help, my hair clumping into damp, sweaty tendrils.

"Lila, come join us," said Seth. "Have you met Adil?"

Vik laughed. "Lila and Adil are tight," he said.

"Yeah, we all grew up together," said Adil as his eyes stopped briefly on my face, then traveled to my bare shoulder.

"Adil's the man," said Seth. "Telling me all about the work he and Vik do over at their paper."

Seth reached for me as I came closer, placing an arm on my back, the boyfriend I suddenly had.

"Hi, Lila," the woman said.

"Lila, this is my wife, Silky," said Adil.

I held out my hand. "It's nice to meet you."

Silky enveloped me in a cloud of sleek hair and long arms and a faint whiff of something expensive, the furthest thing I supposed one could get from persimmon power.

"I love your jumpsuit," she said as she held me close and kissed my cheek.

"Thank you," I said. "It's nice to finally meet you."

"I have heard so much about you—you were my husband's first love."

I heard myself laugh. I imagined them reliving the years Adil and I had spent together as he unbruised my heart, dissecting me as an important ex, the way married people might.

"Well, hardly. We were kids then," I said.

"Your first boyfriend, Lila?" said Seth, delighted. "What was she like? Impossible? And impossible not to love?"

"That's exactly how he describes her," said Silky to Seth, the two of them discussing us, as if in on a secret we were not privy to.

Adil smiled, twisting his head as if easing a crick in his neck.

"Lila was like one of us," said Vik. "More a boy than the other girls. The other girls smelled nice and wore pretty dresses, but Lila played cricket like a dude and raced around Nandan with us when we were rehearsing plays."

"That's not how I remember it," said Adil, easy.

Seth laughed, reaching for me. "I'm sure not."

"After you left, he was brokenhearted for years," said Silky. "Went through girlfriends like a cook sifting flour—finally landing on me."

She ran her fingers over his cheek with a quiet sense of possession, this woman whom Adil had trusted enough to tell her the details of our years together. I felt a tightening in my chest.

"Looks like he did well for himself," I said as Silky shone.

"Where did you meet?" asked Seth.

"Our mothers are friends. They hatched a plot," said Silky.

You could tell she had told the story a thousand times, taking pleasure in the quirks of their fate.

"What about you guys?" asked Silky, as if we were two couples exchanging the kind of stories couples did.

Vik leaned against the balcony, visibly bored, as he lit a cigarette. I wished I could share it.

I caught Adil looking at me, the faintest trace of amusement in his eyes.

"At work," said Seth. "It took us a while to get together. New York isn't meant for lovers—it's too quick. Until it isn't." Seth placed a palm on my bare shoulder blade.

I smiled at him.

"That's so sweet," said Silky, her arm going around Adil, a mirror to Seth. "Adil tells me you're in publishing? I've always thought editors had the greatest power of all—to be able to find stories."

"Sometimes even before writers know that they have it in them," said Seth.

"I don't know about that," I said.

"Oh, that's right," said Silky. "You're his editor too. Seth has been telling us all about his book—it sounds fascinating, like something that would win a prize."

"Seth certainly deserves a few of those," I said, feeling Adil's eyes on my face. I looked over my shoulder, a little desperate. "I should go see if they need any help before the ring ceremony."

"Oh stop, Lila. You're allowed to have some fun," said Vik.

Rinki was bustling about Biddy, Arjun, and the larks. As she caught my eye from across the room, I blinked thrice. She smiled and raised her hand in a little wave but went back to her duties. She had forgotten our little code, the signal we used to send each other when we needed rescuing—from a lark, or someone's perfect wife.

"The larks look like they have it covered," said Adil.

I looked up at him, and our eyes locked over the secret name that I had shared with him when we were teenagers.

Silky tugged on Adil's arm. "Baby, do you remember that great book you gave me to read? What was it called again? Seth, your novel sounds just like it."

"Oh no," said Seth, covering his face with his hands.

Vik laughed, putting an arm around Seth. "Silks, don't break the man's heart. Page 454, and now you tell him it's been done already."

We laughed, so genuine was Silky's horror as she struggled to explain her-self, this kind and vulnerable woman who turned to Adil repeatedly—now reassurance, now a shared touch, his leaning over to pick up her bag for her, their nearness.

"*A Heartbreaking Work of Staggering Genius*," said Adil.

Silky looked at me for help, her eyelashes perfect against her arching brows, a warmth to her features against the striking bones of her face—I hated her in the moment.

I nodded. "You're exactly right. The same kind of coming-of-age. Nothing in common with your book, though," I said to Seth. "Unlike *Great Expectations*, which you've rampantly stolen from, obviously."

"And there you have it: my editor, my nightmare, and the love of my life," said Seth, theatrical, as he leaned in to kiss me—Adil and I frozen in place at this declaration, this notion that I was a love of one life, while he was that of another.

"No kissing, or you'll have Geeta Kaki calling the police on you, my friend," said Vik.

"Are you a journalist as well?" I asked Silky, desperate to say something.

"Oh, no. I have no creative talents. I'm a lawyer."

"Technically, journalists aren't supposed to be creative," said Vik, "even though this country offers them no other alternative."

"That's nice," I said.

Adil was a lawyer. She was a lawyer. They were both lawyers, who talked about law and practiced it in harmony, in the same way they stood close to each other, both too tall, occupying all of the breath I had left.

Seth reached for my hand next to him. It was the smallest of motions, undetectable almost under the darkness and shadows, behind Vik and Silky's chatter, but I saw Adil's eyes flicker, as my palm met skin, my fingers curling around good, kind Seth.

It would have been easier if Silky were not effortless around men and women, with an inherent simplicity and goodness to her that I felt a sear-ing twist of envy toward, the kind that made Seth and Vik and Adil lean in toward her, to bask in some of her natural sun.

Rinki stuck her head out onto the balcony. "Lila, what are you doing over here? Come on. We need your help with the damn priest."

RINKI DID INDEED need me: the priest needed payment, and I was in charge of settling all the vendor accounts.

"He demands the money in advance of performing any pujos now," said Rinki.

"How godly of him," I said, following her into the crowded great room.

"Well, it's his living," she said. "And Hari Mama has forgotten to pay him—a few times."

I counted the cash from my wallet. "Three thousand, correct?"

"Yeah," said Rinki. "What did you need rescuing from, anyway? Was it Silky? Is she awful?"

I felt a sweeping rush of love for Rinki, who had remembered everything that was important to us as girls.

"She's fucking perfect," I said.

"Disgusting," said Rinki, pursing her shimmering magenta lips, an arm firmly around me. "Oh no, Lila, they're coming here," she whispered.

Adil's mother, Janani, had descended upon us, with her son and daughter-in-law in tow. She who had made me more lunches and dinners and snacks than I could count when my mother worked all afternoon and evening at the school.

"Lila, my darling," she said, and folded me into her plush chest—this big-boned, warm woman, whose laugh was deep and guttural and filled with the joy that Adil had been raised in, that I had longed to never leave whenever I was there. Removing me from her breast, she examined me as the larks might have, but with love. "My goodness, you're all grown up. But of course you are—look at my own son. Taller than most buildings. Have you met my wonderful Silky yet?"

"Lila and I are old friends now," said Silky.

"Good. Once upon a time, Lila was more of a regular to my dinner table than my own son."

"How are you, Janani Aunty?" I asked.

"Getting on. Knees going bad, but the spirit is fine," she said with joy. "Speaking of spirits, I must get another glass of this beautiful wine. Excellent choice to serve, Lila. Now, you must promise me you'll come for dinner next week."

"I promise," I lied, as Rinki tugged on my arm.

"Look, it's starting," said Rinki.

We craned our necks to see Biddy and Arjun exchange rings above the crowd.

"Silky, you're going to spill your wine on me," snapped Adil, straightening the teetering curve of Silky's flute.

"Sorry, baby, I can't see anything," she said with a frown.

"Just be careful," he said.

"What's with the mood? You've been like this all evening, and it's really getting to me," she whispered, angry.

I looked away, guilty to have overheard, and could not help looking back at them. He had leaned to whisper in her ear, and in a second she had forgiven him, transformed by the uncomplicated happiness that came naturally to her. Her glass tilted again, and he straightened it before spillage again, the practiced routine of married people.

"Look how beautiful and happy Biddy looks," said my grandmother, in front of us.

"First time I've seen her without her phone in years," said Rinki.

AS BIDDY'S COHORT milled around her and a beaming Arjun, documenting every instant, and the priest muttered his blessings over the hazardous little fire in the center of the room, I slipped away from the smoke, the crowd, and the celebratory cheering. In a rare moment for the house, every single person in it was gathered in one place, and the hallways and stairs and courtyards and bedrooms were all empty, lit by Mr. Das's yellow-crystal lamps, which cast flickering shadows onto tiled floors, throwing up dancing shadows on the walls. I needed darkness and silence, and climbed the three flights up to the main terrace.

Before I reached the recesses of the Secret Sixth, my mother called out.

"Lila?"

"Ma?"

I tried to make out her shape in the moonlight. She was sitting at the base of the Secret Sixth's thin metal stairwell. Could she be smoking? No, it was just her breath, curling out against the cool air.

"What are you doing here?" I asked.

"I'm not needed downstairs," she informed me stiffly. "Gina is very capable, and so are Mishti and Rinki."

I sighed. Someone or something had offended my mother, likely unbeknownst to them—an imagined slight that meant weeks of silence ahead.

"Ma, an hour ago Gina said she could have never done the flowers without you. Biddy will be sad if you disappear in a huff."

"I am not in a *huff*, Lila," she said, seething.

I did not want to interrogate my mother tonight, so I slipped past her and climbed up the narrow rungs. It was a quiet night, and the streetlamps had begun to dim.

"Where's Mr. Roy?" I asked.

My mother remained silent beneath. I had not seen Mr. Roy for a week now and assumed that my mother had probably taken offense to something he had said. My grandmother had told me that at times like that, Mr. Roy would vanish from their lives, emerging later, cheerful as always.

"Why would I know where Mr. Roy spends his time?" said my mother.

I said nothing, soaking up the dizzying, dangerous little square of solitude that was the Secret Sixth.

"What are you doing here?" she said, suspicious, possibly only just clocking that I, too, had decided to leave the party.

"Just needed some air."

"I saw Janani talking to you. That woman is so loud. Always the center of attention."

Her voice floated up, ringing through the stillness. My mother had never liked Janani, whose motherhood I had vastly preferred to hers.

When I said nothing, she asked, "How is Adil?"

Despite my very best efforts, my mother had discovered that I'd loved Adil, as a girl. She had called me "loose" for having stayed out late with "the

Sarkar man" (he was sixteen at the time). I never knew how or when she had discovered it, only that there was hell to pay and that I took to hiding and loathing my mother even more than before. It had been one of the final straws for our relationship, shortly after which I left the country.

"He's downstairs," I said.

"No, I meant how is he doing? Rumor has it that the wife and he fight in public, and Malati once said she went on vacation last year without him. Maldives or something."

I felt as if someone were squeezing the air out of me. "They look happy to me, Ma."

"So what if they look happy? People put on faces. I try to be pleasant to everyone—that doesn't mean I'm always serene inside, now does it?"

I withheld the urge to laugh. Music floated up from the party, accompanied by shreds of Hari's voice, louder than Janani's ever could be.

"Plenty of people go on vacation alone," I said as I heard my mother climb the rungs up. The courtyard swam six floors below me.

"No, this was after a fight or something," said my mother, a faint friendliness to her, familiar from occasions when she wanted to bond with me. "They fight in public, I promise. Malati was there."

"Oh? They went over to Malati's house for the occasion of their fight?"

"No, no," said my mother. "Malati's maid cooks for them. The maid was in their house and told Malati."

"That's not public, and that's not Malati being there."

"You don't have to be so silly, Lila. Of course it's true."

"Okay," I said, despite my desire to leave my mother's company. "It's true. So she went on vacation the next day?"

"Yes," said my mother, triumphant. "She left him and went."

"Well, maybe he deserved it."

"Deserved his wife going to parties without him, going on a vacation without him? What sort of a woman does that? I mean, look at Rinki's marriage. That Bashudeb refuses to go anywhere or do anything, and he's always depressed, but still, she understands him and they have worked it out, as married people should."

"Ma, you know nothing about the situation. You, of all people, should not be speculating about someone else's marriage. And what the hell is wrong with a woman going to a party alone?"

My mother's eyes narrowed, her irises glittering in the moonlight. "What do you mean, me, of all people?"

I shook my head. "I didn't mean anything."

"You know, you can be really vicious sometimes with no reason," she spat out.

"I must have learned that somewhere," I said.

"From me?" she said. "From me?" she repeated, her voice rising higher, disbelieving shards toward the moon.

"Ma, be quiet," I hissed.

A figure was walking across the expanse of the fifth-floor terrace just below us, lit by the soft light spilling from the studio. My mother turned around.

"Lila?" called Adil, uncertain as he reached the bottom of the Secret Sixth.

"Adil," I said, walking to the top rung, where he could see me.

"I knew you'd be here."

"I needed some air."

"Lila, we should talk. I can't—"

"My mother is here," I said as I went down the rungs, quicker than I should have, silencing Adil immediately.

"Careful," he said as I almost tripped on the last one. His arm reached out to catch me, his fingers folding naturally around my waist, as he steadied my feet on the floor.

"Hello, Maya Aunty," he said, smiling up at my mother, who cast a shadow over us on the top rung.

"Hello, Adil," said my mother.

Adil let go of my waist as I straightened the neck of my jumpsuit.

"What did you need Lila for?" asked my mother.

"Oh, no, I just came up for a cigarette," he said, patting his pockets. "Big crowd downstairs."

"But you called her name," said my mother.

"Oh. Yes, I thought I heard voices."

She came down the stairs, carefully holding up the bottom of her sari from the rungs, clutching the metal rail with the other.

"You shouldn't smoke," she said to Adil.

I looked at her, our eyes meeting in certain knowledge that, once again, I had been discovered. My mother walked away from us, crossing the expanse of the fifth-floor terrace, and finally, descending the stairs, back toward the party.

Adil breathed deeply. "Your mother scares me."

I said nothing, and he took my hand. I pulled away, as if singed.

"No," I said. "You can't have it both ways. You can't just take my hand when you feel like it and coochie-coo with your beautiful wife the rest of the time. Your wife, who appears to adore you."

"I *feel* fucking awful."

"Do you have that cigarette?"

"I don't smoke anymore," he said.

I laughed, bitter.

"Lila, I've been honest with you."

"Yes, you have," I said, walking quickly across the terrace, Adil following me a breath behind. "Honesty is your fucking specialty. Hide in plain sight. A lawyer's best advice."

"You're here with your boyfriend," said Adil, furious now.

"He wasn't my boyfriend until a week ago," I said as we reached the top of the stairs.

"Glad to have played Cupid," said Adil. "Lila, stop." He held my hand on the curved banister of the fifth floor, the noise of the great room and the party of the second floor drowning him out, his fingers digging into my skin. "You appeared out of nowhere. All these years later. It was like you had never left. But you did leave."

The sharp pang of acid reflux or heartbreak rose in me.

"Who is to say that two teenagers would have ended up together?" he asked. "Maybe this is the way it was meant to be." He let go of my hand. "I love you," he said.

I nodded. My hand hurt where he had held it.

"I can't leave her. It doesn't work that way here. This is my home."

"Lila? Adil? What are you guys doing here?" Seth and a visibly drunk Vik appeared on the stairs.

"Guys, we have been looking everywhere for you—I have hash," said Vik, swaying. "Scored from my new best friend, the YouTube celebrity Aman Salim, one of Biddy's thirty-five best friends."

Seth was laughing, but there was a look in his eyes, a flicker of recognition as he saw Adil and me on the staircase, on the same step. I moved to the stair below.

"One of them is going to make a YouTube video that will set your career on fire. You do know that, Vik?" said Adil good-naturedly.

"My career is already on fire, bhai. One of these days they're going to come for me and set me literally on fire. You can't be a liberal journalist in this country anymore."

Seth, Adil, and I stood in silence.

"Come on, bhai, just a couple of drags?" asked Vik.

Adil ran his hand through his hair. "Fuck it. Yes. Why not?"

"Whoooooooop," said Vik as he bounded toward the terrace.

"Careful," said Adil, going after him. "Don't go up to the sixth. Last thing Biddy needs is you falling off a terrace at her party."

Vik began to loudly sing "American Pie."

I heard Adil laugh.

Seth climbed the three steps to where I stood.

"Hello, beautiful."

"Hi," I said, putting a palm on his cheek. Immediately, he rested his head, leaning into my hand.

"You abandoned me to the larks," said Seth.

"Did they grill you?"

"Like a shish kebob. I may have agreed to let them plan our wedding." After a pause, Seth said, "I'm joking."

"Ka-bab," I corrected.

He leaned in to kiss me.

"What were you guys doing up here?" murmured Seth against my ear.

I looked over my shoulder at Maya's studio.

"I came up for air, then my mother found me, then Adil came up to smoke, and then it got too crowded, so I'm going back down."

"No hash for us, then?" said Seth.

"You can if you like. It makes me too tired, and I'm already wiped out. See you downstairs?"

"No, I'll come with you."

We had started down when Seth, on the step below me, turned around. "Lila, I have to ask you something."

"Let me guess—the larks want you to take one of their daughters to Biddy's wedding."

"Not just yet," he laughed. "Are you and Adeel . . . Is there some sort of, I don't know . . ." Seth was growing more flustered with every word. "Is there some leftover . . . feelings situation . . . there?"

"A-dil. A 'feelings situation'?" I raised an eyebrow.

"Yeah." He laughed, embarrassed. "I sound like an idiot."

"I do love the expression," I said, flirtatious. I shrugged. "I mean, it's always a spark, right? First love, you know? Nostalgia more than anything, really. But no. No feelings situation. You have noticed he's married right?"

"Yeah, yeah, of course," said Seth hurriedly. "I didn't mean anything by it. I like the guy. And his wife is lovely. It's just that—"

"What?" I asked, a sourness spreading across my insides.

"It feels like intruding, when I walk into a conversation with the two of you. Or find you alone, talking. I've never seen you argue with anyone else. I guess I'm a little jealous."

"I'm happy to argue with you." I smiled at Seth, leaning into him.

Seth kissed me happily.

"Adil's married," I said, "but if he wasn't, we would never get together now. We're different people now. But we still have a friendship, you know?"

Seth nodded.

"Back to the larks?" I asked.

BUT THE LARKS had gone home to roost. The after-party had dwindled to Biddy and Arjun's inner circle, who were spread out on every surface of the great room, arms and legs and sequined pieces of clothing flung casually across the Turkish carpet, every available piece of furniture, and the floor. I felt a twinge of envy at their inveterate belonging to each other, their natural intimacy as a group.

Most of the older guests had gone home at the acceptable hour of eleven, and even Hari had made his way downstairs, very drunk, helped by a mildly contemptuous Bari. The caterers and lighting rental vendors were packing up. I yawned and asked Seth if he minded if I left.

"You can finish the party," I said to him. I'm sure Biddy and Vik would love you to stay."

Seth smiled. "No, I'd like to get up early to write. I'll come with you."

Downstairs, Silky, her shawl around her shoulders, the sheen of her bob catching the flickers of the dimmed courtyard chandelier, velvet purse in hand, stood in the courtyard with Janani, waiting for their car.

"Going home?" she asked me with her quick smile.

"Yes, we're exhausted. I hope you had a nice time."

"Lovely jubbly time," said Janani. "The Lahiris always throw a wonderful party. Reminded me of the grand old days. And the house looks beautiful, Lila. These pillars look exactly like when I would come and study with Bela and your grandfather. I am so sorry for your loss."

She enveloped me in another hug. A blue Ambassador pulled up, its silver crest shining in the night. Janani's uniformed driver hurried out to hold open the door for her.

"I think we saw Adil upstairs with Vik," I said to Silky.

"Oh, he never comes home with us if Vik is around. I'll see him in the morning." She looked up at the terrace. "Who knows what they talk about. He'll be home at dawn."

I thought about the nights Adil had spent with me till dawn, when he would return home to this wife who offered the gift of easy trust.

"Silky, let's go home before I fall asleep," called Janani from the car.

Seth leaned over to kiss Silky's cheek.

She put a hand on each of our shoulders. "You must both come over for dinner, or my mother-in-law will never forgive me."

"Just say when," said Seth, radiating visible pleasure at having made friends with another couple, as part of a matching set of couplehood, here in my own land, where he had forged his own identity even before I could understand mine.

THE LAHIRI HOUSE, the tallest on the block, had been strung with lights to mark the occasion of Biddy's wedding. The light spilled out into the streets as Seth and I left, a soft glow spreading over the neighborhood even after the party had ended.

"Is someone in charge of switching those lights off?" asked Seth as we started the walk home.

The night was quiet enough that we could hear Biddy's friends, raucous from a floor up.

"It's custom to have them lit for the whole month of the wedding festivities. They'll come down next week, after the actual wedding."

"Jesus," said Seth. "That's gotta be one hell of an electric bill."

"It's custom," I said, annoyed.

The truth was that I had argued with Hari and my grandmother incessantly about the matter but eventually had bowed to their outrage. Why would I want to change even this revered Bengali tradition? And did I want to bring shame upon my young cousin, the youngest daughter of the house, leaving the house in darkness when a sacred celebration was in progress?

"I bet Biddy would be fine with having lights only during the party," said Seth.

"It's not a party."

"I know. I'm just saying she cares about the environment."

"And I don't?"

Seth looked surprised at my anger. "I'm just saying that it's a waste."

"Seth, I really wish you wouldn't try to wade into our culture and traditions and consider it your moral duty to rectify our ways."

My voice rang through the empty street as I picked up my pace. A rickshaw puller, Amir, raised his head to look at us, from where he had been sleeping on his mat on the street.

Seth held up his hands. "Lila, I'm not trying to rectify anything. I was just—"

"Then don't."

We walked side by side—me mutinous, and Seth frowning in the way he did when he had stumbled upon a problem in the crossword that might need further investigation.

Amir smiled at me, now a familiar face, as we passed.

"I'm sorry," said Seth. "I didn't realize that it was important to you."

I said nothing.

After a moment, Seth said, "You're right. I shouldn't be making comments on this stuff."

"It's important to them. Not me. I'm sorry. I'm just tired."

"What if I come back to your apartment, make us popcorn, maybe we watch a show?"

"I don't have popcorn," I said.

I took in a breath of the night air, letting the smells float into my lungs: flowering jasmine, smoke belched from a passing taxi, someone's kitchen reheating a late-night dinner, likely a potato curry, strands of incense from a bedroom, the air released from the grip of incessant traffic.

"But that sounds nice," I added with contrition.

Seth put his arm around my shoulders, relieved that the odd spell of friction was past us. Lala, the patriarch of the Bandyopadhyay house, stood on his balcony, shirtless, in a dhoti, a toothpick in his teeth as he looked at us.

"What do you want to watch?" asked Seth.

"Something light," I said.

"Oh, what about *The Adversary*? I downloaded it after you said you finished the book."

"I don't know. I don't want to watch a guy kill his entire family tonight. Is that your idea of a laugh?"

Seth smiled. "What about that documentary on whales? I've heard it's spectacular. Should be soothing too."

"I just want to watch something fun," I said, exasperated. "What about *Curb* or the baking show? Or *The Good Wife*. You pick."

Seth squinted, as if trying to remember.

"C'mon, it'll be fun. How about it?" I said, enthusiastic suddenly.

Seth hesitated. "What if we rewatched *West Wing*? We both love it, and it could be fun to start again."

"Have you seen *The Good Wife*?" I felt a stab of anger that Seth would want to take away the only sign of happiness I had felt the whole night.

"Well, no. But I've looked at it here and there, and I don't know that it's my speed."

"How do you know something's your speed if you won't give it a shot?"

"What about *West Wing*? C'mon, it'll be fun. You thought it was brilliant."

"I did. Just don't know if I'm in the mood for brilliant tonight."

"Right," said Seth. We had reached the apartment.

"I mean, is a doc on dying whales what you do when you're miserable?" I asked.

"I didn't know you were miserable," said Seth. "I don't get it. What have I done to make you miserable? This is so out of character for you."

"Seth, you have no idea what is or isn't in character for me. Just because you decided to come thousands of miles east to make some sort of harebrained grand gesture doesn't mean that you actually know anything about me." I felt a white-hot glare blinding me, unsure if the words were from my own mouth.

"All I suggested was that we find something we both like to watch. Can't we just find something we both like?"

"No. You tried to foist your choice on me. We always watch what you want to watch. We always do what you want to do."

We were standing in the open street, and a thousand eyes might have been on us, but something had possessed me, and there was no escape. I remembered my mother's voice: *They fight in public.*

Seth was blank with his own anger, his jaw set, his eyes narrowed. "We always do what I want to do, Lila? Where the fuck is this coming from? I'm not here, away from everything I know, in a country where I can't hold your hand in public or go anywhere without being photographed like a monkey in a cage, to be told *we* do things only for me."

"When exactly did you spend all this time getting to know what I like to watch or who I was, enough to 'fall in love'?" I made air quotes around the words, as if enrobing them in contempt, like an orange slice in melted bitter confection. "When you were fucking me and everyone else in Manhattan? When you were talking about your books and writer's block and your latest fucking endless character problem, that's basically a litany of drivel about how you think everyone in your family was horrible to you, despite the fact that you have lived off their trust fund for your whole life?"

Seth raised a palm and turned toward the street as if I had struck him, his cheek bright against his pale skin, lit by the streetlamp. The heat left my body in one long gush, leaving my palms cold and sweaty as Seth began to walk away from me, toward Malati's guesthouse.

I breathed in, refilling my lungs. With a rising panic, I ran the few steps to catch up with him.

"Seth, I'm sorry. I didn't mean that."

"Yes, you did," he said, quickening his pace as if reluctant to be near me.

"I did not," I pleaded. "I was angry. Seth!" I grabbed his wrist. "When have I ever done that before? Come on."

He crumpled. "You sounded like you *hate* me."

"I don't, I don't." I threw arms around him, holding him, waiting to feel his come up around me.

"I'm not some spoiled idiot," he said. "I work really hard."

"I'm your editor. I know that."

"I was never anything but honest with you when we were lovers."

"I know that too," I said with urgency. Twice in one day—all men wanted to be was honest with me.

"And I'm being honest now," said Seth.

Bright-red splotches of feeling clumped across his face.

"I love you. I feel nothing but love for you. If you think of me the way you just sounded—"

I held him close, sorrow flooding every part of me.

"I don't. I'm so sorry, Seth."

This time, his arms came up, uncertain but in an encircling that swept relief through me, though I could not comprehend any of my own reactions beyond being witness to them. He rested his head against the top of mine. I began to cry.

He stroked the back of my head, trying to calm me, muttering soothing words, as if to a remorseful toddler.

"Will you come back with me? Home?" I asked.

He nodded. "Yeah."

"We can watch *West Wing*."

"No. You don't have to."

"You know I think it's wonderful."

He looked uncertain. "Well, yes, but—"

"And raid my dad's stash of snacks."

His eyes lit up. "What if we watched the last two episodes of the second season. I mean, you've got to love that?"

"Absolutely," I said against his chest.

Seth looked transported in relief. It was enough in the moment that that was true.

The world was so rapidly in motion that to hold on to what appeared real was of paramount importance. Otherwise, it would have sent us flailing, limbs without gravity, into the vast unknown.

I kissed Seth's cheek as Ram Bhai coughed in the distance, opening up the gate of the apartment building, letting us back in, to temporary refuge.

26

THE NEXT MORNING, Palekar called me at seven. I unpeeled Seth's arm from my waist and tried to unravel myself from the sheets without waking him. Champa, stirring something in the kitchen of the house across, waved at me from her window as I went into the living room, shutting the bedroom door behind me.

"Palekar Uncle," I whispered into the phone. "Is everything okay?"

"Good morning, Lila. Why are you whispering?"

"Oh, I just . . . I just woke up," I said, clearing my throat. I was fond of Palekar, but he was a homegrown Bengali man in his fifties, and I was not about to tell him that my lover had been sleeping beside me.

"I am sorry to call this early."

"Is everything okay?" I repeated.

"And you are not at your mother's house presently, correct?"

"Palekar Uncle, I'm at home. My father's apartment. Can you tell me what's wrong?"

"My dear, there is no reason to be upset. I just wanted to make sure the Lahiris were not around you at the moment."

I looked toward the closed bedroom door.

"I'm alone," I said.

"Very good, very good." He cleared his throat. "I must now regretfully say that what we had expected has come to pass."

I wondered if Hari had stolen money from the trust. If Biddy's wedding would have to be canceled. Was the terrace of the house about to collapse? I felt a sharp pang in my stomach lining, my ribs tightening against the cotton of my pajama shirt. There were daffodils all over it, an Iva purchase.

"The Lahiris have filed a lawsuit contesting the final will and testament of Tejen Lahiri," said Palekar, abruptly all business. "As your legal representative, I have received the claim from their lawyer, Bhaskar Gupta of the legal firm Chand and Sons. He has been the executor of the trust, and I am well acquainted with him, as well as the founder of the firm, Param Chand, who in fact was my classmate at the National Law School in Karnataka, Bangalore. In fact, Param Chand greatly respected your grandfather Tejen Lahiri—"

"So they think my grandfather had lost his mind when he made the will?" I cut Palekar off with more than a little desperation. "Have they been able to find medical evidence?" I felt a curious detachment from the news, oddly relieved that it was not some sort of fatal blow to the family or the house.

Palekar paused. "Well, they believe that the existing will—the version that names you as heir and executor of the estate—was not his final will. The Lahiris claim that they have the most recent version of his will, one that he created and signed and stored in the jewelry compartment of your grandmother's Godrej. She discovered it, the suit claims, two weeks ago. According to Bhaskar, the signature and writing are identical to that on your grandfather's other wills and they feel that they have a case strong enough to take to court. Bhaskar also claims that your grandfather indicated to the firm that he wished to change the will and terms of the estate, but he died before he sent it to them. In short, the family believes it was signed right around the time of his last dialysis, before his health weakened beyond repair."

"That's impossible," I laughed. "My grandfather was the most organized man I know. There is no world in which he suddenly changed his will and locked it up without telling anyone."

The bedroom door pushed open, and Seth emerged, shirtless, his hair in wild curls. Champa, a metal cooking utensil in one hand, looked up at us from her window.

I covered the phone and whispered, "Pants."

Seth, locking eyes with Champa, froze, then turned around, disappearing into the bedroom.

"Yes, I agree," said Palekar. "But, Lila, he was very unwell. He was fully in his senses, sharp as his own razor, which he made the nurse utilize for him until his last day on this earth. But he was unable to even lift his head, so excruciating was his pain."

I felt a tightness in my chest. Palekar said nothing for a moment, a rare silence between us.

"He was a wonderful man, my dear," said Palekar gently.

"Yes," I said into the phone, the salt of tears running into my mouth, soaking the thin material of my shirt.

"Lila, there is one more thing. The will that the Lahiris have produced names Hari Lahiri as heir and executor of the estate."

I shook my head in disbelief. "I don't understand. They all know he is reckless with money. He's got loan sharks after him, credit card debt. But my grandmother loves Hari like her own son. Is it possible she swayed my grandfather into leaving it to him?"

"I cannot imagine a sane man viewing Hari Lahiri as anything but a problem," said Palekar.

I took a breath. "They must really hate me."

"Lila, this is their home. Their birthright, survival, call it what you will—in their minds. How they feel about you has nothing to do with it."

I SHOWERED AND dressed, emerging to find Seth accepting a plate of malpuas from an effervescent Champa at the front door.

"I came to see if you were all right, didi," she said. "Something about the way you were walking around—you looked upset."

It was more statement than question, the ordinary directness of a boundary-free, cheerful Kolkata.

"I'm fine, Champa."

"Well, I made malpuas and wanted to bring some over for you . . . And saheb here."

Champa examined the length of Seth with her eyes, filing away details for the neighborhood, one hand on her hip, a reporter's body language.

"Thank you for the malpuas, Champa," I said.

I meant it. Through our window, Champa and I had formed some sort of bond, her watching my every move at first, later morphing into her becoming a self-appointed watcher-over of me. Her deep-fried sweets were a language of love I understood immediately. In return, she could have a little of Seth if she wanted.

As Champa left, Seth handed me the malpuas without enthusiasm.

"You okay?" I asked. He was fully dressed.

He nodded unhappily. "It's hard to snap out of it, you know?"

I did know. An unpaid looming bill, or days of gray weather, or a panic about his writing could send Seth into an abyss. That a fight with me would create a mist of unhappiness over us that might not be dispelled for hours or days had kept me awake even after he had fallen asleep in my arms.

I took his hand, an uncertain low dread filling me, as it always did when Seth's sadness leaped over from his body and settled into mine.

"I'll walk you back to Malati's," I said.

AT ELEVEN, I walked to the Lahiri house. I felt part anticipation, the way one might at a pivotal point of a movie, and part detachment, as if witness to a set of proceedings that felt more theater than life. My mother was outside the main gate, dressed as if she were headed for the university.

"Aren't you coming to the meeting?" I asked.

"I had a morning lecture—I've just come back. I was waiting for you in the sun, and now it's given me a headache."

"Why were you waiting for me?"

"I heard that you and Seth had a fight."

"Ma, I really don't want to get into it," I said, feeling a surge of fury at Ballygunge Place, where all of my wounds were on public display.

"What was it about?" she asked, unrelenting, one hand clutching her tote of books, the other on her hip.

I sighed. "Just a silly thing—about a show I wanted to watch."

My mother looked relieved. "Oh, good. Nothing else, just a show?"

"Yes."

"Did he not want to watch it? Was that the problem?"

"There's no problem. He wanted to watch something else. We resolved it."

"How?"

"What do you mean how? We compromised. We watched something we both liked."

"You mean you both chose a different show than the one you originally wanted to see?"

My mother was capable of holding me pinned under her microscope until I stopped struggling.

"Ma, for god's sake. The show he suggested in the first place was the show we watched, because it was something we both liked. The show I wanted to watch wasn't something he would have enjoyed. That's all. Now, please, let's just go to the meeting."

My mother's eyes widened.

"You mean you gave in? You did what he wanted? You must love him, then," she said softly, looking around as if this was the only this piece that she did not want overheard. "Lila, it is dangerous to always be the one to give in. I worry that you give in too much—to everyone, to your impulses, even to this family."

"Ma, I'm going to the meeting," I said walking away from her.

"I'm certainly not," she called after me in anger. "In what world would I be part of a case that was against my own child? I'm going upstairs to my studio, where I belong."

THE LAHIRIS HAD assembled around the long dining table. As I entered with Palekar, Bari brought in trays of snacks, as if we were gathering for afternoon tea. Bhaskar Gupta, the bony, large-eyed lawyer whom the Lahiris used for all their estate dealings, grabbed a cup of tea from the tray that Bari offered.

"Sweetened properly, I hope?" he asked Bari.

She nodded.

He laughed. "You can't be too careful these days. Bengalis are losing their standards. They use weak strains of leaves and poison the liquid with fake sugar like Equal. Absolute garbage. Aha, Madam Lila, Palekar Saab, you have arrived. Welcome. Sit. Have some tea. Good morning."

He held his hands up in a folded namaskar, his high-pitched energy filling the room.

"You don't have to welcome the child to her own house, Bhaskar," said my grandmother. "Have you eaten breakfast, Lila?"

I nodded.

"What did you eat?"

This was a question my grandmother asked every time I saw her. She would dismiss my reply of "Toast" or "An orange" or "An omelette," and command Bari to make me a meal or a snack. I had made eggs for Seth that morning, and we had shared Champa's malpuas, their blackened edges chewy yet crisp, syrup dribbling down our fingers, Seth momentarily transported from despair by the taste of my childhood. My grandmother would have approved, but I did not want to tell her about it.

"Just breakfast," I said, taking a seat at the table next to Palekar.

Hari sat sipping tea moodily at one end, Mishti next to him. Rana read a newspaper on the sunlit bench next to the window, Gina correcting exam papers on the armchair next to him. My grandmother sat at the other end of the table, next to Bhaskar Gupta and Rinki.

"Hi, Rinks," I said.

"You smell of Persimmon Passion," she said, sniffing the air.

"I thought I needed some today," I said.

Apologetic, she smiled. I presumed Vik had declined to be involved in the meeting and Biddy dismissed on account of youth, but the specific absence of my mother gave me an odd happiness. The summons that sat in front of Palekar on the table read in large print:

THE CASE OF LILA DE VERSUS HARI LAHIRI, GEETA LAHIRI, RANA LAHIRI, AND BELA LAHIRI (DECEASED AND REPRESENTED BY HER DAUGHTER, RINKI BOSE NÉE ACHARYA).

"Well, now that we are all here," began Bhaskar Gupta as if opening a trial, "let us—"

"Bhaskar," said Palekar, putting both his hands on the table. "There's no need for formality. The Lahiris are a family. Lila is one of them."

"That is correct," said my grandmother. "But this is not a dispute about the family. This is a dispute about the house. Lila is a daughter of the house. We want her here. But the house itself belongs to us, the Lahiris, who have lived in it for decades. It is only fair that ownership remain in the rightful hands."

"And by that, we mean Hari's hands?" asked Palekar, pleasant.

Bhaskar Gupta, displeased at having lost the opportunity to say his piece, responded, "Correct. Tejen Lahiri's final will indicates that the estate should go to the oldest son of the family, i.e., Hari."

"Hari and Rana are twin brothers," snapped Rinki.

Bhaskar, perplexed at this, began to leaf through his notes, frowning.

"Lila, Tejen Mama was very ill in the final year of his life," said Rinki. "Hari Mama looked after the house. He looked after us all. Before Ma died, she wanted to make sure I always have a place to go, should I need it. This house is mine too. I can't let you sell it."

"Sell it?" I asked.

"We know you had a meeting with the property developer. Das let it slip." Hari looked triumphant, as if he had caught me red-handed.

"Lila had a valuation meeting, as estate heirs frequently do. Nothing out of the ordinary," said Palekar.

"Is this true, Lila?" asked Rana, putting down his paper. "Are you planning to sell the house? How can you think of doing that? You grew up here. This is our family's legacy." Rana's eyes filled with tears, as he took his glasses off.

"Is that why you wanted to repair it?" asked Gina, putting a hand on her husband's elbow.

"Yes, is that what your fancy elevator is for?" asked Hari.

"And the chandeliers," added Bhaskar Gupta, writing in his notebook.

"Lila is not on trial here," said Palekar. "The issue at hand is that of the will. Tejen Lahiri sent an executed will to the law firm of Chand and Sons, and to our knowledge, that was his final legal testament."

"Certainly not," said Bhaskar Gupta, thudding a fist onto the table.

Rinki let out a nervous giggle and looked at me, her mirth subsiding when I did not smile back.

Bhaskar narrowed his eyes at Rinki. "Tejen Lahiri informed me that he was in the process of making a second will, which in fact he did, which he then stored in his wife's office cabinet—"

"Jewelry safe," said Hari, clearly irritated.

"Jewelry safe, yes," said Bhaskar. "Jewelry safe, where one day Geeta Lahiri, in storing her jewels, discovered said will."

Palekar lifted the document. "And this is that document you found, Geeta Madam?"

"A copy. Bhaskar has the original," said my grandmother.

"I see. And when did you discover it . . . in your office cabinet?"

"Jewelry safe," said Hari.

"My mistake," said Palekar. "Jewelry safe."

"Let's see. I went upstairs after lunch on Friday after talking with Mishti about Biddy's wedding jewels. Mishti asked if Biddy could borrow my rubies, a necklace of floral design that had belonged to my mother-in-law's grandmother, gifted to her, it is said, by Lord Dalhousie—"

"Yes?" said Palekar, seemingly impressed.

My grandmother continued. "I keep the necklace at the bottom of the drawer in a velvet case, which sits alongside all the other jewelry cases. When I pulled the case out, I saw that there was a sheet of paper under it."

"Just one?" asked Palekar.

"Are you interrogating her?" demanded Bhaskar Gupta.

"Just making sure," said Palekar.

For a fraction of a second, my grandmother's gaze slid to Hari. She frowned, looking away. "Yes, just one sheet. I recognized his writing immediately and lifted out the other boxes, thinking he must have left a letter to me"—at this, she shook her head, grieving—"but it was a will. Tejen knew that Hari was like our son, that he would take care of me in my old age. I must die in this house, Lila. It is only proper."

"And you think I would take that away from you?" I asked, my voice rising. Palekar put a hand on my shoulder, but I shook it off.

"Did any of you think to try to talk to me about your fears? You would have screamed at Hari Kaka if he had dared entertain the thought of a property developer, but you feel it necessary to bring me a lawsuit."

"The house is mine," said Hari. "Ours. My brother left it to me. That is all there is."

"Lila, this is just about the legal matter of it," said my grandmother.

"No, it isn't. You trust him and not me."

"We just don't want you to sell the house," said Gina.

"But you didn't come to me with that, did you? Because I'm the outsider. It doesn't matter what my grandfather wanted. You're willing to do anything, just to keep it in the family."

"That's not true. You are part of this family," said Rinki, tearful.

"Enough," said Bhaskar Gupta. "This is turning into a circus."

"Sit down, sir," said Palekar, stern. "This is a family matter, and the family is entitled to talk."

For a second, Bhaskar Gupta looked as if he might charge headfirst at Palekar, his almond-shaped nostrils inflamed.

Hari stood up. "You can examine the signature yourself, Palekar. Bhaskar has said that Tejen Da discussed it with him. What more do you need?"

"An executed will," said Palekar. "This one lacks Bhaskar's signature. As we all undoubtedly know, a will is only valid if it is executed. Only then does it render a prior version of the same will null and void."

I looked at Palekar, my ears and face burning.

"Rubbish," said Bhaskar Gupta, pounding his fist on the table again. "Here I am, telling you myself, that Tejen Lahiri told me his dying wish."

"Bhaskar, that table has been in this family for generations," said my grandmother.

Palekar stood up. "Lila, there is nothing more to be achieved here. Legally, you are the heir. If the family wishes to pursue it in court, they are free to. The law will be the final word, as it usually is."

"Would you really erase your grandfather's final wishes?" Hari asked me, suddenly transformed from belligerent heir-dethroned to loving uncle.

"It's what he wanted, Lila. The house belongs to the family," said my grandmother.

"It doesn't make sense, Li," said Rinki, bewildered. "Why would he leave it to you?"

I thought of the call I had missed the Sunday before my grandfather's death.

"Lila, let's go," said Palekar.

I felt my hands shake as I stilled them, crossing them over each other on the table. "When I went to meet the property developer—"

"Lila," warned Palekar.

"When I went to meet the developer, it's true I considered selling it. I may still sell it."

My grandmother let out a little wail.

"But not once did I imagine that I would not have fairly divided the money between us all. I repaired the house because I love it. I wanted to see all of you happy. When was the last time you went downstairs, Mummy? A year ago? I put in the elevator because of you. I'm still going to do that. Because my grandfather would have wanted me to."

"We don't need your charity," said Rinki, her face bright with anger. "We want our house. We don't want money off a shopping mall or apartment complex. We want *this* house. And you don't get it. *That's* why we don't want you to be in charge."

"Great. I guess I'll see you in court, then. Let's go, Palekar Uncle."

PALEKAR AND I walked through the courtyard in silence. Once in the safety of the traffic and the sunshine outside, a block away from the main gate of the house, under the shade of Mukherjee Sweets' canopy, Palekar placed a hand on my shoulder.

"Lila, legally, they know they do not have much of a leg to stand on."

I looked over my shoulder. A Lahiri could emerge at any minute.

"What if they are right?" I asked, my voice low. "What if my grandfather did make another will and just got too sick to remember to tell my grandmother about it? Bhaskar said he began talking about it in early January, midway through dialysis. It lines up—that's when he began to lose mobility."

"Even if that is the case—and I doubt it—that does not change the fact that you are still the legal heir. The will they have was not executed."

I shook my head in panic. "The only reason I'm here is because I thought he wanted me to do this. That he had some grand vision for my life that I could figure out by doing what he wanted. If he didn't want me to do this, if he wanted Hari, I can't do it. I don't want to."

Chandra Babu, the sweetshop owner, looked at me, curious, from where he was serving rasmalai to a customer. Palekar guided me behind the champa tree that had stood on the street since before my grandfather was a boy, out of Chandra Babu's earshot.

"We must be patient and wait for the facts," he said.

"I don't know." I looked at him in desperation. "Rinki wouldn't lie to me. It's things like that—I just don't know."

"Maybe I can buy you some shondesh. Do you like shondesh? I often find that a good piece of kachagolla, not too sweet, with just the right texture, is a great antidote to anxiety. Chandra Babu makes a good one. Not the best, but acceptable."

I looked at him in disbelief, unsure if he was making fun of me. But Palekar had walked back to the sweetshop, his stomach pressing against the glass pane of the store's display as he placed his order.

I leaned against the tree, breathing in the heavy sweetness of the year-round flowers, cars honking as they jostled past each other on the narrow lanes, bumper to bumper. I saw Hari emerge from the Lahiri house in the distance. I was grateful to be eclipsed by the ancient tree—he was the last person I wanted to talk to. He crossed the street to the tea stall and settled onto the bench.

Palekar returned, balancing two pieces of sweet shondesh on a plate of dried sal leaves. I nodded across the street, to where Hari sat.

"The boy has spent a lifetime drinking tea and gambling at that stand," said Palekar. "My dear, are you sure you don't want a shondesh?"

He looked shocked at my waving away of his sweet.

"I have never known a real Bengali to refuse a sweet," he said. "It is good for your anxiety."

Across the street, Bhaskar Gupta had joined Hari at the stand. The two of them, heads bent low, were absorbed in conversation.

"They're probably going to take me to court right in the middle of Biddy's wedding," I said, bitter.

Palekar, frowning, said nothing.

I exhaled. "Fine, I'll eat the shondesh. Malpuas for breakfast, shondesh for lunch—I really am in Bengal," I said, resigned, as I put the sweet in my mouth.

"Correct," said Palekar, pleased.

"Just make sure we are prepared for whatever they have planned, Palekar Uncle."

Palekar looked at Bhaskar Gupta and Hari, still deep in conversation across the street.

"I will," he said, his voice so soft that I had to strain to catch it on the busy street.

I WANTED TO see my mother; I felt a wave of gratitude that she had not participated in the lawsuit. Perhaps for the first time in my life, I felt a sense of what it might have meant to be my mother, constantly overlooked and underloved and underestimated because of the presence of a male heir. She and I might be allies after all, bound by my grandmother's inability to see us as equal to men, able to lead, or deserving of the same things. It was not my grandmother's fault, and instead a flaw of her conditioning, but I felt closer to my mother than I had in a decade as I climbed back up the stairs of the Lahiri house, now quiet in the postlunch hour of the afternoon siesta, when even the maids were asleep in their rooms.

On the fourth floor, out of breath, I paused outside the prayer room. As I recovered my breath, Mishti, kneeling in front of an idol of the goddess Durga, raised her head to look at me.

"Lila," she said, going from prostrate to fully upright before I had the chance to get away. "I'm so glad you came back."

"I came to see Ma," I said.

"Yes . . . ," she said, faltering at my tone. "I just . . . I wanted to make sure . . . that things . . . that the wedding . . ."

"What?" I asked, still cold.

"That you won't stop . . . managing it."

"If you mean the money, it's already been paid out to vendors," I said, turning toward the stairs.

"No, Lila." She caught my wrist on the spiraling banister, made slippery by its recent polish. "I want you to keep managing it. You've done a wonderful job, and this big wedding has somehow become something to look forward to, instead of a financial and logistical nightmare, like everything usually becomes. I . . . Biddy is my only child, and you being here—it's meant that I can enjoy the wedding and feel emotional without . . . too much worry."

Mishti had a way of searching for words, even as she simultaneously blurted them out, and it gave her the awkwardness of a young child, wrestling with difficult concepts, though she was almost fifty.

"Of course," I said, feeling a rush of gratitude at being wanted. "I love Biddy."

"And we love you," she said at once, relieved. "All of us, even in all of"—she waved her hands around as if bewildered—"this."

UPSTAIRS, MY MOTHER'S doors were closed. My mother did not believe in naps during the day, preferring instead, even on vacation, to pace with the coiled-up energy of a panther. I knocked once, then pushed the doors open, as I had so many times as a child—my secretive mother's greatest contradiction was that she did not lock doors, nor answer them, expecting instead that the world, and I, would find our way to her. The room was dark, curtains drawn against the blazing afternoon sun, the air cool from the many plants.

"Ma?"

She was lying on the bed, an arm over her eyes.

"Yes?" she asked, without removing the arm, her curls a tangle on the pillow.

"Were you sleeping? I can come back. Just came to say hi."

"I have a headache," she said from beneath her arm.

"Is there anything I can do? Do you have medicine?"

"I don't need medicine," she said in the darkness. "I just need some peace."

I felt the inevitable stab of pain go through me: familiar wound, familiar source, even the darkness was familiar. I turned to leave.

"I hear you're going to sell the house," she said.

I looked back at her.

"I haven't decided anything," I said. "I'm going to go home now. I just wanted to say hi."

She sat up, her tangles a frightening halo around her face, lit by the thinnest sliver of sun escaping through an intangible space between the heavy curtains.

"I don't know what you are thinking," she said, vicious.

Rage coursed through my neck and shoulders, swift and hot.

"If you mean the house, as I said, I have made no decisions."

"To think you can just walk in here and behave like you have the right to do what you want—"

"I do have that right," I said. "And I haven't decided what I will be doing. When I do, you'll know along with the rest of them."

"I don't give a damn about the rest of them. They hate me. Rana's dog peed all over my doorstep in the morning, and the smell made me throw my guts up. My head is burning. The smell has given me a burning headache."

I turned around and pushed the door open, sniffing the air. "What part did he pee in? I can't smell anything. That dog is so old I've never seen him climb the stairs up here."

"Are you saying I'm lying?" Her eyes were wide open, nostrils flared, as if she might attack me at any second.

"I'm asking where he peed. I can try to help clean it up."

"I don't need your help. Do you think I wasn't on my hands and feet washing every inch of the balcony? That lazy Bari was taking a nap. And that bloody Rana has not even apologized."

"Did you tell him?"

"Oh, he knows. Like you, he doesn't care. Nobody cares about me," she raged as the room grew hotter, the light now pouring in through the lace, the many-layered material no match for the Indian sun.

"Ma, I don't have any plans to sell. If I do, I won't do it without your consent. Everyone's consent."

"Who cares about them?" demanded my mother. "They don't care. Not about me. All your grandmother has ever cared about is being a Lahiri, this house, and Hari."

"Ma, please. This can't be good for you. If you're unwell, let me get you something for it."

"He should have left it to me," said my mother. "For him to leave it to you or Hari is a slap in my face."

I sat down on her rocking chair, feeling as if her rage might find its way into my body if I did not allow my legs to give way, so intense was its force.

"We don't know what happened, Ma," I said.

"You silly girl," she sneered. "You don't see them, all rotten to their core."

The beautiful, imperious academic was gone, replaced by hatred that could scorch the earth. It had been a decade since I had felt the full force of her unraveling, and even though I knew it would pass, because it had passed before, I felt the outsize fear that my mother was insane, capable of all that madness brought with it.

"Why are you silent?" she shouted. "Is that what you came here for? To mock me? Don't think I don't know all about you. Your cozy conversations about me with your grandmother. Who are you to judge me? Don't think I don't know the way you are dragging the Lahiri name through the mud like a common prostitute."

For a moment, the breath left my body, as if she had indeed punched me in the face or stomach.

Her eyes narrowed to slits, glittering with pleasure. "Oh, yes, did you think I didn't know? That the family does not know? And I have a feeling your boyfriend knows too."

"Knows what?" I asked, my voice calm in my ears, as if a stranger's.

"You have been sleeping with Adil Sarkar. You are his mistress," she pronounced, triumph in her words.

"That's an interesting theory," said the stranger inside my body. "I thought you said the family was rotten to their core. What do you care what they think?"

I imagined the Lahiris having found their way inside me, jostling for space, for ownership.

"You bring nothing but shame on the name of the family. The Lahiris have a legacy."

"I'm not a Lahiri," I said, willing my feet to straighten, my body to lengthen, to rise above my mother.

"I saw you," she breathed from between her teeth.

I turned away from her, unable to lie or confront any part of her any longer.

"Bringing shame to the Lahiri name is not new. Least of all for you," I said, pushing her doors apart, letting the cool terrace air rush onto my face, even as I did not dare to stand in place, escaping down the stairs in rapid flight, exactly the same way I used to—two, three steps at a time—my grandmother's voice floating in the distance, traffic blurring my vision, every blare of a horn making its way into my veins. Nothing had changed, nothing ever would here. The city, my mother, the Lahiris, the house, the language of shame, and I—we were all frozen in time.

27

MAYA LAHIRI HAD been seven when she first ran away from the Lahiri house. It had been a hot summer day and she had spent the afternoon climbing the guava tree in the backyard, occasionally throwing the hard, unripe fruit at the watchmen who guarded her home. Their curses at her were repressed only by the fact that Maya's grandfather was Krishna Lahiri, the richest man in Ballygunge, who would think nothing of sending them back to their villages with a beating and sans a job. Even as a child, Maya knew the power of the upper hand.

When she tired of the watchmen, she climbed down the tree and began her usual afternoon excavation of the Lahiri house, sliding down the gleaming banisters, finding pigeon eggs in forgotten nooks of the vast terrace, slipping in and out of rooms, unsupervised by her mother, who was either committed to an afternoon siesta or attending to Hari.

Her mother pretended to be Maya's mother, but really she did not have any motherhood left in her after attention to Hari's schoolwork, his reading, their board games, whether he had been fed, what he might like in his lunch box, or how she might get him out of the trouble that he usually was in. It did not matter how much trouble Hari got in—her mother would still worship him.

Maya was the brighter student, the better behaved, the fairer, neater, *biological* child, and yet her mother favored Hari because he was a boy, and that meant he would always have the upper hand. With Maya, her mother was the other mother—dutiful, strict, and rule-bound, instructing one of the family's maids, Molina, to pack Maya and Rana's lunches and asking teachers and tutors how Maya was doing at school.

But with Hari, Geeta came alive—she would laugh at his idiotic drawings and soothe his endless scrapes and bruises, and, once, when he had tried to set a pigeon's nest on fire, the eggs in shards all over the green octagonal tiles of the third floor, the pigeons and Rana screeching alarm all at once, Geeta had doused the fire out herself, cleaning up the ashes and eggshells and singed pigeon debris before Maya's father could return home.

Maya liked her father, who scolded his much-younger brother often, once even threatening to send Hari away to boarding school. And Tejen Lahiri always had a kind word for Maya and would read to her on occasion.

That afternoon of the guava tree, slithering down the banister, Maya wondered what it might be like to run away. The problem was the house, which contained Hari's constant needs, and her mother's cold rules for her, and even with her father's sweetness and Rana's occasional pat on the head, Maya suspected that nobody in the house liked her books or her thoughts or, really, her at all. She wondered if there might be a mistake and she really belonged to beloved Molina, who despite Maya's pinching and tantrums, never failed to tell Maya how smart and pretty a Lahiri she was.

"What are you looking at Maya, shona?" asked Molina, wiping sweat from her brow with the end of her soft cotton sari.

The oil in which she fried luchi bubbled and spat up at her, though Molina seemed to never feel its burn. To Maya, Molina smelled of sweat and luchi and all of the delights of the Lahiri kitchen, a comforting constant in her life.

"Are you my real mother?" demanded Maya as she braided her doll's hair into the same braided loops as Molina's.

Maya had heard on the radio about a girl who had been adopted from the maid, and this seemed a rational explanation for why her mother loved Hari and not her.

Molina laughed, her hand over her mouth, wiping more sweat. "The things you say, Maya Didi."

Maya took her doll and went down the stairs, each high step a steep climb down for her short legs. There was no way Molina would tell her the truth.

Maya knew that servants lied—that was their habit; she had heard it from her mother and grandmother with her own ears.

The farther Maya climbed down the stairwells of the house, the more she felt a kind of electricity flow into her legs, as if the house was egging her on to escape. She did not stop when she reached her aunt Bela's room on the second floor. At seven, Maya had never been out in the streets alone, and on this quiet afternoon while everyone slept, she felt as if she might finally find more people who liked her. Maybe her schoolteacher Sister Agnes would let Maya live with her. Maya reached the bottom of the stairwell and, exhilarated, ran into the courtyard, through it, and down to the entrance of the house.

Just as she was nearing freedom, Katyayani Lahiri passed through the ornate gates, her marble-and-wood walking stick tapping on the cement of the entrance, her driver, Somnath, behind her.

"Maya, what are you doing here?"

She swept Maya up in one arm, imprisoning her against the silk of her sari and the faint whiff of paan and cigarettes, her diamond pendant digging into Maya's flesh as she struggled against her grandmother's sweaty cleavage.

"And in your underwear like this. Where are your slippers? A car could have run you over. My god, that Geeta is not fit to rear a child. Somnath, go and find my daughter-in-law. That no-good son of mine doesn't need her to fawn all over him and make him more of a rogue than he already is. She might want to spend some of her time on her own child."

Later, Maya remembered that day as the first time her mother had locked her up. Seething in rage, Geeta had dragged her seven-year-old daughter by one arm back up the stairs, until she felt like her arm might stay in her mother's grip and she might then be able to run away, albeit armless. Geeta had taken her into the bedroom she shared with Tejen, slapped Maya across the face with such force that Maya's entire body felt like it might shatter like the pigeon eggs, and locked her up in the dark bedroom, the lights and fan out of reach, until her father came home and opened the door hours that night.

Later, her parents had screamed at each other and Maya, despite the burning stain over one cheek that had spread like fire across her face, had been pleased. For once, it was her at the center of their lives.

AS MAYA GREW, she noticed she felt things intensely, as if that cheek bruise at seven had set the tone for the amount of emotion she might experience as a reaction to events: A bruise felt like an amputation. An imagined slight was a spiral into worthlessness. Praise from Sister Agnes triggered indescribable joy. Everything was heightened, the syrup of the ice-cold orange lollies she would buy after school a pleasure as intense as the guilt after her first accidental orgasm—an accident of fingers and boredom that had quickened and escalated.

Maya knew that sex was another lower-class delight—she had heard the maids talk about the size of the lobster seller's penis in that gossipy, furtive way of theirs, so different from the disgust her mother had expressed when at nine, Maya had asked Geeta what oral sex was. (Nayana at Maya's Catholic school had outlined the details, but Maya was unsure if it had all been a lie.)

"Decent people do not do those things," Geeta had said in horrified disgust, gripping Maya by the ear and demanding to know where she had heard the term.

Two weeks of no radio had resulted in Maya's permanent decision to be less forthright with her mother.

As Maya grew taller, it felt like Geeta grew more suspicious of her every move, so determined was she to raise an unspoiled Lahiri heiress. But Hari could do no wrong, even when he was found with the youngest maid on the Secret Sixth, she screaming for help, her breasts in the sun, red fingernail marks around her large nipples, Hari kicked to the floor by an enraged Krishna Lahiri, Hari screaming as his father's cane came down again and again on his back. Maya never saw the maid again, and on that day everyone else looked at a teenage Hari with a mixture of fear and disgust, but even so, Geeta offered him the largest piece of fish at dinner.

AT ELEVEN, MAYA once more began to contemplate the idea of running away. This time, she chose to do so during the wild melee of Durga Pujo: a quick loosening of Geeta's iron grip on her daughter's palm in the throng of the crowd, hordes of men and women dressed in new clothes, swarming to admire the goddess at each of her many pandals across Kolkata, the perfect stage to slip away unnoticed from the Lahiris and melt into the populated throng of Bengal.

It took the Lahiris three hours to find Maya that night, aided by the chief inspector and seven police officers. She had climbed a banyan tree on the crossing between Phari and Ballygunge Place, only a kilometer or so away from the Lahiri house, instead of the great distance she had imagined, and so her eyes filled with watery rage when they found her, her father scooping her into his arms as the inspector lifted her off the branches, all of them mistaking her tears for fright, excepting Geeta, incandescent with fury, in full possession of the certain knowledge of her daughter's crimes.

THAT YEAR, IT was not Hari who was sent away to boarding school; it was Maya. Despite the relief of no longer being around Geeta's gritted teeth and hard slaps, their mutual hatred solidifying like burned sugar, stuck to the very fabric of their relationship now, Maya found the first year at Welham School an abyss of loneliness. It was as if the demon of her mother would not shake itself from her. She would frequently call home and ask what her mother was doing that very moment—if she was with Hari, and if not, what Hari was doing.

Eventually, Maya found professors who admired the intensity she poured into her homework and the breadth of the intellect she had sharpened while reading from her grandparents' library: first editions of Joyce, Tagore, Chaucer, and Shakespeare, the last being her favorite. To her, it seemed as if Shakespeare had understood the dark mechanics of family histories like no other, and quickly she fell in love with the idea of becoming a professor herself.

Her father visited her on prize day and parent-teacher conference weekends, watching her with pride as she excelled at academics and won horse-racing and tennis prizes. But every time he would try to cajole his wife into visiting, she was either beset by illness (first, menopause, and then migraines), responsibility (in Tejen's absence, Geeta ran the house, now that her mother-in-law and father-in-law had passed, making her one-half of the Lahiri family's head), or a social commitment that inevitably centered around

Hari (thread ceremony, engagement, marriage, yet another attempt at a business venture).

It was only after an afternoon coffee with Maya's teacher at Welham that Tejen stopped trying. The silver-haired nun, her green eyes pools of compassion in a sea of wrinkles, looked at him with admiration.

"Such a remarkable child, with such a rigorous discipline to her lessons, so polite and well-mannered. You have done a fine job, Mr. La-hee-ree," she said.

"Thank you, Sister," said Tejen Lahiri with pride, his head bowed, reverential even thirty years after leaving his own Catholic alma mater.

"And to have done it all alone, to have raised a motherless infant to such pedigree—you should be very proud."

As the nun went on talking, pointing out that, despite her excellence, his daughter needed to work on her jealousies and frictions with other girls, that when slighted, she had a mean temper, Tejen Lahiri realized that since the day his daughter had left the Lahiri house, she had considered her mother dead and had presented herself as such, and now, two years in, there was no rectification of this Catholic woman's assumptions, and so he never spoke of it again, to Maya or Geeta.

To his daughter's delight, Tejen discouraged his wife from attending an annual Welham end-of-year play (to which Geeta readily agreed), and in the five years that Maya spent away, she only saw her mother when she returned during summer breaks. But increasingly, she began to spend those breaks at riding or piano or study-abroad camps, or at a school friend's home in a different city.

The other students found Maya's single-mindedness odd and her ability to fly into a rage at a prank or slight went from rumor to reputation quickly. Yet as the years went by, she found friends among the children of the oldest families of India, haunted by the legacies of their own histories. The years at Welham became her happiest, free of the beasts that roamed within the Lahiri house.

When Maya returned from school, graduating at seventeen as valedictorian, Geeta barely recognized the elegant woman who turned heads as she opened the door of the car, stepping out into a neighborhood full of admirers, polished diction with a faint British clip, her body full yet demure under her lace salwar, her shoulders thrown back with a new confidence, her hair cut into the short, smart style that the Queen herself favored. It gave Geeta a sudden thrill to think that after all, she had succeeded, that after all, she, Geeta, had raised a real Lahiri, with no traces of her own mother's strange madness. The child's persistent, bitter hatred of Geeta, Hari, the house, and the family seemed all but erased. In her place, a beautiful English-speaking prodigal had come home.

But when Maya stopped in front of the gates of the house and looked at her mother, Geeta recognized the unmistakable brilliance of enduring hatred in her daughter's dark eyes.

MAYA LAHIRI HAD no shortage of suitors in Ballygunge Place—the result of a potent combination of beauty, money, pedigree, and education. The job at hand was to find her a husband quickly, after which Maya's new family could decide if she was going to have children immediately or postpone it and go to college, like she insisted she wanted to. Tejen and Geeta enlisted the help of the Lahiri female cousins and aunts, and within two weeks, Maya had forty-three photographs of upstanding Bengali boys at her disposal, each more well-groomed than the next, all poised to become the lawyers and bankers and doctors of their generation, most of them ready to abandon the motherland for American shores after acquiring a suitable wife.

Maya, exhilarated at the influx of attention, a first in her life, went on chaperoned dates for a full six months, making witty conversation and talking about her dreams of becoming a Shakespeare scholar at Oxford, drawing out even the most reticent of her aspiring grooms, most of whom adored their mothers and had strong political opinions on what Indira Gandhi should do with her life (stop being a masculine bitch to start, they mostly expressed, it seemed to Maya). But for all the delightful outings to Victoria and the urgency she felt at staging a final escape from the house, she could not bring herself to choose a husband. Every bone in her body wanted a life of freedom away from Geeta and Hari, to be queen of someone else's mansion, and yet, despite the sailboats and the phuchkas and the romantic walks around the watchful neighborhood and the promises of allowing her to continue her education, Maya could not imagine herself as any of their wives. Even the most persistent of her suitors began to wear looks of mystified rage.

It was only on the evening when Tejen Lahiri invited the young new lawyer at his firm, recently orphaned of his parents (heart attacks, in quick succession, leaving behind a son in need of taking care of) and the owner of a flat only a few blocks away from the Lahiri mansion, that Maya understood that you had to wait for a man who might send a lightning bolt through you when he introduced himself. His open delight lit up his whole face when he smiled at her, as if floodlighting some long-forgotten dark room inside her, and Maya's desire for him was almost an acute relief.

Mihir De was not a suitable boy. He was a non-Brahmin, to start, from the second-rung warrior caste of Kshatriyas. He was not handsome, and compared to The Suitors, might have blended into the background of a crowded watercolor. He was not tall, and not short either, a rounded man with boyish features, with a sense of wonder whether he was speaking of rabri or Robert Frost or the Rolling Stones. And most of all, Mihir De had something Maya had never seen before: a happiness inside him, ethereal light such that when it touched her, it swept her up in its helium, lifting her off her feet, immune to her mother's protestations of a Lahiri marrying a lower-caste De, her father's hesitation at handing her over to a boy without a family, and the neighborhood's shock at their unbridled romance—kissing behind sweetshops, holding hands in the cinema, a mad renegade love, the likes of which Maya had never experienced before, to which she felt entirely justified, having been poverty-struck her entire life with love, and so now to claim this bounty as her own, was the natural order of things.

THE FIRST THREE months after the wedding were the sweetest. Mihir was madly in love with his young bride, who seemed to him like a bruised jewel. He had seen the enormous hurt that her mother's slights had caused. At the wedding, Geeta had insisted on saving money by serving two desserts instead of the five that had been served at Hari's wedding; and at the reception, she had remarked that Maya should have had a professional tame her hair for the occasion; and before their honeymoon, Geeta had said to Mihir that he had to watch out for her temper. And so all that Mihir wanted in the world was to see Maya smile.

It was a triumph of a fresh start—free of the Lahiris, Maya took on the shorter, lighter De name, feeling a release of darkness that she had never experienced before. Even when his parents had been alive, the De family was wildly different from the Lahiris, almost American in their ways, allowing intercaste marriages and second wives and anticolonial political ideas as if they were the norm.

Mihir De had a law degree from the University of Michigan, and his income at Tejen Lahiri's firm, combined with some family money, allowed them a lifestyle of restaurants and parties and boat trips and holidays to Darjeeling. Their apartment was filled with contemporary fiction (Mahashweta Devi, Philip Roth, Bibhutibhushan Bandopadhyay, John Updike, even Joan and Jackie Collins), Lichtenstein prints, and Jamini Roys. And it was as if the must and the gloom of the Lahiri pomp had lifted and the new Maya, this butterfly, could now fly through Kolkata, a brilliant, smiling creature filled with the promise of a happy life.

AT FIRST, IT was his parents that Maya began to fear. As someone with a life-long suspicion of motherhood, Maya could not understand what she viewed as Mihir's unhealthy obsession for his dead mother and father. He would talk of them, especially his mother, and begin to tear up—their deaths, only a year before, had left a gaping void within him. But Maya wanted no voids inside Mihir De. She wanted to fill him up entirely and have him fill her back, and any reference to the incomparable presence of his parents only served to feed a gnawing fear that she was not good enough to occupy all of Mihir's heart, that in fact when he spoke of his mother's virtues, he was really launching disguised barbs at her insufficiencies.

One night, at dinner at Trincas with another young couple, Janani and Bijoy Sarkar, Mihir chose to tell an anecdote of a vacation with his parents in New York, where his mother had been photographed in a crisp silk Nehru jacket and slacks and later showed up in *Holiday* magazine's Street Spotted section. Maya, grim, had risen midstory and, after twenty minutes in the bathroom, had returned refusing to look or speak to Mihir for the rest of the meal, until a disturbing silence descended upon the entire table. It was their first real fight, and Maya was determined to win it—she had not come all this way down the street to compete for love again. A bewildered Mihir eventually relented, the tears of his young bride too much for him to bear.

When he left the house to spend time with his cricket friends or colleagues, Maya would imagine the worst—that he was enjoying time away from her more than the time they spent together. After a bitter fight, remorseful, she would cook and clean and love him more than ever. These postapocalyptic moments were bliss—they would feel an intense, charged love for each other, as if double the size of the original, and all would be forgotten in a haze of food and sex and sweetness.

At nineteen, Maya found herself pregnant, seven months after her wedding. Mihir threw himself into the law firm, determined to become senior counsel before the end of the financial year—this, he felt, would adequately prepare him for fatherhood. As he came home later and later after work, Maya grew increasingly afraid that she would lose her husband entirely to his colleagues and their celebrations of deal after deal at Olypub and Trincas.

Gripped by fear and hormones and the growing swell of her stomach, which felt like a distended, alien part of her, she would spiral into vicious barbs and accusations: Who had he been with? How was there yet another deal closed so quickly after the last one? Did Arindam not have a wife to go home to? Who was the new white woman on the team? She would rail and attack, while inwardly crumbling, as if witness to her own fury instead of participant, in increasing despair that she would drive Mihir away.

Mihir, descending from his own fury and his exhaustion at his wife's silences, which could last for days—once, even weeks—would break down and beg for her to take him back in their bedroom. And so the cycle would end, and Maya, experiencing pure relief and joy that Mihir did in fact love her, did in fact want her, would welcome him into a cocoon of love that seemed stronger, deeper than before. And for a few days or weeks, they would be happy—until it began again.

WHEN THE BABY came, Mihir fell in love, besotted from day one. But Maya did not want to cuddle the child or soothe her screams, and so Mihir installed Rahelamma, a young, sturdy hospital nurse to keep a watchful eye on both mother and child. Marriage had delivered nothing but a weariness in Mihir's bones. He no longer wanted to understand the complexities of his wife. While ecstatic when he held tiny Lila in his arms, he found fatherhood a burden more than anything. If he could only go back to Michigan, breathe in clean lake air, and shrug off the mountain of responsibility he had brought upon himself.

And as far as Mihir was concerned, the country too, had gone to the dogs. Shah Bano, a seventy-two-year-old Muslim woman, had filed for alimony when her husband had divorced her after forty-three years of marriage. When the Supreme Court ruled in Shah Bano's favor, sectors of the Muslim community were outraged that the sharia law, which did not provide for alimony, had been slighted. As a result, the prime minister, Rajiv Gandhi, had reversed the Supreme Court decision, removing Muslim divorce cases from India's civil law, thereby recognizing the jurisdiction of sharia, which in turn enraged Hindus, who prided themselves on India's secular civil code.

Mihir spent hours debating the laziness of the ruling Gandhi family with his colleagues Iva and Arindam at Olypub. (Mihir privately considered Rana and Hari Lahiri with the same contempt, as privileged men born into money without the desire to earn anything.)

By then, the prime minister had further tried to appease the Hindus by opening up the Babri Masjid to Hindu worshippers who nursed a theory that the mosque was, in fact, the birthplace of the Hindu god Ram. At his office Christmas party, Maya by his side, Mihir proclaimed that India was caught up in shit of its own making, with all the gods and goddesses screwing logic and science, and that he, like so many of his generation, was ready to flee the ship.

Maya had dressed up for the occasion, radiant in a soft pink chiffon sari and lipstick, drawing admiring glances from men who looked at Mihir with envy—yet all Maya saw was the way Mihir talked to Iva, the third senior counsel who had come from New York.

Filled with foreboding rage, Maya said, "We've always coexisted as a nation of many religions. Tension is natural because our identities are complex. That doesn't mean we've gone to the dogs."

"People are complicated. That doesn't mean they're not worth your time," she had protested hotly, fighting back tears.

It was Iva Lechner, the white woman, who had come to her rescue, a soothing hand on Maya's burning shoulder, remarking on how Indians were able to coexist in harmony, especially in Bengal, unlike in the South of the United States, where Iva had been born.

A chastened Mihir went in search of a second whiskey. And Maya felt ashamed that she had ever insinuated that Mihir had any chemistry with this horse-faced, plain-speaking, kind American woman.

On the way home, Maya had held Mihir's hand to his surprise, leaning into him in a way that she had denied them both in the months after Lila's birth. Confiding now in Mihir, she said that their child, she could see, was in need of her, and though every bone in her body wanted to extend the natural function of motherhood, Maya knew that the maternal gene was broken or missing and in its place was despair.

About six months into motherhood, when Lila began to crawl, Maya began to feel the fog lift. The occasional spark of joy would hit her like a ray of strong sun when her baby would smile up at her. Maya would work on her research for her PhD while Lila lay enclosed in the playpen, and Maya would feel a sudden sense of well-being that life was finally starting to fall into place for her, that here was a true happiness, meant for her.

So when Mihir came home at nine fifteen one night to the chicken in white sauce she had kept warm for him, and said through tears that he wanted a divorce, that he could no longer pretend that he wanted to live in the marriage or in the country, Maya felt nothing except a hard certainty that the world was out to get her.

The next day, she packed a suitcase for herself and Lila, and promised Mihir that he could hire all the lawyers in his firm but she would make sure he never saw the one thing he still loved—his daughter. At the age of twenty, Maya Lahiri returned to the home she was born in, that she now knew she would die in, and as her infant daughter ran into Geeta Lahiri's arms, Maya recognized the look in her mother's eyes as she held her granddaughter in her arms, the look that Hari Lahiri had exclusively enjoyed from Geeta, the raw, instant love that Maya had been denied entirely. If this child from her own body had the right to Geeta's love, perhaps she, Maya, would also be entitled to some portion of it.

But when her mother lifted her eyes from her cooing granddaughter to Maya, she said, "Well, this was bound to happen. Your room is exactly as you left it."

With that, Geeta turned away from Maya and took me up the stairs, into the Lahiri house.

28

INDIA HAD NOT sparked in Seth the productivity he had hoped for. The saturation of color and noise, unfamiliar language at every turn, and my big messy family's incessant invitations had disrupted his writing routine. Yet the chapter he finally showed me was extraordinary, with an attention to the character of the father in a way that he had not been able to depict in the previous draft. Now, the man was a breathing monster, with an unshakable love for his country and son.

"I don't know how you did it," I said to Seth, as he rubbed his eyes next to me in bed.

I put the pages down and looked at him.

"There's such a *tenderness* to him. I want him to be my dad. And then, minutes later, he's an evil politician, capable of sleeping with a teenager. It's remarkable."

Seth was awake now. I was genuinely moved and he heard it in my voice.

"God, that feels good to hear. Half the time, I'm gripped by the anxiety that I'll never produce another sentence."

"It's very good," I said.

Seth pulled me into his warm blanket cocoon. Being his girlfriend now meant separate blankets, since he pulled on his during the night, something I had never noticed as a sporadic lover who thrilled in the unfamiliarity of a too-small sheet.

"Seth," I murmured against him as his hands roamed my body. "Seth?"

"What?" He unbuttoned the shirt I was wearing—his shirt.

"I think you should leave."

"Now? Why?"

Seth's head dropped to my breasts. Suddenly, he stopped.

"Wait, is your mother coming over?"

"No." I laughed as his worried head came up for air, out of the sheets. I pushed him away gently. "Although she's expecting me in half an hour. There's been some issue with the elevator. They haven't been able to finish work on it yet, and apparently, it's been making noises in the middle of the night. My grandmother is convinced there's an evil spirit trapped inside."

I kissed the top of Seth's head and slid out of his arms, swinging my legs over the side of the bed.

Seth sat up, frowning. "That's all I get? A kiss? I thought you loved the pages."

I laughed again, picking out a pair of jeans from the closet. "This book is going to get you in the *Times*."

"I can see it now," said Seth. "Another white guy writes out his daddy issues."

He came up from behind me, his arms encircling me. I turned around and kissed him. "Seth, you have to leave."

He let out an exasperated breath. "What is up with you this morning?"

"I don't mean here—I mean Kolkata. India. This is no way to finish a book. Yes, it's an excellent chapter. But you've got at least six more to revise. And you're not going to get it done going to movies with Biddy and Arjun, learning the harmonium from Rana, or hanging out with my grandmother. It's all too much. And as your editor, I need you to go somewhere and focus."

Seth frowned, petulant, toddler-like. "What about as my girlfriend?"

He sat on the edge of the bed, despondent.

"I will be very sad. But as you know, nothing makes the heart grow fonder than a published book," I called to him, turning on the shower. I shut my eyes as the water rushed over me. When I opened them, Seth was standing in the doorway.

"Promise you're not trying to get rid of me?"

I shook my head. "I can't think of a single reason why I would want to get rid of my wonderful boyfriend."

Seth grinned. "I like being your boyfriend."

"Good. Now let me shower, or my mother will consider it a personal attack on her if I'm late."

"The wrath of Maya," said Seth, railing a fist in the air. "All right. I love you. See you later."

"Hey, Seth?"

"Yeah?"

He turned around.

"If I ever decide to open my own publishing house, would you consider coming with me?"

He lifted his eyebrows. "What? Are you serious? "

"No, I just . . . it's just a thought. And of course you don't have to. It's just a thought."

Seth paused, frowning.

"I think I would," he said slowly. "You make my work what it is. But I'm not sure."

I nodded quickly. "It's just a random thought."

He nodded, and I regretted my inchoate, sudden impulse intensely.

"I love you," he repeated as he opened the front door.

"Bye, sweetie," I said.

Seth told people often that he loved them—his mother, his sister, even his friends sometimes—and I was now on that list, because in the world of Seth, redolent with kind, easy love, that was a natural step for his heart to take.

As much as I wanted to, I could not make myself say the words back to him.

THE WALK FROM my father's apartment to my mother's house was littered with evidence of an election campaign gathering steam. The National Popular Front, with its conservative platform, had never won in Bengal before; the average Bengali prided themselves on being secular, born of the colonial British Raj's shaping of local men and women who thought and dressed like them. Bengal had disavowed right-wing religious ideology and censorship and had embraced Muslims and Christians and Parsis as their own. But the NPF was determined to win this year, appealing to notions of patriotism, outlining Hinduism as true Indianism, and mounting over ten thousand public campaign rallies in the past month alone.

As I passed the sweetshop, Hari was reading the paper at his tea stall. The street itself was nearly obscured by flyers, like leaves in the fall in Brooklyn. Inside the gates of the house, my mother, grandmother, and Gina were sitting in the courtyard, cups of tea in their hands, watching two artisans build an ornate bamboo construction, inside which the Lahiri priest would perform Biddy and Arjun's wedding ceremony in two days' time.

"Outrageous," said my mother. "Just outrageous. To think they would come here and imagine that we would vote for them. That will be the end of Bengal, of freedom of speech, of women's rights and secularism."

"Far be it for your freedom of speech to come to an end," said my grandmother mildly.

My mother glared at Geeta. "This is not a joke, Ma. You should educate yourself—"

"Oh, here's Lila," said Gina hurriedly. "Lila, what do you think about the National Popular Front? "

"My Lila is an American," said my grandmother fondly.

"Hi, Mummy," I said, giving her a kiss.

My mother and I had not spoken since the last time we had met, the afternoon of her migraine, and neither of us looked at each other. I sat down, and almost immediately Bari appeared.

"Tea, Lila Didi?"

"Yes, thank you, Bari," I said in Bengali.

"The whispers of approval for the NPF in the university worry me," said Gina.

"They're all fat cats, just looking for a reason to hide their bigotry in their fiscal excuses," said my mother hotly.

"The problem is that the left has its own problems of corruption and laziness. There's nobody to vote for," Geeta said, sighing.

"Ma, stop talking like that. The choice is clear. The NPF believes in ethnic cleansing," said my mother, the tips of her ears beginning to redden.

"I think there might be a real danger, though, of the NPF winning," I said. "Every sweetshop owner, electrician, and flower store has their flyers."

"That's right," said Gina. "I'm sure the NPF is slipping a little something into their pockets in return for the favor, maybe even in return for the vote. And remember, the prime minister won the nation because he campaigned so hard, even used a hologram in the villages—they think he's a god of sorts."

"It'll be important for the People's Left to get citizens to vote," I said.

"Bengalis are famous for being lazy. This is not your American Obama election. If the left loses and the right wins, we will shrug and eat a second shondesh," said my grandmother.

"What nonsense, Ma," said my mother. "You're correct, Lila. The key is to mobilize the vote, especially the youth. Gina and I are part of the university movement, and I know Vik is leading the local council chapter in Ballygunge and Howrah."

"Even if they lose," said Gina, "the support they're building worries me. It's true that the left is complacent and forgets that they must serve the people."

Like my mother, Gina was considered a voice of authority at the university, and I felt a wave of pride for the fearless women of my family, my rage at my mother forgotten momentarily.

Hari strolled in, newspaper under an arm, toothpick in his mouth.

"Lila Ma," he said. "How fresh you look today, like a little flower. The pollution of Kolkata is doing your cheeks wonders. Are these two talking politics again? Tell me, what are the three kinds of people in the world?"

My grandmother looked at Hari fondly as he crouched by me.

"Can you guess, Lila Ma?" he said.

"Good, bad, and worse?"

"Those who can count, and those who can't."

Even in the face of the silliest joke, there was an effortless goofiness that was charming about Hari, and I saw my mother struggle not to smile.

"Now tell me, what's the most terrifying word in nuclear physics, Gina?" said Hari. "Come on, give it a try."

"'Bomb'?" said Gina.

"No. 'Oops,'" roared Hari, and we collapsed in laughter around him.

My mother stood up. "Lila, it is time for lunch."

Apparently, in her mind, we had made up.

Hari sat down next to me. "Why are you stealing my Lila Ma away so quickly? Lila, tell me how your dear father is—it's been so long since I met him."

My grandmother and Gina stilled with discomfort. Mentioning my father in the presence of my mother was akin to lighting a fire. It had been twenty-eight years, yet my mother's pain at having been infinitely wronged by an immoral man and his white girlfriend remained a fresh welt.

"He's fine, Hari Kaka," I said.

My mother's open hate enveloped us as she walked away, up the stairs, disappearing.

"Such a good man, Mihir Babu," Hari murmured.

"Really, Hari," said Gina, gathering up her teacup and rising. "Is there no limit to your insensitivity?"

Hari laughed as even my grandmother shot him a reproachful look. "She's going to take all her anger to the grave," he said. "Now tell me, Lila Ma, are there business opportunities in America for someone such as me?"

IN THE AFTERNOON, the entire family except my mother was crowded in a circle around the elevator, in various stages of outrage at its incompletion. Mr. Das and his men were riding in it, testing its machinations and making notes as they went up and down, the elevator emitting horrifying shrieks, as if on its dying, last lurch.

"Last night, there were wails coming from inside the machine," my grandmother muttered in Bengali, ominous. "I'm telling you, something dark lives in there. When I came out to see what the crying was, it began to rain."

"It's not just a machine, Geeta Kaki," laughed Biddy, gazelle-like as she lounged under the banana tree, filming us with her phone. "It's a *time* machine."

"You're sure the crying wasn't from one of your TV shows, was it?" I asked.

"Be quiet," said my grandmother. "You can laugh at me, but something evil is trapped inside. Those sounds are not of this world." She tapped her father-in-law's cane on the ground. "In this lifetime, I will not ride in that thing."

"That thing will make your life a lot easier," I said. "You'll never have to take the stairs again."

"Boudi, we've called the priest. Once the machine is ready, he will come and perform a pujo and cleanse the air inside," said Rana to my grandmother as he stared unhappily at the elevator.

Mr. Das waved cheerfully from inside. My grandmother frowned, her face dark in the shadow of the banana tree behind us.

Gina smirked. "Is the priest going to break a coconut on the glass door and assure us that the ghost of Krishna Lahiri has finally found its way to heaven? I'd prefer Lila assure us we won't plunge to our death if we get on that thing."

"Don't you dare talk of my father-in-law like that, you disrespectful girl," said my grandmother in Bengali, her face reddening, a map of patches of blood and brown skin.

As she walked away, leaning on her cane, Rana frowned at his wife. "I don't know why you have to be so unkind," he said.

"God, I was only joking," said Gina. "Anything to do with the honor and glory of the Lahiri kingdom sets her off. Except the plunging-to-our-death part. Lila, tell us that won't happen?"

"That bloody priest is charging seven hundred rupees for the inaugural pujo," said Hari. "Bloody crook."

"Are we sure this will not permanently damage the foundation of the house?" asked Rana, frowning as if the thought had just occurred to him.

"Guys, could you turn a little bit toward me?" asked Biddy, lowering her sunglasses, her long legs tucked under, her gauzy caftan billowing around her as she writhed to find the perfect angle of the family squabbling. "I'm trying to make a video."

"Biddy, shut that thing off at once. We are your family members. Not actors in a YouTube TV serial," said Hari.

"That 'thing' pays my bills, not you," said Biddy as she and Hari glared at each other. "I make more than anyone in this house."

The glass-chambered elevator creaked to a halt midflight, an outwardly panicked Mr. Das consulting his notes, high above us. Bari let out a little scream from the kitchen on the third floor as the pulley groaned diagonally across her window alongside the eastern wall of the house, seventeen feet in the air. I swallowed.

"It's just a small hiccup," I said. "Mr. Das has planned and designed an extremely safe lift. These are just teething pains. It'll be ready before the wedding."

I LEFT THE house immediately afterward. I had a headache, brought on in equal measure by the Lahiris and the afternoon sun, and I wanted the peace of my father's apartment. As I walked past the awning of Mukherjee Sweets, I saw Hari and Bhaskar Gupta in deep conversation at the tea stall, bhars of tea in hand. They were in exactly the same position that Palekar and I had seen them last, the week before, as if they had not moved, their necks bent toward each other swanlike.

I must have slowed or stopped, because both swans simultaneously looked in my direction. At first, they stared back, then their bodies separated from the single organism they had been only moments before. Hari stood, waving at me with his whole arm, as if we had not been discussing the doomed elevator only half an hour ago. Bhaskar Gupta stretched his legs and arms, his mouth open in an enormous yawn, as his hawklike eyes examined me from a distance, something cold and bored and dangerous in them.

I shuddered. *The evil spirits have made their way from the elevator into the streets,* I thought as I turned into the throng of the sweetshop, thick with the clamor of children and their parents screaming for doi, rabri, and milk cake.

ONCE HOME, I drew the curtains, allowing the quiet darkness of my father's apartment to settle over me. I chewed on the dark, sticky-sweet milk cake I had treated myself to as I held my cell phone to my ear.

"Lila," answered Palekar on the first ring. "Is everything okay?"

I laughed. "Do you know, that's exactly how Baba answers the phone, as if I could never call just to ask how he is."

"Well, do you?"

I paused. "Not often enough," I admitted.

Suddenly, I missed my father fiercely. Kolkata was far away from everything and everyone I had learned to call home. Yet the city had begun to take me in, made me part of its daily landscape, without my knowing when I had been assimilated.

"I'm going to change that," I said.

"Good," said Palekar with a chuckle. "Now, tell me why you called this old man."

"I saw Hari Kaka with that lawyer from Chand and Sons—"

"Bhaskar Gupta," said Palekar immediately.

"Yes, the one who did my grandfather's will. They were just sitting there again and drinking tea."

"They know we're contesting the will they've produced," said Palekar. "They know they'll have to prove in court that Tejen Lahiri told Bhaskar he meant to sign it. That he was mentally sound. They've said he wasn't when he produced the signed will claiming you as heir. Now they're saying he was sharp as a razor a few days before his death and changed his mind. No doubt it involves several bhars of tea, my dear, for Hari Lahiri to prepare his case."

I said nothing.

"I know you hoped they would give up on it," said Palekar gently.

Palekar's unruffled exterior irritated me. "Bhaskar's been the family's lawyer for years," I said. "If he says he was witness, surely that makes their case stronger." I felt my voice rising, shrill.

"My dear, you must trust that I am investigating this to the fullest. In fact, I have enlisted the help of a retired policeman we have on payroll at the firm, to get to the bottom of things."

Could I trust Palekar? I felt a wave of paranoia, on unfamiliar terrain, where nobody felt known to me, least of all the Lahiris or my mother. What if they were all in on it?

Palekar sighed at my silence. "You must trust me," he repeated.

"What if they win?" I asked. "What if they bribe the judge? Or find my grandfather's diaries or something like that?"

"Unless they produce a fully executed will, it will be very difficult to contest the legal one your grandfather left behind."

Palekar was my father's friend, and his firm had been my father's firm. I relaxed into Iva's rose silk cushions, the sweet melting and sticky in my mouth. I let out a breath.

"You're right."

Palekar cleared his throat. "Would it not be easier if Hari were to take ownership?"

"No. He would run them into the ground."

I felt a certainty wash over me.

"My grandfather intended me to have it," I said. "And even if he didn't, I'm better equipped to take care of it. At least for now." I felt as if I were defending myself in court as I spoke, my cheeks burning. "And . . . and . . . it's my house. My history. My family too. I can't let Hari force his way into this—who knows what he would do to it? To them."

"I agree, my dear," said Palekar quietly. "I'm glad you do too."

After he hung up, I must have slept for hours, enveloped by my father and Iva's things, evil spirits and milk cake and lurching elevators, my grandmother's face and my mother's tears, and Seth's repeated claims of loving me, swirling together in a fevered dream.

29

MY EIGHTH AND final week of leave from Wyndham also saw the start of Biddy's three-day wedding celebration, a prolonged marathon of parties that everyone except me had the stamina and appetite for.

"Why can't it be a one-day affair?" I said to Rinki as I examined the accounts book at the Lahiri house.

We were seated in the courtyard, vendors and workers milling about us. Seth was helping Rinki pack little gifts for guests into silk boxes. He had taken my advice and booked a flight back to New York, right after the wedding and reception, which he was under no circumstances willing to miss.

"Like, a wedding in the morning and a party in the evening," I said. "A quarter of the cost and headache. What's the point of the gaye holud today, wedding tomorrow, reception on day four? Feels endless. And why is there a day in between where nothing happens?"

Rinki looked at me, incredulous.

"To recover after the wedding, so you can have the time of your life at the reception," she said. "Why would anyone turn down the opportunity to celebrate for four days? Americans are crazy."

"Not me," said Seth. "I'm one hundred percent here for this extravaganza."

"Wait till you see the guests all dressed up, the rituals and pujos, Biddy and Arjun lifted in the air by the family as he tries to garland her," said Rinki dreamily.

"Wait till we get the bill," I said.

Behind us, I noticed a man leaving the house.

"I'll be right back," I said to Rinki and Seth.

Outside the Lahiri gates, I called out across the street: "Mr. Roy?"

Mr. Roy looked up from opening the door of his car, surprised.

"Lila," he said. How nice to see you. "I didn't recognize you for a moment. That's a beautiful Dhakai sari."

I crossed the street to where his modest cream Maruti stood. "Thank you. It's Mummy's, from when she was in university. Aren't you staying for the holud?"

"Oh. No," he said, embarrassed. "I just . . . I just came to see your ma. She's . . . Well, she's having a hard time, the poor dear."

This took me aback. That someone would say a kind word about my mother was wholly unexpected—an aberration to the norm. I had forgotten that this was what a person who loved my mother might look like. Something felt heavy against my ribs—what might it be like to be my unloved mother? I looked away, suddenly uncomfortable in front of this good man.

"We have our differences," I said.

"You are the person she loves most in this world."

And did you know she takes yearlong silences from me, as if I were a boyfriend tossed to the curb? I wanted to rail at him.

"You should stay," I said instead. "You have every right to be at the wedding."

It was his turn to look away. "Maybe another time," he said.

The man had a sadness mixed into his whole body, and yet he seemed content.

"It's not fair that she won't acknowledge you to us, or anyone," I said.

After a fraction of a pause, Mr. Roy got into his car.

"I must be going, my dear. But I will see you soon."

"At the wedding tomorrow?"

He looked at me, as if curious about the shape of my face.

"As the head of the family, I'm inviting you." I had the urge to laugh as I said the words, imagining Krishna Lahiri's face at the idea of his twenty-nine-year-old great-granddaughter calling herself that.

He nodded, solemn. "Well, then. Yes. I will be there."

I stood there on the street in my starched sari as the sun began to take on its full morning strength, the feeling as if it were lighting me on fire.

Mr. Roy smiled at me from inside his car. "Your mother is a very special lady, Lila. She has brought me a lot of happiness."

With that, he held his palm up in a quick wave and drove off, disappearing around the corner of the sweetshop as it began to open up its storefront.

THE HOLUD WAS a ceremony for friends and family to smear pastes of turmeric onto the faces and bodies of the bride and the groom the day before their wedding so that their skin might glow the next day, enriched and cleansed. It was the equivalent of a facial administered by your entire social circle. In the Lahiri house, it also meant piles of fried kochuri, to be eaten with the slender jilipis brought in hot from the sweetshop, and Bari's famous niramish alur dom, spiced with whole garam masala and made without onion or garlic. There were enormous quantities of spiked shorbot and Kingfisher beer, cooling in a bathtub filled with ice in Hari's bathroom.

The sound of laughter and shouting rang through the courtyard, Biddy protesting the excessive turmeric on her cheeks and arms and forehead, flecks of it in her hair, in all of our teeth, stained into our fingernails and palms, as we came together to celebrate. The house, like Biddy, felt fresh and young, its ancient walls and polished doorknobs gleaming, the granite coldness of the stairs and banisters transformed by garlands of marigolds, the sun streaming in through every crack it could find. I felt a joy that made its way through me, seeping into my skull and ears, lighting up my insides.

"You're a vision," said Vik, a marigold behind one ear, flecks of holud on his cheeks and eyebrows.

"That shorbot is potent," I said. "Tastes like lemonade and runs through your veins like gin."

"Aha, the infamous Lahiri shorbot, a recipe that survived world wars and the British. You think it's gin, but it's pure feni, brought back in every Lahiri suitcase from Goa since the beginning of time."

I giggled. Vik too, was swaying a little.

"Here, have a kochuri," I said, scooping a few potatoes into the fried dough and raising it to his mouth.

Vik took a bite, and I finished the rest, both of us chewing in eye-watering pleasure.

"God, that's good," said Vik. "Bari should start her own shop. Get the fuck out of this place. She's too good for the Lahiris. I'd like to see them function for a full day without her."

"I've missed you," I said, putting an arm around his shoulders.

Vik sobered. "I've been busy," he said. "The paper thinks secular Bengal will come through in the election. But the NPF is feeding neighborhoods a cocktail drug of what patriotism and Hindu pride means. They're making it clear that they want to destroy anyone who challenges the Hindu agenda. They're inciting a mob, winning local seats. And the People's Left is too cocky to take real action. They're the old guard, assuming they'll win anyway."

Hari looked at us from where he was standing in a circle with Biddy's parents, who had been laughing at whatever entertaining speech he had been making. He nodded at Vik, who looked away immediately, his jaw clenching.

I touched Vik's elbow again. "It's Biddy's wedding. Relax. Tell me what I can do."

"About what?" asked Vik distractedly, his shoulders rising, taut around his body.

"The election, Vik. Is there anything I can do?"

"I didn't think you were interested."

"Of course I'm interested," I said with some anger, surprising myself. "Of all the things to say."

"Fine, fine," said Vik, amused. "The next time there's a rally, you can come with me. Just don't wear those heels you wore to Trincas."

I shoved him. "Asshole," I said. "Just don't get killed."

Vik put an arm around me as Seth, balancing a plate of sweets, resplendent in a purple kurta, joined us.

"Seth Schwartz, my man, you look like those white fellows who model Indian clothes in our magazines," said Vik.

"That doesn't sound like a compliment," said Seth, cheerful, his days of gloom erased.

I linked my fingers with his; Seth smelled good, and for a moment it felt like his sweetness was the antidote to the world.

AT LUNCH, SETH was served the largest helpings of dessert, despite his protests, and soon became the object of amusement for the younger generation, especially Vik, who made a thousand colonial jokes, and Biddy, who called him "the real blushing bride."

Rinki leaned over her husband, Bashudeb, and said to me approvingly, "What a good sport he is. An equal match for the Lahiris."

"The very inappropriate Lahiris," I said. But I took pleasure in Seth's easy assimilation into my family, the uncomplicated way in which people loved him and, in return, he reassured them of his own affections.

"Don't try to teach me about bookkeeping, you moron," screamed Hari at Rana from across the room. "I ordered three hundred chairs, and that asshole bokachoda shuorer-bachcha vendor charged for five hundred. He would have never got it past me, but he knew who the moron of the family was."

Hari slammed down the heavy accounting book I had left on a plastic table, which threatened to crack under his shaking fist, the veins of his forehead bulging. Rana took off his glasses, speechless under his brother's wrath.

"Even Laltu at the paan shop would be able to trick you into paying for ten paans for the price of one, you good-for-nothing son of a bitch," spat Hari in his brother's direction as he stormed out of the courtyard, toward the tea stall.

It was not Hari's words themselves, I realized, as much as his ability to shrivel his brother's existence into the smallest that it could be. Rana stood motionless, as if physically struck, more pitiful than the tormented street dogs outside the garbage dump who would trade a kick for every scrap they foraged.

I turned to Vik, who was shaking in fury, his jaw clenched and twitching. He pushed his chair away and went to his silent father, who stood still, looking at the glasses in his hand as Vik put an arm around him. Rana laid his head on Vik's shoulder, their roles suddenly reversed. Seth and I were frozen in place, even as we looked away—Rana's sorrow was too much to look at directly, and even my mother and Gina were still.

My grandmother turned to Seth, her voice loud and chatty, a fist through the stillness. "Now tell me, young man, have you ridden the ferries at the ghats yet? If not, my granddaughter will have to arrange an outing for all of us as soon as the wedding is over."

"I... No. Not yet," said Seth.

No one else said anything. Biddy went to Rana and Vik, murmuring softly under her breath.

Mishti rose slowly, as if worried she might break something if she moved too fast. "Bari. Come and clear the plates please," she said.

"What part of America are you from, Seth?" asked Bashudeb, his high, pale forehead creased into furrows.

Seth, still shaken from Hari's spectacle, cleared his throat.

"Manhattan," he said. "Though I live in Brooklyn now."

"Ah, New York. Yes. A fine place," nodded Bashudeb, approving.

ON THE WALK back to Malati's, Seth was subdued.

"Are you okay?" I asked finally.

He took a deep breath. "That... That was pretty terrifying. Your uncle... He can get really mad."

"That's one way to put it," I said.

Seth shook his head slowly, as if to try to shake Hari out of his ears. "Has he tried talking to a professional? About his anger issues?"

An auto screeched past us, startling Seth.

"Listen, I'm sorry you had to see that. All families are fucked-up in their own ways. It's never as simple as it looks."

"But there's no excuse for that kind of rage. He needs help. Poor Rana."

As we walked, Seth took my hand. "It must have been hard for you ... growing up."

"There were lots of good times too," I said immediately, my heart picking up speed.

"Still."

He shook his head again, and I prayed he would leave it there. It was another two or three minutes to get to Malati's.

"You're sure you don't want me to come over tonight?" Seth asked.

"No, I have an early morning call with the New York office."

"But I'm leaving on Sunday."

When Seth grew distressed, he became petulant, more willing to pick a fight than let go of me, in need of reassurance before we parted. I knew how to tend to him as his editor, but as his girlfriend, I felt as if I lacked a specific skill.

"Are you nervous about flying?" I asked.

Once, when we had traveled to an event for his first book, Seth had taken three Xanaxes, slept through the flight, and woken in a haze that had dispelled only on the flight back the next day.

"I'm nervous about leaving you here, Lila," he said, frowning.

I laughed. "Why? This is my home. I grew up here."

"I think you should come back with me. Come back to New York. Your whole life is there. Your apartment, Wyndham, me, your friends. What are you even doing here? How much time off do you have left?"

"I thought you were willing to live here with me. Why the change of heart?" I laughed.

Seth's eyes widened. "Is that what you really want?"

"No, but come on, Seth. "You know I have a responsibility."

"To whom? To them? They're suing you. And you don't even like the house enough to live in it. Li, just come back with me on Sunday. I . . . I love you."

I felt anger, but it also seemed impossible to look at what was on Seth's face and respond with any measure of unpleasantness.

"You are going to come back?" he asked, suddenly fearful.

"Of course I am," I said. I touched his cheek.

He breathed in. "I'm just worried about you."

"And I appreciate that. Thank you."

He nodded, holding my hand against his cheek.

"You'll have to take an Uber from JFK, because there's a yellow-cab strike that day."

"The Ubers will be thrilled to have me," said Seth happily, at the thought of New York.

"Yes," I said with affection. "Vik and I will take you to the airport. It's all sorted out. All you have to do is get home and write."

Seth relaxed visibly. This is where we excelled—my organizing of his writerly existence and appeasing his fears. In return, he provided me with his many reserves of kindness and empathy, when he was able to think clearly.

"And you'll come home to me soon," said Seth, yawning with a childlike happiness. "God, that lunch was good."

I kissed his cheek. Malati waved at me from inside the guesthouse.

"See you tomorrow," I said.

30

ON THE MORNING of Biddy's wedding day, I had a very early Skype session with Dr. Laramie. I was ready with the dozens of reasons that had prevented me from weekly therapy, yet when the screen flickered to life and he appeared, he felt like an old friend, glad to see me and curious why I had suddenly called out of the blue. He settled into his chair, his thin face pleasant, his mustache a little overgrown as usual, giving him the rumpled, learned air of a nice, somewhat-interested college professor.

"Tell me how you're feeling, Lila," said Dr. Laramie.

I wish he would learn a little small talk, I thought, irritable. Yet I began to talk, and then I rambled on, presenting events in jumbled order, my feelings about them as fragmented as the narration—the house, the case, the men, the Lahiris, Wyndham, Molly, even the elevator. Laramie nodded in his earnest way when I stopped, out of steam.

"And your mother? Do you not see her often?"

"Of course I do. Why?"

"You haven't mentioned her."

"There's nothing new to report. She's exactly the same."

He nodded again. "So you see her often?"

"I see her as much as I see any of them. She has her university, her work."

"But surely, being near her, after all these years . . . has made some impact?"

He squinted at the screen, as if looking for something.

"It's not that I don't want to talk about her," I said. "But there really is nothing new to say. She gets angry, doesn't talk to me for a while, forgets why she was angry, gets angry with someone else, falls madly in love with me for a few days, rinse and repeat, same old, same old."

Laramie cocked his head. "Yes, but now she is near you. Not on the phone."

I exhaled. "In a way, it's easier. It doesn't matter that she hasn't spoken to me for a week—I still see her come and go." I shrugged. "It matters less."

"Does it?" he asked, cocking his head to the other side.

"I really wanted to use the time we have today to di—"

"Lila," said Laramie, writing in his notebook. "Do you think it is easier because now you have some reassurance that she physically cannot leave your life? When she stops speaking to you, you are no longer afraid that she has disappeared into the ether, never to return? Being in her house perhaps means that she cannot disappear on you, no matter if she tries?"

"Well, I guess this is what happens when you pay for psychoanalysis," I said. "You suffer psychoanalysis."

Laramie smiled.

"I was hoping to talk through the difficulties I'm having with my ex-boyfriend."

"The childhood sweetheart?"

"Yes."

"The one who loves his wife?"

I looked at Laramie as he nodded.

"Tell me," he said. "When you feel love for someone, what does that feel like to you?"

I wished I hadn't requested the session, so filled with potholes and riddles.

"I don't know," I said.

"When you think of this man, what does that feel like to you?" Laramie said gently, with another nod. "Close your eyes, if you like. Just tell me how you feel."

Resolving never to seek his services again, I closed my eyes.

"Good. Now tell me how you feel."

"I don't know," I said, images of Adil—rain-soaked, at work, in my apartment, inches away in my bed, as a teenager—engulfing me.

"Just describe the way you're feeling now, the physical sensations in your body," said Laramie, light-years away.

I felt a pricking, like an insistent shard under my skin, in my chest. I opened my mouth to let in some air, but the pricking did not go away. Instead, a sadness made my heart beat faster—like fear, but heavier, sinking into my stomach. I opened my eyes.

"Do you want to stop?" asked Laramie.

"Aren't you going to give me a tool, some sort of exercise or breathing, to help with the situation?"

Laramie looked reflective. "You could do a chair exercise when you want answers. Imagine he's sitting opposite you. Ask him a question, then put yourself in his shoes and answer it as honestly as you think you can. But I'm afraid you might have to let yourself do more of what we just did. Allow the feeling to descend, note the physical sensations in your body, then try to let them go."

"Should I be writing these descriptions of feelings down?" I asked.

"Sure, if you like."

"Just tell me what you need me to do," I said.

Laramie looked up at the sharpness in my voice. "Yes, write it down, and maybe toss it into the trash after. But even if you just name it in your head, with practice, it could get easier to deal with."

"So no solutions. Shit just gets easier to deal with?"

Laramie shrugged. "Pretty much. But this might get you there a little quicker. Maybe even in one piece."

He looked at the clock. It was 7:54 p.m. in New York, 5:24 a.m. the next day in Kolkata, and right on cue, Laramie said, "That's all we have time for today, but I hope you'll schedule something before another eight weeks pass us by."

I nodded, fidgeting, eager to leave his screen.

"Lila," said Laramie, as if outlining a genial afterthought. "People tend to develop narratives about love, based on their early perceptions of it. For example, if a child had an absent parent, he or she might grow up associating neglect with love, even confusing one for the other. Our neural networks love to form patterns, and without attention, it's easy to let those patterns deter-mine what we think we're feeling."

"Adil doesn't treat me badly," I said, suddenly furious. "I'm not confused about the way I feel about him. He's always taken care of me. I just need a little help getting over him."

"Yes," said Laramie, agreeable. "But it may well be that if someone creates a situation that may result in trauma, your body and brain might be trained to mistake your response to that as love. Just a thought." He looked sympathetic yet again. "As you so rightly point out, analysis is what one must suffer if they come to me. It doesn't always mean that the analysis is set in stone. People are far more complex than that."

"You don't know our history," I said.

"No," said Laramie.

We sat in silence for a few minutes.

"Now let's have you breathe in and out a few times, just to relax as we end the session," said Laramie, his eyes floating to the clock on the unseen wall across from him. "Breathe in . . . hold . . . breathe out . . . hold."

THAT AFTERNOON, PALEKAR had called, four hours before the wedding. He said that he had news but refused to tell me what it was, only that I should meet him at the Lahiris' law firm, Chand and Sons, at two.

"If it was bad news, Palekar Uncle would have waited till after the wed-ding," pointed out Adil in the taxi.

"Thank you for coming with me," I said.

In the aftermath of Dr. Laramie, I had gone back and forth on whether he should accompany me to the office. In the end, I succumbed.

"We're in this together, Lila," said Adil.

I felt a flash of rage and longing.

"Do you ever think about leaving Kolkata?" I asked as we flew by Birla temple, auto rickshaws, Opel Astras, a pumpkin seller precariously perched on his mountain of pumpkins on the cross street at a busy intersection, in the hopes of a traffic-light quick sale.

"Yes," said Adil after a pause.

I turned to him, but he was looking outside his window, where it had begun to drizzle and the mongrels on the street were running for cover.

THE CHAMBERS OF Chand and Sons had recently undergone renovation, expanding across two floors of the building they occupied on Old Post Office Street, in the oldest part of Kolkata. Adil and I were shown into Param Chand's office, where, laughing, he leaned back in his leather swivel chair, his pale skin striking against his green-rimmed glasses. A Warhol silkscreen hung on the bright-yellow wall behind him, the interior of the office in stark contrast to the bustle of the Old Kolkata landscape outside.

"Lila," said a beaming Palekar, seated across from Chand. "And Mr. Adil. How nice to see you both. Please meet my dear friend Param, who is the latest in the long line of Chands who have handled legal matters for the Lahiris."

Param Chand rose, elegant, his silk shirt patterned with tiny flowers, extending a manicured hand, a peculiar agelessness to him.

"I've been waiting a long time to meet the new Lahiri heir," he said. "Adil, it's good to see you again."

"We've met at various law conferences over the years," Adil said to me, smiling at Chand with real pleasure.

"We seem to have interrupted something," I said.

"Just a little anecdote I was telling my old friend here," said Chand. "Do you know the Hindu conservative party, the NPF?"

"Of course. I lived here till I was a teenager," I said.

If he heard exasperation in my voice, Chand did not show it. "One of the NPF party members went to a high court judge and said that they were going to file a case against the court for having a mosque on its premises. He said it was confusing the identity of the Hindu state of Bengal."

"The high court mosque, by the way, stands right next to the high court temple," said Palekar, his eyes alight with merriment.

"The judge asked the chap how he got into the high court chambers in the first place," said Chand, sitting back down in his seat. "The NPF man fidgeted for a while and finally admitted to bribing a guard. The judge said with a smile: 'He won't be here the next time you attempt to break into our judiciary.

And furthermore, I look forward to hearing the case you will be filing against the court's sacred buildings that have stood here for centuries. After all, it is the court who will be hearing the case, is it not?'"

Palekar and Chand roared with laughter.

Wiping an eye, Palekar shook his head. "They'll be waiting to have their cases heard for three decades, if our judges have anything to do with it."

"True," said Chand. "My only worry is that if they win the election, they could put right-wing judges into the court. That's when it will start becoming serious."

"Param Bhai, we will all be dead and gone before Bengal succumbs," said Palekar. "Anyway, we better get to the matter at hand. Biddy Lahiri is getting married tonight, and Lila must be there."

"Yes, many congratulations, Lila," said Chand. "In fact, I will be attending the reception the day after tomorrow. The groom's family are also clients of ours."

"Did Hari Kaka not invite you to the wedding tonight?" I asked, aghast.

In Kolkata, one invited everyone one knew to a family wedding, risking certain offense if not.

"I'm very sorry," I said. "He must have forgotten in all of the madness and only invited Bhaskar."

Palekar and Chand exchanged a look.

"I don't think it was a mistake," said Chand. "I think it is in Hari Lahiri's best interests to keep me out of the picture for as long as possible."

"I don't understand," said Adil.

"Lila, my dear," said Palekar, sitting up a little straighter. "Param is a dear friend of mine, and your father's, from our university days."

"A fact that Hari perhaps did not count on," said Chand, smirking.

"Is that how you became my grandfather's lawyer?" I asked Chand, wishing that they would dispense with their small talk and camaraderie, as if building up to a giant joke that felt like it could be on me.

Adil placed a palm on the small of my back.

"And why isn't Bhaskar here?" I asked.

"My father and grandfather were both lawyers for the Lahiris. My firm has served your family since 1935," said Chand. "In fact—"

"Mr. Chand, Palekar Uncle, I don't mean to be rude," I said. "I just really need to know what is going on. Are the Lahiris filing their lawsuit? Have they found a loophole?" I felt a small shred of something like relief pass through me. Perhaps I could just go home and let them all go to hell.

Chand and Palekar looked at me, taken aback. Bengal was not an anxious state—it took its time with words and life, a lazy luxury to all that passed through its sieve. My urgency felt foreign in the room. Adil's fingers tightened against my back, his shoulder touching mine.

"Bhaskar Gupta is facing charges, from Chand and Sons," said Palekar.

"We have hired external parties for the express purpose of reviewing all of Bhaskar Gupta's dealings with Tejen Lahiri," said Chand.

"So Bhaskar was lying about my grandfather changing the will?" I asked, the beginnings of a headache crawling into my temples.

"The fact is," said Palekar, "when the Lahiris claimed—when Geeta Lahiri claimed—to have found a new will, and Bhaskar Gupta said that it was a legal will, since your grandfather had spoken to him about it, it raised a few suspicions in me, as you know."

"There are two separate matters here," said Chand, leaning forward. "First, the matter of Bhaskar Gupta claiming that Tejen Lahiri told him that he intended to change his third and final legal will to name Hari Lahiri as his successor."

"Given that there were no witnesses, that fact is only submittable in court for any consideration if Chand and Sons had authorized Bhaskar Gupta as a representative of their firm to be an executor of the estate. I had done no such thing," said Chand.

"At the moment, Bhaskar Gupta is facing potential charges of inheritance fraud," said Palekar with the delight of a revelation.

"So he was lying?" I asked again, with an air of idiocy.

"It brings me to the second matter," said Chand. "The will that was found by Geeta Lahiri in her jewelry box, claiming Hari as heir to the Lahiri estate."

"Which Bhaskar did not sign," said Adil.

In my struggle to parse through the performance of the meeting, I felt a flicker of happiness at the concern in his voice.

"That is correct," said Chand, examining Adil with interest. "While that will was not executed, its existence, together with Bhaskar's testimony, might have complicated matters for you, Miss Lahiri."

"De. My name is Lila De."

"My mistake, of course," said Chand, shaking his head.

"That will is a forgery, though a very good one," said Palekar. "Tejen Lahiri has only ever discussed his wills with Param here, who is listed as his official legal representative. Bhaskar Gupta was simply assigned the day-to-day management of the estate affairs as an associate of the firm. Tejen Lahiri's first will was created in 1964, the year that he inherited the house from Krishna Lahiri. That will named Hari Lahiri as the legal heir to the Lahiri estate. Tejen Lahiri's second will was created in 1986, naming his daughter, Maya Lahiri as heir, when she was nineteen years of age. His third and final will was created ten years ago, in 2005, naming his granddaughter Lila De, as heir. All three wills were attested and signed by him in the presence of Param Chand, as well as members of Chand and Sons, providing witness. A fourth will was never created or discussed with any member of the firm, outside of Bhaskar Gupta's claim. When I mentioned the fourth will to Param yesterday, it was the first time he was hearing of it," said Palekar.

"The truth is, your grandfather could not have made Bhaskar privy to any wills, because he knew that Bhaskar was not authorized to oversee inheritance matters," said Chand. "And the way the Lahiris, or any of these old Bengali families work, is that the head of the family oversees all legal matters. After Tejen's death, none of them knew that Bhaskar was only supposed to handle basic administrative affairs of the estate. As far as they knew, Tejen had dealt with only Bhaskar for years. And Bhaskar assumed that nobody in the family would check with the firm as a result. A thin scheme concocted by an idiot. Only in Kolkata could he have very possibly gotten away with it."

"Yes, the Bengalis do not always concern themselves with paperwork or details," said Palekar, amused.

"Incredible that Bhaskar passed his law exams," said Chand, contemptuous.

"I was nineteen when he decided to leave me the house?" I said.

Adil looked as taken aback as I felt.

"My dear, your grandfather was a man who knew more about people than they often did about themselves," said Palekar with a gentleness.

Chand nodded. "Certainly, he seemed to have a keen understanding of Hari, when he changed the will from him to Maya."

Why had he changed it, then, from my mother to me? What had he seen in her that had changed his mind? The past weeks had shown me so much of Maya in myself that the thought only distressed me further, the idea that there was some generational malaise that lay dormant inside me, which my grandfather had believed I might not have inherited.

"Tejen always wanted you to come back," said Chand to me. "To manage the estate. And because you were a child, and I did not know you well, I asked him, on the phone, in emails, in person, over the years if he was sure, if he wanted to change his mind. He never did. The last time I asked him was a week before he died. He was clear about his wishes."

I said nothing as they all watched me.

"But why would Bhaskar lie?" I asked after what felt like an eternity. "What does he have to gain?"

Chand shot Palekar a look.

"It appears, my dear," said Palekar, "that Bhaskar may have been in partnership with Hari Lahiri."

"What?" said Adil, outraged.

"It appears they created the fourth will hoping to appeal to Lila's sentiments around her grandfather's wishes. Bhaskar knew that putting his signature on it would have been too great a crime, but the presence of a will created on Tejen's deathbed, his final wishes per se, they hoped would be enough for you to let Hari have ownership. If you had returned to America quietly and let Hari take over, no one would have been the wiser."

"Bhaskar would have undoubtedly made a tidy profit for his efforts," said Chand.

I felt only a sense of rejection. Had my family loved me more, surely they would not have resorted to theft.

"Was my grandmother involved?" I asked.

"Bhaskar maintains it was just Hari Lahiri and himself," said Chand, impassive as if stating the color of the walls. "As of now, it appears the family had nothing to do with it. He has confessed that the fraudulent will was placed by Hari Lahiri in Geeta Lahiri's jewelry safe on the same day she discovered it. The two of them planned it together, bungling fools that they are."

I wondered what my grandmother might have done if she had known. Her bond with Hari ran deeper than blood or wills, or the easy rationale of the right side of history.

"How did you get Bhaskar to confess?" asked Adil, standing up, filling the room with a radiating anger.

"We have our methods," said Palekar. "Hari Lahiri does not know yet."

"That bastard will never practice law again," said Chand in a neutral voice that reminded me of the National Popular Front leader's, cold and flat, on television. A shudder went through me.

"They should all go to jail," said Adil. "Bhaskar and Hari. Thieves. Stealing from Lila."

"They certainly can be prosecuted," said Chand.

"That is a matter for Lila to decide," said Palekar quietly.

Adil, glowering, nodded. He must have known that I had no answers for any of them. Hari was my family, the love of my grandmother's life, the Lahiri scion, Biddy's father, my grandfather's brother. As if suddenly blind, I remembered, aching, his enveloping kindness to my grandmother, his ability to make anyone laugh.

"Take your time, Lila," said Palekar. "You don't have to make any decisions immediately. What happens to Hari, whether or not you want to sell the house, and who finally runs its affairs—these are all matters to think over carefully."

Palekar must have thought that I would be grateful for all their efforts, but I could not muster even the effort of pretense. I stood up.

"Thank you," I said. "I must go now. I have to help with the wedding."

31

THAT EVENING, BIDDY was married, sindoor streaming from the middle part in her hair to the bridge of her nose and her cheeks, the fine red powder mixing with her highlighter and her sweat, the same color as her Banarasi sari. The soaring wail of the shehnai wafted through the high ceilings and the old walls, simultaneously ecstatic and melancholy. The neighborhood was dressed to the nines. Two hundred people had been invited to the wedding, but it felt like many more had streamed into the Lahiri house that night. Beggars stood outside, waiting for the sweets that the maids were distributing in exchange for blessing the new couple. The priest poured hot ghee into a fire, flames leaping out, crackling dangerously near the silk of Biddy's sari, her face flushed from the heat as she repeated the Sanskrit mantras that would marry her to the man next to her. I thought of what she had said about escaping the house. Afterward, Mishti cried as Biddy and her husband bent down to touch her feet.

"My little girl, leaving me," said Mishti in Bengali, through her tears.

"I'll be back by lunchtime tomorrow for leftovers, Ma," said Biddy as she hugged her mother, but she was crying too, rivulets mixing with the sindoor, bloodlike, on her face.

My grandmother hurried over to me, anxious, draped in another of Katyayani Lahiri's Kanjeevarams, the effort leaving her slightly winded.

"Lila, really. Where have you been? You disappeared in the middle of the day. I was worried you weren't coming."

"It's Biddy's wedding. Of course I was coming."

"I'm an old lady," she said, ominous. "If you worry me like this, who knows what could happen."

I narrowed my eyes at her, laughing despite myself.

As I made my way through the crowd of guests, people chattered and mingled around me, a crackle of joy in the air, the heavy smell of jasmine mingling with perfume, cigarette smoke, and fried chicken cutlets. I felt a lightness—that my inheritance could no longer be contested, that my grandfather had been sane when he chose me, and that, no matter what, the family and I were irrevocably bound by the brick and mortar of the house.

I LOOKED AROUND for Seth, but he was nowhere to be found. I had seen him as I had come in, happily enjoying the festivities in Vik's clutches, and I assumed that his great Indian wedding experience was continuing to give him much pleasure. At a table near the bar area, Janani was seated alone, rubbing the sole of her left foot. After making sure Silky was not in the vicinity, I got myself a gin and tonic and made my way to her table.

"Hi," I said, sitting down. "Biddy's feet are killing her too. We really should do parties barefoot."

"Lila," said Janani. She looked around, hesitant. "How are you?" she asked.

"Me? Fine. I really enjoyed the ceremony and garlanding. Did you have fun?"

"Yes," she said.

A silence hung between us. Usually, Adil's mother had the loudest laugh in the room, throwing her arms, opinions, and affections around anyone who struck up conversation.

"Is everything okay, aunty?" I asked.

Janani reached for the glass of wine in front of her, letting her foot drop. As she took a slow sip, her eyebrows knitting together, I felt a sharp sensation at the top of my head, and my heart beginning to beat faster. In that instant, I could not fathom how it had never occurred to me that my affair with Adil would make its way to his mother. She set her glass down, placing both her elbows on the table, her hands laced together under her chin, where she rested her worried, kind face. She looked at me with the clear, frank manner I had loved so much as a child, so unlike the mysterious complexities of my own parents.

"Lila," she said, "I am very fond of you. And I know you and Adil . . ." She stopped here for a moment as if remembering us, the teenagers she had loved, a faint breath lifting her chest, then leaving it. "You were very special to each other when you were"—she stopped again—"younger. But you are not children anymore."

She leaned forward.

"He's married to my daughter-in-law, who is a wonderful girl," she said. "They are happy."

There was a pleading in her voice that burned into me, the once-teenager turned homewrecker who sat across from her. I looked away, swallowing the hot disgust at myself. Janani's hand closed over my fingers on the table.

"You're a good girl. I know you. Please, just stop seeing him. He doesn't know what he's doing."

"He's not doing anything," I said, taking my hand away, knocking over my glass, which then crashed to the ground in shards before I could rescue it.

People turned to stare, as one of the waiters hurried to scoop up the pieces.

"Sorry," I said to the waiter as he brushed up pieces into a dustpan. "I'm sorry," I said to Janani as I looked up at her.

I thought of Silky, the sharpness in my chest severe. She must not have come to the wedding.

"Does Silky know?" I asked.

"I asked Adil to tell her, before she heard it from someone else."

I stood up, my skin on fire. Janani slipped her feet into her sandals and rose quickly.

"I don't blame you," she said, so quiet that I had to strain to catch it. "I just want my son to be happy. He hasn't been happy since you arrived. And if this turns into a full-blown Kolkata scandal, he could lose his whole life."

"Are you okay, Lila?" asked my mother's voice from behind me. "Hi, Janani," she said, suspicious.

"It's a beautiful wedding, Maya," said Janani after a pause.

"I heard a glass break," said my mother, frowning at me.

"Just an accident," said Janani. "I'm going to ask the driver to bring the car around. But I'm looking forward to the reception the day after tomorrow."

My mother looked at me, ignoring Janani. "Are you okay?"

"I can ask for your car, Janani Aunty," I said as my stomach began to contract into a familiar cramp.

"That's okay. A little walk will do me good. See you both at the reception."

As she left, my mother sat down in her place, a detectivelike energy to her. "What's the matter with you?" she asked.

"Ma, stop," I said. "You didn't have to be rude to her."

"I wasn't rude. I don't like her. She's always acted like she's your mother, giving me advice. You have a mother. Now what did she say to upset you like that?"

"I don't know what you're talking about," I said, pushing back my chair.

"I don't like seeing you upset," said my mother. "When children grow up, what they do is not always the business of parents. Although," she added hurriedly, "you can always tell me anything."

I had the urge to laugh, even with this obvious reference to my indiscretions. This mother of mine, who did nothing but upset me, was outraged at Adil's mother for tampering with her daughter. It felt wildly incongruous yet also completely natural for my bizarre, conflicted mother. She would not mend any of the burning bridges between us, and yet she exercised her right to me—to motherhood—at will. When she did, it was something to see.

I SLIPPED AWAY from the wedding, the night cool on my skin as I walked quickly, the unfamiliar sari and petticoat rustling between my shins. Outside my father's apartment, I stopped. Seth was sitting on Ram Bhai's stone seat, outside the gates.

"Hello, stranger," I said, comforted by the thought that I would have him next to me that night. "I texted you. I thought you were in the middle of shenanigans with Vik. Did you get tired of the endless parties?"

He stretched his neck, the tendons rising on pink flesh, and stood. I saw then that the wheels of a shiny black suitcase rested against his feet.

"Moving in?" I asked, flirtatious. But a tremor snaked through my ribs as something in his face shifted.

"I'm going home."

"But your ticket is for Sunday, after the reception," I said in confusion.

Seth looked at the bag, then at the dogs bathed in the light of the streetlamps, sleeping on the street a few feet from us, and then back at me. "I saw you kiss him. On the terrace."

The trouble with love, or what felt like it, was that it made you reckless, dizzy with need. Adil and I had sought corners and bedrooms and car seats that were free of others, free of decrees and families. In these spaces, only the need existed; it was stolen time, thefts made from others, and we knew it.

That Seth had seen us today on the Secret Sixth, when I had arrived and immediately looked for Adil, was not surprising. What felt like a slap of consciousness was that in a house that contained our whole families, it had never occurred to me that we might be caught, might have to pay full price for what we had stolen, that the most obvious, natural conclusion would come to pass.

There was nothing I might have said that Seth could not see on my face. He nodded, with grief.

"Of course it was him," he said. "I should have seen it. I didn't, because I didn't want to."

"There's nothing to see, Seth. He loves his wife."

Seth's face twisted in anger. "Why would you do this? What are you doing all of this"—he gestured in the direction of the Lahiri house, blocks away—"for? Why can't you . . . Why can't you just . . ." He shook his head as if confronted with the inexplicable.

"Why can't I just what?"

"Let yourself be happy. It's like you tell yourself you want love, but it's an idea. Real love—there's something about it you have contempt for."

"Don't psychoanalyze me," I said, cold. "I'm not a character."

"Okay, I won't," he said, incandescent. "You just keep all that . . . stuff . . . in there, where nobody can see it, touch it, love it. You're afraid of what happens if you let someone in. You're afraid of the person you really are."

"For fuck's sake, Seth. If you want to go, go. It didn't take long, did it?"

"Actually, it took forever." He spots a passing cab. "Taxi!" he yelled.

For the first time since I had been in Kolkata, a cab stopped on the first try.

"Airport?" asked Seth, his crimson cheeks golden in the overhead streetlight.

"Domestic na international?" asked the cabbie, staring at my bare legs.

"International," said Seth, hauling his suitcase into the seat. "You know," he said to me, "since I've gotten here, you've been trying to prove to me that this is idiotic—that we couldn't possibly be real, that I meant nothing to you. Congratulations. You've finally succeeded."

Seth got into the cab and slammed the door.

"Dada, please. Old taxi. Door will break," said the outraged cabbie.

But as if intuiting that the conversation, clearly a war, might not be over yet, that unfinished sentences hung in the air before an irreversible trip to the airport was made, the cabbie waited—for one of us to say something, some sort of goodbye.

I waited too, for my words to form. *Don't go, Seth. I'm sorry. I love what we could become. I am someone I don't recognize sometimes. When I am with you, I am a self I recognize.* But no words came, and after an eon, the cabbie turned, first looking at me, then at Seth.

"Ready, dada?" he asked with an awkward kindness.

Seth nodded, and, quickly, they disappeared into the night as I stood under the streetlamps, my shadow stretching in front of me.

32

I LAY AWAKE that night, the lights still on around me in the living room. At five, I turned off the lights, drank water, and sank again into my parents' bed. I felt the rising tide of loss—there were to be no texts, no easy laughter, no more many small kindnesses that Seth had shown me daily. I tried to think of his worst flaws—entitlement, solipsism, negativity, the fact that he did not organize or plan or tidy up or know what to do or say in crisis—but they were no balm for the fact that I had not loved him enough, that he was good and kind and I had deceived him. I could not find a way out, or bring myself to write or call with the words that might yet change my grief. Finally, at seven, I fell asleep.

I WOKE TO the afternoon sun streaming in on my face, hot and blinding, and the doorbell ringing. I stumbled to my feet, my first thought to see if I had a text or email from Seth, but there was none.

"Stop it," I yelled as the bell rang again, and I pulled Iva's flamingo dressing gown around me before opening the door.

Adil stood in front of me, pale-faced and drawn. Even in despair, I felt a rush of white-hot longing.

"You have a key," I said.

He was holding the key in the fist he uncurled as he stepped inside. We looked at the key as he placed it on the end table by the couch.

"You're returning it," I said pointlessly as I sat down in the nearest chair, my knees suddenly giving way.

Adil came toward me, and I held up a palm.

"Lila," he said, quietly.

I could hear the hurt in his voice.

"I did what I thought was right. For myself and Silky, for our families. For you."

"Yes," I said, bitter. "You do what's right, no matter what."

"That's not fair," he said, standing over me.

"Get out, Adil. Take your right and wrong and black and white, and get out."

"You're this angry with me because I told my wife about us? Lila, what if she had heard from someone's maid or cousin or friend? Do you think that's fair to her?"

"You told her because your mother told you to. Because you think telling her absolves you from cheating on her."

"Is that what you think?"

His anger was the kind you couldn't see, but its wound rippled through me.

"Yes," I said. "You don't care about my life or hers or anyone else's. You want your guilt gone, and then you'll be just fine, with life trotting along at a steady pace. No great feeling or emotion or purpose that could rock your boat."

I wanted badly to see him in pain, but even as I did, I felt a stabbing in my own gut. For a long few seconds, he stood there, silent and enraged.

Then, slowly, he said, one word at a time, "So if I were to say, 'Let's go, Lila. Let's ride into the fucking sunset together. Take me to New York with you, Silky be damned, our families be damned. Better still, stay here, love me, have my children—we'll make a family, right here in Ballygunge Place, your mother's house a kilometer from us,' you would say yes? You would want to love me for my lifetime and live with the consequences?"

He crouched down next to the arm of my chair, holding my knees.

"Because if that's the truth—and I have not once thought it is, and you know that—then correct me, please. Tell me you really know what you want, and what you want is me."

I sat paralyzed in the long, hard silence between us, his breath so close that I felt it on my arm.

"Because if you can really do this, Lila, I'm here, right in front of you."

I closed my eyes and felt him nod, his voice say, "I didn't think so."

It was the first time we had both acknowledged that too much had passed between us, that we would never find our way back to our younger selves again. At some point, his head folded onto my lap, my own leaning on his, our sorrows merged into one. We stayed like that, a long time. Eventually, he disentangled himself, stood up, and looked at his watch.

"I should go home," he said.

I nodded.

"Do you need anything?" he asked. "Before I go?"

"No," I said, grieving.

He nodded, turning to leave.

"What finally made you tell her?" I asked.

"Silky? We're married. We wouldn't stand a chance if I didn't. Ma asking me to was just a push over the edge."

I exhaled, trying to purge some of the pain his words caused me. "No, I meant your mother. What made you tell your mother?"

Adil looked at me with the expression of someone trying to piece together a puzzle.

"I didn't."

Even before he said it, I knew it from somewhere in my subconscious.

"Your mother did. Maya came to our house last week and told her. I thought you knew. She said it was her and my mother's responsibility to try and fix this." His face crumpled. "You didn't know," he said. "She didn't tell you."

I shook my head. It was only reasonable to expect the elements of a pattern to recur, as they always had. Of course it should have been unsurprising that once more my mother had used blunt force to assert her power over me.

33

AT FIVE, MY mother had felt a lot like Ma Kali, my favorite character in a television show we watched about our gods and goddesses. All of the powers of the Hindu universe had combined to make Kali, a powerful, beautiful, enraged goddess who had defeated all the asuras, and she had a great deal in common with Ma. An aura of power hung perpetually around Ma, at the university where people worshipped her, and at home, where nobody wanted to incur her wrath.

When I grew older, I understood that like with Kali, with Ma you had to extinguish your ego to make way for light. When the goddess (as per our priest) was happy, we could be assured of joy in every corner of our existence. It was the same with Ma. When someone's evil doings (or my own) had caused the goddess pain or grief, the skies opened up, and there was no mercy for the wicked. Kali in the graveyard, born of fire, child of war, garlanded by skulls, would come for you, consume and destroy you.

When people (police officers, friends, therapists, Reiki masters) asked me about my childhood, I began with the truth—that my parents had divorced and Ma and I had moved to the fifth floor of the house. I did not tell them that the scandal of her divorce hung around us like a smell; family members and the parents of my friends and teachers at my school said nothing, but their bodies and faces betrayed them. Ma was a single mother, unheard of in the '80s and early '90s in India, and wives looked at her body and career with suspicion. I omitted all of this, instead fast-forwarding, straight to sixteen from five, when I had moved across the Atlantic, adopted by my father and his wife, a proper American dream in the works. The in-between years I did not dare to touch, even with the fingers of my own memory. Those years that I spent alone with Ma were so effectively buried, so far gone into the abyss, that if you asked me about them, I could only measure it in objects:

The shoe. A brown leather sandal, the sensible, not-too-expensive kind a professor with a depleted family trust and a mouth to feed might wear to university, but it had a gold clasp on one side, a touch of the unusual, because Ma had taste. The heel was an inch, maybe just a little higher—enough for her to assert herself around her colleagues with her big vision for the new texts, the more liberal ones like Rushdie and Amos Oz. After a meal that I had chewed slowly, cud-like, for two and a half hours after she had spent ten hours at the university so that she could pay for my dance classes and sports-day outfit, she flung the shoe (*just the one*) at my head. She must have meant to miss, but it was high enough that it swerved to the right of my left ear, a tap dance in the air next to my eye, a sliver of time during which she might have taken out the whole eye, half of my entire vision. Instead, an elegant failure, the heel, bound by its own gravity, bounced along the edge of my eyebrow (*I would never wear sandals as an adult*), purple-thudded lanes forming on my flesh, the shoe skimming as it landed, still graceful on impact, on the top of my cheekbone (*another near miss*), where my teeth could feel the rhythm and rattle in their sockets, the sound then making its way inside my head, and should we just bow now to regal force and end the performance, but no, my mother would fling in possessed rage (*no longer herself*) the second shoe.

The belt. It unwound itself one clear morning in the wardrobe we shared, where everything we owned was intermingled—shirts and underwear and her kurtas over my uniforms, our desks overrun with our common pens and pencils, my textbooks, her copies of *Hamlet* and Henry James and *Femina* magazine. We were one organism in those years, fused together in blood and bone. I was eight or nine, and she seemed the kind of beauty that bloomed every decade, a kind of cactus flower, the kind that men admired and feared. I learned this early, in the way she used rejection with them, her biggest weapon against the harm they might do—to her, to me, to the unit of us she protected in the only way she knew, by standing fierce guard at its door. In those years, we were also happy. Kali was both the divine protector and the goddess of destruction. If I wanted a slice of cake, we would walk two neighborhoods to the bakery we liked and order one slice of pineapple and other of chocolate and share both, and she would let me eat all of the fruit that studded the whipped cream and brush the hair from my eyes, reveling in the sun of my gluttony. In those years, my mother wore jeans that flared a little at their bottoms, exquisite in their timeliness, a doyenne of style to me. I would pull on spangled tights in the late afternoons and try to imitate her walk, pirouetting across the terrace, and we would laugh until the pigeons scattered against the sunset. At home, the curtains drawn, she would unhook her bra, unbutton her shirt, the smell of her day wafting toward me, her stretch marks like bolts of lightning across the cesarean scar on her flat stomach, the tops of her breasts—the price of motherhood, she would say—sliding the belt out of the loops of her denims, it uncoiling slowly, then slithering for a second or two onto the bed where she had tossed it before it fell silent. I watched the belt closely, always. It was an inch wide, elegant and polished, the color of my great-grandfather's mahogany chair, and it had belonged to him, a man's buckle adorning the center, an oval long-horned beast made of iron. My mother would have given anything to have been born a man instead of a woman in Kolkata, and the belt gave her a degree of masculine, personal Lahiri power. I knew the belt could not be trusted. The belt was a serpent that could slither over a shoulder or a shoe and attack, springing from nowhere, suddenly enraged, filled with venom over a husband who had left, a bad grade that would prove that I was a failure on the résumé of motherhood, or punishment for an accident I had caused—a broken vase, flowers and glass everywhere, or ink spilled like blood on a fresh linen sheet. In those years, the serpent lived quietly, dangerously, under the surface, and I had to learn how to trick it, to sidestep and tap-dance and present illusion, such that it did not feel fear or anger or hopelessness or rejection. If the very worst happened, and it did raise its hood and prepare to attack, and there was no removing myself out of its way, then I had to do what the charmers told you to do—stand very still, close my eyes, and hope that the snake would eventually slither away from my arms and legs, streaked with red welts, yellowing lesions, a majestic sunrise across my back, would feel mercy, even as I soared higher and higher into the sky and clouds, away from all sensation, leaving only my body behind on the fifth floor of the Lahiri house.

The scale, lingo for what we called a ruler. I did math with it, geometry, and the simple graphs we began learning in middle school economics. I cannot remember where it came from (maybe the university, and she had brought it back home for me, or it might have belonged to her or Hari or Rana when they were children), but it was the object that had lived with us the longest—light-colored wood, not heavy at all, but at least half an inch in thickness. (*Have you ever felt a half an inch of wood slap against a thigh, the area beneath an ear, against cheek and bone, the underside of an armpit, the backs of shins and thighs, and a folded fetal self—again and again—so hard it became fiction?*) I had begun a period, rough and wild, the kind that stained my white uniform or the shorts I wore to science coaching, sweaters pulled hurriedly across my waist—everything I felt was heightened. When the wood broke in half against the back of my leg (*I wouldn't eat the dinner she had rushed home to stir into existence*), I felt a roar of pain in my ears, making its way into my eyes, a haze of something red and thick, my rage as viscous as period blood, and in that moment, Kali lived no longer in my mother; she leaped into my still-flat chest as I raised both palms, and that was how my mother went flying across the fifth-floor studio and crumpled into a child version of herself, against the bamboo of the laundry basket, her head hitting the side of the steel Godrej cupboard. The other Lahiris did not interfere, because they were parents too and had children who needed to be disciplined in the ways that our community disciplined children, and even if it was rumored that Maya went too far, that one of these days that child would crack her head open and Mihir Lahiri would arrive with the police, they largely shook their heads in disapproval and left us alone. But that day that the scale broke and my mother lay crumpled on the floor, something must have sounded different. My grandmother pushed the door open and rushed to my mother and helped her up, and suddenly it was them, in a unit, mother and child, both of them staring at me in a mirrored, haunted image, and I was on the outside, looking in.

There were other objects that defined our years together. The badminton racket slammed onto a table by one of us, bending under the force into an odd curve, like a hunchback, that we laughed at afterward. A certificate of excellence from my English teacher that my mother had ripped up and spent six hours putting back together, which we then laminated and filed away in the special red cabinet's drawer of pride, where she saved all my academic prizes. We had painted it red together when at six I had said that I hated all of the brown (teak, mahogany, mango wood) "stuff" in the Lahiri house; after a pause in which I'd felt a familiar urgent fear that I had invoked the demon, she had laughed and agreed. Wherever she went, I went, and we grew into the same height and body, and you could not tell us apart from behind as the objects collected around us.

WHEN I WAS taken away, as we had both known I might be, my childhood finally began, at sixteen. There were books and magazines, siblings and an American private school, tennis lessons and prom, and hard lemon candies I was allowed an endless supply of. I was, in my mind, the tragic orphan who had been rescued and reunited with my true family and given warm milk, a pretty bedroom, new objects like makeup and backpacks, a car, and a second chance. My father and Iva gave me more love than I needed, so it felt just—as though excess was the answer.

And yet in those years after, I longed for my mother with a broken heart, acutely aware that she was long gone, free of me and free of our objects and free to be Kali elsewhere. Free of the birthday parties she had painstakingly organized year after year, of the ugly donkey piñata that had to be hung so it would explode right over my head when I least expected it, enveloping us in Styrofoam and sweets, and we would laugh so hard at the sight of everyone scrambling for the prize on the floor, our eyes locked in secret joy that the prize was mine, that she had kept it for me in the drawer of the broken chipped red nightstand, which stood, even now, by the bed we had slept in together.

34

AFTER ADIL LEFT, the sky darkened quickly. It felt impossible to be alone, so I pulled on jeans and a sweater and left the apartment. I walked without a goal—through the neighborhood, past the school and the temple and the new restaurants that dotted the main street and jostled for space with the raddi stores, past the old peanut seller's shop in the alley behind the sari and blouse repair shop, past the field where Rinki and I would sneak off to play badminton together after school.

I walked all the way into Gariahat Market, through the winding lanes of shopkeepers who sold everything under the sun, their stalls fluorescent-lit and overflowing with gadgets, clothes, pickles, sweets, books and magazines, toys, and incense, and then the fruit and flower vendors who sat hunched over their baskets, shelling peas or threading rows of jasmine on string. Until that night, I had been too wrapped up in the house, the family, in my own head, to wander without purpose through the streets I still knew by heart their smells, untouched by the years I had spent away.

Despite myself, I eventually stood in front of the Lahiri house. It was eight thirty, an hour that was usually quiet, as each family unit began to eat dinner. Tonight, the night before the wedding reception, the house hummed with activity—contractors laying out chairs, extended family milling about, executing various duties. I walked through the entrance and into the courtyard, where Rinki and Biddy wore face masks as manicurists painted their fingernails and pasted gemstones on.

"Lila," called Rinki. "Just in time. Come and get your nails done. Since Biddy's husband's family is paying for the reception, we are going all out."

But I did not stop. Instead, I walked as fast as I could, up the stairs, past the second floor, where Gina and Rana were preparing another batch of little gift baskets for the groom's family, and then the third floor, where my grandmother's room was. Bari, with Ami on her hip, stood over Mishti, my grandmother and my mother, surrounded by the tea roses that were my present to Biddy, baskets of them, at least five hundred flowers, exquisite, fragile dusty-pink buds that they were snipping into small bunches and sliding into little glass jars filled with water. Ami, clinging to Bari, watched me silently, immediately alert to my presence.

"Lila, there you are," said my grandmother.

"We're drowning in your roses," said Mishti. "It's going to be a beautiful party."

"Really, we should have used them instead of the marigolds for the wedding. We—Lila—shouldn't be paying for anything for the reception," said my grandmother.

"What's the matter?" asked my mother, looking at me like a bloodhound.

"Bari, could you take Ami and give us a few minutes?" I asked in Bengali. "Mishti Kaki, you too, please. I need to talk to Ma and Mummy."

"We need to finish these before morning," protested my grandmother.

But my mother nodded to Bari, who left right away, Ami's gaze still on me until she could not see me any longer.

As Mishti closed the door behind her, my grandmother propped her elbow on her knee, sitting upright on the floor, conspiratorial.

"What is it, Lila Ma? Has the beautiful white boy asked you to marry him? Oh, you absolutely must."

"You told Adil's mother about us," I said to my mother.

For a long moment, we looked at each other, and I saw my mother come to a decision.

"I did what I had to," said my mother, her voice hard. "But I made her promise to keep it quiet. She wasn't supposed to tell you."

"Told her what?" asked my grandmother.

"They were sleeping together," said my vile mother.

A silence filled the room as my grandmother's face crumpled.

"Oh god," she said.

"We had stopped," I said. "I was going to leave. No one was going to get hurt. But you couldn't have that, could you?"

"I did not do this, Lila," my mother said, cold. "You did. The situation was born of your actions."

Even in my hatred, I felt a dazed wonder at her cruelty.

"You are a terrible person," I said.

"Lila, my dear," said my grandmother, her eyes filling with tears. "You cannot say these things to your mother."

My mother looked at me unflinching. "He would have been caught, one way or another. It isn't my fault for doing the right thing."

I laughed. "The right thing. You think you did the right thing? You throw a man's life away, you don't care about my feelings, you hide your boyfriend in the fucking alleys of Ballygunge Place. My god, you're such a fucking hypocrite, *Professor De*. Maybe you can start telling the truth by changing your name back to Lahiri. You haven't been a De for twenty-eight years. You were never really a De."

My mother straightened her spine as she held my gaze.

"He doesn't love you," she said.

"It must be hard to be someone that nobody loves," I said to her.

"You want it to be my fault. You hate that it isn't," said my mother, venomous.

"Shut up," I said, my screaming ringing in my ears. "Don't you get it? It's all your fault. All of it."

My grandmother looked terrified.

"Both of you, please," she said, pleading. "Lila Ma, I am sure it was an accident. Your mother never intended to harm anyone."

"You want to come in here and make a scene, because for you, I am to blame for everything," said my mother. "This is why I stay away from you. You've hated me since you were a girl. Your father taught you to hate me."

She rose to her feet, the folds of her starched sari billowing and crackling around the piles of roses that surrounded us, their smell pervasive and heavy and claustrophobic in the airless room, as she stepped over the baskets, trying to get to the door.

"You think my father taught me to hate you?" I asked her.

She must have stepped on something, a thorny stem or a piece of wicker, because she stilled with a soft scream and crouched to examine her heel.

"Do you remember the way you would slap me?" I asked.

I sounded inaudible to my own ears and raised my voice.

"The way you punished me for every misstep and hit me every chance you got? You don't think that's why I hated you?" I said.

My mother looked as if I had struck her. I watched as rage swept over her, in that familiar way in which she could not articulate all of the words she felt and so she would give free rein to her fists and palms. But now that she could not (she dared not), it was like watching her struggle to breathe.

"I did what I had to," she said, her nostrils flaring. "I gave you a few spankings to discipline you, and you've made me a monster because of it. It was for your own good. Name one mother you know who did not do the same. You just need me to be the monster in your life."

"Do you remember when I was eight," I said, relentless, "and my teacher asked why I had cuts and bruises everywhere? That's what Baba saw when he came here when I was sixteen. That's what he took me to the police station for. But you've always pretended that you let him take me away for my education."

I examined the stone of her face, for any sign of feeling. My grandmother began to wail uncontrollably.

"You're incapable of remorse," I said to my mother.

It felt good, as if verbally I was doing the equivalent of taking a belt or a shoe or a series of slaps to her, adrenaline coursing through my veins.

"You'll never be sorry for what you did to me as a kid, or what you've done today," I said. "You're incapable of love. You disgust me. You hate your own mother, when all she does is make excuses for you and try to love you."

I felt my face burn with fury and the satisfaction of finally hurting her.

"And you have the nerve to tell me, to pretend to yourself, that you tortured me for my own good," I said.

Something extinguished in my mother, like a light had been turned off, a blackness, empty and dangerous, descending in her eyes. She turned to my crying grandmother.

"Do you hear that, Ma?" she said, contemptuous. "I disgust her. I am evil. You are kind. You are a mother."

"Stop it," I said. "Stop trying to turn this on her."

Suddenly my mother's face scared me.

"Did you hear that, Ma?" my mother asked, screaming now. "Did you hear her say that you try to love me?"

"Stop it," I said again.

But my mother had begun kicking the roses aside, thorns and stems attaching to the bottom of her sari, in a frightening stampede toward my grandmother.

"Do you hear that, Ma?" she screamed as she shook my grandmother, holding her by her frail shoulders.

I screamed too, a sound foreign to my ears. "Get away from her."

I kicked aside the baskets of roses, placing my body between my mother and my grandmother. My mother sank to the floor. Debris must have pierced her, but she did not care.

"Stop crying," she screamed at my grandmother. "Stop crying, and tell her the truth."

"Tell me what, Mummy?" I asked my grandmother.

My grandmother shook her head, bewildered. "I don't know," she whispered in fear.

"You want my daughter to hate me the way you hated me," said my mother. "You won't tell her that you punished me because I wasn't a boy, wasn't the son you lost, wasn't Hari. You pretended that I committed some crime, when you did so much worse to me, and then you tell her you love me. At least I did it out of love, Lila. She did it out of hate. Do you remember your beloved cane cracking over my back, Ma? Do you remember making me strip naked, throwing me so hard against the wall that I broke my arm and couldn't play badminton for the school team for a year? She was only satisfied when she sent me to boarding school and never saw me again till I was seventeen, Lila.

I found myself a husband the first chance I got, to run away from her. From this godforsaken family."

My mother sat on the floor, her sari in a heap around her, crying like a child. I felt dizzy, the sickly smell of roses in my lungs.

I turned slowly to my grandmother. "You hit her? When she was a child."

"No, no," said Geeta through her tears. "It was only a few times. I don't know why she says such terrible things about me."

"You said you hated what she had done to me. You told me there was something wrong with her. You said you tried to make her see reason," I said, piecing my sentences and memories together, stupidly, agonizingly slow. "But you did the same thing to her?"

Something flashed in my grandmother's eyes as she straightened the hunch of her back.

"Lila, be quiet," she said. "You are a child. You don't know what you're talking about."

"You taught her to be this way," I said, horror spreading through my insides.

"You have no idea what she was like as a child," said my grandmother with real hatred, a fearsome Kali in her own right, a Geeta I had never witnessed before, as my mother flinched in the corner.

I turned away, unable to look at my grandmother.

Behind us, the door opened quietly. "Downstairs . . . they can hear you . . . ," said Mishti, softly.

I looked at her. "Leave him," I said. "Leave that man. I can help. I can get you out of this. You have to leave this house."

"Lila," said my grandmother, the rage rising in her voice. "You don't know what you are talking about."

Mishti looked at me, her large eyes filling with tears.

I turned back to my grandmother. "You abused your child until she ran away. You let her do it to me. You let Hari do it to Mishti. You raised him to believe he could. Where will it end? When will you stop?"

"Be quiet," said my grandmother. "It's not my fault your mother is the way she is. It's not my fault Hari is the way he is. You never knew his father."

She raised her cane in my direction—my great-grandfather Krishna Lahiri's cane.

"This was his weapon, and Hari learned how to use it from him," she said as she turned to Mishti. "Tell Lila it isn't my fault."

"You do nothing about it," I said in disgust. "You let her have *accidents*, and you turn away. Just like you did with me."

"I have tried to make him see reason a thousand times," said my grandmother, beginning to cry again.

"Lila," said Mishti. "Hari is my husband. This is my life. I don't know what you think you know, but I make my own decisions."

I looked at her in disbelief. "You're telling me, those were . . . accidents?"

"You can't just come in here and think you know everything about us and try to fix things you don't know anything about," said Mishti. "We're not geysers or chandeliers. We're a family."

Mishti radiated a quiet strength. I felt a shame descend over me.

"It is time for you to go home, Lila," said my grandmother from behind me.

I did not know if she meant my father's house or New York.

I looked at my mother. "Is this where you want to spend the rest of your life? In this house? Keeping their secrets?"

"It's my house," said my mother, looking at me with an odd sympathy I had never received from her before. "Our lives are here."

I peeled roses off the bottoms of my jeans, taking care to leave the surviving ones whole. I left the room as Biddy's laughter floated up to the balcony.

Trauma does not leave our bodies easily. It is inherited by our children and translated, an inevitable language in our genes and blood, insidious in its ability to lie in wait under newborn skin, always at the ready to eventually morph and strike, and in that moment you will be unfathoming of how certainly and quickly you might have turned into your mother. There was to be no freedom for us—not for my grandmother, my mother or myself. This I knew finally. Our unending cycles of hatred looped around us, a circular, rhythmic beat clanging on the prison walls of our violence, as we passed them on, calling them our mansions, generation after generation.

35

IN MANHATTAN, A lifetime ago, Dr. Laramie had sat on his leather chair, the tips of his fingers touching each other, as he explained the merits of chair exercises, a part of the Gestalt therapy he practiced.

"You sit facing an empty chair. In the chair, you picture the person with whom you are experiencing conflict. Or, you may picture a part of yourself. Then, you speak to the empty chair. You explain your feelings, thoughts, and understanding of the situation. Then things get interesting. You move to the other chair. And you respond to what you just said, from the other person's or your other half's perspective, taking on their role. You may move back and forth between the chairs several times to continue the dialogue."

I had laughed. "I spend a lifetime trying not to become her so you can get me in her head?"

"It actually can give you an extraordinary perspective," he had said. "Demons lose their powers when we understand where they come from."

"You sure the saying isn't 'When you see a demon, run before it kills you'?"

"Demons have a fantastic way of catching up when you're out of breath."

I sat in one of Iva's armchairs now, deep and plush, and imagined my mother across from me, on the couch. She would be making barbs about the way my stepmother had decorated the apartment, and I would be chafing back at her.

"Stop it, Ma," I said aloud, into the empty living room. "Stop it," I said again.

I felt a tide of grief.

"I'm sorry, Ma," I said, my breath catching in my chest, trying to imagine her look of satisfaction. "I hate you, Ma," I said, my hands over my face as I tried to release the image of my young, fragile, tormented mother from my brain, from my body, where it felt like she had infiltrated every bone, where it felt like my heart might disintegrate from the sorrow I felt for what she had endured, where the pain felt like it had woven itself into the fabric of our DNA, never to leave.

IT WAS THE night of the reception. I had an email from Aetos. My eight weeks were up in a week's time, he reminded me, jovial, noting that I would see more than a few meetings landing on my calendar for the week I was expected to be back in the office. *In 2016, we've got to get Wyndham to be just a touch more commercial and global!*

Hi, said an email from Molly. *Let's try to text and email if calling doesn't work. I need your advice on a thousand things. Seth called. Tell me how you feel.*

Even in those few words, she gave me an odd reassurance that she would make sense of what was beyond me. Molly had always known to take what she needed from life before it was too late; I seemed perpetually to be lying in wait for life to reveal itself to me.

I pulled out the sari that my mother had earmarked for me to wear that night—pale-rose silk with gold embroidery work—which I remembered her wearing at a wedding herself once. In the mirror, I looked like her, and it was impossible to recognize myself anymore. The thought of Seth flashed through me, a lingering sadness rising in my chest, a dull ache of guilt that refused to fade.

At seven, Vik picked me up.

"At least it'll be over tonight," he said as I got in the passenger side of the Contessa. "I'm all weddinged out."

I nodded.

"You okay, Li?" asked Vik. "You look tired."

"Didn't sleep well."

"Me neither. The election is this weekend. Feels like all our lives hinge on it. If the right wins, I could be out of a job, on my way to Brooklyn," he said, playful even as I heard the fear in his voice. Vik and I both knew what a right-wing administration would mean for the *New Statesman*, but more so for his life in India, already fraught with denials.

"You're always welcome in Brooklyn," I said.

The band was in full swing, playing Hindi and English songs that guests were swaying to or humming along with. The reception was a modern party, a lighter revelry in contrast to the traditional rituals of the wedding. Adil and his wife made a brief appearance, but I avoided the room they were in as soon as I spotted them.

Many rounds of speeches and toasts were made, the most prominent being Hari's. It was one of those nights when one understood the true extent of Hari's powers, the way he filled a room with his presence, as he alternated between making his guests double over in laughter at his quick-witted humor or moving them to tears at his description of what it felt like for a father to watch his only daughter depart for her new husband's home.

Rana's speech was more poetic, with less of a point. And just as he had begun to ramble into a description of his own wedding, the band launched into a spirited rendition of "Khaike Paan Banaras Wala," a raucous Amitabh Bachchan classic that roused even my grandmother to her feet.

The dancing went on for hours, accompanied by cocktails made of shrubs of roasted raw mango and date syrups and jamuns, and even my mother seemed like she was transported to another universe, one where we might leave behind our problems for a little while.

AFTER THE LAST guests had left, all of us—the whole Lahiri family, plus Arjun's parents and Biddy and Arjun—gathered on the terrace to eat a late dinner together. Mr. Das's men had brought the long table up from the great room. I had barely spoken to my mother or my grandmother—Vik and I had spent the evening largely huddled together and were now at one end of the long table. We all were a little drunk, raucous and exhaling from the days of planning and celebration. The clear air of the night filled my lungs, the expanse of the city sprawling below us.

As I looked down at the streets, on a dark streetside corner across from the main entrance of the house, I saw my mother talking to Mr. Roy. I looked at them, illuminated—they would have been under cover of darkness were the moon not so high that night. There was at least a foot of distance between them, yet it was clear that they were lovers, and I averted my eyes quickly, something rising in my chest at the reality of seeing my mother as half of a couple. She was so effective at keeping secrets that even if you knew something to be true, you might doubt its existence from time to time. I looked again, and they were gone, as if I had not seen anything in the first place.

I remembered the things I had said to her the previous night. My grandmother, too, had been watching them, and as she met my eyes, I felt something hard and cold settle into my stomach. I did not know if I could ever love her in the same way, she who had created my mother, so full of pain and secrets, who then had created me.

"ARE YOU GOING to stay the night, Li?" asked Rinki, leaning over Gina.

I shook my head as I felt my mother join us, sliding into a chair too near me.

"I can drop you home—I'm not staying either," said Vik.

"And why not?" asked Gina. "Can't a mother ever expect her son to spend a night under her roof?"

"I was hoping to stay up with you and Lila and have a little fun for once," said Rinki to Vik, crestfallen.

Vik took Gina's hand. "Ma. Come and spend a weekend with me at my apartment."

"You better take your socks and dirty jeans off the floor before I step into that place."

Their banter made me smile. Somehow, Rana had found himself a family that managed a simple, unconditional love for each other. What Rana, Gina, and Vik shared seemed almost too fantastical to be true; Vik's hatred of Hari and his refusal to spend a night in the house while his uncle lived in it seemed far more natural to me.

Gina leaned over, whispering to Vik. "He's your uncle, and he's not going to change now. If your father can make his peace with him, why can't you? For my sake."

"Ma, he calls me a faggot. He calls Baba a faggot, for fuck's sake. God knows what he thinks the word means. He takes every opportunity to humiliate us. Have you considered that maybe Baba *shouldn't* make his peace?" whispered Vik, furious.

Rinki and I exchanged a look, uncomfortable at being seated between the two of them. Before I had arrived, it was as if the Lahiris had agreed to coexist in harmony, hatred and secrets merely seething below the surface. In the past few weeks, everything seemed to boil over into plain sight. I wondered if, after all, my grandmother was right—that unsightly secrets were better buried if you were unprepared to wrestle with their consequences by day.

Gina leaned back in her chair, tired. "Don't swear in front of your mother," she said.

Under the table, Biddy slipped her hand into Arjun's hand. Rana, animated, was talking about poetry to Arjun's mother. The moonlight, more clear with every passing hour, gave even my own bruised heart some peace. I closed my eyes.

A volley of curses and shouting from the fifth-floor staircase, near the end of the terrace, erupted into the night. Hari, who had gone missing for most of the meal, appeared, followed by the frightened caterer.

"But, sir, it is the price we had agreed on. I will never be able to pay my boys at that rate," said the caterer, his fingers twisting together.

"Did you see the size of the mutton chops, you lowlife bastard?" said Hari, breathing through a haze of rage and liquor. "Do you think you can trick me into paying you double what you deserve?"

As if in practiced choreography, Rana, Gina, and Vik rose simultaneously as my grandmother chattered louder to Arjun's horrified parents and Rinki called out to Bari to bring up more pots of mint tea and a plate of paan, as if nothing were unfolding in the backdrop. Vik and Gina brought a disgruntled

Hari back to the table—years of practice had taught them how—as Rana patted the caterer on the back and handed over cash, nodding in acknowledgment of what was owed.

Hari sat down, shaking his head as if to loosen water from his ears, suddenly so genial and coherent that I wondered if he was drunk after all. "Can't get a fair rate anywhere, eh, Ghoshal Saheb?" he asked, an air of resigned mirth to him.

Arjun's father nodded as Mishti pushed a cup of tea toward Hari. With calm restored as quickly as it had left, the table settled back into conversation. When he wanted to, Hari could return to being the life of the party, his charm making its way into even his skeptics' veins, as evidenced by the Ghoshals' reluctant laughter at his many jokes about the wedding.

Biddy got up to pour herself a cup of tea. Vik had disappeared, and I patted the empty seat next to me. She made her way to my end of the table and slid into Vik's seat as I put an arm around her.

"How does it feel to be married?" I asked.

She huddled into my side, like a child, breathing in the mint from her cup, raising her face to me. "Exactly like yesterday," she said, wrinkling her forehead.

I laughed. "I'm told it takes a while."

"What even is being married? I mean, it's just us trying to be good roommates who have sex, right?"

"I wouldn't know," I said, amused.

She sighed and rested her head against my shoulder. "I hope my marriage works out."

I squeezed her shoulder.

"Arjun seems like such a great guy," I said.

"He's wonderful when he's happy," she said, so softly that I barely caught the words. I could not see her face, but I knew that she meant her father, that she had been watching him reign over the table, people roaring at his jokes, even his family, whom he terrorized, his Hyde forgotten, forgiven as Hari knew he would be, lighting up like one of our chandeliers as he drank more whiskey. I could feel Biddy's sadness (or maybe I imagined it, transferring my own), wishing for the best parts of a parent to be the truth, wishing that their demons would fade from our existence.

IT WAS ALMOST midnight when the Ghoshals stood up. It was as if everyone but Vik was reluctant to end the festivities and reenter ordinary life.

"Arjun, aren't you staying the night with Biddy?" asked Geeta.

"He's going to drive his parents home and pick me up in the morning."

"Really, Biddy, must you defy tradition all the time?" said my grandmother. "A new bride, sleeping in her mother's bed on her wedding night."

"The wedding night was two days ago. And I'll be sleeping in Ma's bed often," declared Biddy, her eyes floating in the direction of her father. "Nothing will change. I'll visit often."

My grandmother and I looked at each other involuntarily, some shudder of recognition passing through us at the warning in Biddy's voice. I looked away immediately, unwilling to have a connection with her.

Hari, too, had caught the edge in Biddy's words; a flash of rage skittered over his flushed face.

"Marriage changes everything, Biddy. Just you wait and see," said Rinki, teasing.

"I'll FaceTime Arjun at bedtime if it helps, Geeta Kaki," said Biddy with a wink.

I recoiled inside at the idea of Geeta playing the part of doting grandmother and aunt. To me she was altered.

Vik looked puzzled. "You okay?" he asked me.

"Yeah," I nodded. "Should we go soon?" It was just the family on the terrace now, languid over the last remnants of tea and paan and whiskey, as Bari and the maids cleaned up downstairs.

"I'm just waiting for my parents to wind down," said Vik. "Maybe ten minutes?"

"Rana, what the fuck did you tell that moron of a caterer?" asked Hari, as if the question were a punch line to a joke.

Rana, who had been chewing on paan contentedly, listening to Gina,

Rinki, and Mishti's dissection of who had worn what at the wedding, looked up. "Ah, we just haggled a bit, and then I settled his bill," he said, mild.

"God, if the Ghoshal idiots hadn't been here, I would have broken that moron's nose," said Hari.

"Baba, those are my in-laws you're talking about," said Biddy, annoyed.

Hari doubled over with an unusual amount of laughter—as if a cartoon version of himself, but grotesque instead of funny.

"Come on, you have to admit they're jokers. That Ghoshal Babu looks like his dhoti is going to come off any second—he's such a Durgapur simpleton. And Mrs. Ghoshal, famed for her constipated face." Hari scrunched all of his features into a concentration of wrinkles, collapsing into paroxysms of delight.

Vik stood up, one hand on Biddy's shoulder. "It's late. We should get going, Lila. Maybe everyone should go to bed."

I looked around for my bag as my mother, too, stood up, pushing her chair back.

Hari thumped his fist on the table, startling Mishti, next to him, the bones of his face rearranging themselves into rage. "Am I the only man with a backbone in this family? Can I not leave one small unpaid bill to my retarded brother and expect him to do it properly? I bet that caterer got you to cough up three times what he was owed," he said, speaking to Rana but looking at Vik with a challenge in his eyes.

Vik's nostrils flared, and it felt like he might charge at his uncle. This was Hari in his element, spoiling for a fight, a potent mix of whiskey and self-loathing.

"It's not your money, Hari Kaka," I heard myself say. "It's the trust's money and the family's money, and Rana Kaka can do what he likes, because I approved it. I'm the legal heir. Nothing is going to change that."

Our eyes met across the length of the table, and even in the haze of his fury, I could tell he knew that I knew about the will. But it was not in Hari's nature to feel remorse; instead, he swelled in outrage at having been discovered, that in his own house he was not allowed to be himself.

"Look at how you talk to your uncle, to your elders, you disrespectful little bitch," he snarled. "You walk in here, and you think you can take what you like. You treat us like renters and behave like the landlord, trying to fix the toilets so you can spray your American backside in it. We don't need your help, maharani. This is our house. The last time the British came to loot us, we sent them packing. This time will be no different."

In wrath, Hari often lost the plot, threads of hatred loosely woven, because he was also usually drunk. The Lahiris sat frozen, a rising horror and dread at what else he might expel into the night air, things that could not be unsaid.

"How dare you talk to my daughter like that," said my mother, her hands shaking in fury.

"Maya, don't make it worse," hissed my grandmother.

"Don't talk to her like that," I said to Geeta, feeling a cold anger slide into my throat. Maybe I was infected with whatever the rest of them had, but I was rooted to the floor of the terrace, blood-tied to whatever was to come.

Hari turned on my mother, the sudden motion of a viper. "Do you remember how after Lila was born, you would leave her on the terrace, hoping the sun would bake her to death, forgetting to feed her, crying to every maid in sight that you didn't want to be her mother, that you wished Mihir had let you get an abortion?"

"Stop it, Hari," said my grandmother. "She was not well. Are you mad, bringing these things up?"

"I'm going to kill him with my own hands," said Vik, his knuckles white against the chair he was gripping.

"Baba, stop it," said Biddy, tears streaming, bringing makeup and glitter with them. "You're spoiling everything."

Hari thumped his fist down on the table, hard. "I am not spoiling anything. Your wedding has ruined us. The trust has withered to nothing."

Untrue, I corrected him in my head. The trust had enough interest left over for the Lahiris to live off until the next financial year.

"But what do you care?" he said. "You had to have three kinds of dessert served to your friends, who dress like overpriced hookers. While my impotent brother sat and ate those fucking tiramisus, pretending that his wife's fancy degree makes up for the fact that he has a homo son."

"Bari," he yelled, "bring me another glass of whiskey."

But Bari knew not to come up now. Years of working for the Lahiris had taught her when the family table needed to be members only.

"You've turned into a madman," said Mishti in disbelief. "It is our daughter's wedding."

In all of the years that I had existed on the fringe of the Lahiris—a semi-Lahiri, not quite whole—privy to their secrets and lies and all that went unsaid, yet still an outsider, I had never actually seen Hari hit Mishti. It was whispered gossip that ran through the network of neighborhood kitchens and tea shops that the Lahiri scion was a wife beater, that if you stopped still in the night near the house, you could hear muffled screams. But none of us had ever witnessed it, and so three generations, each taking cues from the last, had looked the other way, in a myriad of directions other than the straight one, accepting her stories about her injuries, taking her to the doctor, and, on occasion, resorting to gentle interrogation, with a gnawing suspicion that we could not look the other way for much longer.

But Mishti may have already known that what we—all of Ballygunge Place—were seeking was a confirmation that nothing so terrible could be going on under our own roof and noses, that, ultimately, a marriage was a private matter between man and wife, and that the demons that existed between them were their own to exorcise. When Mishti had an accident, the women of the house would walk silently past Hari in the hallways, checking on her, producing sympathy and tea, a laugh or two at her detailed anecdote of how she had stumbled or slipped or sliced or bruised herself, yet again, yet again, yet again, because in Mishti's version, she was a Chaplin-esque caricature, bumbling and clumsy, addled by a violent routine of slipping and sliding through life, and, boy, could she laugh at it, and "Here, have another biscuit, another cup of tea," and soon, even this pink scar, that purple welt, will ebb and be forgotten.

So expert had we all become at enabling Mishti's skills at carrying on this charade that the truth only lurked beneath our subconscious, never rising fully to our eyes; as a community, we swallowed it whole, and so Mishti and Hari Lahiri were allowed to be just another upper-class Bengali couple, Lahiris and Brahmins and good citizens of Kolkata, who had a daughter for whom they had found an excellent match.

Only Biddy, too young, too near, and too fearless, refused to leave her mother's side as she grew older, sliding into her father's side of the bed by night so that now Hari was accustomed to her placing a perpetual wedge, a human barrier, between her parents. And tonight, on Biddy's last night in the Lahiri house, she was seated across from her mother when her father's ire burned bright under the moonlight, his face a terrible map of violence.

In the moment after Mishti called her husband a madman, there was a silence, because we had never heard contempt for Hari in her voice before. Then, his palm and fingers splayed across her cheek, producing a terrible crack, its confirmation finally shattering all of our cowardices. Biddy let out a sharp cry of horror as her mother's chair fell sideways, the force of the blow to her body too much for the lightweight aluminum to bear.

The terrace exploded into pandemonium. Geeta slapped Hari across his face, shaking him by the shoulder, as Gina bolted out of her chair to her sister-in-law's side. I knelt on the gravel of the terrace floor, where Mishti, eyes closed, lay fetal, almost peaceful in her inertia.

"What is the matter with you?" said Geeta, hissing at Hari, even as she turned around, a human shield between her beloved nephew and a charging, inflamed Vik. "Vik, please for god's sake, just go home."

"Vik, please," said Rana, restraining his son by the shoulders. "He's my brother."

Vik shook his head, blinking, restrained by Rana's arms. "You people are lunatics," he said.

Gina and I held Mishti in our arms as she opened one eye, and then the other, and raised her neck. "Oh, I'm fine," she said, gentle, even as the spots of red on her cheekbone took on color, readying to darken and sear overnight.

"Apologize to your wife immediately," said my grandmother to Hari, as if to a toddler for having refused to share a snack with a sibling.

My mother looked at me, on the floor with Mishti, her eyes childlike, as if to say *This is what I have lived with. This is the lot I have had.* Or perhaps it was grief that I should witness her family's unraveling, or that I was by Mishti's side and not her own.

"I am sorry . . . Sorry," flung Hari, bewildered, as if he were apologizing on behalf of someone else. "I didn't think . . . The whiskey . . . I'm sorry." He looked around, a horror dawning that there was no place left to hide, and then at Mishti, a pleading in his eyes.

But when she refused to return his gaze or hurry to his rescue or accept his apology, instead occupying the silence, his face twisted again. Wrenching his shoulder free from Geeta, he spat on the ground.

"Fucking drama. I'm tired of this family looking at me like I'm a murderer. I got a little angry, I said I'm sorry. What more do you want, you lot of lazy, no-good ass-kissers."

Stomping away from the table, Hari climbed the thin metal steps to the Secret Sixth. One heavy step at a time, he swayed uncertainly, moonlight bouncing in shards off his navy silk kurta.

Geeta looked up at the Secret Sixth in concern. "Should one of us go up there with him? He's had a lot to drink." But when she turned around to face the disgust of her family, she shook her head, as if confused by her own words. "Mishti, my darling, are you all right?"

Mishti, sitting back up on her chair, free of my arms and Gina's, looked at my grandmother, saying nothing. Geeta looked away, tears filling her eyes. I remembered that in every one of her arguments with my mother, my grandmother would begin to cry and I would take her side.

Biddy had been frozen in her seat. "Ma, you have to come with me," she whispered, her voice breaking. Vik put an arm around her.

"She's right," said Gina. "Go live with Biddy and Arjun. This can't go on."

"Why should she go anywhere?" asked my mother angrily. "This is her house. That man should go to jail."

"That man is our family. We don't send family to jail," said my grandmother.

I had a brief flash of my great-grandfather, the patriarch Krishna Lahiri, the man who had created Hari Lahiri.

"If it were your father, would you send him to jail?" asked Geeta, facing my mother.

Mishti sighed and leaned against Gina's shoulder. "Nobody is going to jail," she said.

Her statement seemed to bring some relief to my grandmother, whose gaze kept sliding to the Secret Sixth.

"I'm going to bed," announced my mother, standing up. "Mishti, come to my room for a cup of tea if you like."

This sudden dispatch of kindness startled me, but Mishti nodded. "Thank you, didi."

"I'll come too," said Gina.

"Lila?" asked my mother.

"No, thank you," I said stiffly, my first words in what felt like an eon. "Vik, will you take me home?"

Vik nodded.

Rana put a hand on his son's shoulder. "I'll come to see you tomorrow, Bikram."

It was surreal, as if the Lahiris were practiced at this extending of apologetic affection, regretful at the bad apple in their midst, but united in their belief that he was, under no circumstances, to be expelled.

Finally, only Vik, Rinki, Biddy, and I were left on the terrace. The occasional clink of glass from above meant that Hari was occupied with one of the bottles of whiskey he kept stashed in a corner of the Secret Sixth. We could not see him, which meant he was probably sitting on the floor, licking his inflamed wounds.

"I should go to bed too," said Rinki, subdued. "Biddy, I'm looking forward to the bidai in the morning. What will you wear?"

Biddy said nothing.

Rinki looked at me, stricken. All she wanted was to restore some degree of happiness to the scene, but something had shifted that night, a recalibration. Tomorrow, the family would need to understand how to live without looking away, or with the certain knowledge that they were culpable. Our silence bewildered Rinki—she had spent too long in the Lahiri way of life.

"Good night, Rinks," said Vik quietly.

After Rinki left, he turned to Biddy. "We'll find a way to get her out of here. I promise. And till then, I'll make sure Ma doesn't leave her alone for a minute."

I wondered if Hari, only a story above, could hear us.

Biddy nodded. "I feel like I'm abandoning her, to this hell."

Hari began to sing, a low rendition of a Rabindrasangeet song. His pure, high voice was striking in the silent air as it floated out from the Sixth, his mother's love of music in his veins. That he was capable of beauty felt unjust, like a betrayal.

"Let's go, Vik," I said. "You coming, Biddy?"

"No," said Biddy. "I just need to be alone for a bit."

"Are you sure?" said Vik, looking at the Secret Sixth.

She nodded. "He's going to be up there all night," she said, bitter. "This is what he does. Tomorrow, he will be good as new."

We left her on the terrace, her wedding dress fanning out around her. As we passed my mother's studio on the far end, Vik leaned his head in.

"We're going. Biddy's still sitting out there."

Gina, Mishti, and my mother had been talking, and they sprang back as if we had interrupted, a hush filling the air.

"I'll go get her in a few minutes," said Mishti. "Good night, darlings."

From the door, I could see the fresh welt of her bruise, like a sunrise over her cheek and ear. Were it not for all of her bruises and scars and welts, you might have thought she was entirely content with her lot in life, an easy, unassuming happiness emanating from her even now. I felt as if I were in a house of tricks—illusions and magic acts that felt so much like reality we could not tell them apart any longer.

Hari's singing had progressively become louder, like a musician paid to perform for the night. Startling in its loveliness, it set my body on edge.

"I'm going to kill myself tonight," shouted Hari. The announcement floated to us in my mother's studio like an idle threat he might have wagered at the tea stall. Then, with more conviction, he repeated, "I'm going to kill myself tonight."

Mishti's shoulders sagged. "He just wants me to go and get him," she said.

"The nerve of that haramzada," said my mother.

"How about I go help him do the job," Vik said.

"Be quiet," said Gina. "You can't talk like that."

"The entire neighborhood can hear him, and I'm the one who needs to shut up?"

"Vik, just take Lila home, please," said Mishti. "We need to end this night. It was such a beautiful wedding, Lila. Thank you."

I tried to smile back at her, but all I saw was her bruise.

"All of you are responsible," screamed Hari from the Secret Sixth, Shakespearean in his outrage. "My wife and daughter hate me, my mother hated me, my father hated me, everyone conspires against me—I may as well die tonight, or they'll kill me in my sleep someday."

Mishti got to her feet. "I'll go to him. It won't end unless I do. It's okay," she added. "He's just feeling alone."

"He's not a five-year-old child, kaki," Vik said, furious.

"Vik, let's go," I said. The least we could do was not add to Mishti's inescapable grief.

"Do you know what bad luck it is to be born in this house?" shouted Hari. "My American niece is trying to steal my property from me under my nose while she lures all the men of the neighborhood into her bed. My own brother just gave away the house like it was his to donate to an outsider."

My aunts stared at me, stricken. My mother stood.

"I'll kill him myself," she said.

Thus far, we had only been able to hear Hari, catching only occasional glimpses of his hunched back leaning on the guardrails of the Sixth, from our vantage point of my mother's studio's window. But now, in the clear moonlight, his kurta shining as if he were an actor on a stage, taking a bow, Hari stood outlined against the sky, the floor of the Sixth beneath him.

"He's climbed up on the ledge," I said, my heart beating faster.

"Don't worry, Lila," said Mishti. "He gets up there all the time. It's a good thing. it means he's sobering up. Something about the air sobers him up."

"Hari's been terrorizing us from that ledge since he was a boy," said my mother. "He wouldn't fall from there if we wished it on him."

"Vik, go and get your father," said Gina. "Rana is the only one who can get him down from there."

"Faggot brother, faggot nephew, faggots all," screamed Hari. "Spinsters and faggots and whores under my roof." He was playing to an imagined gallery, a performer entertaining his glittering audience, except that eighty feet below stretched nothing but the emptied Lahiri courtyard.

Vik disappeared down the stairs. The moon flitted between clouds, making our view of the Secret Sixth murky.

"I can't see him any longer," said Mishti. "Did he climb down?"

"He's still there," said Gina, looking up from one of my mother's *Femina* magazines.

"I'm going to get him," said Mishti, rising.

"Where the hell is Rana?" asked Gina. "What's taking Vik so long?" She took off down the stairs, presumably in search of her son.

Mishti, my mother, and I (nobody was going to let Mishti go alone—in this, at least, my mother and I were united) stepped out from the patio of my mother's studio onto the terrace. The thought of climbing the stairs to the Secret Sixth—to Hari—sent a shudder through me.

My mother looked at me, sharp. "Are you cold? Go get a jacket."

I shook my head. As we were crossing the expanse of the terrace, we heard muffled rustling from the Secret Sixth, and then a series of thuds, as if something heavy had dropped.

I stopped. "It sounds like he jumped down from the ledge back into the Sixth," I said. "Maybe we don't have to go up there."

"What is that noise?" asked my mother. "Is he dancing up and down now, the moron?"

For a moment, there was silence, a pause in which I felt relief. "He's probably sitting in the corner with his bottle now," I said.

My mother, Mishti, and I had stopped walking toward the Sixth, unwilling to engage with Hari if we did not have to. We stared at the slim four-legged structure, and I imagined my great-grandfather standing on it, taking in the view of the whole city.

And then, in the still of the night, only our breath floating through the air, we heard another series of thumps amidst more rustling, followed by a sharp crack, far-off and simultaneously heavy and acute, unlike anything I had heard before.

The three of us stood frozen, halfway to where the thin metal staircase to the Secret Sixth began. Mishti clapped her palm over her mouth. Biddy—still in her wedding dress, her eyes large in her face, like the ghosts that I imagined haunted the Lahiri house—stood on the Secret Sixth, staring at us.

A long, sharp scream spiraled up from the courtyard below. Bari's voice, each scream longer and louder than the last, rang through the quiet.

"Hari Babu," she screamed, again and again.

My mother ran to the balcony and leaned over, looking into the courtyard. As she turned back to us, Mishti looked up and whispered fiercely, "Biddy. Come down."

Biddy descended the metal staircase in one gliding rush, the sequins of her heavily embroidered skirt making tinny sounds against the metal stairs. Mishti took her by the wrist, and together, mother and daughter ran past us—past Gina and Rana, and Vik, who had returned—and into my mother's studio as a scream from the third-floor balcony, this one unmistakably my grandmother's grief, crashed into the night, the moon once more emerging brilliant from behind the clouds, as if to shine a floodlight on Hari's body lying eighty feet below us, cracked open in the bloodied center of the empty courtyard.

36

SUB-INSPECTOR MOIZ KHAN of the Kolkata Police Force had a new boss. Commissioner Abir Chatterjee, formerly special commissioner of the Mumbai Police Force, and who, it was said, had *run* Mumbai, had been awarded the top job at the KPF headquarters a month ago. The KPF headquarters were, ironically, the historic brick-red Lalbazar building where John Palmer, the wealthy British merchant of colonial trade, had once lived in luxury. Moiz made note that Commissioner Chatterjee prayed to the Hindu god Vishnu at the small shrine he had had installed in his new office before he sat at his desk each morning, and chewed gutkha violently, such that his teeth glowed orange in the station's stark white lighting. Even the more hardened cops felt a surge of fear at what the new boss might be capable of. But Moiz had seen a few commissioners come and go, and all he was interested in, as he told his wife, Ambreen, at breakfast that morning, was a promotion, so he could buy a secondhand car for them to take little trips. After sixteen years in the KPF and still earning only a little more than minimum wage, who could blame him? Besides, the commissioner had been nothing but friendly to Moiz so far.

"I don't know, jaanu," said Ambreen, doubtful. "I've heard he's killed a criminal once with his bare hands. Snapped his neck." She made a cracking sound, with her throat and teeth coming together in one guttural motion as she took a bite out of her buttered, sugared toast.

"This is why I tell you not to gossip with the other wives," said Moiz as he rolled up his omelette in a paratha. "I've solved hundreds of cases, I'm on time every morning, at eight a.m. sharp. All we need to think about is how to make sure I look good in front of him. I don't want any of this nonsense getting back to Commissioner Chatterjee."

"Is it true he wants the National Popular Front to win?" asked Ambreen, leaning forward, a little breathless, her morning hair unraveled over her shoulders, softening Moiz immediately. Moiz had met and married Ambreen only three years ago and was as yet not immune to her charms. Life finally seemed to be shining down at Moiz at thirty-six, with a lovely wife who could cook and an impending promotion.

Moiz cleared his throat. "I think he's a patriot."

"So it's true he's going to target the Muslim neighborhoods? God, Moiz, what if they start targeting our street, our friends, or my mother's neighborhood in Khidderpore? Allah save us."

Ambreen had been five during the Hindu-Muslim riots of 1992 and had seen her father and uncle dragged out of their fabric store by their limbs and their hair.

"What if they win?" she said, her voice rising. "We'll never feel safe again in our own homes."

"That's enough drama," said Moiz, standing up.

"Every few years, the Hindus decide this is their country, and they forget that Muslims are their friends and lovers and colleagues, that our children play together. If the party comes for us, they will kill us, jaanu, they will hunt us down."

Ambreen's flair for the theatrical came mainly from starring in a number of neighborhood plays, and Moiz put a hand on her cheek, affectionate.

"I am a police officer, not a political man. I'm telling you, jaan, if you keep talking about this nonsense with the other inspectors' melodramatic wives, it'll only bring ruin into our lives. At the KPF, there are no Hindus and Muslims. Only the uniform. The ultimate power lies in this khaki shirt."

Pretending he did not see the flicker of an eye roll from his wife, he squeezed her shoulder, inhaling the scent of her shampoo, and headed out toward the bus station.

Just outside his building, the butcher was holding up a chicken, preparing to slaughter it. *You would think the creature would squawk, as it did all day long, disturbing my naps, instead of being mute only seconds before its death,* thought Moiz as he walked on.

THERE WERE RUMORS, of course, that Chatterjee did not like Muslims, that he had been homegrown by the NPF in Mumbai and was going to be their man on the force while the party tried to gain control of Bengal and Kolkata, and that Muslim neighborhoods were already under target, but so far, Moiz had felt respected, even liked, by his boss and put the whole thing down to the endless rumormongering of politicians. After years in the KPF, Moiz felt invincible in his uniform, feared and respected wherever he went and though he was known for his fairness, on a bad day Moiz knew that even Ambreen would stay out of his way. The uniform made you feel like a man.

So when the Lahiri case came in, in the dawning hours of that Monday morning, and Chatterjee assigned him to it, Moiz knew that he had to make an impression, no matter what. It was too bad that he had been partnered with Jai Pathak, who had worked with Chatterjee in Mumbai. Even so, an investigation involving a prominent Kolkata family could be just the shine that Moiz's career needed.

"Beautiful, isn't it?" Moiz said as he and Inspector Pathak stood outside the Lahiri house, the morning light bouncing off the arches and pillars. "They must have painted it for the wedding. It used to look old and decayed."

"It's still pretty ramshackle," said Pathak. "Look at those weather-beaten walkways and telephone wires. They could spend some real money on it, if it's all that historic."

"I don't think they have the kind of money they used to," said Moiz, feeling a stab of hurt. The inspectors from other cities would never love Kolkata the way he did, he thought.

"Was it reported as a suicide?" asked Pathak.

"An accident," said Moiz, reading the report. "Hari Lahiri, the younger brother of Tejen Lahiri, who died two months ago."

"Any chance of foul play?"

"They are one of the oldest, most respectable families of Kolkata. It would be a scandal."

"They have money," said Pathak. "That's always a motive."

Moiz nodded. "The patriarch, Krishna Lahiri, died a while ago and left his son Tejen in charge. Tejen left the house to his granddaughter, skipping over his own child. An American woman."

"A series of deaths," said Pathak, sinister. A Hindu bhajan in praise of Shivaji rang out from his phone, flashing a call from Chatterjee.

"Yes, sir," said Pathak, stepping away from Moiz as if in private conversation. "Okay, sir . . . Okay . . . Okay . . . Yes. Got it, sir. Don't worry, sir."

Pathak came back to where Moiz was standing, at the Lahiri entrance gate, still strung with wedding lights, looking up at the five stories above, nobody in sight. Moiz turned around—the maid who worked in the house across the street was staring down at him from a window.

"What did Commissioner Saab say?"

"Nothing," said Pathak, kicking aside the NPF and People's Left pamphlets strewn on the pavement as he strode toward the Lahir house.

INSIDE, MITRA, THE forensics guy, was leaning over Hari Lahiri's body, tapping it with the mild interest of someone asking the dead man about the weather. Moiz hated forensics, with their degrees and their instruments—as if they knew more information and had an edge even before anyone else got there. *What they do is act as if they are better than the rest of the police force,* Moiz thought as Mitra looked up, a sneer settling into the pockmarks around his nose.

"Well, look who's here," said Mitra.

"There was traffic," said Moiz.

"How long has he been dead?" asked Pathak, impatient.

Mitra shrugged silkily at the question, looking at his watch. "It's six thirty a.m. now, so anywhere between four and a half and seven or nine hours."

"Goddamn it, are we supposed to solve a case with three different times of death? Is this your first day on the job?" Pathak snapped.

Mitra, who had been on the job far longer than Moiz and exposed to every kind of police officer there was, allowed his features to settle into the bland map that Moiz knew to be fury.

Moiz put a hand on Pathak's shoulder. "The maid is listening," he said.

They looked up to where a woman in her midthirties with softly rounded features stood, watching them. She was in a shiny hot-pink sari studded with glass flowers, which had clearly been worn for the wedding reception the night prior. She nodded, reverential, as if in the presence of celebrity.

"Some tea, sahebs?"

Pathak lifted his chest in the face of the woman's prettiness. He nodded. "No sugar. With Britannia biscuits if you have them. But come here first."

She moved toward him, wiping the sweat collecting on her upper lip with the nylon of her sari. Pathak's eyes rested briefly on her bare waist.

It was a cloudy, humid morning, and the wedding lights were still on. *In a photograph, you could not have told what time of day it was,* thought Moiz, staring at the dead man. He was grotesquely broken in places, his body at odd, sharp, jagged angles. There was little blood around him, but Moiz knew of the internal flood inside the man's once-whole body, betrayed only by the fine sprays of expired spatter around his head. Even in tragedy, rich people looked more rested than the poor.

"What's your name?" asked Moiz.

"Bari," she said.

"Bari," said Pathak, in more of a baritone than usual. "Where were you when Mr. Lahiri fell—"

"Jumped," said Bari.

Pathak frowned. "That is for us to decide. Where were you when he landed on the ground floor?"

"I was downstairs, having a paan with the catering boys. They had just been paid, and we were having a laugh about Janak the head caterer having to chase Hari Babu for the payment."

"Chase him for the payment?" asked Pathak.

"Yes. Hari Babu"—Bari paused, raising her eyebrows—"didn't love it when it came time to pay up, so we knew it would be a chase. Hari Babu and Janak got into a bit of the usual fight—"

"At what time?" asked Pathak.

"About eleven," said Bari. "Yes, eleven I think. My sister had just taken my daughter home. She's only six."

"Get on with it," said Pathak.

"Then Janak came down and said Vik Babu and Rana Babu had paid him. Rana Babu looked like he wanted to punch Hari Babu in the face. But he didn't, of course."

"Vik. That's Bikram Lahiri, Hari's nephew," said Pathak, looking at the file. "Rana Lahiri, twin brother of Hari Lahiri and Bikram's father."

"Rana Babu couldn't harm a fly," said Bari. "He's so gentle, and besides, I took him a glass of Bournvita, because he went to bed right after dinner. The only time he gets angry is when talking politics and the NPF. Says they are a band of thugs."

An odd expression—Was it impatience or anger or a stifled yawn? Moiz couldn't tell which—passed over Pathak's face.

"Then at about midnight, Hari Babu began to shout and joke loudly, like he does after a party." Bari's eyebrows lifted again. "And then I don't know what happened, but he went on the secret terrace, the small one, and kept drinking—he keeps a special bottle in the corner. I saw earlier in the afternoon that there wasn't much left in it, so he might have been angry about that too—"

"What the hell is the secret terrace?" asked Pathak.

"Oh, we have a tiny little terrace built on top of the main terrace on the fifth floor—you'll see it when you go up. Krishna Babu, Hari Babu and Rana Babu's father, had built it to be able to see the whole city and feel like he owned it." Bari laughed, contemptuous. "Rich people love to feel like they own things."

Pathak and Moiz nodded at this, the three of them in familiar recognition of a truth. Moiz tried to prompt Bari to speed up. "So Hari Lahiri was on this secret terrace, and the rest of the family—"

"Was on the main terrace, just below him, with drinks. They don't like us up there cleaning or anything if they have arguments, but we can always hear them loud and clear, airing their so-called secrets. Especially Hari Babu," said Bari, giggling.

"And when did the body fall?" asked Moiz, staring at the five floors above him.

A thin, pale woman with the kind of bony face and plucked eyebrows he didn't like, was watching him from the third floor, fear in her eyes. He nodded at her, and she disappeared from the balcony. *The American,* he thought. You could always tell when someone didn't belong.

"Must be the foreigner granddaughter," said Pathak, who had seen the woman too. "Looks like she hasn't been fed in days."

"Yes, that's Lila Didi. She runs the house now," said Bari, lowering her voice. "Hari Babu hated her coming and taking it over from him. And besides, she's having an affair with Adil Sarkar of Kasba—everyone knows, including his wife. The family is furious about it."

"These rich fuckers just can't enjoy their money in peace, can they?" said Pathak with a laugh.

"They don't have too much money left, though. Always a few days late on my salary," said Bari with disgust. "Hari Babu gambled with most of it when he could. The Lahiri men know one thing, and that's how to piss away their fortunes." Bari stopped here, a little breathless, confident in the powers of her storytelling.

"Lila Didi runs whatever is left in the trust," she continued. "She's like a policeman with it—won't let her own grandmother buy an extra gold necklace. Insists it's all for repairing the house and groceries and whatnot."

"I heard a rumor at the tea stall that she sends your daughter to school," said Moiz.

"Oh, come on," said Bari, turning a dimpled cheek to him, sweet. "These people are all the same. She paid my daughter's fees, and then the grandmother checked to see if I'd spent it on a new sari. They'll give you leftovers from their dinner and consider it redemption for all the shit they do. Them with their fancy English sentences that they think my daughter needs to know. Motherfuckers. If the second earring goes missing from the jewelry box, I'll be turned out without any of you showing up at the door, maybe even thrown in jail—even though I've worked here since I was ten. The only reason I can't be blamed for whatever happened to Hari Babu is because I was downstairs eating a paan and ran out to see him like that on the courtyard floor. I screamed loud enough to wake the dead, thank goodness, so everyone knew where I was."

Moiz and Pathak exchanged a smirk.

"Anyway, I better go make tea before Geeta Boudi begins shouting for it," said Bari. "I'll bring you both some. Be prepared, they're going to act like they're saints and angels, perfume coming out of their assholes, one at a time."

THREE AND A half hours later, Moiz and Pathak sat down on the tea stall bench that Hari had frequented, where the shop owner and his helper boys scuttled to serve them free tea and biscuits. Pathak looked perplexed.

"The women of that family are like men," he said with distaste. "Even the American."

Moiz nodded. "The Lahiri women have always been like bulls. Katyayani Lahiri could shrivel your balls off if you offended her. I once came to investigate a neighbor's complaint that they were making too much noise at one of their parties, and she made me feel like I was a five-year-old."

"You've known them a long time?" asked Pathak.

"You work in the KPF long enough, you get to know the palaces as well as the streets," Moiz said. "And besides, Hari Lahiri gave us reason to come and visit them a few times over the years."

"For beating his wife?" asked Pathak, dunking a nankhatai in his glass of tea. "That was some shiner on that woman. She must have really said some shit to him to deserve that."

"Never that," said Moiz. "Nobody ever complained about that. Not even the neighbors. But he would gamble and owe people money, get in fights—things like that. He had been helping the NPF campaign too and would get into fights with People's Left supporters. The nephew, Bikram Lahiri is a leftist journalist. Hates—hated—his uncle."

Pathak and Moiz met eyes briefly, both looking away quickly.

"Every family member tells the same story," said Pathak evenly. "Seems fairly clean. They were eating on the terrace after the guests had left. He got into a fight with the caterer. Came upstairs drunk. Slapped his wife, behaved badly, got shouted at by his mother—"

"She's his sister-in-law, Geeta."

"Whatever," snapped Pathak. "She acts like his mother. You made me forget my thread."

"Sorry," said Moiz. "After that, Hari went off to sulk on the sixth-floor terrace with his bottle."

"Yes, and at some point he got drunk and climbed the ledge and fell off," said Pathak. "Geeta Lahiri was in her bedroom, Rana in his, Rinki Bose was on the phone with her husband, and the rest of them were in the studio, watching him sway on the ledge with his bottle. They all said they saw him fall."

"That's Maya De's studio," said Pathak. "They built it on the terrace for her after she came back to the house. After her divorce. She's a strange one, that woman. Something off about her eyes. A little mental, the way she talks."

"She became a little strange after her divorce. Respected at the university, though," said Moiz. "Good heart. Makes sure all the beggar kids in Ballygunge stay fed."

"She was in her studio with the two wives, Mishti and Gina," said Pathak, signaling for another round of tea to the alert owner, who had abandoned all other customers. "And then the newlywed daughter, the American, and the nephew joined them."

"Well, that's what they say," said Moiz.

Pathak laughed. "What is this, a Bengali television show? You think the whole family is lying to us? Poisoned his whiskey?"

"If one of them is involved in any way, they're certainly capable of it. These old families, they don't betray their blood."

"But Hari Lahiri was their blood, you idiot. You're contradicting yourself," said Pathak, taking a glass of tea off the tray that the teaboy held, the latter's head bowed. "Eh, motherfucker, this glass is dirty," Pathak said to the boy. "Get another one before I whip your ass."

"Sorry, sir," said the boy as the owner appeared with a fresh glass of tea.

"Sorry, sir. That boy needs a slap," said the owner.

"Thank you for the tea," said Moiz.

Taken aback, the stall owner retreated.

Pathak frowned. "Well, I think Hari Lahiri got more drunk than he had ever been and realized his whole family hated him and jumped. It's not a new story with these good-for-nothing sons of rich liberal Bengalis. Lazy, spoiled soft sons of bitches."

"Where was the nephew? Rana's son, Vik?" asked Moiz.

"The servant girl said she saw him go into his father's room to ask him to talk some sense into Hari."

"Rana Lahiri worshipped the ground his brother walked on, even though Hari spared no opportunity to bully and blackmail him as a kid," said Moiz.

"I'd be surprised if that stopped when they grew up," said Pathak.

Moiz nodded. "Rana's wife, Gina, hinted at that."

"That one again, like a man," said Pathak.

"She's a professor too," said Moiz.

"They have too many things to say, these women," said Pathak, disgusted. "Still, Gina wasn't lying about being in the studio—you can tell. And she wouldn't have revealed her dislike of her brother-in-law so easily when we grilled her if she had something to hide. And the mother—I mean, sister-in-law—couldn't have done it. You saw how Geeta couldn't even get out of bed. Wonder if she and Hari were having sex or some weird thing. You never know with these Western-type families. Corrupt morals."

"He was like her son. After her infant son died, Hari became a replacement. It's well-known," said Moiz.

"Well, I'm sorry I haven't read the Lahiri history book like you," said Pathak, glowering. "I was off doing real police work in Maharashtra. The Kolkata Police Force have no idea what we deal with in Mumbai."

"Yes, of course," said Moiz.

"And why should anyone want to kill Hari Lahiri besides his wife, since he was beating the crap out of her?"

"It's true. If anyone wanted him dead, it would be her," said Moiz.

"Why are you speaking so slowly, like a child?" asked Pathak. "Clearly, she did no such thing. She couldn't raise her voice to a baby."

"Sorry. I get slow when I'm thinking things through. Yes, I agree with you. I don't think it was her."

"Can't afford to be slow in this business, Sub-Inspector Khan," said Pathak, mollified. He looked at Moiz, curious. "I always forget you're a . . . a Mohammedan . . . until I say your name."

Moiz smiled. "That's what I told my wife, Ambreen, this morning, sir. The uniform has no religion. I am not Muslim. You are not Hindu. We are KPF."

Pathak looked amused. "What about the American? Seems like Hari wanted her dead, not the other way around. She already had the house."

Moiz began to shake his head but thought better of it. "Well, that's right in many ways," he said, agreeable. "The thing is that they all, including Hari, felt sorry for Lila. Her parents got divorced. The dad went off and married a white woman—"

Pathak made a sound of disapproval with his tongue and the roof of his mouth. "The servant girl said there's a rumor that Maya De practiced witchcraft on the girl, trying to cast a spell on her father," said Pathak. "Mental, this family. Divorced witches, murderous wives. Too bad the American didn't push her mother off the terrace—now there would be a case." He stood up to stretch his legs. "Look, Khan, I like your style of detailed police work, but the KPF's problem has been too much attention to some areas"—here, Pathak frowned, ominous—"and not enough in others. And just between us, Commissioner Chatterjee would prefer to wrap up this matter as quickly as possible."

"Oh?"

"Yes. It so happens he is an old friend of Krishna Lahiri's and was at the daughter's reception last night. Not that it has any bearing on the case, of course." Pathak snapped his fingers in the direction of the tea stall owner. "One pack of biscuits, parcel," he said to the nodding man. "But since it is clear-cut that it was an accident and that he was drunk and the family saw him fall, I see no reason to let the press get wind of it. It will be an unnecessary scandal around a family that the boss is acquainted with. The press are vultures—they love to make a stink about nothing. They'll say Hari Lahiri was an NPF supporter, and that's why the boss was at the wedding. They'll say our commissioner secretly plans to support the party once they come to power. All sorts of bloody conspiracies."

"Well, there's a chance the NPF could lose, isn't there?"

Pathak flexed his neck as if he had a crick in it, clockwise and counter. "Only Vishnu knows what the future holds."

Moiz nodded.

"Besides, the daughter is a YouTube superstar. Global," said Pathak, rolling the *l* off his tongue. "It could look bad for us if we mess this up. Nowadays, the internet is enemy number one."

They stood in silence. When Moiz did not respond, Pathak let out an impatient little bark.

"Where did you park? My car is around the corner. I didn't have time to get in a KPF jeep this morning."

"Oh, er. I came straight from home as well. I parked my scooter outside the Lahiri house."

"I'll see you at the station, then," said Pathak. "Let's be prepared to wrap this up with Commissioner Chatterjee."

As Pathak turned to leave, Moiz said, "Inspector Pathak, what type of car do you have presently?"

"What? A Toyota Corolla. Why?"

"My wife and I, we were thinking of buying a car soon. It's nice that you already have one."

Pathak gave Moiz a stiff nod and strode off.

THE MAIN STREET of Ballygunge Place was tentacled with narrow alleys and lanes, providing refuge for lovers across age and class who could not canoodle at home, truant schoolchildren, and mongrels with one eye open to casual cruelty or danger. At a sleepy crosswalk between the local high school and a spate of one-story houses, Moiz stood, trying to look inconspicuous but aware that every passerby's body went on alert at his uniform. He leaned against the thick trunk of a banyan, taking refuge in its shade, his temples throbbing under the sun. If Pathak had a car and a cell phone, why didn't

Moiz, who had served the KPF since he was a boy? As he contemplated this, a thin, frightened face floated into his periphery.

"Bilquis Apa," Moiz said quietly. "As-salaam-alaikum."

The woman, in her fifties, stopped, her eyes searching, until, reluctant, they settled on him under the tree. She came nearer.

"Wa alaikum salaam, janaab," she said, stopping about six feet away from him.

"Thank you for coming. It is a private investigation, so I could not be seen coming to the house," said Moiz.

"I can never be seen on a street corner with a man, much less a policeman, janaab," said Bilquis, sharp.

"Yes. I'm sorry to ask you to come like this. But it is important."

"You've always been kind to my family, janaab. But ask me your questions quickly, before the household wakes up and wants their tea." She pulled the sari farther over her head.

"You've seen Hari Lahiri shout from the top of his terrace before, haven't you?"

"Janaab, the whole neighborhood has. We can hear him in our kitchen."

"Did you see him last night? Before he fell?"

"A terrible business. We are so used to his fits of shouting, usually after he's had a drink, that I barely paid attention. The master and mistress had gone to the Lahiri wedding and come back about an hour before he started. They were watching television in their bedroom, and I was on the kitchen floor eating dinner, because they brought me back some food from the wedding. The food was good, so I didn't bother getting up to see Hari Babu's antics, like I usually might have for a laugh. By the time I got up to wash my plate, he had climbed up onto the ledge."

"Weren't you worried about him falling?"

"Well, that's what's odd," said Bilquis, leaning forward as the school bell rang out, piercing the air.

Moiz also leaned in, straining to hear her over the sound.

"The ledge is wide enough for him to stand comfortably without losing his balance. It's about six feet wide, like a whole sidewalk. Biddy Didi sits there all the time, and so do Bari and I when I go over to have a cup of tea. Hari Babu's father, Krishna Babu, used to stand on it for the view. Hari Babu gets drunk and pretends like he's Krishna Babu up there." Here, Bilquis had the hint of a laugh, but, quickly sobering, she said, "But he always stays on the side far from the edge, even when he's shouting about the family like he was last night. He would have had to walk quite a few steps further to reach the edge and then fall off."

"A drunk man is not in possession of his senses," said Moiz.

"No," said Bilquis as they stood, silent, in a moment of agreement. "But, janaab, the moon was so bright. I could see him clearly. He was at the far side of the ledge, as usual. He had been singing. Such an angelic voice. Although then he said horrible things, as usual, as if the devil possessed him. I won-der . . . I wonder if he just decided to jump, and it wasn't an accident?" Bilquis's eyes filled with horror at the thought.

"When did you go to bed?"

A stream of children and teenagers dressed in identical blue uniforms poured into the street, milling around and past Moiz and Bilquis, like a swarm of noisy bluebottles.

"At about midnight," said Bilquis. "He was on the ledge. I said a prayer for his soul, as usual, and rolled out my mat on the kitchen floor and went to sleep."

"You didn't hear him fall, or Bari scream?"

"Janaab, my bones are old, and I work from five to midnight. Nothing wakes me anymore, not even my own dreams." She looked around. "It's almost four—can I go?"

Moiz nodded. "Thank you, Bilquis Apa."

"Just remember that you promised to help my son get a job after he fin-ishes his exams next year, janaab."

Moiz laughed. "Yes, I remember. Allah hafiz."

"Khuda hafiz, janaab."

Moiz's scooter, a red-and-black Yamaha Ray-Z that he kept shiny with polish, was leaning against the sidewalk outside the Lahiri house. Moiz stopped in front of it and, for a long moment, stood on the hot street. Then, he turned and went back inside the Lahiri house.

THE COURTYARD WAS empty except for Mitra sitting on one of the benches next to the pillars. The house was silent, as if nobody else was in it.

"Are they at the ghat?" asked Moiz.

Mitra looked up. "To do what? The body's gone for an autopsy. It'll be at least two days before they can cremate him. I'm just packing up."

"Why an autopsy?"

"Just a few fresh scratches on his hands and palms. Routine. He probably got them losing his balance, trying to grab the edge of the ledge. It's going to help us rule out suicide."

Moiz nodded amicably, pleased that in the absence of Pathak, Mitra had decided to be cordial.

"Funnily, his blood alcohol wasn't all that high," said Mitra.

Bari appeared at the bottom of the stairs leading inside the house. "You're back," she said, disapproving.

"Can I look at the terrace one more time?" asked Moiz. "The small one, the Secret Sixth."

"God, the family hasn't even been able to eat yet," said Bari, shaking her head. "Follow me."

As they reached the fifth floor, Moiz stopped, entirely out of breath. "These people need to install a lift."

"Oh, Lila Didi has put a lot of their money into one. Next time you come, it may even be running—up and down, up and down, on the back wall of the house. Hopefully, they'll let me ride in it too. Although I hope you don't come back soon." Bari giggled as they walked across the terrace, passing Maya's studio. "She's gone to school," said Bari, gossipy. "Won't miss a day, not even on a day like this."

Moiz nodded. "Is the daughter going to live in Kolkata now? Or go back to America?"

"Oh, I think she'll stay here," said Bari. "I think Adil Babu will divorce his wife and the two of them will live in her father's flat. She sent her boy-friend back to America, you know." Bari lowered her voice. "He was a white saheb."

They had reached the bottom of the Secret Sixth.

"I'll go up," said Moiz. "You stay here."

"Why?" asked Bari, suspicious immediately.

"Because I'm the police, and I said so," said Moiz, climbing the thin iron stairs.

ON THE WAY downstairs, Moiz passed by Mishti Lahiri and her daughter, Biddy, on the ground floor, sitting in armchairs in their living room. They were still in the clothes they had worn to the reception, even though it was late afternoon. Moiz stopped in front of their door and saw the American girl, changed into Western jeans, sitting across them on the bed with that haunted look on her face, and Vik Lahiri, unshaven, next to her. Bari made an annoyed click of her tongue behind him.

Moiz nodded respectfully at Mishti. "Madam, I just wanted to thank you again for your cooperation. We were able to gather everything we needed. The rest of the process should be smooth."

She nodded back, the purple bruise on her face giving her an odd mask of villainy, her other eye red and swollen. "Mitra Babu said we could plan the funeral for the day after tomorrow."

"Yes." Moiz looked at Biddy Lahiri, who was watching him. "Madam, I congratulate you again for your marriage, and I am so sorry that this tragedy had to occur on the same night."

"Thank you, Inspector Khan."

"It feels like only a few years ago that you were running through these halls as a girl," said Moiz.

The Lahiris smiled strained, polite smiles at him.

"And what a beautiful bride you are today. A breathtaking dress."

"Thank you, Inspector Khan."

"Of course, of course. A pity that you tore it."

Biddy looked down at her sequined skirt.

"The arm, Biddy," murmured the American in her accented English, her bony legs and arms huddled into her body. Something about the woman reminded Moiz of the chicken in the morning, mute right before slaughter.

The thin gauze of Biddy Lahiri's lehenga top had ripped under her elbow, spreading to her forearm, a flap dangling under her arm, her skin visible through it.

"I must have ripped it during dinner at some point," she said, raising her clear, bright eyes to meet Moiz.

Vik Lahiri stood up. "It's been a long day, as you can imagine, Inspector. Our family is tired. But if you need any more assistance, I can come down to the thana tomorrow."

"Of course, of course," said Moiz. "Again, my condolences to all of you. We will be in touch."

Bari followed him all the way to the entrance.

"All right, all right, I'm going. You don't have to act like the police," said Moiz, "or we'll have to give you a uniform."

Bari giggled. "I just need to sleep for ten hours."

"Make sure you do."

Bari turned to leave.

"You said his bottle, the one that he stashes up there, didn't have much alcohol in it, when you went to the terrace yesterday morning?" asked Moiz.

"Yes. It was only about a quarter full," said Bari. "Sometimes Mishti Boudi goes up there and pours half into the stones so that he won't get as drunk."

"Right. Okay, I'm off now."

"Finally," said Bari, closing the door with a laugh.

IT WAS DUSK by the time Moiz's scooter reached the busy street on which the KPF headquarters stood. The brick building glowed crimson against the setting sun, yellow taxis crowding through rush hour in Lalbazar.

As Moiz stepped inside, he felt the familiar stab of pride in being a KPF man. Pathak was interrogating someone, looming over the old man, almost certainly a beggar.

"Just tell me what you saw, chacha. There's no point in protecting anyone. We will find out anyway," shouted Pathak, his face inches away from the beggar's face as the man rocked back and forth on his heels, crouched into his own bones. "Khan, there you are. Where the hell have you been? Did you walk back or what? Chacha, I'll deal with you when I come back. Have some tea and think about the side of justice you want to be on."

THE COMMISSIONER HAD a wide, cool office that always had its blinds drawn and gave Moiz the impression of an expensive massage parlor. A little water fountain trickled in a corner, and the chairs in front of the granite-topped presidential desk had white cushions on them, a bizarre departure from the plastic chairs, bhars of tea, files and wires, and paan-stained floors and walls of the rest of the thana. Moiz thought of how violent inmates were held in damp cells only three floors below as he admired the intricate carvings on the stone-carved Vishnu and Krishna on the shrine in the corner.

"Sir, we spent the day at the Lahiris, and forensics should have a report back to us by tonight," said Pathak. "We can wrap the whole thing up and clear the family to cremate the body."

"Excellent," said Chatterjee. "Good work. What a tragedy, the day of his daughter's wedding."

"Yes, sir. But we made sure it was efficient for the family."

Chatterjee shook his head. "A bad year for the Lahiris. First Tejen, and now Hari. At least now that the investigation has concluded, I will be able to send Geeta some flowers."

Moiz cleared his throat, which felt as if it had never experienced water. "Sir, I actually feel there is a small matter to address. In the investigation. The Lahiri case. Sorry." Moiz cleared his throat again.

"What is it, Khan?" asked the commissioner.

"There may be foul play in the Lahiri matter, sir."

Pathak, apoplectic, turned his whole body toward Moiz, disbelief radiating from him.

"Inspector Pathak and I undertook a full investigation, but as we were leaving, I went back to collect my"—here, Moiz looked uncomfortable for a fraction of a second—"scooter, and some new information has come to light."

"Abir Sir, Khan and I should discuss it before we waste your time," said Pathak.

Chatterjee ignored Pathak. "Khan, speak up, and for god's sake, do it quickly. You are aware I went to the wedding and knew Krishna Lahiri, yes?"

Moiz nodded. "I felt I had to make you aware, sir. Before someone else did. Or the journalists begin to dig around. My suspicion is that Hari Lahiri died because he was pushed over the ledge by his daughter and we should open a formal investigation," said Moiz in a rush as all the air emptied from his lungs.

A silence enveloped the room. "What the fuck, Khan," roared Pathak.

"Be quiet, Pathak," said Chatterjee.

Moiz began to talk, as if it were his last chance to do so. "Sir, the family maid said there was barely any whiskey left in the bottle, and Mitra in forensics agrees that Hari Lahiri's blood alcohol was too low to impair judgment to the point he might fall. Besides, the Bangladeshi maid across the street, Bilquis Islam—I trust her—told me he stands on that ledge all the time and he never goes to the far edge of it. He was practiced in climbing off and on— he had been doing it since he was a boy."

"How wide is the ledge?"

"About six feet. He would have had to take at least a few long steps forward to reach the other side. If he lost his balance from where Bilquis saw him shouting, he would have safely fallen on the ledge, and not over it."

The commissioner's reflection shone in the granite of his desk, creating a smooth second commissioner radiating out of the torso of the original.

"Hari Lahiri was a not a suicidal man," continued Moiz, shaking his head to clear the ringing in his ears. "He had made plans to campaign for the National Popular Front the next day, and at the wedding, he said that he was looking forward to seeing the new Shah Rukh picture next week. "

"You went back and talked to the family?" asked Pathak, a vein throbbing in the center of his forehead.

"Because I felt we had new information," said Moiz, apologetic.

"Pathak, I won't have you get in the way of police work. Stop threatening Khan. Leave my cabin immediately."

"But, sir," protested Pathak, shouting, despite himself, "this is my case."

"One more outburst, and you're going home for the week," said Chatterjee.

After Pathak left, Moiz stood alone with the commissioner, the coolness of the evening creeping in through the thin shirt of his uniform.

"What's this harebrained theory that it was the daughter? Biddy Lahiri is always posting videos about her father."

"Sir, the others did not see him fall. Every one of them said the moon was behind the clouds just before he fell, but she did not. She described him falling over in clear sight. I went back to the terrace, the one that Hari Lahiri fell from, and I found sequins from her dress, though they tried to clean it up. She never once mentioned going up to the sixth terrace in her wedding dress. Furthermore, she has a rip on her dress. Sir, the family is covering for her. I promise you, if we go back and grill them properly, one of them will buckle. And given his scratches, we should do a DNA test under her fingernails or on the terrace," said Moiz, his eyes shining. "You just had to see her this afternoon—not a trace of crying in her eyes."

"What possible reason could she have?" asked Chatterjee after a pause. "There's no property motive here. Lila De holds the title to the trust."

Moiz looked at his feet. "Hari Lahiri was not kind to his wife, sir. The daughter had taken to sleeping with her mother in the past few years, to avoid . . . incidents. All the servants know."

A long pause stretched between them, punctuated by the even tide of the commissioner's soft breath, which seemed to be in step with the trickle of the fountain. The ringing grew louder in Moiz's ears, and he began to discreetly massage the area where his left ear met his jaw.

"Well, Khan, you've certainly done some good work today," said Chatterjee, bringing the tips of his fingers to his forehead, as if smoothing over his wrinkles.

"Thank you, sir," said Moiz, grateful.

"You recommend we investigate, correct?"

"The facts point in that direction, sir."

"Have you considered what the situation might be if we were to be wrong?"

Moiz straightened, the clammy fabric sticking to his ribs. "Wrong?"

"I mean, if we go charging back into the Lahiri house and open a case, get

DNA testing, the press will find out. We'll have to open the autopsy records. We'll put the family through hell. And imagine if after all that, you happen to be wrong. The ledge is still just a ledge, and that old Muslim servant was just making it up or imagining that he was farther back than she thought. How on earth can we take her word for it? Who knows what she was on.

"And the autopsy results would have to be made public then—the press love a story where they can take apart a legacy family. Or better still, take the KPF apart for terrorizing a legacy family. Either way, the press will be out for someone's blood.

"Then, imagine if the autopsy showed no evidence of Biddy Lahiri's DNA. And even if it did, she is his daughter. There are a thousand ways a legal team—and, mark my words, the Lahiris will get themselves a legal team"—here, Chatterjee paused to take a breath after the stress he had laid on the word *team*—"will take that one apart. All you are left with, then, are a few sequins shining on a terrace floor, probably gone by now, but in the process, a slithering can of worms has been opened. If you are wrong, Moiz, it could take down the force. The whole KPF."

Moiz shifted his weight from one foot to the other.

"Can we ever be sure, a hundred percent sure, of our . . . theories, Moiz?" asked Chatterjee, a soft sadness emanating from him.

Even in that moment, as he felt a lightheaded chill, Moiz felt a dull throb of pleasure that the commissioner knew his first name. "One can . . . One can never be sure, of course," said Moiz. "But my—"

"Moiz, you have a young wife, correct?"

"Ambreen," said Moiz.

"What do you think she would say to all this? I mean, I would have to fire the person who made such a huge mistake, if it were a mistake," said Chatterjee. "The press, the internet, will want to see someone pay. With Vik Lahiri and Biddy Lahiri's reach, this could go global."

Moiz noticed the commissioner rolled the *l* at the end of *global* in the same way as Pathak.

"Justice is not black-and-white, Moiz. It is often about looking at the bigger picture. Going after the bigger villains. The real ones. A man beats his wife for many years. Gambles. Drinks. A man falls to his death. Think about it. You can tell me what you decide in the morning."

"The morning, sir?"

"Oh, yes," said Chatterjee, rising to his feet. "Nothing more to be done tonight. And besides, I have a function to attend."

"Sir, was Hari Lahiri a friend of yours? He . . . He worked for the NPF, is that right?"

Something passed between the two men, a recognition of the knowledge that each possessed.

"I have no friends, Khan. I'm a policeman," said Chatterjee quietly. He came around the giant expanse of his table to where Moiz stood. "I know how hard you work, Khan. I see the dedication to the force you've had for all these years. How long has it been?"

"Sixteen years, sir."

"Sixteen years," murmured the commissioner, his orange-stained teeth glowing in the sunset. "You're due for a promotion soon, is that correct?"

"Yes, sir."

"Inspector?"

Moiz closed his eyes, suddenly very tired. He tried to conjure up Ambreen, but it was Bilquis's face, old and afraid, that floated in front of him. He remembered where he was and opened his eyes; the commissioner was smiling at him, like a friend.

"Deputy superintendent, sir. Since I have not been promoted in seven years, I technically should skip one rank."

"That would put you above Pathak," said Chatterjee.

"I have served the KPF for sixteen years, sir. Pathak is five years younger than me."

Chatterjee looked at him with those eyes of his. A man screamed somewhere in the depths of the thana. Moiz put a hand to his own throat to make sure it was not him, even as the fountain trickled a few feet away.

"You see, Moiz. Justice is about the bigger picture," said Chatterjee finally. He stretched his arms out, above his head, and yawned, a terrific snarl of a yawn, like the tiger in the NPF leaflets, then picked up his laptop bag from the bookshelf it rested on. "Congratulations, Deputy Superintendent Khan. Go home to your wife. Celebrate."

Moiz swallowed, trying to wet his throat enough to form words, but nothing came out. He nodded and took a step back, bumping into the metal of the Vishnu shrine. A moment later, he felt his arm yanked forward so hard that it felt like the socket had traveled ahead of the rest of his body.

His back had been shoved in the direction of the commissioner's heavy office door, and a dull ache spread into the base of his neck from the impact.

"Careful," hissed Chatterjee, so close that Moiz could smell the sweet gut-kha on his breath. "What kind of idiot are you, letting your fucking body touch my gods? You've got what you came in here for—but know your limits, Khan. At the end of the day, we have to know our place in the world." He spat an orange stream into the bucket near the fountain and then, laptop bag in hand, pushed open the door, past Moiz, leaving behind only the smell of his gutkha and a faint trace of cologne.

Moiz, alone in the office, stared at the idol of Vishnu. "Deputy Superintendent Khan. Deputy Superintendent Khan," said Moiz softly, rolling the syllables around in his mouth, like Hari Lahiri might have swirled alcohol. "Someday, I, too, will have a water fountain in my office."

But as he said the words, Moiz could not concentrate on the trickle of happiness in his chest. A larger swell of dread began to creep into his arms and fists and fingers, even as the clear eyes of Biddy Lahiri and the haunted American girl and the misshapen bones of the dead Lahiri man fused itself with Ambreen's words—*they will kill us, jaanu, they will hunt us down*—and began to throb against his temples, a steady beating drum eclipsing all that he had known before.

37

THE DAYS FOLLOWING Hari's death were a suspended fugue state. It was as if the wedding, for all its unending ceremonies, had never happened, so erased was any sense of celebration, only my grandmother's mourning punctuating the silences that hung in the hallways of the house. Biddy had not left to go to Arjun's house—instead, he had brought two suitcases and moved into her childhood bedroom. Unlike my mother, Gina took time off from the university and its rumor mills. Rana sat huddled in his armchair or on the ledge of the Secret Sixth, with an air of dazed confusion, as if something of his had gone missing.

After the funeral, Biddy refused to touch the silver jewel box that held Hari's ashes, and it was Rana who shook them into the Ganga, where almost immediately, they disappeared beneath the murky green of the water.

"Baba's gone," said Biddy, breaking our silence as we huddled around each other, staring at the water, chilled, on the riverbank.

The wet wind blew Mishti's hair around her face as she stared at the water, as if making sure. After a while, she nodded, taking Biddy's hand in her own.

WE LIVED IN a bubble of silence and fear in the days that followed, waiting at every turn, terrified of everything—ghosts and blood and policemen and the way that the servants whispered. The neighborhood had decided to be kind, and instead of speculation and scandal, we were confronted by a steady stream of condolences and flowers and visitors who described how they would miss Hari's bonhomie—his big, deeply felt laughter at parties, the manner in which he could make anyone feel at home, the many ways in which he filled rooms.

It haunted the Lahiris, who mourned and exhaled simultaneously, existing in the strange ether of missing the member of the family that had made them laugh more than anyone else, even as he had terrorized them for an eternity. Death had exonerated Hari even if our memories said otherwise. His many creditors and loan sharks only spoke of how charming he had been, the lifeblood of every gathering, the brother they had lost, as Palekar, Rana, and I began to deal with extricating the family from the many deals and debts and promises that Hari Lahiri had made with abandon, across Kolkata.

Mishti lived as if with a phantom limb—a phantom Hari, for whom she would set a place at the table and when she would jerk awake from the fugue, the truth would bring her to her knees in desperation, a new life stretching out before her, filled with both freedom and void.

The family did not talk much, preferring to exist on the fringes of ordinary conversation—the size of a fish, the price of onions, Brad Pitt's rumored marital troubles, the university's unending politics, the close shave with which the People's Left had won the election, defeating the National Popular Front, but the unease of how close they had come to winning Kolkata, the many seats that they had won in local districts, promising to rule the city one day in the near future as Bengal's ideology shifted to the unfamiliar far right—these were the conversations we could endure.

Even so, our usual patterns of hiding beneath placid lakes had been ruptured to their core, a disturbing new intimacy between us, a volatile sense of hope and dread permeating the air, the truth rearing, like underwater creatures, in Biddy's nightmares, in Mishti's screams that she had spent a lifetime holding in, in my grandmother's constant breakdowns, in the way Bari tiptoed around us, in the way Mr. Roy spent hours reading to my fearful mother in her studio, uncaring of rumor or scandal, and in the way I ignored email after email urging me to go back to work, to return to my life at Wyndham, in Brooklyn, in the alternate universe that called for me—until it, too, began to be silent.

IN ALL OF this, Mr. Das remained a steady force around us, never treading on the many walls we erected around ourselves in those weeks, yet orchestrating his men like a symphony humming away at construction on the outside of the house until the repairs and the elevator were complete. After days of unseasonal rain and wind, one cold afternoon the Lahiris emerged from the house, blinking in the sunlight as I stood next to a beaming Mr. Das.

"At long last, the day is here that we have all been waiting for," he said.

The Lahiris and I stood in silence.

Mr. Das's smile faltered.

"What's the matter?" he asked, looking at me. The elevator slid up the wall of the house, in an elegant glide, a combination of brass and glass sparkling in the sun. For the first time in days, I felt my heart lift.

"It's so beautiful," said Mishti. "The buttons and sides look like they were made in the fifties."

Mr. Das nodded, enthusiastic. "Lila Madam wanted something that would look like a part of the house."

"Will I be safe inside?" asked my grandmother, her voice hoarse from crying. She moved nearer to the elevator, peering at it where it stood, opening up into the fifth-floor hallway.

"Can people die from lift crashes?" asked Rana, looking upward.

"It's such an old house," said my mother. "How can we be sure?"

"This is the safest, strongest structure I have ever designed and built," proclaimed Mr. Das. "And I have built a few. Latest technology from Germany, 350 rpm motor, energy-saving, top speed."

This did not have its desired effect on the doubtful Lahiri faces in front of him.

"Greater speed does not mean greater danger," Mr. Das added. "The last time a lift may have entered free fall was in 1945, Otis officials say. That was when a B-25 bomber hit the Empire State Building between the seventy-eighth and eightieth floors, severing lift cables. A cab dropped seventy-five stories, but the only passenger, a woman inside, survived."

My grandmother gasped.

"Relax, Mummy," I said. "What he means is that safety is dependent on the quality of the lift cables and ratchets. And we paid for the best ones possible. There's no chance of this elevator—lift—ever falling."

My grandmother looked at me, relief in her eyes.

I had all but stopped speaking to her since the day of Biddy's wedding. When I tried, it was difficult, and a hard ball formed in my stomach, despite Dr. Laramie's many cautionary remarks around transferring anger or hatred from one person to another, because, really, what you wanted to do was let go of the original anger, but life wasn't that easy, and Laramie had sat there looking smug.

I nodded at my grandmother, looking away, my heart racing in my ears suddenly.

As a family, here we stood, in free fall, worrying about falling to our deaths.

"Well, then I suppose we must go for a ride, then," said my grandmother, a tremor of bravery in her voice. "Maya, you will come with me. And Lila."

"Only four at a time," said Mr. Das.

"I thought you said this thing couldn't fall if a bomb hit it," said my grandmother as she stepped into the elevator.

"No need to try," said Mr. Das, stepping inside with the three of us—my mother, my grandmother, and I. We slowly made our way upward, the rest of the Lahiris beaming at us.

Quickly, the elevator became a fixture in their lives. They argued over it, caused delays on every floor, and behaved as though they had not known a life without it, much the same as they treated me.

ONE AFTERNOON, I lay on my stomach in the courtyard on one of the mattresses that Bari had put out to soak up the last few rays of the afternoon sun, the disinfectant of choice in Kolkata. I was reading for pleasure, something I had not done in at least a year, a copy of *Silas Marner* that had belonged to my mother when she was a girl, the pages yellowed and breaking, her notes in the margin—*Silas is bone-deep lonely! Individual versus society!*—then three emphatic underlines under this sentence:

*Year after year, Silas Marner had lived in this solitude, his guineas
rising in the iron pot, and his life narrowing and hardening itself more
and more into a mere pulsation of desire and satisfaction that had no
relation to any other being.*

When I looked up, the sun in my eyes, I found Mishti watching me, sitting on one of the courtyard ledges, by a pillar. She held out a naru.

"I was making these and saw you from the kitchen window and thought you might want to try one."

I sat up and took the little globe-shaped sweet from her. "Mmm," I murmured, the naru's coconut and jaggery giving way in my mouth.

"Good," she said, pleased.

I chewed with pleasure while she sat in front of me.

"Lila," she said eventually.

In my chest, I felt a quick stab of fear at what she might want to talk about. There was so much we had, as a family, agreed to leave unspoken.

"I just wanted to say I'm sorry. That day, when you and Geeta Boudi were . . . arguing . . . you offered to help me."

I swallowed, the memory of the roses and carnage returning. "You have nothing to apologize for," I said.

"Tejen Da had said to me that if I left Hari"—Mishti stumbled on her dead husband's name—"he would help me. Find a place, take care of Biddy. He tried to talk to Hari. He tried to protect me."

"He should have done more," I said. "We all should have."

Mishti leaned against the pillar, the sweetness of her peaceful face lit by the sun, her eyes closed. "It is so nice to feel the sun on one's face. To feel anything at all, really," she said before she left.

I got off the mattress, pulling my sweater around me. The house was quiet, Mishti in her kitchen, my mother and Gina at work, Rana and my grandmother deep in siestas. I made my way to the fifth-floor terrace, then I walked all the way across and climbed the stairs to the Secret Sixth.

Bari, combing out her waist-length, oiled hair, grinned at me from the ledge. A shudder went through me.

"Be careful on the ledge, Bari."

She laughed, looking behind her, where the wide ledge sprawled over the courtyard. "It's impossible to fall off this thing. I could lie down and take my nap right here, and I would be fine."

Something passed between us, and quickly, she looked away, picking up her bottle of coconut oil, shaking it to melt the hardened liquid inside, and squeezing some out on her palm before rubbing it into her hair.

"You have such beautiful hair," I said. "Mine falls out by the clump every time I wash it."

"Really? You should try some coconut oil. I can give you some of mine if you like."

"Sure," I said, running my fingers through my bangs, pushing them back. She nodded, pleased.

"Bari," I said, clearing my throat. "I just want you to know that if you ever have any trouble in life or need any help, you can come to us."

Bari lifted her eyebrows. "Like money, you mean?"

"Anything. You're part of our family. Your daughter too."

She laughed. "That's nice of you. You're a sweet girl." Bari went back to combing her hair. I felt like a teenager.

"My grandmother . . . she once said that your husband . . . that there was trouble at home . . . that he wasn't good to you." I was having difficulty getting the words out, but I pressed on as Bari looked at me with puzzled sympathy. "I just want you to know that you have options," I said. "That you can live here if you like."

"My husband?" asked Bari.

"I've heard he . . . that he can be mean."

"Oh god, that old scumbag pig." Bari burst into laughter, the coconut in her hair perfuming the breeze that had begun to swirl gently around us. "I threw him out months ago, sent him packing the day he came home blind drunk and dared to slap me for not having his dinner ready," she said. "I slapped his stupid face back and tossed him out into the street, that garbage bag. Hasn't dared to show his face in our village since."

"Oh. That's good."

"Oh, yes. There's no way my family was going to stand for it."

I stood up, my face warm. "I'm so glad," I said.

"I mean there's always the chance he comes back and murders me in my bed, but he probably doesn't have the balls for that."

I nodded. Bari went back to her hair, and I climbed down from the Secret Sixth as the city spread out around us, vast and relentless, refusing to be contained by the bubble we had decided to live in, because it had been easier to do so, inside the house.

MY CELL PHONE rang that night at 3:37 a.m. My first thought was that something had happened to Molly. Then, in the time that I'd thrashed around in my bed looking for my phone as it vibrated furiously beneath many layers of duvet and pillows, scattering them on the floor as I hunted, the fear that something had happened to my father had taken greater hold of me. But the number on the flashing screen was Biddy's.

"What's wrong?" I said into the phone.

"It's Geeta Kaki," said Biddy. "She's had a stroke. We've called an ambulance."

38

AT ELEVEN THAT morning, Vik, Rana, and I sat in the fluorescent-lit waiting room of a private hospital, Ruby General, famous for its discretion among a section of Kolkata's families. We had been there for hours. Mishti, Gina, Arjun, and Biddy had gone home to change and eat and bring us food.

My grandmother had woken up in the middle of the night to go to the bathroom, where, suddenly dizzy, she had fallen. Rana, unable to sleep, had been on the Secret Sixth when he had heard her call out for help. When he had found her, she was lying on the bathroom floor, her eyes closed as if sleeping. Rana had thought she was dead.

But my grandmother did not die that night, her natural steel climbing to the surface even when she would rather it hadn't. Her husband was gone, Hari was gone, but her will to hold on to life was, despite herself, tethered to her formidable character and not her frail body.

I watched her through the window of her room, where my mother sat in a chair next to her, her head on the hospital bed my grandmother lay on, both of them asleep, like figures in a painting.

AN HOUR LATER, my mother emerged, rubbing her eyes.

"She's awake," she said. "She doesn't seem to have any paralysis, because you got to her so quickly, Rana. But they're running tests to see if her neurological function is impaired in any way. She can't speak clearly, except to say Hari's name, but she drank a little water."

Rana clasped his hands together. "Thank the lord. I'll make sure the priest does a pujo in the evening. Death has haunted our doorstep this year. This is a good sign—it may leave our home yet."

"Oh, be quiet," said my mother, irritable. "The truth is that that woman refuses to act in a responsible manner. I have told her a thousand times to wear slippers in the bathroom, but just to spite me, she won't. And now she's lying there muttering Hari's name while I have to take leave from work."

Rana, chastened, stood up. "Oh, er, well . . . I better go see to the pujo, then. Some oranges for the goddess perhaps."

"I'll take you to the market, Baba," said Vik.

"Bring me back a coffee, Vik. And maybe an idli?" said my mother.

He nodded. "Lila?" said Vik.

"Coffee," I said. "Thanks."

We exchanged a look, united in our incomprehension of our parents. My mother slumped into the plastic chair next to me, the smell of blood and sanitizer in the air, as patients on gurneys were wheeled past us.

"Dean Ravi called," I said.

My mother looked up, her eyes wide. "Oh god, did they forget to tell the students my classes were canceled?"

"She called to check on how you were doing."

"Oh, how nice," said my mother, pleasure on her face. "She can't really be bothered, of course—she just wants to know when I'm going to be able to go back. I'll call her later and tell her I'll be in tomorrow."

"When are they releasing Mummy?"

"Not for a few days, but she won't care if I'm gone for a few hours. She can make me feel bad about it when I'm back," said my mother with a laugh. "The doctors said she's going to be fine, god help us all."

I saw pure relief on my mother's face. "Dean Ravi said she was inspired at how devoted you were to your mother," I said. "That you talk of Mummy all the time at school."

My mother's back went rigid, embarrassment and then anger knitting into her brow. After a pause, she said, brusque, "I don't like your tone, Lila."

"I'm sorry," I said, suddenly regretful. It dawned on me that my mother had presented the version of the daughter she would have liked to be to Dean

Ravi, and the mother that she'd wished she had. Like my mother, I had spent a lifetime wishing for a different mother and felt a surge of emotion for the one I had. But I could not have touched her, to take her hand or express any traces of love, even if I'd tried.

"Have you eaten?" she asked.

I shook my head.

"I hope that Vik has the sense to bring us more than one idli. But you will eat half if he does not."

"Okay," I said.

We sat there next to each other in silence for a while, her eyes closed as she leaned back into the chair, stretching her legs out, her jeans the same color as mine—we might have been mistaken as sisters.

"Ma, I'm going back to New York."

She opened her eyes. She said nothing for a few minutes, and then she nodded slowly. "When?"

"In a few days, if Mummy is okay," I said.

She nodded again. "Your leave has ended?"

"Yes." I took a small, silent inhale. "And I want to go home."

At this, she looked pained. "You have more than one home," she said, a flash of rage in her eyes. But she did not scare me. Something between us had been altered the day I had found out that my mother and I bore the same wounds.

"Yes," I said.

"Durga Pujo is in a few days. Don't you want to stay for the goddess?"

"Like her, I want to go home too, Ma."

My mother was silent for a moment. "What about the house?" she asked. "How will we manage without you?" She looked genuinely worried.

I laughed. "Oh, please. You'll be delighted to run the ship without interference."

"Me?"

"You love the house. You should manage its affairs. I've talked to Rana Kaka, and he agrees. The last thing he wants is to deal with Mummy in one of her tempers because the pigeons got into her room again."

My mother did not smile back. "But the trust is in your name now," she said.

"I'll give you power of attorney. I've discussed it with Palekar Uncle. He'll help you. And once a month, we can check in, you and I, to see how it's going."

My mother gave me an accusatory look. "You've thought of everything."

"I think it's what Dadu would have wanted if he was here."

My mother looked away. "Well, he didn't leave me the house, did he?" My mother fiddled with the strap of my leather handbag.

When she looked at me again, it felt childlike. "You'll come back?" she asked.

"Yes," I said. "You could also come and visit me."

She took a long breath. "You would get sick of me in a day."

"I wouldn't," I said. The truth was, she was probably right, but I wanted her to come.

She looked at my grandmother. "Maybe next year. Ma needs me here."

I felt a little shard of pain, but my mother did not see it.

"Maybe she'll finally make some room for me now," said my mother with a brittle little laugh. After a pause, she said, "I'll need a visa. To come and see you?"

I nodded.

"Your father, he will be happy. You must miss him. You were always such a team. From the moment you were born. Sometimes I felt left out."

We watched my grandmother's chest rise and fall through the window.

"Lila, I feel like I've never been able to give you anything. I've never been able to do anything for you." The words came out of my mother in a jumble. "But the house . . . it's yours. As such, it is ours, of course," she said, hurried, "but equally yours. You grew up in it. Your grandfather wanted you to have it. And you—you are the most important thing to me."

I felt my throat constrict. "Dean Ravi certainly thinks so," I said, light. "She said you're always talking about me too. Even when you don't call me for months."

My mother frowned. "That tone again," she muttered.

Vik arrived, a steaming newspaper-wrapped package of idlis and two coffees on a tray in his arms. "I come bearing gifts," he said.

"Good boy," said my mother.

"Oh, Geeta Kaki is up. I'll go say hi," said Vik.

Through the glass of her window, my grandmother smiled at me, wincing at the effort. I raised my hand in a small wave. Vik went into her room, and we drank our coffees, the South Indian filtered kind, sweet and strong and hot, as we ate idlis, my appetite emerging with a roar.

"Do you remember when I was little, Ma?" I asked. "You had that bed with the headboard that was also a shelf, with all those books in it. The abridged classics."

"*Jane Eyre*, *Silas Marner*, all the Brontës, Jane Austen. Edith Wharton. Dickens, said my mother, her mouth full. "Remember that copy of *The Godfather* I found you reading when you were eight?"

"You let me finish it."

"Censorship is the death of imagination," said my mother, breaking open another idli and putting it in her mouth. "That is the problem with the country. Do you want the books? For your own children?" she asked, hopeful.

"If I hadn't been allowed to read and think about whatever I wanted . . . ," I said slowly, wanting to get my words right. "If you didn't have all those books, if you hadn't told me to read them, I wouldn't have my career. Or the life I do. Books were my escape, my superpower. They still are. You did that for me."

My mother ate quietly, her eyes reflective. I thought that she might reach out to touch me, or look up so a moment could pass between us, that surely something in our skin gravitated toward each other, but instead, she looked away, the flicker of emotion in her eyes as quickly gone as the crumbs of idli she brushed from her mouth and lap.

"Well, that's good," she said.

I nodded. "It is."

39

OUTSIDE THE OFFICE of the *New Statesman*, there was a small park, where dogs and children and power-walking senior citizens took refuge in the only spot of green around for miles. In my childhood, the park had felt bigger, the streets surrounding it wider, but Kolkata was a jagged, clustered metropolis now, skyscrapers jostling for space next to Café Coffee Days at every corner, an unmistakable hustle constantly in the air. It was a peaceful time, before the melee of rush hour took over, only a handful of toddlers in a sandbox crawling over each other for real estate, their family's maids gossiping nearby with one eye on the children, the other on Adil and me. We were a man and woman, on a park bench at five thirty in the evening, eating ice cream, igniting their imaginations.

"Can I try yours?" he asked, leaning over before I could respond, scooping away a curl of chocolate from my cup, his intensely familiar aftershave sending a tremor into the soles of my feet, his nearness too much.

I looked at the side of his mouth, the bottom of his lip. "You have chocolate . . . ," I said, raising my thumb, gesturing in the direction of my own lip instead of his.

He rubbed at the wrong side. "How's that?" he asked.

When I said nothing, he rubbed lower, where the cleft of his chin met the underside of his lower lip. I gave in, reaching for him, my fingers on his cheek, as my thumb stroked his lip, the ice cream absorbing into my skin and his, the women eagle-eyed in the background. He let me finish, and I took my hand back as we sat there in the melancholy of the fading light, our ice creams melting in their cups.

"Why won't you let me take you to the airport?"

I shook my head. "It's too much. This is about as much as I can do."

"Will you write?"

"I'll think of you."

He was silent for a few seconds. "Ever since I've known you, you've wanted the perfect version of everything, and love, it can be ugly." He was quiet for a moment, the fading light bouncing off the gleam of his well-shined office shoe. "But it's still beautiful for the few minutes it's ours to have."

"There's the poet I fell in love with," I said, light.

"You mocked me endlessly at fifteen, you mock me now," he said, shaking his head.

"That's what teenagers do when they're madly in love," I said, desperate to touch him.

He looked away, his chest rising with his breath as he reached for my hand. I blinked at the relief of feeling his skin on mine.

"Lila, I know you must not think much of me, the choices I make—"

"I think everything of you," I said. "You're the best person I know. Duty, commitment, love—all of those things—they're abstract shapes to the rest of us, and somehow you put your hands around those shapes and make sense of them and understand what you have to do, to live the life you want. I wish I was you."

We were both crying, his hand on my cheek as he drew me close, and even the women in the distance averted their eyes. It was the end of something, they must have known, and gathering up the children in their arms, they left us alone, lovers on a park bench, in each other's arms for the last time.

40

DELIGHT, A LIGHTNESS in my lungs, as I breathed in gulps of Brooklyn's crisp air—I was home. My plants were alive; Harriet had watered them. My apartment felt airier, bigger, with more room for me. I stood still, the green of McCarren Park stretched out in front of me, the trees already a deep rust. Children in jackets milled about me, their parents taking in the fleeting sun, garbage bags and trash cans fighting for space on curbsides outside bodegas, my bookstore and laundromat and Italian restaurant exactly where I had left them. On my windowsill, where the hummingbirds hovered, once at war with each other, and absent now that the season was turning too cold, was a note from Harriet welcoming me back and reminding me to read her manuscript, the exchange for tending to my home in the time I had been gone.

I sorted through an avalanche of mail and packages—manuscripts and galleys for the next season—stacked on my dining table. One of them, a modest size, the weight of a four-hundred-page novel, with a familiar looping writing on the label, sat on top of the stack, a recent addition to the pile. I slid it off the other boxes and sat down, ripping at the soft paper envelope. Inside, a sheaf of bound pages, and a simple note, with neither warmth nor chill.

Lila, a finished draft of Sinking. I look forward to your comments.
Seth

IN THE AFTERNOON, my body still adjusting to New York, I walked to the train station, stopping to wave to every familiar face—my newspaperman, the people at the deli, the café—as if to reassure them and myself that I had returned, that my absence had only been temporary. I had returned in time for the dazzle of late fall, the bleak early winter, the cycles of fresh snow mixing with muck. I took the L train into Manhattan and the 1 to Eighty-Sixth, then I walked west to Riverside Drive. Unusual for October in New York, it had rained the night prior, and the streets were still wet, branches still occasionally dripping overhead, the sun reflecting off the marble Madonnas that dotted the park's edges. At 110th Street, I headed to the yellow-taxi-dotted clamor of Broadway, the gray stone Cathedral of Saint John the Divine sweeping into the blue sky, the Hungarian pastry shop where Molly was waiting for me inside.

She was hunched over a book in the bustle of the coffee shop, her now-long hair twisted into a swirling bun low on her neck, some sort of old-fashioned jeweled pin holding it together, tendrils of curls escaping everywhere, her sweater a soft camel. When I stood in front of her, casting a shadow over her paperback, she looked up with her generous smile and then stood and wrapped her arms around me, a look of relief on her face that must have been mirrored on mine.

"Lila, I've missed you," she said, leaning her head on my shoulder.

As I sat down, she said, "I hope you're not mad."

"What for?"

"Not stopping Seth from barreling after you."

"Not even a little."

She sighed. "He was on a mission. Only you could have stopped him."

I looked away.

"You didn't know, Li," she said gently. "I should have told you."

"Tell me how you've been. Have you been happy?"

She blinked, the warm light bouncing off her curls. "Yes. But it's so good to see you. When you were gone, I was lonely."

I nodded, feeling my throat constrict. "Me too. It was hard not to have your opinion on my life. Or talk to you every day. Even when you're a pain."

She laughed, blowing her nose on a small cream handkerchief. Even when we were girls in college, Molly had always carried little things like coins and handkerchiefs and flashlights, ever prepared to take on anything.

"Did you end up selling the house?" she asked as the warm, familiar buzz of the coffee shop settled into me.

"No. The house is still ours," I said.

"Oh?" Molly looked curious. "What was saying goodbye to your family like? Do you miss them?"

I thought for a few moments. "I feel like I grew a second head," I said. "One that belongs in India. Belongs to them. I think they knew it wasn't goodbye."

Molly looked at me for a long moment, examining me as only she knew how to. "You sound happy," she said.

I took a breath. "I quit. I wrote Gil and Malcolm an email this morning."

Her eyes widened as she inhaled sharply. "What? Why on earth would you do that?" she asked. "You just got promoted."

"I wouldn't have been happy. I would have been in a bunch of meetings, managing that department and figuring out budgets and deciding who needed to be fired. Finding the writer, finding the book, helping to shape it, getting it out into the world—there would have been no more of that." The words rushed out of me, unanticipated. "What they want out of the business now, all of their large-scale plans, that's not for me."

She nodded. "You know, Gil said that about you. That you wouldn't be happy in the gig."

I looked away. Gil had known from the start; he had not needed to go around the globe to discover it.

What will you do?" asked Molly in her direct way.

"I want to start my own place," I said. "Just a few writers at first. Maybe rent a small office. A tiny press."

She stared at me. "What?"

"I know. It makes my head spin. But I'm going to do it."

"Doesn't that . . . Doesn't that need a lot of money or something? Are you rich now? Is it from the house?"

I laughed. "The only way that house could make me slightly rich is if I ever sold it, and if you met my family, you would know that hell would freeze over before that was a possibility. That house is going to be in the family for the rest of all our lives."

"So where would you get the money?"

I swallowed. "I have some saved up, and my dad, well, he's giving me the rest. He's going to sell the apartment he has in Kolkata—he kept it for me, so that I had a place to go, to hide from my mother when I visited Kolkata, I guess." I looked at the case of pastries, the perfect little squares of shortbread across from us, a throng at the counter, like at the sweetshop across the Lahiri mansion. "He thinks I don't need it anymore."

Molly frowned. "It's still going to be a lot of the same headaches, you know? Any business comes with its share of crap if you want it to actually do well."

I took a breath. "It'll be my own place, though. My own books. I think . . . I think I'd be happier dealing with the crap that way."

Molly stared at me. "God, Lila. You're the bravest person I know."

"That, I promise, is not true."

"But you are. You're doing exactly what you need to do for your life. I am so fucking happy for you," she said.

"I was wondering if you wanted to do it with me," I said.

She was quiet. After a few seconds, she frowned. "But I'm not entrepreneurial at all. And I do kids. Wouldn't you be better off with a literary-fiction person?"

"You're the best editor I know. And you have more taste in literature than most people I've met. You throw an incredible party and bring people together like nobody else. We'd go fifty-fifty, own it together, take decisions together. And kids and YA should be an important part of the focus."

Molly sat back in her chair. She moved her coffee cup in concentric circles on the table. "I thought you were going to say you wanted to go off and write a book yourself."

"I don't," I said. "I never have."

We did not talk for a few minutes. Molly stared at the table, cradling her coffee cup.

"You don't have to," I said. "I won't take any offense. But I think you'd be good at it." We looked at each other, my eyes shining with thrill, an uncertain glimmer in hers. "You're the only person I wanted to ask."

"Let me think about it. I have some money saved up too. If we went bust, I could survive a couple months."

"True," I said, laughing.

"You'll have to tell me more about this trip," said Molly, leaning back into her chair. "It feels like you slayed a few demons and came back queen of your manor. Should I call you Princess Li from here on?"

But as Molly and I laughed in that coffee shop, the beauty of the moment, the joy I felt to inhabit the city and its freedoms and all that my life could be, drained from me. I ran out of breath, all of it emptied from my lungs in one quick slither, so hard was the longing that gripped me for Kolkata—for the walls of a house that stood, despite itself, for its people and their lives, which existed so far away from me and yet felt as if they were made from my own bones.

41

THE NEXT DAY was a Saturday, and I was going to take the afternoon train into Hartford, in time for dinner with my father and Iva. A tropical storm, making its way from the coast of Africa, was scheduled to weaken and land with heavy showers in the city on Sunday, and I planned to spend the weekend indoors with my family. At seven in the morning, clutching a paper cup of tea that periodically scalded me, the gray weather cold enough for a woolen scarf around my neck, I took the train in the opposite direction from Hartford, the as-yet-empty 2 to Brooklyn Heights instead, where once I got off at Clark Street and took a circuitous detour past Orange Street and Love Lane to get to 54B Pineapple Street, where Seth lived on the first floor of a historic brownstone.

I stood outside the flight of steps that curved up to the old wooden front doors that were painted a welcoming yellow and outfitted with a state-of-the-art security system that involved having the person you were visiting buzz you up via an app. I had not thought this through, and cell phone in hand, I stared at Seth's number.

We had not talked in over a month, since he had taken a taxi to the airport from outside my father's apartment, and to call him for the first time and hear that he might not be home, or not want to see me if he was, felt worse than turning up unannounced.

The door pushed open, and a beautiful, long-limbed woman, with her hair in a printed turban and a tote over one shoulder, came out.

"Hi," she said, holding the door open. "Did you want to go up?"

"Yes," I said, rushing toward the porch stairs. "2B. I'm going to 2B."

"For Seth, right? I've seen you around. Have a nice day."

"You too," I said, grateful for the nights I had spent in Seth's bed, a number large enough that even his neighbors might recognize that I was of some significance in his life, enough to at least be let in for now.

I felt my heartbeat quicken as I climbed the stairs. A yellowish cat sat in one of the second-floor stairwell window boxes.

Outside 2B, I took a breath and rang the doorbell before I could convince myself to leave. A few moments went by. A man passed me by as he went down the stairs. I felt like an intruder, everyone's eyes on me and all that I had done.

I rang again. This time, footsteps thudded through the slim hallway that connected the bedrooms to the living room, matching my heartbeat, closer, until the door opened and Seth, still pulling on a T-shirt over his sweatpants, still sleepy, stood in front of me.

"Lila?" he asked, incredulous, as if I were in the last place the world might imagine I should be in.

"Hi."

He shook his head in disbelief. "What . . . What are you . . . When did you . . . Are you back?"

I nodded. "I got in Thursday night."

"I see," he said, the surprise on his face dissolving into something harder, as if a memory had come back to him, his features settling into an impassiveness.

"I came to say how sorry I am. I am so sorry."

Seth looked away from me, his eyelids flickering, to the floor.

"When I think of how I treated you, how I behaved, I just . . . I can't bear it. I'm not here to be forgiven. I just want you to know how sorry I am."

For a few seconds, we did not break our gazes, neither willing to acknowledge the truth or let it go. Finally, he shrugged. "You didn't love me. It happens."

"I behaved terribly. I'm so sorry."

From behind him came the patter of footsteps, soft and even, a flash of a striped pajama shirt, the glimpse of bare leg, dark hair, as a woman disappeared into the warm light of the kitchen. Seth looked at the kitchen, then back at me, a frown knitting his brow.

"Lila," he sighed.

"I'm sorry. I know it's early. I should have texted, but I didn't know what to say. So I came here because I thought it would be easier."

He nodded.

"I . . . Also, I wanted to say, to tell you, I quit. Wyndham. I resigned. Before I got back."

"What?" Seth's features flared in shock.

"I'm starting my own house. Well, Molly and I are. It'll be small. But I'm excited. It . . . It could be cool."

He ran his hand through his hair, blinking his eyes. "Wow," he said.

"Gil and Malcolm at Wyndham are really excited about your book, of course."

"They sure seem to be," said Seth slowly.

I nodded. "But I was hoping that for the next one, you would come with me." I swallowed, and let the words rush out. "I think we work well together. We always have. It's the best version of us."

Seth said nothing.

"And I'll completely understand if it's impossible for you to work with me, given . . . given everything that's happened. And given that it would be a smaller advance. But I wanted to come here and also say that if you wanted to come with me, I would make your books my priority. I read *Sinking* last night. It's wonderful. Anyway," I said, stepping backward, "that's all I came here to say."

I heard the whir of the coffee maker, the smell of a breakfast routine wafting toward me. "You don't have to say anything right now." I lifted a hand as Seth continued to stare at me, as if uncomprehending.

"Bye, Lila," I heard from behind me, quiet, short words, as I rushed down the stairs, the cat still asleep in the same place, the world around unchanged except for us.

I WALKED QUICKLY to the subway station, a burning in my cheeks, my boots slapping against the puddles on the sidewalk. As I turned the corner of Pierrepont, I heard footsteps behind me.

"Lila," called Seth, out of breath, a half-zipped jacket over his T-shirt, sneakers without socks. "Lila," he said again as he came to a stop in front of me, gulping in air. "Fucking hell, I am in the worst shape of my life. And apparently you walk at the steady clip of a cheetah."

I waited as he caught his breath, his palms holding the sides of his ribs. After a few moments, he straightened and looked at me.

"No one takes the 2 train unless they want to be forgiven," he said.

I nodded.

"My book. It wouldn't have been what it is without you. I, the writer I am, wouldn't be here without you. You believed in me before anyone else did."

People hurried past us, the sounds of the subway in the distance, steam rising out of a grate on the street.

"I'll come with you," said Seth. "Aetos might be very mad, but he can't do much if I turn down whatever he offers me for the next one. You should talk to Gil, though."

"I can do that," I said. "What if Aetos offers you the moon?"

Seth cocked his head to one side. "You'll just have to make this hare-brained scheme of yours work. And I can get some revenge from all those digs you made about my trust fund when you're the reason I have to dip into it for the first time for rent."

I laughed. "I'll try very hard to keep your trust fund safe, I promise."

He nodded. "You and Molly—this is a good idea."

He zipped up his jacket to his neck, shivering in the cold, his dark hair blowing in every direction, the winds suddenly taking on a force.

"It wasn't on you," he said. "I knew you weren't looking for more than what we had. I went chasing after you."

"I let you," I said. "I could have been honest."

Seth looked into the distance, where the water below the promenade over-looked the Manhattan skyline. "Call it even?" he finally said.

I blinked back tears, swallowing as I nodded.

Seth exhaled. "I better get back."

I nodded. "Friends?" I asked, hearing the tremor in my own voice.

"Not so fast," he said jokingly. But I knew he meant it—that it would take a long time before Seth Schwartz was willing to be my friend again. Yet a relief filled me.

"Thanks for coming after me, Seth."

"I seem to be an expert at it," said Seth over his shoulder. "See you in a few weeks. I'll have questions about our new business arrangement. I'm a difficult celebrity author, you know."

I laughed, the sharp, cold wind icy on my cheeks, my eyes watering as gusts whipped around me, an unreasonable happiness running through my veins at what the future might hold.

42

IT BEGAN TO rain again, this time a diagonal onslaught that I could barely see through, which brought with it icy shards that crumbled before they landed on my hat. My eyes, my hair, and my coat were soaked, my overnight bag covered with soft hail, during the half-mile walk from the train station to my father's house—usually a picket-fenced idyll, but today a Sisyphean task.

At four, the sky had already begun to darken into the neon rose that promised the storm would only increase in might. Cars moved even slower than I did, drivers inching past me at a crawl, hazard lights blinking through an opaque storm, a feeling of real fear in the air at what nature might be capable of, the occasional lightning bolt splitting the sky open.

After what felt like an hour, I walked past the iced-over rosebushes and sturdy hedges, until I was at the front door. Before I could raise my hand to ring the doorbell, my father opened the door, his face creased into lines of worry.

"Lila, for god's sake, I called your phone so many times. Why don't you pick up?"

Iva appeared behind him. "My god. We were so worried. What train did you take? Why didn't you tell us what train you were coming on?"

"Ma, stop shouting at Li. She's drenched," said Avi from behind them.

"Be quiet, Avi," said Iva.

It occurred to me that I had never seen Iva furious with me before, her pale cheekbones tinged with patches of red, the tip of her nose red, her lips pressed together, a look I recognized as having been directed at my siblings a thousand times, but never at me.

My father shepherded me inside the door. Could it be possible that he had become older in the few weeks I had been gone, his face more lined than I remembered it? I felt a rush of relief at being near him, as if something of my own had gone missing for too long and suddenly, by a miracle, I had found it.

"You should have picked up your phone," he said under his breath.

"I'm sorry. I fell asleep on the train. The storm wasn't supposed to land until tomorrow."

He looked mutinous, but I could see a relief in his eyes too.

Iva, still incandescent, plucked off my hat. "Avi, get a towel instead of just standing there. We thought you were taking the noon train. Who takes a train in inclement weather, Lila? It is not responsible. Do you know how frightened your father was? They don't make those trains or stations with freak storms in mind. If you paid attention to the Weather Channel, you would have known it was traveling much faster in our direction than they initially thought."

"What if you'd had an accident?" said my father, the two of them a double act of outrage.

Avi grinned at me as he handed his mother a towel, with which she swiped off the melting hail from the back of my shoulders. "Welcome back," he said.

"Take that coat off and come into the kitchen. You have to drink something hot or a brandy immediately. And next time, please tell us what train you're coming in on."

"The day got away from me," I said. "I'm so sorry." I reached for her, embracing my stepmother, who for the first time in her life, had treated me exactly as she would one of my siblings.

"Well, you're here now," she said, hugging me back, her face still upset. "Mihir, get her inside," she said as she turned toward the kitchen.

My father helped me out of my coat. "Look how wet it is," he said, still frowning. "I would have come and picked you up."

I nodded as he picked up my bag, my coat and hat, and my scarf.

"You're staying until the storm settles," he said. "There's no guarantee it will be gone tomorrow."

I nodded again.

My father softened a little. "They're predicting eight inches of rainfall. Something is happening to the weather. Everything is upside down. It doesn't hail in October."

"I brought enough clothes for a few days," I said.

"Good," he said.

We were both silent.

"Palekar called me," said my father. "It seems your mother has a lot of plans for the house."

I laughed. "That sounds about right."

"Does she need your approval? For things like a security system and so on?"

"Technically, yes. But the others will have a say too, so as long as she gets them to agree to it, I'm okay."

"Sounds like you're going to be involved," said my father.

"It's my house too."

"I'm glad you went," he said. "Maybe next time, I can come with you. Show you the city I grew up in."

"That sounds really good, Baba."

We stood there, my father and I, not hugging, both of us radiating a peculiar happiness at being in the same room together.

Avi reappeared in the hallway and threw a second towel at me. I caught it, inches away from my face.

"Avi, really," said my father, annoyed.

"The folks were going to launch a search party if you didn't turn up in the next ten minutes," said Avi.

"Please call Robin and tell her your sister is here," said my father. "She's at school, but she was worried too."

As my father went to hang my coat up, Avi lowered his voice as he hugged me. I hugged him back.

"These two have been impossible the last few weeks," he said. "Especially after your . . . uncle died. I think they thought you might not come back.

Another few days, and Mom and Baba would have been over there, descending on you."

"Glad you're back," said Avi, holding me by the shoulders now. "I was worried about you, but here you are, looking happier than before you left."

"You mean you're glad you're not plowing through the snow looking for me right now?"

"Exactly," said Avi. "C'mon, let's go get you a drink. Mom's been cooking all day. I'll call Robin."

As I followed Avi, my phone vibrated in the back pocket of my jeans. I pulled it out, the screen cold against my fingers. I stared at it.

"I've got a call. I'll be in in a few minutes."

Avi turned to nod at the entrance of the living room. I walked to the bottom of the hallway stairs, just above the basement, where the memories of our lives sat in boxes, next to furniture and old bikes and my father's latest DIY project.

"Hi, Ma," I said, sinking onto the step.

"Lila," she said, as if I was sitting next to her, her voice loud, with a familiarity that lacked any boundaries. "You haven't called me at all."

"We talked yesterday."

"But you said you would call back. There are so many things to talk about. Do you know the university is having me host Theater Day this year? What modern texts do you recommend? I was thinking *The Shape of Things*. Have you read it? Of course at least one Shakespeare. Also, I am raising the issue of a security system. German. Like the lift. We will need your input. Next Saturday at the household meeting. I've decided to do it at seven a.m. so you can attend."

"Ma, that would be Friday night for me. I don't want to be on Skype with the family on a Friday night. And I bet they don't want to do it at seven a.m."

"Lila, I need your help," said my mother irritably. "Sunday, then? Also, what is so important every single Friday night that you have no time for your family?"

"My life?"

"Fine, live your life. But you must attend. What about Mondays? It'll be Sunday night for you."

"Fine."

"So you will attend on Monday?" she asked, a faint note of worry crackling through the connection.

"Yes, I will," I said, laughing despite myself. The storm had slowed to a brief halt and the puddles outside were deep, their surfaces almost blue in the moonlight.

"Are you okay, in New York?"

"I am, Ma. It's beautiful here."

"But you miss us too," she said.

"I do."

My mother launched immediately into a tirade about Bari taking a month-long leave, the problems of *King Lear*, the university's new historian, and her new, excellent lipstick, of which she had purchased a second, identical tube, so that I would have one when we next attended a wedding together. I could hear the chatter of my family upstairs, the smell of dinner floating down to where I sat. The memory of what I had once said to Dr. Laramie came back to me suddenly. In that moment, it felt like we had all burned something down, razed it to the ground, and in its place, something altogether new, wholly unrecognizable, had emerged from the ruins.